THROUGH THE
WHITE WOOD

Also by Jessica Leake

Beyond a Darkened Shore

THROUGH THE WHITE WOOD

JESSICA LEAKE

An Imprint of HarperCollinsPublishers

Library of Congress Control Number: 2018952750
ISBN 978-0-06-266629-1 (trade bdg.)

Typography by Michelle Taormina
19 20 21 22 23   PC/LSCH   10 9 8 7 6 5 4 3 2 1

First Edition

To Kelsey, my cousin who is more like a sister, who helped me turn my love for telling stories into a reality

Chapter One

There are countless monsters in this world. Some with fangs, some who skitter in the darkness just out of sight, some who wear human skin but whose hearts have turned dark as forest shadows.

And as my fellow villagers dragged me, bound by rough rope, from the cellar of the elder, I knew that these men and women I'd grown up with—they thought of me as a monster, too.

I wasn't sure they were wrong.

"Haul her to her feet," said Anatoly, the village elder, with arms crossed over his black fur coat.

Yury and Peter wrapped strong arms around me, and I tried to wrench out of their grasp, stumbling in the deep snow. "Her skin has turned to ice," Yury answered, his lip curled in disgust.

"Then pull her by the rope," Anatoly said, irritation clear in his gruff voice.

The rope grew taut as they forcibly brought me to a standing position. I was still exhausted from my long flight through the woods, but as the sleigh that would take me away suddenly came into view, pulled by magnificent white horses, I strained against my bonds. The ice, my only defense, spread all over my body.

A group of villagers had assembled to watch the sleigh arrive, and I made a pitiful sound low in my throat as I caught sight of Babushka.

"Babushka, please," I cried out as I fought more wildly against the men who held me captive.

Her ruddy face was stern, the red-and-orange kerchief on her head colorful against the backdrop of the smoky wooden huts. Dedushka, who would normally be by her side, was painfully absent. The fact that it was entirely my fault he was missing tore through me, like a blade in my chest.

Though Babushka's eyes weren't as cruel as the others', she did nothing to protest my treatment. Pain as sharp as ice pierced my heart. Did she condemn me to my fate?

A shriek above us drew our attention. An enormous golden eagle was swooping toward us, talons outstretched.

No, Elation, I thought desperately, and the bird banked and rose again to the sky. But her gaze remained on me as she circled above. I wouldn't be the reason for more deaths or injury in this village—not even to save myself.

My attention returned to the sleigh, from which the driver had stepped down. Anatoly hurried to meet him.

"Please," I begged again, and I wasn't sure who my pleas were directed toward. Tears fell from my eyes and froze upon my cheeks.

All too soon, Anatoly beckoned for Yury and Peter to bring me forward. I fought them until I was half-dragged all the way to the side of the sleigh.

"She is kept bound?" the driver asked, his dark eyes narrowed.

"She has escaped once already," Anatoly said, lip curled beneath his beard. It seemed now when anyone looked at me, it was with a sneer or a curled lip.

"That won't be necessary," the driver said, and he retrieved a small knife from within his coat. I tried to back away, but the men held me immobile before him. With one clean movement, he sliced through the rope binding my wrists. "Come," he said as I stood trembling before him. "There is no other choice for you now."

The men held tight to my arms, but I turned back toward Babushka, desperate to speak to her one last time. I didn't think she would—didn't think that I even deserved the chance—but to my surprise I saw she was making her way toward me, leaning more heavily on her gnarled walking stick than I'd ever seen her do.

"Babushka," I said, and her name was breathed out of me like prayer and a plea, "forgive me."

She shook her head as she came beside me. "We don't have

time for that now, devotchka." I searched her familiar face, wrinkled and worn and stern, wondering if I'd ever see it again. "If you stay here, these men will kill you," she said, her voice a desperate whisper, and I strained to hear her. "There is hope in Kiev. Sometimes the place we do not want to go is the best place for us after all." I tried to puzzle out her meaning—I couldn't imagine she thought my destination would be good for me by any stretch of the imagination. Was it an old proverb, then?

"Babushka," I said, my voice breaking, "I don't understand."

She touched my face, her skin rough from years of hard work. I waited—whether for explanation or forgiveness, I didn't know. But the village men would not wait for an old woman's words, nor did she seem to want to offer any.

Before I could say anything else, Yury and Peter dragged me to the side of the sleigh and threw me into it, so that I stumbled and nearly fell. I glanced back at their faces, triumph and relief plain to see there, and I knew they felt glad to see me go.

Babushka stayed close to the sleigh, her lips pressed tight as though she was in pain.

"May the grand prince have better use for her," Anatoly said, his gray beard now dotted with snow. "She has brought us nothing but misery and destruction."

The driver nodded but didn't offer any other response, merely turned back to the sleigh. To me, he said, "My name is Ivan Petrov, and I am to bring you to the grand prince."

I thought of the sleigh's eventual destination at the grand

prince's palace, and the frost on my skin turned to ice.

He waited as though expecting some sort of answer from me, and as I looked around my village—at those who had arranged all of this, who wanted me gone—I knew I had no other choice. Not right now—not unless I wanted to unleash something better left chained within me forever.

I settled for nodding once.

He grunted and leaned over to the driver's seat. I tensed, expecting him to have changed his mind about keeping me bound. Perhaps he was retrieving his own length of rope. But when he straightened, he brought with him a long, crimson coat trimmed in fur. "The road will be cold."

I hesitated, wondering why I was being given such a thing. What use did a prisoner have for fine clothing? But he only handed it to me more insistently, so I reluctantly pulled it on. The fine fabric would hide my rougher peasant clothes from view, but even its heavy wool would do nothing to keep the cold wind from biting deep.

Then, without another word, he climbed into the driver's seat, gathered the reins, and pulled us away from the only home I'd ever known, to a prince they said was a monster.

But then, they said I was one, too.

I promised myself I wouldn't look back, but I did it anyway, squinting through the snow at the thirty-seven villagers who silently watched me leave. It was easy to note the ones who were missing. While the ones who remained stared at me accusingly,

I reached down to rub my wrists where the ropes had once bound them.

Babushka stood apart, looking frail and alone. I could still feel her hand on my cheek, her words in my ear—were they absolution?

I am not your babushka, she'd told me long ago, *but you may call me by that name.* My life with her had not been easy or warm, but at least it had been mine.

I turned to face the front of the sleigh and squeezed my eyes closed. I thought I'd known loneliness, but it was nothing compared to this . . . this utter exile. The cold seeped in, hardening my already icy skin, and I wrapped my arms tighter around myself. I tried desperately not to think of the one time I had felt warm, the only time I hadn't felt as though I was carved from ice. But the memories surfaced anyway.

Screams echoed in my mind as the tingling reminder of the cold fire crept over my palms. That terrible power that was nothing like my usual ability.

I pinched my arm to keep the sensation from spreading, but it did nothing to stop the memory of how I'd felt that night. How I'd felt none of the nagging feelings of guilt . . . only blissful warmth.

I felt regret now.

Above me, my golden eagle let out a soft cry, and as I glanced up at her, my spirits lifted ever so slightly. Elation, I'd named her long ago, because she never failed to bring me joy. Now she followed the sleigh from the sky, and I suspected she was my only remaining friend and ally.

After the horror of what had happened in the village, it was almost difficult to be afraid of what awaited me with the prince. Almost, but not quite. Rumors hammered at my thoughts as the sleigh traveled farther and farther into the deep woods that surrounded my home.

People disappearing into his castle, never to return. People with abilities beyond human limits. People like me.

Worse still was the knowledge that I went to him having committed crimes whose punishment was death.

You deserve it, the nasty part of my mind said to me, the one that sounded like the village children I grew up with. *It will be a fitting punishment for what you've done.*

We will not execute you as you deserve, the village elder had said, dressed in his long black shuba—the bearskin coat he was so proud of. *Instead, we will hand you over to the prince. He's always searching for people with your abilities*, he'd said with a look of disgust. *Let him deal with you as he sees fit.*

Standing in the elder's own izba, the clay oven blazing with a warm fire that could do nothing to pierce my frozen skin, I had paled at the announcement.

But Babushka—I'd stuttered, trying to think of anyone who could save me.

She has agreed to it, Elder Anatoly had interrupted, his voice brooking no argument.

Beside me, Andrei, one of the men who held my ropes, leaned toward me. *They say the prince will cut your heart out and eat it.* I had looked at him, this man I'd seen walking cheerfully to work in the lumber mill every day of my life, with eyes wide with fear. He'd looked back at me with a terrible sneer instead of a smile. *And you will deserve it, Ice Witch.*

While I swayed with the images of such violence, the man on the other side of me had added, *I've heard he does it slow, cutting you and letting you bleed into a golden cup.*

Either way, Andrei added, dark eyes flashing, *you'll be dead.*

Deserved punishment or not, I couldn't contain the shudder of fear that wracked me as I was held captive in the prince's sleigh.

I glanced at Ivan. He sat tall and straight, his steel-gray hair covered by a black fur hat. I stared at his broad back for a moment, an urge for contact moving me—to at least ask him why I'd been given the coat—but the wind was too strong, and the moment passed.

We traveled ever farther into the woods, the trees towering above us, snow clinging to their piney branches. I watched animals flee from the oncoming sleigh—birds flitting from tree to tree, squirrels chattering reproachfully, even a fox and hare interrupted from a deadly chase.

I imagined myself jumping down into the snow and escaping into those woods, and I went so far as to shift closer to the edge of my seat. I glanced down at the ground, moving so quickly beneath us. I could jump now, but would I manage to stay on my feet? If I stumbled, I risked serious injury. Still, wouldn't it be worth it to try rather than be brought before the prince like a lamb to slaughter?

I moved still closer to the edge, gathering my skirt in one

hand. I glanced at Ivan, but he continued to face forward.

I will jump, I thought, my gaze shifting to Elation in the sky. As always, she seemed to understand and flew lower to meet me.

My heart raced in my chest, pounding painfully against my ribs. I could see in my mind's eye what would happen: I would jump, and run, and Ivan would stop the sleigh and follow. What would I do then?

A flash of the destruction my power had wrought on the village lit up in my mind, and I winced.

Again, I thought of being brought as a criminal before a prince everyone said was a cruel and heartless murderer, and I knew my mind was made up.

I gathered myself to jump as we rounded the next bend, my skin hardening at the anticipation of hitting the snow at such a speed.

And then a heavy hand landed on my arm. I yelped in surprise, jerking my head up to find Ivan's eyes trained on mine. My mouth went dry.

With his other arm, he pulled the horses to a stop.

The icy cold spread all over my skin, hardening it to marble.

He climbed down from the sleigh and came over to my side. I met his gaze from my lofty perch, the blood pounding in my ears.

"I didn't want to have to do this," he said, and I flinched in spite of myself when his hand moved.

He reached behind me and retrieved a length of rope. It was

attached to the sleigh by a metal ring, and as he gathered the rope, I gritted my teeth.

Elation, I thought, and the eagle flew to my side.

Ivan watched the eagle impassively, as though it wasn't a creature with talons and a beak sharp enough to tear him apart. "There is a reason I was chosen to bring you to the prince," he said, his face stern but not twisted with cruelty. "I alone am enough to stop you—even with your abilities. Even with your eagle."

I held very still. I knew what he was implying: that he, too, had power. The idea of that sent a little shard of cold shock and fear through me. There had always been talk of others with abilities, though none like my own destructive power, but it was hard to know what to believe. The whispers of stories were traded as often as furs, and as they traveled along the breeze to the far-flung villages, they couldn't always be trusted to be accurately retold. I couldn't know for sure what power he was gifted with, but it was the veiled threat to Elation that stopped me.

"Do you understand?" he asked.

After a moment, I nodded.

"Then I won't have to restrain you," he said with a terse nod to himself. He coiled the rope again and replaced it.

The sleigh dipped under his weight as he returned to the driver's seat and urged the horses on again.

Elation stayed by my side on the seat, her gaze trained on Ivan, as though she'd like nothing better than to rip the flesh from his bones.

I held her back; Ivan's threat weighed heavily upon me.

What if his power was as terrible as mine? What if Elation was harmed—even killed? I shuddered to think of such an outcome. I never wanted to be responsible for the death of someone I loved again.

The trees slipped by endlessly as we traveled through the heavy fir and pine forest. I had been unlucky enough that this had happened in winter, when travel was even possible. If this had been late spring, there would be no means of journeying to Kiev due to the muck and lack of any decent roads. As it happened, though, the snow was thick and firm enough still in these few weeks before spring that a sleigh could travel easily. By the sun, I could see that we were heading roughly southeast, the sleigh gliding smoothly over the snow. As I watched the dark forest on either side, far from any other village or town, my thoughts turned to my last failed escape attempt. The men in my village had hunted me like hounds and caught me just as easily.

I'd meant to stay awake that night as I fled, and I thought I'd almost succeeded, but I fell asleep near dawn. A single cry from Elation woke me, the light from the weak winter sun turning the sky a pale peach, my small cooking fire long since died out to ash.

I meant to get moving again, but then I heard the men crashing through the woods. I tried to run, which was fool-ish. I should have melded back into the trees while it was still dark and found another place to hide, but I was as terrified as a flushed-out hare.

Elation had tried to help me. She had swooped down on

them, talons outstretched like she meant to hurt them—maybe even kill them in my defense—but I'd cried out and stopped her.

My heart twisted in my chest as I remembered the looks in the villagers' eyes: like I was a creature they'd thought docile, only to have it turn out to be a mad dog. As they knocked me to the ground, my skin had hardened defensively, but gone was any trace of the terrible power I'd unleashed on them only the night before.

Bound and physically weakened, I was dragged back to the village. I'd felt only relief that they hadn't killed me then, but I feared now, as I sat in Ivan's sleigh bound for a malevolent prince, that what they'd chosen instead might be far worse.

Because there was another rumor about the prince, one that was far more frightening than all the others: that he had murdered his own parents while they slept, naming himself grand prince before his father was even cold. And now he was gathering people with power, people who could help him take over the rest of our snowy-white world. I had no hope that such a cruel prince would pardon me for what I'd done. My crimes against the villagers were enough that I would surely be sentenced to death, but as I rubbed one hand across the thick wool of my coat, I wondered if the prince had a worse plan for me:

To make me join his dark army.

I glanced down at my hardening skin—which was turning to ice at the darkness of my thoughts—and wondered just how long my natural defenses would hold out before I, too, was killed.

After traveling until the sun hung low in the sky and the chill in the air took on a vicious edge, Ivan finally slowed the sleigh. I sat up a little straighter, taking note of our surroundings. We were still deep in the forest, enormous pine and fir trees on either side of us, no hint of a city nearby.

Babushka taught me at a very young age not to ask stupid questions, so I didn't ask whether we'd arrived at our final destination. It was clear that we had not.

Ivan slowed the horses to a plodding walk, and up ahead in a clearing, I saw the points of tents with small gold flags flying from their tops. The sounds of men and a large, crackling fire greeted us, and our horses perked up noticeably.

So many others waiting for us made my shoulders tense. I'd become used to Ivan's silence—at least enough that I no longer feared he would suddenly attack me—but I didn't relish walking into a circle of strangers.

"The horses need rest," Ivan said without turning around. "We will stop here for the night."

I said nothing, only glanced at the sky to be sure Elation was still with me. It took me a moment to find her, but then I saw the gleam of her feathers against the green of the pine trees. I closed my eyes in relief. She had flown away on our journey once or twice—presumably to hunt or find water—and each time she returned I was nearly moved to tears.

Ivan guided the sleigh to the very center of the camp, so close I could feel the warmth from the fire, and then jumped down in a surprisingly agile way for his age. He held his hand out to me as a small company of men surrounded us.

I forced myself to meet their eyes unflinchingly even as memories of the last time I faced a contingent of men threatened to drag me under.

"The grand prince has ordered you to be escorted to Kiev with enough men to keep you safe should we encounter any raiders," Ivan said. "The road to the city is not always secure."

I nodded once even as my mind raced ahead. As frightening as they might be, raiders could provide the chaos I needed to get away. I had enough knowledge of the woods that I could keep myself alive; I could find food, at least, and shelter, and make a fire. I wasn't helpless. And I had Elation.

I came back to myself only to find the men still staring at me, their air expectant. Only then did I realize that they had been asking questions I'd failed to respond to.

"Is she mute?" a man with a pointed sable beard asked with a sneer. "Is this the power we've sought? The only woman in Kievan Rus' who does not speak?" His close-set eyes narrowed slyly as he laughed, making me think of Sergei and Rodya—brothers in my village who'd taken great joy in tormenting me.

Both dead now.

The other men joined in laughing, all save Ivan. He'd been so quiet that I'd almost forgotten he was there. He stepped forward now. "It is not for any of us to question what Katya's powers are. We have our orders."

"Right. I'll take the girl to her tent," the man with the

pointed beard said, and I felt my heart sink.

Ivan nodded. "That's fine, Grigory. I need to look after the horses."

Grigory grabbed hold of my arm, but my skin immediately turned to ice, and even beneath my thick coat, I think he could feel the blast of cold. He dropped my arm like a hot coal. "Follow me," he growled.

I kept my head held high even as my stomach quivered. Would they restrain me again, as my villagers had?

I hadn't used that terrible fire again on my villagers, even when they'd captured me. The thought of using it here and now entered my mind, a little shudder of horror going through me. Never again did I want to be responsible for that much death and destruction.

We walked past the roaring central fire, and I noticed an iron pot steaming with some sort of stew. A few of the men sat around the fire while still others tended to the horses. Several tents were set up in a half-circle around the fire. But Grigory led me past all of these. My skin grew increasingly icy until my breath came out in plumes of cold air.

Soon we were well out of earshot of the other men, and Grigory whirled on me. "Your village made some wild claims about you, but I know they are lies." His eyes flashed angrily at me, his bushy eyebrows drawn low. "The prince has searched the world for someone with that kind of power, and I can tell that someone isn't you."

I didn't understand his anger, but it made me want to make

a run for it and damn the consequences. Instead I faced him. "I wish it was a lie."

He took a step toward me, and the cold within me spread, protecting my skin as though anticipating a blow. "Had I been there, I would have demanded you prove yourself. No doubt this is a waste of time—something the prince, with all his riches, has very little of. Even now, his enemies plot to move against him. Yet here we are, spending more than two days away from the palace, hunting a girl who will prove to be yet another charlatan."

How I wished I was a fraud! I'd already spent countless hours begging God to turn back the hands of time, to take away this hateful power. And now, to stand accused of faking it for my own profit brought pinpricks of anger on the heels of my fear. "Then take me back to my village and fail to bring me before the grand prince. It makes no difference to me."

Like a snake striking, his hand darted out and grabbed hold of me. This time, his grip was strong enough to hurt—if my arm hadn't already been well protected by ice. He flinched in surprise, but soon his surprise turned to cruel amusement. "So, you do have power—your skin can turn to ice. How impressive," he added wryly. "Still not quite the talent that was promised. We were told you could wield an ability slightly more . . . destructive."

I could, and I had. Faces of villagers frozen in death flashed before my eyes. The death that I had brought about. "Once my ice-cold skin was all the power I had, and I wish it was still true."

"Prove it to me," he said in a tone dripping with venom. "Prove that you aren't another charlatan drawing interest from the prince only to trick him again."

I swallowed hard. "I cannot."

"You see!" he shouted, practically in my face. I tried to yank away, but he held me tenaciously.

Suddenly, a girl appeared beside us, and Grigory dropped my arm like it burned him. She watched us both, her eyes as dark as her hair, with her slender arms crossed over her chest. At first glance, I thought she was younger than I was, but as I took in the worldliness hidden in the depths of her gaze, I realized she was probably older, though not by much. I wondered how I hadn't noticed her approach.

"What are you doing, Grigory?" she asked, and her accent immediately identified her as from the steppes in the east. There was a traveling trader who sometimes visited our village who was from that far-off place. I remembered his face, wrinkled and kind.

Grigory's mouth opened and closed several times, leading me to believe he was as surprised to see the girl as I had been.

She narrowed her eyes at him. "Katya Alexeyevna is to be brought before the grand prince, unharmed."

"I wanted to be sure this girl wasn't another fraud," Grigory said with an accusatory glare at me, like I'd somehow provoked him into acting this way. "And she told me herself she can't demonstrate her power. The prince shouldn't waste his time on her."

Grigory's unprovoked anger at me had been strange enough,

but the fact that he seemed most upset about my supposed lack of powers both confused and worried me. As far as I knew, I was being brought before the grand prince for sentencing. But there had been no mention of that so far—only my power. Were the rumors about the prince seeking out people with abilities true?

The girl's gaze shifted to me briefly, and I tilted my chin higher. Everything had been taken from me, but I refused to cower. "The prince can decide for himself," the girl said. "But we must follow our orders."

Grigory looked like he wanted to argue, but apparently the invocation of the prince's name was enough to dissuade him.

"Ivan needs your help with the sleigh," she added.

Grigory turned to me, his face still dark with anger. "Come on, then."

The girl let out a snort. "As if I'd let you lead her to her tent now. Of course I'll do it. You should have fetched me the moment she arrived."

Grigory shot me a look but thankfully relented. It wasn't until he was well on his way back to the entrance of camp, though, that the ice on my skin receded.

"I'm afraid Grigory only has two moods: hostile and disgruntled," the girl said with a faint look of disgust. "But he does have his uses." She turned to me. "You aren't hurt? He looked more hostile than disgruntled today."

I thought of the way Grigory had grabbed my arm. If it weren't for my defenses, I'd likely have nasty bruises. "No, he didn't hurt me."

"Good. I'll show you where you can rest," she said, gesturing for me to follow. "My name is Kharankhui, by the way," she tossed over her shoulder at me with a smile, "but you can call me Kharan."

"Katya," I said.

Warily, I continued to follow her until we arrived at a round tent that could easily sleep five men comfortably.

"Here we are," Kharan said, gesturing toward the enormous tent.

"I am to sleep here?" I asked, unable to keep the incredulity from my tone. "Alone?"

Kharan smiled. "The grand prince sent this tent to be used only by you."

"It's . . . beautiful," I said truthfully, gazing up at its deep-blue sides trimmed in gold. As I looked closer, I saw that gold stars had been embroidered throughout, so that the whole thing resembled the night sky.

She held aside the front flap, and I found I didn't even need to duck my head to enter. Once inside, my boots sank into plush silver fur. The inside of the tent was nearly as elaborate as the outside, with tapestries, a wide bed with richly brocaded blue-and-gold coverings and a midnight black fur, a small table with a bowl for washing, and two ornately carved chairs.

I hadn't seen such finery in all my life; Babushka's humble izba was furnished with far less.

"I don't understand," I said, and it was the confusion that made a prickle of unease trace down my spine. I was being brought before the prince as a criminal, yet I was given my own lavish tent?

"Did you think we would keep you chained like the cruel people of your village?"

"I don't know what to think."

"It's clear you don't know the value of your abilities," she said with a side glance. "I can tell you that they make you worth more to the prince than any of the fine things found in this tent."

Her answer so surprised me that I let out a quiet, self-deprecating laugh. "Does he value monsters so highly? Murderers, too?" Perhaps he did, if the rumors about him were to be believed.

She appeared unperturbed. "A dog may be kicked so many times before it turns around and bites. Are humans any different?"

Yes, but does a dog revel in it once he has bitten? "I should think humans would be held to a higher standard than animals, so yes."

She looked at me appraisingly. "You have a very noble view of humanity."

I tried to silence myself, but I was genuinely curious. "And you don't?"

She shrugged. "It depends on which particular group of humans we're discussing."

My gaze continued to roam before finally landing on a chest big enough to hold a full-grown man.

Kharan must have followed my line of sight, for she walked over to it and threw open the lid. "The prince wanted to be sure you had clothing."

Inside were garments that glittered like gemstones: deep carmine, sapphire, emerald, and lighter colors like jade, aquamarine, and topaz. I could tell from a few feet away that they were all heavily brocaded and embroidered, trimmed in fur and silk.

My chest at home contained two outfits, and I was wearing my nicest one—usually only worn for festivals. I thought of my own clothes now hidden under the fine robe Ivan had given me—my white linen rubakha, embroidered with carmine-colored thread that trimmed the neckline and wide sleeves, the one I'd always been so proud of, now looked like what it was: peasant clothing. Even my lovely red wool skirt with what I had always thought of as intricate white embroidery might as well have been moth-eaten compared to the fine garments within that chest.

"Surely this is too much for someone like me," I said, my eyes still on the chest. The gowns were lovely—lovelier than I'd ever seen, but they were intimidating in their beauty. *All this for a prisoner?* But I thought I knew the reason for such finery, and the whispers of worry in my mind intensified. Were the tent and the gowns bribes? Was the prince trying to entice the poor peasant girl to join his dark army with gifts of more value than she'd ever seen?

I also couldn't help but fear, like Kharan's kindness, that it was some terrible deception. Like the old tale of a witch in the woods feeding children all kinds of delicious treats . . . only to fatten them up and eat them.

"The prince can afford it, so why not take advantage of his generosity?"

Because these were clothes fit for a boyar's wife, not a peasant like me, I responded in my head.

My expression must have still been one of dismay, for she arched an eyebrow and said, "Would you have been more comfortable with rags?"

"I don't mean to sound ungrateful, but in my experience, people don't usually do things for me out of the kindness of their hearts."

"No one here is trying to trick you, Katya. You're safe here with us. And not even Grigory would dare cross the prince. The prince said you're to be protected."

I didn't know what to say, other than I knew it couldn't simply be out of the goodness of his heart. He had to have a purpose for treating me so well. I just wasn't sure I wanted to find out what it was.

A rustle at the flap of the tent drew our attention, and in the next instant, the flap was blown aside to reveal Elation swooping over our heads. Kharan took a step back, surprise and alarm clear on her face, but then Elation landed on the top of one of the chairs, perching there as though it was especially for her.

A moment passed, and the three of us stared at each other, one after the other. The strangest urge to laugh gripped me.

"I hope this eagle is yours and not some poor confused bird who has mistaken this tent for her tree," Kharan said finally.

I smiled. "I wouldn't say she's mine, but I do know her."

"You're a falconer, then?"

I shook my head. "Not exactly. She's more a friend and companion than anything."

"It's been too long since I saw someone who had such a close relationship with an eagle. There were many in my tribe who hunted with them, but I never had the affinity for it." She watched Elation with a wistful look. "The prince enjoys falconry and keeps many birds of prey, but none so large as this."

Finding that the prince and I had birds of prey in common did nothing to comfort me. I didn't want to see him as human at all. Not with such a beastly reputation. I wanted, suddenly, to ask her opinion of Prince Alexander, but something stayed my tongue. Kharan might have been courteous, even friendly, but I also couldn't forget to whom she owed her loyalty.

Keep your own counsel, Babushka always said, and so I did.

I said nothing, my hand gently stroking the soft feathers on Elation's head.

"How long has the eagle been with you?" Kharan asked.

"For as long as I can remember." The eagle had appeared one day in the woods just beyond the village, where I often gathered herbs, and had watched me, but I'd thought nothing of it. Until she was there the next day and the next, and then I'd find her watching from the trees closer to the village— her beautiful golden eyes interested and, to my lonely mind, friendly. It had seemed just a figment of my imagination, really. But soon I began to think of her as my friend.

I'd started talking to her then. First, only in my own head, but later, in whispered confessions.

It wasn't until recently that she had shown any sign other than her constant vigilance that she cared for me at all.

I thought of that dark night in the woods, alone and hunted, terrified of not only my pursuers but of my own self—of what I'd done. The eagle had descended from the sky like the firebird of legend, her feathers illuminated by the glow of my small campfire. She'd brought me a hare. She kept me alive. But most of all, she offered me what I wanted most: companionship.

"An eagle is a good friend to have, falconer or not." Kharan's voice broke through my thoughts. She nodded to herself once, her gaze turning faraway again. After a moment, she gestured toward the flap of the tent. "I'm sure you're thirsty after that journey. I'd meant to have water waiting in a pitcher, but it took them longer than they expected to set up this tent—they only just finished before you arrived. I'll return shortly with water and news of supper."

"That's kind of you—thank you."

When she left, I took better note of my surroundings. I ran my hand over the softness of the fur on the bed, examined the comb made of bone upon the small table, and ultimately found myself drawn to the chest of beautiful clothing.

Whoever had packed the chest was clearly familiar with dressing wealthy ladies, for it was filled with not only the gowns but with glittering jewelry, embroidered and gemstone-studded belts, silky veils, and two woolen cloaks trimmed in fur. Three pairs of slippers were included, each more impractical than the next: two made of soft deerskin and one of gold silk. I glanced down at my leather boots lined with rabbit fur that, while not as pretty, were much more capable of handling a sleigh ride through the snow.

More important, it was Dedushka who had made them for me.

It's usually the city dwellers who wear boots, he'd said one cold night when he'd returned home with doeskin and rabbit fur, *but I thought you should have a pair to keep your feet warm when you're in the woods.*

You'll spoil the girl, Babushka had said, eyes narrowing in disapproval. *Get her used to a life she can never have.*

Dedushka hadn't responded for a moment, only continued to sharpen his skinning knife. *It won't hurt to give her something special for once.*

Babushka shook her head but didn't argue anymore. For her, that was as good as giving her blessing.

Thinking of them made me homesick, though I'd been gone only a few hours. Our village was small, only a derevnya with no church or even a place to buy supplies, but it was built around a lumber mill, and there was no shortage of work to be done. Dedushka had been a hunter as well as a logger, and Babushka was a weaver as well as an herbalist. I pictured her now: her hands moving quickly over the loom that sat in the very center of our izba. Many times had I woken from my small cot by the window to find her already awake and weaving, her gnarled hands still agile enough to work the loom. It was the herbalism, though, that she'd passed on to me. We'd spent countless hours in the forest beyond our village, searching for everything from pine needles, which could bring down swelling in the body when brewed and drunk as a tea, to violets, which could be used to help relieve congestion in the chest. After gathering the herbs, we'd return home and spend hours categorizing. I didn't have much skill in drawing, but I learned to draw and write well enough to keep a journal of medicinal herbs and their uses. Yet another thing that had been left behind when I'd been exiled.

I thought of our izba now. It was small, and nothing compared to this celestial tent, but it was beautiful in its own way. The eaves and window frames were carved with woodland scenes: deer and leaves, squirrels and nuts and berries. The elegant lines of a horse head watched over the many people coming and going from the ridgepole of the roof. Dedushka always said he'd carved it for good luck.

It hadn't brought him luck in the end.

Elation made a little whistling sound, and I went to her side. She closed her eyes and leaned her head into me, and I did the same.

"The accommodations here are very fine," I whispered to her, "but I'm afraid it may all be a gilded cage."

Chapter Two

Long after the sun had set and the candles had burned down nearly halfway, Kharan returned with water. I'd spent the entire time wondering about my fate and trying unsuccessfully to understand why I'd been thus far treated like I was a guest and not a captive, thoughts that left me anxious.

"My apologies for taking so long," she said, setting the pitcher down on the small washing table. "I was coerced into helping prepare supper."

She poured water into a copper cup and handed it to me. "Thank you," I said, immediately taking a drink.

"Supper is ready if you're hungry," she said. "It's only hare stew, but Boris takes his stews very seriously."

This seemed yet another example of being treated decently, which only served to put me further on edge. Though Kharan had told Grigory I wasn't a prisoner, I couldn't help but still feel like one. Did I have the freedom to leave if I chose? Ivan certainly made it clear that I didn't. But then again, I knew a normal captive wouldn't have a tent like this one. "Supper would be lovely," I said, "only, I'd like to ask you something first."

She tilted her head. "Of course."

"Why am I being treated this way? Can I expect the same treatment from the prince when we arrive in Kiev?"

She blinked at my questions as though surprised, but I didn't regret my bluntness. I'd rather know my fate than wait for it to play out before my eyes. "The prince isn't cruel like he is rumored to be," Kharan said after a moment. "You have committed a grave crime, but yours is a rare ability." She leaned closer as if imparting a secret. "I would use that to your advantage."

"It's a monstrous ability that I want nothing to do with." My words seemed to fill the space around us, echoing like a declaration.

Silence followed, and then Kharan said gently, "Then we will speak no more of it tonight. Will you still eat?"

I hesitated, running my hand over my frigid arm. The hunger within my stomach roared to life, reminding me that it had been at least a day since I'd last eaten.

I nodded.

She walked over to the tent flap and held it aside. "Come, then. I can't promise the company will be what you're used to, but the food will be good."

The moment I stepped outside, I took a deep, cleansing breath. The vastness of the sky above, dotted with countless bright stars, relaxed muscles I hadn't even realized were tense. It was the same sky I'd seen from my izba, and from the forest beyond our village. *As long as I can see the stars,* I told myself, *I won't feel so far from home.*

Kharan led me toward a blazing fire, toward the rich smell of food, toward the low sounds of men talking.

"Cold fire, they called it," one of the men was saying just loud enough for me to hear. I stopped. He leaned toward the others and lowered his voice. "It was so cold it shattered anything it touched."

Before he could say more, though, he caught sight of us and paled under his scruffy brown beard.

"I thought it would be best to have Katya enjoy her supper out here with us," Kharan said, interrupting the heavy silence that had overtaken the camp. "Don't make me regret my decision."

Ivan stood and offered me his seat closest to the fire. "Sit. Join us."

Not wishing to offend him, though the spot was in far too conspicuous a location, I took the proffered seat with a small smile. "Thank you."

Kharan brought me a steaming bowl of the stew, a hunk of dark bread, and a mug of kvas. A bite of the stew revealed it to be just as flavorful as its smell suggested, with herbs and vegetables that made it both savory and aromatic. "This is delicious," I said, and the man who was speaking when we first arrived smiled.

"I did the best I could with limited ingredients," he said.

"Boris is just trying to impress you," Ivan said beside me. "He brought an entire bag full of food for just this simple meal."

I smiled and took a drink of my kvas, which was as good as the stew: both tangy and mildly sweet. "I'm impressed either way."

The others turned back to their meals, and I quietly ate mine. Slowly, they grew used to my presence among them, and conversations cropped up around me. They talked of ordinary things, work and family and hunting, and mentioned nothing of fire—cold or otherwise. And I was able to relax and enjoy my meal, the feel of a full stomach, the lingering taste of the kvas on my tongue.

"Finish up," Ivan said after the men's bowls remained empty and no further trips to the kettle were made. "We leave at dawn."

"How much farther to Kiev?" I asked.

"An easy day's ride."

Not much longer, then, to enjoy my relative freedom. What would the palace be like? And the prince? I glanced up again at the stars above me.

As though reading my mind, Grigory said, "Soon enough you'll meet the prince." It was the first he had said to me since the moment Kharan had interrupted his attempt to intimidate me. "Let's hope he finds you worthy."

The guard with the scruffy beard and love for cooking scoffed, "How could he not? Did you not hear my tale?"

I winced at this as the others shifted uncomfortably. In just those few words, the relative camaraderie I'd been enjoying around the campfire was shattered.

"I did hear it, and we've heard many tall tales like that before," Grigory said, and again, the ice began to spread over my skin.

"Grigory, not again." The warning came from Kharan, who shook her head in an attempt to silence him.

Grigory held up his hand in peace. "I have only an innocent question. If you're so powerful, then why didn't you save yourself when the villagers captured you?"

I stayed silent. Why answer? What was the point? I knew Grigory's type: they trod on anyone they considered weaker than them just to inflate their own egos.

"Is that a tear I see shining in your eye? Did I touch on a sore spot, dearie?" Grigory continued with a laugh.

I lifted my gaze to meet his cruel smile, and for just a moment, I fantasized about releasing my power on him—just to see the expression wiped from his face. After what had happened in the village, though, these thoughts so disturbed me that I came suddenly to my feet.

"By all the saints, that's enough, Grigory," Kharan snapped.

Eager to escape, I thrust my bowl at the cook and mumbled my thanks. My hands shook as the ice in my veins grew stronger, colder.

I turned on my heel and hurried back to my tent. As my mind produced image after image of the many ways I could take revenge on Grigory, deep down I knew the answer to his question:

Just because I had power didn't mean I had to use it.

❖ ❖ ❖

Elation turned her head toward me as I burst through the flap of the tent. She made a sound that could have been one of greeting or surprise—or both. I was too agitated to decode it. The cold had hardened my skin again, dropping the temperature of the air around me, and making the flames of the candles dim as I passed by. The ice only appeared when I was upset in some way, and I was definitely upset now. My heart was pounding in my ears. I wanted to escape—could see myself turning around and fleeing the way I'd come, Elation by my side. But I wasn't so foolish as to think that just because I had been given luxurious accommodations and good food, I wasn't being watched. The moment I set foot outside, they would track my every step.

There is *one way I could escape*, I thought, but then I shuddered violently and pushed such malevolent thoughts aside.

I couldn't do that. Not even to save myself.

"Katya?" a voice called from the other side of the flap. It was Kharan. "May I enter?"

I answered by pulling aside the flap for her.

She held up two mugs of kvas and a piece of fine cloth. "Pry-aniki?" she offered as she opened the cloth to reveal four glazed cookies. The sweet smell of honey and spices wafted up.

They were my favorite; I could practically taste the sweet gingerbread now. At home, they were a special treat that I only ever got to eat at Christmastime.

"This is kind of you," I said, and stepped aside so she could enter.

Kharan came in and sat on one of the many furs carpeting the ground, folding her legs under her. I joined her, and she handed me one of the mugs.

She placed the cloth with the cookies closest to me, and I took one and bit into it.

"I didn't want you to miss out on the pryaniki," she said, taking a bite of one herself. "I thought it would be too cruel of a punishment."

"They're very good," I said with a small smile.

She watched me take a sip of the kvas. "Grigory can be a miserable little snake, but I hope you won't judge us all by his actions."

It wasn't Grigory I was concerned about. Not when I thought about the person such a man was guardsman for. "Grigory is no different from many I've met before. But the prince . . . how would you describe him?"

She looked at me pointedly. "You are asking, I'm sure, if the rumors about him are true."

"Yes."

She shrugged one shoulder. "It depends on the rumor. Is he searching for those of us with abilities? Yes. Is he drinking our blood? Not that I know of."

I looked at her in surprise. "You, too, have an ability like mine?"

"Not as strong as yours, but yes."

It was rather shocking to find out that not only Ivan had power, but Kharan, too.

"What is your ability?" I asked as she took a sip of kvas.

"I'd have to give you a demonstration," she said with a glitter in her eye. "Not here, though. Perhaps when we return to the palace."

I was almost afraid to find out. I didn't wish my own ability on anyone else. Once, it had only made me the object of derision, but then it had manifested in such horrible destruction that the villagers had no choice but to turn me out. To me, abilities had always been something to be feared. It was odd to hear Kharan speaking of her own ability so lightly.

"One thing I will say about the prince," she said, "he is driven to protect his people. Some find him aloof, even cold, but that's because he is always focused on his goal."

"And what is his goal for me?"

Her eyes danced a bit, but not in a mean way. "We'll have to wait and see." She brushed off crumbs from her skirt as she finished the last bite of her gingerbread. "Have you ever been to Kiev?"

I shook my head. "I've barely been farther than the woods surrounding my village."

"It's one of the greatest cities in the world," she said fondly. "Traders come from all over, bringing cloth and food and furs. Almost anything you could want to buy is right there in the marketplace. The palace serves meals like every day is a feast day, and the fires and braziers burn brightly all day and night."

"It does sound exciting."

She nodded. "You'll be safe there."

Safe from what? I wanted to ask, but at that moment, Elation flapped her wings. I turned to look at her and could tell she wanted to fly. "She wants to hunt," I told Kharan, coming to my feet.

She looked at me curiously. "An eagle that hunts at night?"

I pulled aside the flap for her and she flew through gracefully. "I'm not sure what she does, honestly. She always returns, though, which is all I care about."

She stood, too. "I should let you rest. Ivan will be barking orders for us to pack up before the sun has even made it past the horizon."

"Thank you for the pryaniki."

"I hope it allowed me to make amends for supper," Kharan said with a smile.

I let myself smile back. "That wasn't your fault, but I'm glad you came anyway."

Kharan might have been loyal to the prince, but I found myself thinking of her as someone I could talk to. I'd never had someone I could confide in, not really, and especially no one close to my own age. There was something about her that put me at ease—not enough that I could confide everything; I didn't think I'd ever feel that close to anyone—but at least enough that I wouldn't fear for my life tonight.

But tomorrow . . . tomorrow I would face the prince.

Chapter Three

I awoke before dawn, and for one blissful moment, I thought I was back in the izba with Babushka and Dedushka. But then I remembered.

And once the memories began to flow, they were so painful that I pressed my eyelids closed with my fingers. Desperate to distract myself, I threw aside my bedding and fumbled around for the candle in its little golden holder. I'd left one candle burning, which was possibly foolish considering I was sleeping in a flammable tent, but I couldn't bear to sleep in total darkness among men I didn't trust. Besides, I knew Elation wouldn't let me burn to death. She'd flown in again sometime after I'd gone to bed and perched on the back of the chair. Even now I could just make out the shimmer of her eyes in the gloom.

I carried the smaller candle by my bedside over to the one on the table and lit it. As I cast my gaze around the tent, the clothes chest seemed to call out to me again. I walked over and stared at the beautifully embossed lid before finally opening it. The fine clothing waited there, even more lovely in the soft light. I glanced down at my rubhaka, now hopelessly wrinkled. Still, as I looked at the gowns, with all their many colors, I wondered which would be appropriate for travel. Would the gown look ridiculous over my boots? Should I wear a veil and the jewelry? What about the belt?

With a sound of disgust, I slammed the lid closed. I had been raised a peasant. What did I know of fine clothing? Kharan said I was being summoned, but it was clear that I was a captive—at least until I stood before the prince. To dress as a princess seemed ridiculous at worst and presumptuous at best—no matter that the prince himself had sent the garments. Perhaps it was merely to play a cruel trick on me, to have me arrive dressed in such finery only to be laughed and mocked.

A rustle came at the entrance of my tent then, followed by a soft voice calling my name. Elation ruffled her feathers and turned her gaze toward the entrance. I walked over and held aside the flap.

There, Kharan waited in the early morning light, dressed for travel in a beautiful long coat, tied at the waist with a golden sash and trimmed in fur. It was as midnight black as her hair, with golden threads embroidered throughout. She wore boots like mine of rough leather.

"The others are already striking the tents. Would you like to eat with me while they take yours down?"

I nodded. "Let me just get my coat."

After I'd retrieved it and returned to her, I nodded toward her beautiful clothing. "Your coat is lovely."

She held out part of the wool fabric. "Thank you. This is a deel. I have two that I was able to bring with me from my village—this one, made of wool, and another, made of satin." She held out a hand and touched the rough fabric of my red skirt. "Yours is beautiful, too." She leaned close. "I think it's a better choice for travel than anything the prince sent."

I gave her a relieved smile. "Thank you. This is one of the only outfits I brought with me from home, but it's my favorite."

"Did you do the embroidery yourself?"

"Yes, only I had the help of Babushka . . ." I trailed off as pain shot through my chest. I remembered her last words to me, and it made me desperate to go back, to speak to her again . . . to ask for the forgiveness I hadn't received.

"There were many people I loved who I left behind, too," Kharan said, and I knew my expression revealed how distraught I was. She reached out and touched my arm. "Would you like hot tea and kasha? It won't make the pain go away, but it will at least fill your belly."

Not trusting my voice with my throat closing on unshed tears, I nodded and managed a small smile.

She led me to the campfire that hadn't been stamped out yet, and as I ate and drank, I watched the men pack up the tents and various supplies on a wagon pulled by wide, shaggy ponies. My enormous tent was rolled and stored, the bed broken down, the chest hefted onto the wagon. Elation disliked the newly chaotic environment and took flight, perhaps to seek out something to eat, or to simply escape because she could.

At one point Kharan left and went to the line of horses tied to low tree branches. When she returned, she was leading a wheat-colored pony. I watched with some surprise as she fed him some of her own kasha.

"Is this one yours?" I asked.

She smiled at him proudly. "Yes, this is Daichin. He came with me all the way from the steppes and isn't as magnificent, perhaps, as some of the desert-bred horses the prince has, but Daichin is the one thing I can call my own."

I thought of Elation, and though she wasn't mine by any means, I could still sympathize with Kharan. "If he made the long journey here with you, then I understand your attachment."

She petted him and I did the same, marveling at his thick coat. "He's a hardy thing," I said, and I could tell just from his flinty hooves that he was tough and reliable.

"He is," she agreed, scratching beneath his forelock. "Strong enough to bring me all the way here without a moment's lameness. Though he has grown fat in the prince's stables. He's not used to being pampered in a stall. At home on the steppes he'd be digging through thick snow for his food like every other horse. I ride him every day to keep him from becoming too sedentary, but it's not enough."

"It takes skill to be fat even in winter," I said with a smile.

Kharan laughed. "This is true, but when the horses are dining on kasha as delicious as any that would be prepared for us, then they can't help but grow rounded bellies." She glanced down at the bowl of kasha she was even now sharing with him sheepishly. "I suppose I'm partly to blame, too."

After a much shorter length of time than I would have thought possible—I had only just finished my tea and porridge—the contents of the camp were loaded.

Ivan walked over to us, his steps quiet on the fresh snow. "Ready to travel to Kiev?"

As if I have a choice, I thought, but nodded.

Ivan had the sleigh ready, and he offered me his hand, roughened by cold winters and hard work, to help me into it. I settled down and drew my coat tight, nerves and fear churning unpleasantly inside me. Despite my treatment here, I knew I wouldn't avoid facing the prince's judgment. The punishment for death and destruction caused in my own village would be unavoidable. I steeled myself for what lay at the end of today's journey.

Kharan mounted Daichin beside me, and Ivan settled in to drive the sleigh, the two white horses stamping their hooves as if eager to be off. The other men formed pairs in front of and behind us without having to be told. Their horses were heavy battle chargers, and I thought uneasily of what Ivan had said about the road to Kiev not always being safe.

Ivan signaled the lead guards to go on ahead, and then our sleigh was gliding over the snow, the sounds of jingling harnesses and horse hooves filling the woods. The sound was cheerful, but it made me think of chains. I couldn't shake my apprehension, however amiable most of the guards had been to me.

It was almost more frightening to be treated with compassion than to have been greeted with aggression. At least then I would have known where I stood. The luxurious tent and even Kharan's kindness made me fear a trick—something I was no stranger to.

I watched the snow-laden trees as we passed by, and it felt as though ice crystals were slowly forming over my skin. I had learned that kindness was usually cruelty in disguise, that those who grew more powerful from the belittling of others usually liked to provide their victims with something they could take away. As a prisoner who had been exiled by her village, I had so very little else that could be taken away from me.

Only a month had passed since I'd lost control. It had never happened before. My power—if it could even be called by such a name—had only ever subjected me to mockery. Sometimes, I could do simple things with it, like freeze water into ice—not a particularly useful skill in winters as brutal as ours. And the village children I'd grown up with found it endlessly amusing to put me in situations they knew would result in me becoming as stiff as a corpse—anything from simple teasing to hitting me with sticks to see if I'd flinch.

But that day was different. For one thing, I'd never been pushed that far before.

Ironically, when I lost control, I wasn't the one being targeted—the victim was the one person other than Babushka who treated me with any kindness: Dedushka.

His given name was Lev, and he had once been as strong and respected as the lion he was named for. That was before he became a world traveler—long before he took me in. He and Babushka had wandered across the snowy world, making trade and accruing vast amounts of knowledge, particularly in the healing arts. But when they finally returned to the tiny village where they had first settled, they were treated with suspicion and disdain. The other villagers wrongly believed that because Lev and his wife had traveled far and wide, they then thought of themselves as superior to the humble people of the village. It didn't help when they took in a babe left for dead in the cold winter woods—a girl with strange powers. Me.

In the end, my adoptive grandparents were only tolerated because of Babushka's gift of healing and Dedushka's hard work as a logger. But as Dedushka grew older, his strength failed him, and eventually he could no longer work as he once had. Then it was his wood carving and stories that provided an occupation of sorts. He spun tales of far-off places we could never hope to see, of magic and monsters and creatures of legend, which held us all enthralled long into the night.

On this particular evening, he'd sat by a fire, surrounded by young and old from the village. He told us of warriors who rode animals several times larger than a horse—war elephants, they called them. Enormous and intelligent, with more brute strength than a warhorse. He told of golden books detailing the strategy of using such animals, of how the Persians had once used them to terrify and destroy whole Rus' military units.

The melodic tone of his voice, the way he used his entire body to paint a picture of his tales—these traits made it impossible not to listen once he started talking.

Though I could feel myself being drawn in, I had remained a safe distance away from the others, hovering just outside the warmth of the fire. Dedushka's sharp eyes had landed on mine, and he grinned and beckoned to me welcomingly.

"Come, join us, dear girl," he said.

Several eyes landed on me and narrowed warningly. The men were in a dark mood that evening already. At the mill, one of the chains holding the logs in place had rusted and broken, spilling many weeks' worth of work. They would be picking up logs for days. "I'm fine where I am," I answered, skin prickling.

Dedushka's smile widened in spite of the tension around the fire. "Nonsense. You cannot be comfortable hovering in the shadows. Come sit by me—surely these fine men will move."

"Not for her," Sergei said, the scar above his lip twisting cruelly with his sneer. Rodya, his brother and his friend, as always, followed his lead.

"Not for the Ice Witch," he said.

Dedushka watched me for a moment, judging my reaction. It had been a long time since I'd come crying to Babushka and

Dedushka after being taunted by others, and I'd done my best to hide it from them once I was old enough to stifle my cries. I remained as still as a statue. "An accusation of power and magic is not one to take lightly," he said finally. "It seems foolish to taunt such a person."

"He has a valid point," Yury, one of the few men of sense in the village, said. "What does it matter to you if she sits here with us?"

"I don't want her to think she's anything other than a burden on this village," Sergei said, his small eyes shifting to mine.

"Katya is no burden," Dedushka said in his calm but firm way. "She has never asked for anything from anyone in this village, and especially not from you, Sergei."

Sergei's hand tightened into a fist at his side, for he was well known for his volatility. "You've always thought you were better than us, haven't you, Lev?" He jerked his chin in my direction. "That you could even force us to accept that Ice Witch no one wanted. Well, you were wrong."

"Go home, witch!" Rodya said, eyes flashing just like his brother's.

"You're letting the misfortune of our work today anger you," Yury said, exasperation creeping into his tone. "If you cannot be at peace, then go home. Leave the rest of us to enjoy the evening."

Dmitri, one of Sergei's friends, glared at Yury. "Why are you defending the witch?"

"Because we only want a bit of peace," Viktor, Yury's cousin, added with a shake of his head.

The others were treating this casually, as though it was only a tantrum being thrown by a child, but I could read the danger in the air. It charged the space around us like the threat of lightning.

And then Dedushka came slowly to his feet, aided by his beautifully carved walking stick. "Take my seat, then. I won't continue until you do."

I hesitated, but I didn't want to leave him standing there alone. As I walked closer, Sergei leaped to his feet and grabbed me.

"Let go," I said as ice spread over my body.

Sergei only grinned, knowing there was little I could do.

"Enough of this, Sergei," Dedushka said, his voice deep with warning, but we all knew he was no longer strong enough to be a threat.

But then Dedushka surprised us both by reaching for Sergei's arm. Sergei jerked it out of his reach, but in doing so he lost his hold on me. I spun away.

The other men shouted as Sergei began to grapple with Dedushka. He knocked Dedushka down, and Dedushka fell painfully to the logs they'd been sitting on with an audible *thump*.

I screamed, and something ignited within me. A rush of cold escaped from my outstretched hand, dousing the fire instantly.

Everyone, including me, was stunned. Never before had my power done anything more than turn my skin cold and hard or freeze small buckets of water.

A flicker of fear passed across Sergei's face, and he reacted as he always had—by lashing out. "You see? He has brought a witch into our midst, just as I said!" He yanked Dedushka roughly to his feet before catching his brother's eye.

Rodya and Peter grasped Dedushka under each arm. Dedushka struggled to escape their hold, but he was no match for their strength.

"Anatoly will never stand for this," Dedushka said. "Unhand me. Now."

"What are you doing?" Yury demanded of Rodya and Boris. They ignored him and pushed past him unheedingly. "Then I will go to Anatoly." And Yury left to find the village elder.

When Yury left, it was as though the one voice of reason left, too. Even Viktor, who had spoken up before, said nothing now. The others who had been sitting around the circle, though they had stood when I'd doused the fire, did not speak. I couldn't tell then if their silence meant they agreed with Sergei.

"We'll leave now," I said, desperation clawing at my throat as I caught hold of Rodya's arm. "Only let him go."

But he backhanded me, the blow strong enough to send me flying to the ground, though the ice of my skin prevented it from causing me any real harm.

"It's too late for that," Sergei said. "We've tolerated him for too long." He stared at me. "He should have never taken in a stray witch."

"Stop," I shouted. *"Please."*

They dragged him toward the trees at the very edge of the village, and I lurched forward to follow. The threat of violence hovered, a dark cloud infusing the men with cruel power.

When someone produced the length of rope, I knew the threat would become a promise of murder. Dedushka fought them, wildly, but he could not escape their grasp. I pushed through the crowd of men, each of them flinching away the moment my hand made contact with them. I was radiating cold, so much that frost hovered in the air around me like an aura.

"Let him go!" I yelled, snatching at Sergei's arm.

He shoved me away. "Shut up, or we will hang you both, witch."

They made a noose and wrapped it around the old man's neck. Dedushka cried out. Rodya wrenched my arms behind my back, and then it was difficult to say what happened next.

I remember the ice in my veins spreading outward. I remember encouraging it instead of trying to stop it.

The power bubbled up from within me like a geyser, cold and ruthless. As the men threw the rope over the branch, the cold fire burst forth in an explosion that illuminated the night sky. Blue in color, blindingly blue—brighter than the sky. My skin was hard as marble, shielding me from its cold.

The men scattered with terrified shouts, but the blue fire clung to them, spreading over their bodies and consuming them faster than the hottest blaze. They shattered when they hit the ground.

Some made it as far as the village, and the fire spread to the huts and buildings. It froze the carefully built structures instantly, and then the people living inside the izby shattered like shards of glass. Half the village was destroyed in an instant.

But the worst of it was that Dedushka had been consumed just as Sergei and Rodya had been. I found his small body, broken in several pieces as though he was a statue instead of a once living, breathing man.

I'd killed him as surely as if I'd fastened the rope around his neck.

It was the suddenly increased pace of the men and Kharan on horseback and Ivan in our sleigh that dragged me from my dark thoughts. As the trees blurred by, and the horses' nostrils flared, both with the effort to pull the heavy sleigh and to carry the men at such a fast clip, a sense of foreboding gripped me. If we were so close to Kiev—an easy day's ride, as Ivan had told me—then why was such a pace necessary?

The rush of wings close enough to ruffle the fur on my hood drew my attention. Elation had finally returned. She let out a low whistle and ascended rapidly into the sky, far above us. There, she banked, making a wide circle around us, one golden eye on me at all times.

She had found something.

"Ivan," I shouted, but my voice was swallowed by the wind.

Still, his back and shoulders tensed noticeably, and he reached for his sword.

Up ahead, a bend in the road revealed the reason for Elation's agitation and the men's breakneck pace.

Armed raiders were pouring from the trees, a wave of men in ragged clothing with unkempt beards, their archers firing arrow after arrow over us as men on foot attacked our guards. The state of their dress and their dirty, unwashed faces made me think they were acting out of desperation. And desperate men were dangerous.

Before long, we were forced to a jarring stop.

Kharan was to the rear of the sleigh on her hardy little pony, and I feared for them both. The prince's men surrounded the sleigh, shielding me with their bodies.

An arrow zipped through the air, perilously close to the hood of my coat. Tension rippled over me, and my skin hardened into impenetrable ice, leaving me with a grim stoniness.

The guards sprang into action around me, cutting down the raiders closest to them. The battle was loud and chaotic, the shouts of men and the twang of metal meeting metal. In the chaos, I lost track of Kharan.

I resisted the urge to shout at the guardsmen to move away, to engage the raiders and not worry about me, but of course it was their job to deliver me to the prince in one piece. My earlier plan to escape during the confusion of the battle flitted through my mind, but as I looked around at the flying arrows and the flashing swords, I realized I hadn't truly expected us to be attacked. Nor had I realized just how terrible a battle would be.

From atop his perch on the sleigh, Ivan cut down one of the raiders—the horses plunging and rearing as raiders attempted to break them free from their harnesses. One nearly succeeded in pulling Ivan, and I fought the warring desire within me to come to Ivan's aid.

Not that way, I thought. *Not when it could mean his death along with the raiders'.*

Boris wielded his sword like a knight out of a fairy tale, but even with his obvious prowess, more and more men surrounded him until I feared he'd be overtaken.

Grigory fought raiders at the base of a tall pine tree, his blade somehow parrying the many that flew at him. Then something unexpected happened. Grigory raised his other arm, and the tree itself groaned, bending and swaying as if under a powerful wind. Next I saw the boughs smashed into the raiders closest to Grigory, sending them flying into crumpled heaps in the snow. I remembered then that Kharan had said others had abilities like mine, and I realized Grigory must be able to control the trees.

Another arrow pulled my attention away from Grigory as it whistled past me and nearly hit its mark: Daichin. At some point he had lost his rider, and as he galloped out of the line of fire, I scanned the battle for Kharan. Finally, I saw her, not far from Grigory. She held a dagger to the throat of the raider who'd fired the arrow that narrowly missed her horse. In the next instant, he was dead, blood pouring from his throat. She turned to another threat: two more raiders, who circled around her with jagged blades. I thought of how kind Kharan had been to me, and the ice on my skin spread; the palms of my hands tingling with the temptation to destroy the raiders the only way I knew how. I shook with the effort to hold myself back.

But then I remembered I had another option. I held out my

arm, and Elation, though she had stayed far above the skirmish, dived at my call.

The loud clash of swords still rang out, but Elation didn't flinch. She glanced at me, her tawny eyes predatory. Waiting.

"Blind them," I said, and sent thoughts of her daggerlike talons tearing into the raiders.

I lifted my arm in the air as she took off, her powerful wings carrying her toward the nearest cluster of enemies. Bloodcurdling screams greeted her outstretched talons as she tore into a man with a curved sword. As he dropped his weapon to cradle his face, she took off only to circle around again for another victim.

Just then, something crashed into the sleigh, distracting me from Elation's battle. I turned to find Ivan slashing the throat of one of the raiders who had managed to almost climb aboard. The raider slumped off the sleigh, the smell of blood coppery in the air. And then another raider succeeded in pulling Ivan from the sleigh. A group of four swarmed him. He took down the first man easily—a quick thrust with his sword, but as he parried the weapons of two at once, the third smashed him with his hilt. Stunned, Ivan fell back against the sleigh, dazed and unsteady. Several times he tried to regain his footing and failed. The raider grinned, and to my horror, continued forward, as though he would finish Ivan off.

All around us, the other guards were being overwhelmed by the raiders.

Time seemed to slow as the blood pounded in my ears. I

could see the choices before me:

I could summon Elation again to come to Ivan's aid, but it wouldn't be fast enough.

I could help him myself, possibly injuring him or even killing him in the process.

Or I could do nothing.

I shook my head—the last was not an option.

I jumped from the sleigh. The raider nearest me was caught off guard. It gave Ivan some room, and he kicked free of the men. "Katya, no!" he yelled as I inserted myself between him and the men. He wrenched at my shoulder weakly, shouting for me to move out of the way, but I ignored him.

Just do it, I thought. *These are bad men—men who will kill you if the guards fall.* I thought of my promise to myself: to never release the full extent of my power again.

But it was our only chance. Surely it was necessary.

I outstretched my arms and willed my hands to stop shaking.

Burn, I thought, as the cold fire poured out of my palms.

CHAPTER FOUR

I WOKE TO GRAY SKIES, THE soft sound of the sleigh rushing over snow, the jingle of horse harnesses, and the smell of snow in the air. I was also warmer than I'd ever remembered being, as though I'd been thrust in front of a blazing fire.

The memories of the attack trickled in slowly. Images of the cold fire burning, spreading from raider to raider until each enemy was a motionless statue.

Ivan, I thought. *Did he survive?* Had I managed to save him, or had I destroyed him with my cold fire? The last thought made me feel so sick I was afraid I'd vomit all over the sleigh. I tried to look around me but found it difficult to sit up.

My eyebrows furrowed, and I winced against the light. What had happened to me? I thought as hard as I could, and

I remembered bits and pieces. Ivan had raised his arms, and a terrible wave of *something* had hit me, and my power had fought back. It made me sick to think of it now: the two dueling forces. My own cold fire, and the *nothingness* that wanted to stifle it.

Let go, Katya, someone had yelled—Kharan, maybe? My memories, I found, were hazy.

As I could only stare up at the sky, I looked for Elation. I breathed a sigh of relief when her familiar form flew past, none the worse for wear despite her brave attack.

Finally, by gripping the side of the sleigh, I managed to pull myself up slowly and held my spinning head in one hand. It throbbed along to the beat of my heart. I gasped at the pain, and Ivan called from the front of the sleigh.

"That was my doing, I'm afraid." He turned to peer at me briefly. "Though we appreciated your intervention, I couldn't let you burn us all."

"You're alive?" I managed, my voice sounding weak and faraway.

"I'm alive."

"What happened?"

"I told you before that I had the power to stop you, so that's what I did. But when it came down to it, I was afraid for a moment that I wouldn't be able to. I can negate another's ability, but it was a real struggle with yours. It seems," he added, "that the villagers have been telling the truth about you."

I thought of the men I'd turned to ice, just like the ones from my village, and a sick feeling filled my stomach. I now understood why I felt so warm—it was the heat that had accompanied my cold fire before. The delicious warmth filled me even now, though it was fading. The raiders had attacked us, and they deserved their fates, perhaps, but what of the other guardsmen? My power was so unpredictable. Fear wrapped cold hands around my throat as I turned to count the guards who rode before and behind the sleigh. All were accounted for— even Kharan's pony, Daichin. "I didn't kill them," I said quietly to myself, my breath coming out in a rush.

"Does your head hurt?" Ivan asked, turning back to me. "That's a side effect of my power."

"Not badly," I lied. Why make him feel guilty for what he had to do?

"I'm glad. We're minutes away from Kiev," he added.

Kharan must have noticed that I was sitting up, for she rode over to the side of the sleigh. "I'm glad to see you're awake." Her expression turned sympathetic when she saw me wincing in the sunlight. "Ivan calls that a headache, but it feels like your head is about to split wide open like a melon."

Ivan shook his head with a dismissive grunt, but I had to agree with Kharan. "Better this than wake up to find all of you dead."

She smiled. "Well, I suppose you have a point there. As it was, we had to do some pretty impressive maneuvering to stay out of the path of your cold fire. Luckily, we knew a little of what to expect. The raiders, unfortunately for them, did not."

The idea that my guards had to scurry out of the way of my fatal power made me feel sick. "I'm so sorry."

"Don't apologize," she said with a wave of her hand that made Daichin toss his head. "You helped us in the end, and we'll be sure to make that clear to the prince when we all stand before him."

The prince. It made my head pound harder to think of being brought before him. What would my sentence be? Would I be condemned for my crimes? Executed as a criminal? Especially now, with what I'd done to the raiders. Would such destruction on my part be viewed as yet another monstrous act? I shuddered, and I could feel myself turning to ice again, as if that could help me.

"Thank you," I said finally to Kharan. She only nodded and urged her pony along.

Ivan was right—in no time, the towering pines became fewer and farther between until finally they made way for snowy fields. Before us, not far in the distance, was a walled city bigger than anything I'd ever encountered. A wide, frozen river led the way in and appeared to cut right through the city itself. I spent several moments just blinking at it dumbly, trying to calculate how many people those walls contained. No less than one hundred thousand, I was sure.

Slowly, my fears of the prince were drowned out by another worry. My assumptions of what Kiev would be like had proven to be horribly ill-informed. I'd imagined a large village—perhaps twice the size of my own—not hundreds of times that size and surrounded by a great stone wall. At home, Elation had remained in the surrounding forest, never far away. The beautiful tent had reminded me of a gilded cage, but how would Elation feel following me to a place completely outside her normal hunting range?

There was nowhere safe for her here.

I looked up at her and held out my arm, tears burning in my throat.

She landed on my proffered arm, and I rested my head on her soft feathers. "You must stay in the forest," I said. "You can't follow any farther, or you'll become as trapped as I shall be. I won't ask that of you."

She tilted her head and gazed at me with one amber eye.

"It was wrong of me to ask you to come so far in the first place. I'll be fine," I told her, though I knew I wouldn't. "I'll come to see you as soon as I can." I hoped that part, at least, was true.

She met my gaze one last time and then lowered her head. I touched my forehead to her soft feathers, trying not to cry.

But when her powerful wings carried her away from me, my shoulders slumped as a sob escaped anyway.

"The prince keeps many birds of prey in his mews," Ivan said, turning to look at me with sympathy. "None are as impressive as the one who's been your companion, but others may remind you of her, at least."

I smiled gratefully and brushed away my tears. "Kharan

mentioned that before," I said, catching her eye. "Thank you. That will help, I'm sure."

Ivan grunted before turning back around.

"I'm sorry, Katya," Kharan said. "I know how difficult this must be for you."

"I don't want her to feel trapped in such a crowded city," I said. *I don't want her to share the same fate as me,* I thought but didn't say.

Kharan must have guessed some of what I was thinking anyway, for she reached out across the side of the sleigh and touched my arm. "I understand," she said.

I sank into my fear and misery as the walls of Kiev loomed closer and closer until finally we rode through a heavily guarded gate.

The city was bustling with activity. Merchants stood in front of colorful tents, and people trudged through snowy ground to buy their bread, or furs, or linen. The air smelled of snow and woodsmoke and baking bread, so much like my own village that I could close my eyes and almost imagine I was home again.

It was loud, though—much louder than I was used to. Animals braying, people laughing, merchants shouting, and a blacksmith beating out horseshoes on his anvil. If this was life in Kiev, then what could I expect from the prince's palace? Would it be just as chaotic and unfamiliar?

A man with yellow teeth and a ratty coat appeared beside my sleigh, hefting a dead-eyed fish in my face.

"Caught fresh just before the freeze," he shouted.

Grigory shouldered his horse into the man, nearly knocking him off his feet. "Be gone with you," he said in a snarl.

I reached out a hand to him, sorry that he was treated so badly, but the man only shook his fish angrily after us.

The man, as it turned out, was not the only one to recognize our party as a potential source of revenue, and we were soon set upon by both merchants and beggars. It was the poorly dressed children, though, the ones trying to sell a single candle or a bit of wool, who wrenched my heart out of my chest and made me beg Ivan to stop for them.

"We can't stop here," Ivan said. "Not with all the trunks and tents. There's nothing you can do for the poor beggars now."

I sat back against the sleigh, sickened by my own impotence. I watched as Kharan slipped them a coin or two, though, and felt my spirits lift marginally.

We progressed through the market and arrived at a wide bridge, filled with carts and people leading animals over a frozen river.

"The Dnieper River," Kharan said helpfully, but I was too distracted by the palace looming in the distance.

Grigory and the others shouted at the people to make way, which they did with wide eyes and curious looks, and then we were gliding over the snowy bridge.

This side of the bridge was clearly where the wealthy resided, with sturdy wooden houses five times the size of the small fletched huts I spied near the marketplace, and a snowy white cathedral with a rounded dome roof and a golden cross.

The horses perked up as we drew closer to the palace, their heads eagerly pointed toward home, where warm stables, hay, and grain would be waiting.

For me, though, there was only a cold dread.

If the marketplace was overwhelming, the palace up close rendered me incapable of speech. It loomed over us, its stone as gray as thunder clouds. It seemed as wide as the city itself, though where the marketplace was colorful and loud, the palace was as still and silent as a mountain. It had two towers and a church—designated with a rounded roof and a smaller version of the golden cross I spied earlier at the cathedral—attached to the central palace building. The result was a veritable mountain of stone. Coming from a village made entirely of wood, such a sight took my breath away.

The men dismounted while servants arrived to lead the horses away, and to retrieve the trunks and tents. The palace courtyard was filled with people—page boys, servants, and attendants, but also men who wore swords at their belts and led great war chargers. They watched me with unabashed interest, and I managed a nervous smile or two, though my focus was on what lay ahead.

Kharan stayed by my side, but I could only think about what was to come.

On who waited for me within.

A woman with a bright-red scarf tied around her head came to kiss Ivan on the cheek—his wife?—and then laughed as he swung her around like a girl.

When he put her down again, he turned and held his hand out to me. "This is my wife, Vera," he said as I climbed down from the sleigh.

"Katya," she said, taking hold of my cold cheeks with both of her warm, calloused hands. "I am glad you arrived safely."

Being treated as a guest was disorienting, but it managed to dim some of my fear—at least for a moment.

"Was it an easy trip?" she asked her husband.

Ivan hesitated. "For the most part."

I was curious why he withheld mention of the raider attack, but I decided it would be better for me not to interfere. Already she watched Ivan with narrowed eyes. She'd no doubt find out on her own.

"Come, devotchka, let's bring you inside out of the snow," Vera said, turning her attention back to me. She directed me toward the palace doors with bustling movements. "The prince has been waiting for you in the throne room."

I slowed to a stop and couldn't convince my body to move.

The soft sound of boots on snow announced someone's presence next to me, and then Kharan put her hand on my shoulder. "I'll go with you, Katya."

Ivan stepped closer to me, too. "And I."

I nodded even as I briefly contemplated bolting, but I remembered the last time I'd considered such a thing. And if Ivan was strong enough to stop my cold fire . . . Besides, where would I go? Who would even help me? I would have to bide my time and wait for an opportunity for escape. If I wasn't sentenced to death first.

Reluctantly, I followed Vera with Ivan and Kharan close behind me. Beyond the double wooden doors, the palace awaited, ablaze with light from sconces all along the walls. The ceiling soared above our heads, and our boots echoed across the stone floors. There were tapestries with battle and hunting scenes, ones of exotic animals and flora and fauna of all kinds. They were beautiful, but I couldn't appreciate any of them. All I could think about was the prince.

Every rumor I'd ever heard ran through my mind. He'd killed his own parents. He collected people with powers to form a dark army of his own. Others—like the men in my village—said he wasn't forming an army at all but was instead drinking the blood of those with power like an upyr. I hadn't allowed myself to believe that last rumor. All accounts said he was cruel, arrogant, and selfish, so ugly inside that his face was scarred and disfigured to reflect the evil within.

But he gave me a tent of my own, and a chest full of clothes, I thought.

Nothing made sense, and it was this feeling of not fully knowing what to expect that scared me more than anything else.

All too soon we arrived outside the doors of the throne room. I tried not to let my fear show as Ivan stepped forward and pulled open the heavy door. I walked into a cavernous hall, the ceilings above me arched, lit by iron chandeliers. More tapestries lined the walls here, and battle scenes with men and swords and horses blurred by me as I passed. Page boys and men dressed in dark tunics with swords belted at their waists lined the walls.

There at the end of the hall was a wooden throne, and the man seated upon it stood as we approached. Even from this distance I could see he was elegantly dressed, all in black—his clothes matched his dark hair. My mouth went dry and my skin began to harden.

Each step seemed to take far too long, as though we were slogging through mud, and I was far too aware of my own shallow breaths. And when we finally got close enough, I saw that the man standing in front of the throne was not a man at all but a boy not much older than I.

He was nothing like I'd imagined. Not the old, heavily bearded man I'd expected—Grigory fit the description more than he. This boy was tall and beardless, his hair thick and dark but with glints of auburn. When his eyes met mine, I saw that while his body might have been young, his eyes were those of a man much older and wiser, piercing and silver as a wolf's pelt.

And he was beautiful—a cold, stunning beauty. But I knew that it was often beautiful people who were the most cruel.

"You are in the presence of the grand prince of Kievan Rus'," announced one of the two guards who flanked him, "Alexander Konstantinov."

Out of the corner of my eye, I saw Kharan bow from her waist, hands steepled in respect. Awkwardly, I tried to curtsy as best I could. The highest-ranking person I'd ever stood before was our village elder—a far cry from the grand prince of all of Kievan Rus'.

"Thank you for answering my summons, Ekaterina Alexeyevna," the prince said, as if I hadn't been escorted here under armed guard. His voice was deeper than I'd thought it would be, with a rough edge, like he wasn't used to speaking much. He turned to Ivan. "Was the journey uneventful?"

"We encountered raiders, Gosudar. On the main path to Kiev. They ambushed us from the forest—perhaps fifty men in total."

Vera stiffened in surprise next to me, shooting her husband a glance, but the prince's expression never changed. He appeared unsurprised—unconcerned, even. And I wondered if Kharan was wrong in thinking that he cared for his people.

"Fifty?" the prince repeated, turning his attention to Kharan now. "This is a bigger band of raiders than you'd heard about, isn't it?"

"Twenty was the original number," Kharan said, her tone grave. "Few enough that they should have been easy to defeat. Fifty, though, was nearly our undoing."

"Yet everyone remained unharmed?" this was addressed to Ivan, who nodded.

"Yes, Gosudar, though we might not have escaped unscathed were it not for Katya's help."

I felt the full force of the prince's attention on me, and I stood up straighter. "It seems I owe you my thanks, then, as it was I who sent all of you on the raiders' path."

A little jolt of surprise ran through me. The prince had

ordered his men to take such a route? One that, by the sound of it, had been almost certain to result in a confrontation. I thought of Ivan becoming overwhelmed, of Kharan's beloved horse nearly being shot with an arrow, of the sheer number of men that had poured from those trees. A cold anger grew inside me. How could the prince put his people at risk like this?

"I'm only glad I was able to save them, Gosudar," I said, trying to keep the censure from my tone.

"The raiders have long been a problem—assaulting and stealing from travelers on their way to Kiev. But I am also pleased to see your village elder was telling the truth about your abilities. I hadn't expected it to be proven so unequivocally and by so many witnesses before you'd even arrived at the palace, and I'm relieved that no one came to any harm."

Admitting that he did care about the others soothed some of my anger on their behalf, but I was still afraid of what he would decide when he discussed the destruction and deaths in my village.

"I am not unsympathetic to the fact that you have traveled far and are most likely tired and possibly even shaken after the attack from the raiders."

His words so surprised me that I managed to only nod mutely, my gaze searching his.

"However, I have always been the type of person who'd rather know my fate than lose sleep over all the things that could be decided the next day. Therefore, I feel it is almost cruel to keep you in suspense regarding my verdict on your crimes." His eyebrow arched, but his expression was not unkind. He truly meant what he said. "But if you disagree, if you'd rather have a day to rest and recover before facing judgment, then I will grant you that time."

"Thank you, Gosudar. That is kind of you," I said, my surprise and a small glimmer of hope—hope that someone who thought this much of someone else's feelings would not turn around and condemn them to death—forcing my voice to come out strained. "I would rather hear your decision on the matter now."

He nodded. "Very well. Your village elder accuses you of using your power to not only destroy homes but to kill nine men. Do you deny this?"

Memories of that horrible night pushed to the forefront of my mind, but I beat them back, tears stinging my eyes. "No, Gosudar," I said, unable to meet his gaze this time.

"Was it your intention to use your power purposefully to wreak such destruction and murder your fellow villagers?"

My head snapped up. "No. *No.*" The mere thought made my belly churn in horror.

"Such an act is punishable by death—do you know this?"

My skin grew still colder, until I could see my breath coming in soft plumes. "Yes," I managed to say.

He watched me for a moment, and something softened in his gaze. "Your actions—they were a matter of control—or lack of?"

"Yes, Gosudar."

He nodded to himself and fell silent, as though deep in thought. "This power—could you learn to control it?"

I looked at Kharan for guidance, but she merely lifted her eyebrows. He hadn't sentenced me to death yet, and I still had hope that he wouldn't, but I was equally afraid of the new direction the conversation was headed. "I'm not sure."

"Ivan?" the prince asked.

Beside me, Ivan shifted his weight. "It took all of my own power to negate hers. Had I not, she surely would have killed us all."

"There is a war brewing that will consume all of Kievan Rus'," the prince said, his gaze shifting to somewhere over my head, like he could see the coming army. "We need every available weapon if we are to survive—even the untried ones. Your power could make the difference between life and death on the battlefield."

I recoiled. Then the rumors were true: he was amassing an army of people with power. "I am no soldier," I said, my voice soft but clear. "Even if I could control it, I don't want to use my power as a weapon."

For a moment, the prince looked at me, and I looked at him, a single muscle in his strong jaw twitching. He was taking my measure, I was sure, and I knew I would be found wanting.

"You are forgiven for the attack on your village," he said, as though I'd never said anything, but even as relief filled my body, he continued, "but in return, you will stay and learn from Kharan and Ivan about the war, about how you can help your country."

It felt as though the floor was disappearing beneath me. I'd escaped the execution, but at what cost? "I thank you for your forgiveness, Gosudar," I said because I didn't dare give him a reason to change his mind.

He waved Vera forward, and she moved toward him before dropping into a curtsy. "Vera will show you to your room," he said, dismissing me.

As I moved to follow, he added, "A warning for you before you go. Ivan will stay close at hand to you at all times. You are in the city now, and though I know you would never intentionally hurt innocent people, we cannot take risks."

I flinched like he'd struck me.

Even the prince thought I was a liability.

Chapter Five

The room Vera showed me to was actually a set of rooms overlooking the courtyard. In truth, the rooms were fit for a princess and as richly furnished as the celestial tent. There was already a roaring fire in the fireplace, the bed was massive and covered in velvet and fur, and three tapestries telling the story of the capture of a golden firebird hung from the walls. The rooms, while beautiful, made me distinctly uncomfortable. The hut I shared with Babushka could fit in a corner of the bedroom, and the cavernous space made it difficult to know what to do with myself.

I stood awkwardly in the very center of the room while Vera showed me all the necessities: a washstand, a small closet with a chamber pot, the trunk with the elegant gowns, and other lovely things.

"I'm sure this is overwhelming for you, devotchka," she said with a kindly expression, "but you'll find the palace to be a comfortable new home in no time at all."

My new home. Did the prince expect me to stay here forever? I thought of the war he'd mentioned and how I suspected I had only been pardoned for my crime because of the power I held. "If this is my home, then am I free to go wherever I like?"

She nodded. "You are free to wander within the palace and its grounds."

I glanced up at that. "And if I should leave the grounds?"

"The prince has not given permission. He still considers you—" She paused as if considering her words. *Dangerous*, I supplied in my own mind. "He knows the limits and the control of your power are untried. He does not wish to risk the city."

I couldn't find it within myself to blame the prince. Not when I knew he was right to fear such an outcome.

"I'm sure Kharan will show you more of the palace, and if you should need anything from me, do let me know." When I remained distractedly silent, she nodded. "Well, if there's nothing else I can get for you, then I'd better be on with my chores."

The moment she left, I collapsed in the nearest chair, my legs completely refusing to hold me any longer. I kept replaying the prince's words over and over in my mind. I tried to convince myself that I'd been pardoned, that I wouldn't be executed as I'd feared for days now, but my body still shook like it didn't believe me.

And perhaps that was because I wasn't entirely free yet. There was still the concern of being asked to train and hone this terrible power—the one that I very much doubted could ever fully be controlled. After all, Ivan had said he'd barely been able to stop me. The brewing war the prince had mentioned must be dire if he would risk my volatile power.

But even as I told myself these things, I remembered being able to save the others, and finally feeling warm. I remembered the men of my village who had threatened me and assaulted Dedushka, destroyed.

Grigory had asked me before why I had not saved myself from this fate—to escape being brought before the prince—and I suppose I could have. Maybe after the villagers had captured me, after they'd thrown me in the elder's root cellar, I could have focused on that terrible power I'd unleashed. I could have tried to summon it again. I could have turned on the villagers just as they'd expected me to. But I was no monster.

Aren't you? a quiet voice in my mind asked, and I winced away from the memories that threatened.

I hadn't set out to be a monster, but what happened when someone was pushed too far?

What happened when the dark swirls of regret were accompanied by a sense that maybe what I'd done wasn't so terrible?

What happened if I liked it?

Despite my exhaustion, my anxious thoughts would not let me rest. Eventually, they forced me from my room, and I found the dark hallway was a welcome escape. Servants moved down the hall, but none of them paid me any attention. Somewhere nearby, I was sure, Ivan was close should I lose control and attempt to destroy Kiev as I once had my own village.

I didn't know what the future would bring with the prince and the army I wanted no part of, but the smartest thing to do—what Babushka would have done—was to familiarize myself with the palace, particularly its exits and entrances.

All around me, palace servants hurried by doing various chores. It was easy for me to blend in simply by keeping to the shadows. Even in the comparatively dim light from the torches, I could see that the palace was ornate. The stone floors were covered with luxurious Persian rugs, the ceilings were painted in golds and reds depicting everything from Christ and the saints to hunting scenes, and the walls were covered in a vibrant fabric that was as smooth as silk when I touched it—so that's probably exactly what it was.

I wandered for what felt like hours.

Voices rang out in the hall to my left, and I made an abrupt right turn to avoid them. It was quieter here, the walls broken by doors and tapestries. Each tapestry told a story, and in spite of my worries, they captured my attention. One was of a knight bound by vines, standing impotently by, his face contorted in a grimace of agony as he watched a maiden being impaled all over her body by thorns as big as swords. The tapestry was done in reds as dark as blood, and both the knight and his lady wore white clothing stained crimson. The sight of it raised the hair on the back of my neck.

As I continued down the hall, I saw a line of tapestries in the same style as the first. The next had the same thorny vine, only this time, a golden firebird blazed in the center. Flames leaped from its wings and tail feathers, setting fire to the tendrils of the vine. Another showed the vine almost obliterated by darkness. I could only just make it out by moving so close to the tapestry that my nose nearly touched the fabric.

But it was when I came to the third tapestry that my skin turned icy hard, reacting to my surprise. The vine was forefront again, but it was no longer green and wicked looking. The artist had instead showed it encased in white and silver, as though trapped within ice. I reached out to touch the vine, almost expecting it to be cold, but then I heard a soft scrape of shoe on the hard floor.

I clutched my hand to my chest and whipped around as though I'd been caught doing something I shouldn't. But when I scanned the darkened hallway, there was no one there.

"It's me, Katya." Kharan's voice came from the darkness. "I promised to show you my ability, remember?"

My gaze still darting around the dark corners, I nodded.

Across from me, the torch flames danced. The shadows lengthened and shrank, and as I peered closer, they began to take on a human form. I jumped back, pressing myself against the wall.

Kharan stepped out of the darkness, coming out of the shadows as though she had opened a door. She solidified before me, her hair so black it had a bluish tint in the soft light of the torch.

"I hope I didn't frighten you," she said.

"You didn't," I lied, running a hand down my still-frozen arm.

She gave my arm a pointed look as though she knew I was lying.

"Have you always had this power?" I asked, desperately curious now that I'd seen it.

"Not always. It didn't manifest until I was five or six, which made for an interesting childhood," she said with a wry smile.

I thought of my own childhood. Of the teasing and jeers from the other children at the coldness of my skin. "And the others in your tribe . . . what did they think of your ability?"

"They tolerated me hiding in the shadows and listening to conversations I shouldn't have, but ultimately, my ability was useless for reindeer herders. I imagine that our ancestors had once been more of a war-mongering people where shadow-melding was useful. Spying for the prince, though," she said, leaning closer, "my power was made for that."

"You spy on his enemies?"

She laughed. "I can spy on anyone I like."

She took a step away from me, and I blinked as the shadows enveloped her like a blanket. I stared at the place where she'd disappeared, my eyes straining for even a flicker of movement, a form in the darkness. But there was nothing.

Just as suddenly, though, she stepped back into the light, throwing the cloak of darkness off her as though it was a physical thing.

"I'm no ice elemental," she said, "but shadow melding has its usefulness—especially in being covert."

"Ice . . . ," I said slowly, struggling to understand and still a little spellbound by the shadow manipulation. "You mean me?"

She tilted her head. "Yes. Surely you knew ice was your element?"

"I've never known it to be described that way—I've only been called an Ice Witch," I said, the words still bringing to mind Sergei's angry eyes. "I'm afraid I don't know much about my power's origins at all."

"That's something we'll have to rectify. The main thing you should know is there are four types of elemental powers: fire, water—ice is a form of water, but it's even rarer—earth, and wind. My own ability is what's considered a lesser power. Boris's, too, for all his strength. Ours probably originated as elemental but have become too diluted over time."

I'd never heard it explained in such a way. "I don't see how becoming a shadow is considered a lesser power," I said with a shake of my head.

She shrugged. "It doesn't give me much power on the battlefield."

"I'd rather have that than a volatile and dangerous ability."

She shot me a sympathetic glance. "I'm sure if we all work together, we can help you learn to control it just as the prince suggested."

I remembered the thoughts that had chased me from my room, the anxiety of how easily I could succumb to the power within me—to be someone who inspired fear instead of ridicule. But I couldn't do that. I didn't want to be responsible for more deaths. "Though I'm thankful the prince pardoned me, I still want nothing to do with his plans for battle."

Her mouth turned down in sympathy. "I understand why you'd be afraid, but wouldn't it be better to learn how to control your power and use it for good?" When I said nothing, she continued. "And anyway, where would you go, if not stay here? Can you truly return to your village? To the ones who cast you out without a backward glance?"

Remember, devotchka, sometimes the place we do not want to go is the best place for us after all. I still didn't know what Babushka had meant by those words, but I took them as a sign that she still cared for me. Even after I brought such pain into her life. But the other villagers . . . I knew they would never forgive me.

"I thought so," Kharan said, as though she could read my mind.

I met her gaze. "Have you ever lost control over your ability? Been trapped in the shadows, perhaps, or disappeared when you didn't mean to?"

"No, but—"

"Then how can you possibly help me? Ivan told the prince himself that he could barely stop my power with his." I shook my head. "No, this isn't the right place for me. You can't help me. Babushka was wrong."

I turned to go, but Kharan reached out and touched my arm. "How can you know this isn't the right place unless you stay?

You haven't even been here a single night."

I let out a humorless laugh. "Can I even leave? The prince made it clear he'd only pardoned me in exchange for my ability. Wouldn't I be imprisoned if I tried to escape?"

She hesitated. "You wouldn't be imprisoned, no." Something about her hesitation and tone made me realize there was more she was leaving unsaid.

"But I still cannot leave if I choose to."

"I can't say I understand exactly how you feel—I came here of my own accord—but I do know what it feels like to be far away from everything you've ever known. That's how I felt when I came here, too."

Something shifted in me at the recognition of another thing we had in common. I tried to push the feeling of kinship away—it'd never served me well in the past. "And you never regretted staying here?"

She met my gaze. "Not once."

"How long have you been here?"

"It feels like years, but in truth, it's only been a little over a year since I first rode into Kiev."

"I can't imagine staying here that long," I said.

She smiled. "Can you at least agree to stay for a few days? There aren't many girls at the palace, and it's nice to finally have someone to talk to. We could go riding together!"

Her grin was infectious. "You're pretty persuasive."

"So I've been told."

"Well, as long as it's a very slow, very simple creature, then yes, I'd love to ride with you."

She laughed. "There are a few of those in the stables, so don't worry. I'm sure you're tired now, but how about I show you around in the morning?"

"I'd like that," I said with a smile I found was surprisingly genuine.

"Good, then I'll come by your room after breakfast. We'll go outside and look around and try to avoid Grigory."

"I definitely want to avoid Grigory," I said, and she just touched my arm and very seriously said, "We all do," before disappearing into the shadows with a laugh.

As I made my way back to my room, I thought of everything Kharan had said, of how quickly she'd charmed me into staying—willingly, since of course I didn't really have a choice at the moment—and I knew I was in serious danger of actually trusting her as a friend.

I wished I could discuss this with Babushka. More than ever, I wished I knew who I was, where my power came from. I was afraid I'd never have the chance to ask her again.

Chapter Six

The next morning, Kharan made good on her word, greeting me at my door shortly after I'd awoken and gotten dressed. Breakfast had been set out for me on a tray in my room—a steaming bowl of kasha—and it embarrassed me to think of how hard I must have been sleeping to not have heard the servant enter with it. The bed, stuffed with down and piled with furs, had been so comfortable that not even thoughts of war, or my village, or Dedushka had kept me from sleeping like a hibernating bear.

"Vera wanted me to remind you to eat if you haven't already," Kharan said as she led me down the stairs from the upstairs chambers to a lower level. "She's overly concerned about whether everyone has eaten."

I smiled inwardly at that. Babushka hadn't been like that at all. We were all responsible for making sure we got enough food to eat, and it was rare that any of us were ever completely full. "There was kasha waiting for me when I woke up, and I ate every bite."

"Ah, what a relief. You missed dinner last night, though. Vera was beside herself over that," she said with a glance over her shoulder at me.

"I was asleep. I went back to my room after talking to you, went to bed, and I've only just now woken up. I don't think I've ever slept so long."

"I did the same when I first got here. It's just what happens when you've reached the end of a journey. It's exhausting." She stopped then at a small wooden door where a cold breeze escaped into the hall. "After you," she said, holding open the door.

When I walked through, I found myself in the dvor. The sun shone down on the snow of the stable yard, and I saw a small wooden house that was surely the banya. For a moment, I contemplated asking to go there; it had been far too long since my last bath, but then other sounds drew my attention away. The familiar animal sounds—a horse's neigh, a goat's bleat—released some of the tension within me. I was drawn to the quiet warmth I knew I'd find within. The stable had always been a place of escape for me—much like the woods beyond our izba. The animals never teased me or whispered behind my back.

The inside of the stable might have sounded like ours in the village, but it looked nothing like it. It was larger than my izba, for one thing, and built of the same stone the palace was constructed of. The animals, too, were no ordinary beasts. Aside from the three sturdier horses that had pulled the sleigh that brought me here, the rest were clearly the prince's riding horses. Even I could see they were extraordinary creatures with arched necks and streaming manes and tails; their coats gleamed in the dim light.

An older man came forward then, his beard dark and oiled. His boots were polished to a high sheen despite being in the stables, and his clothing was richly embroidered. "I am Nicholas Annenkov," he said, "Master of the Horse."

I gave him a slight bow. "Ekaterina Alexeyevna."

"Ah, yes, your reputation precedes you."

I stiffened, though I supposed I shouldn't have been surprised that everyone, including a member of the prince's senior druzhina, would have known about what I'd done. "I understand if that makes you wary of me being around the horses."

"No less than any of the others close to the prince. Even Boris, with his excessive strength, has managed not to injure one of my horses. I can only hope you will prove to be the same." He turned toward Kharan. "Have you come to ride?"

She shook her head. "Not today. I'm just showing Katya around. We came here to admire the horses."

He smiled with approval. "There are many here to admire. Most are friendly, but mind the prince's stallions," he added to me. "They are fiery in temper. If their ears are back, do not approach them."

"I'll be sure to heed your warning," I said.

"Then I'll leave you to it."

I watched him walk away for a moment until he disappeared into a room near the back end of the stables.

Groomsmen remained, but they were busy tending to the horses: feeding them, brushing out their coats, mucking out their stalls. They bobbed their heads at Kharan when she passed by, and I got the impression that she spent a lot of time in the stables. I paused as one horse poked her head over the stall door, her eyes as huge and dark brown as a doe's, and she deigned to let me stroke her velvet nose. Her coat was pure white and silky smooth, even with her heavier winter hair. I turned to move on to the next, but she nickered so softly and beseechingly that with a little laugh, I resumed my petting.

"Aren't they lovely?" Kharan asked as I wandered down the long aisle, admiring sleek coats and silky manes. "Daichin looks a little rough in such illustrious company."

The pony in question was nodding off in his stall, lower lip drooping and eyes half-closed. I smiled. "He may not be as sleek, but I imagine he's a lot warmer in the winter."

"His fat stores help with that, too," Kharan said with a fond look toward the sleeping pony.

The mare's obviously sweet nature made me wonder: If it came down to it, could I take one of these horses and escape? I would cover far more distance and faster on horseback, but it would have to be an exceedingly docile one, for I had very little experience riding.

But it only took a moment of thinking to realize that the vast majority of the horses were far too beautiful to take. The grooms would know immediately, and it would make my crime that much worse. There were other horses that were humbler, but I feared being labeled a horse thief, especially from the prince's own stables. Better to escape on foot.

Stables were usually somewhere close to an exit from the dvor, I realized, and this was true, but it was the main one—the one I'd come through yesterday. The one that was well watched. I would have to seek another way out.

"Are you sure you don't want to ride today?" Kharan asked, interrupting my reverie with a question far too close to my thoughts for comfort.

"I'm sure," I said with a weak smile.

"There's something else you might like to see."

I gave the mare one last pat and then followed Kharan through a side door in the barn. It exited right beside a small building with only two narrow windows, which I found odd until I walked over to them and heard a faint flapping of wings. Inside were hooded birds of prey: no fewer than three gyrfalcons, all snowy white with black markings. They were the largest of the falcon species, but they were still only half the size of Elation. If this would have been her fate—to be tethered to a post by a short length of rope in this dark little building—then I was glad I'd asked her to stay in the woods.

"These are the prince's falcons I told you about," Kharan said. "I prefer horses because then I don't have to worry about having my eyes gouged out by talons."

"No, only falling and breaking your neck," I said wryly, and she snorted.

Just then, we could hear voices behind us, and when we turned, we saw the prince accompanied by Grigory. Grigory spoke rapidly, while the prince's expression could have been carved from stone. A little chill chased over my skin at the sight of him, this prince who held my fate in his hands, but who was little more than a boy himself. I snuck glances at him as I pressed close to the mews, hoping he wouldn't notice me here. He was dressed in a black, heavily embroidered kaftan, trousers, and tall, black boots trimmed in fur. The gold threads of the embroidery reminded me of the tent I'd slept in. With his dark hair, the overall effect was striking.

Kharan, though, stepped forward and raised her hand in greeting to the prince. He said something to Grigory, and then they walked toward us. "I was just showing Katya your falcons," she said when he was close enough to hear her.

"I'm glad you're showing her around," the prince said, while Grigory looked frustrated that their conversation had been interrupted.

"Gosudar—" Grigory began, but the prince shook his head.

"Not now. Perhaps Kharankhui will know more."

Grigory immediately turned to Kharan. "Might I have a word?" he asked, and Kharan shot me an exasperated look that made the corner of my mouth curl up before I could hide it again.

"Yes, fine," she said, following him to the other side of the dvor.

I looked back at the gyrfalcons through the window, and when I next glanced at the prince, I found him staring directly at me. Little shards of ice dug under my skin as I met his dark gaze.

"Hello, Katya," he said.

"Gosudar," I said with another awkward curtsy.

He nodded toward the birds within the mews. "Would you like to see them?"

"If you'd like," I said cautiously. He looked at me with a curious expression, nothing like the one he'd worn in the throne room. It seemed to erase some of that dark, brooding aura he had. He had strong facial features: a sharp, straight nose, angular jaw, a mouth that reminded me of a longbow just barely drawn.

"Perhaps they will cheer you for the loss of your own."

"How did you know?" I asked, trying very hard not to let my disbelief show—I was surprised he cared.

"Kharankhui told me about your eagle—and the bond you have with it. I was surprised your eagle didn't continue to the city with you."

Speaking of Elation brought a lump to my throat. I swallowed uncomfortably. "She wouldn't have liked the mews."

He watched me for a moment, his expression thoughtful. "Then perhaps we could have come to another arrangement for her. I have to admit I'm curious to see your interaction. Kharankhui said the eagle not only slept in the tent with you but came to your defense against the raiders."

"She did; she has always been protective of me in that way." I didn't tell him that I'd asked her to fight them. For some reason, I was afraid of anyone knowing the full extent of our ability to communicate.

"That's an extraordinary bond," he said. "I'm afraid my birds aren't quite so impressive, but I'll show you anyway."

He brought out one of the gyrfalcons into the light, where it turned its head toward me at my little intake of breath, its head covered in a small leather hood.

"This is Reys," he said, allowing the gyrfalcon to rest its impressive talons on his thick leather glove that stretched all the way to his elbow. "She is my least experienced gyrfalcon, so I try to handle her as often as I can."

"She's beautiful," I said truthfully, admiring her snowy plumage. It made my heart ache for Elation. Unable to help myself, I reached out and touched the feathers of her wing, like satin under my fingertips. But then she flapped her wings agitatedly, stirring the prince's hair and making me jump back. "I'm sorry," I said. "I forget that not every bird is like Elation."

He smiled and shook his head. "It's good for her to be reminded that humans are not here to hurt her." He lowered his arm a bit, and Reys seemed to calm. "My mother was like you—she loved birds of all kinds. Being around them always makes me think of her. She would have loved the chance to see your eagle," he said, his voice sounding suddenly gruff, and as I looked at his face, I could see the shadow of loss, the same that held me in its grip. I thought of the terrible rumor that the prince murdered his own parents. Was his grief an act? It seemed real enough.

"I always heard the princess was as kind as she was beautiful. I'm sorry," I said, knowing how ineffectual the words were. "I never knew my own mother," I added quietly, just so he'd know I did understand. "But I think knowing her for a while only to have her die would be worse."

His brows furrowed, and I could feel the threads of shared loss tying us together. I wanted to snip them with sharp shears before they became too strong, but his quiet interest drew me in against my will. "I'm not sure that's true," he said. "I at least have memories to sustain me. It must have been very hard for you growing up."

"In some ways, it was, but not because I didn't have a mother."

He glanced at me. "Who raised you?"

I didn't want to talk about them—the memories were too painful—but as I opened my mouth to change the subject, the truth poured out instead. "I was taken in by an old man and woman who asked me to call them my babushka and dedushka." My tongue tripped over Dedushka's name, and the prince's gaze held mine. "They raised me as their own," I said, the tears trapped in my throat, and I coughed as I tried to hide my grief.

"I'm sorry you had to leave them behind," the prince said, and I didn't bother to correct him—to tell him the truth about Dedushka. "But I can't imagine a small village like that ever being able to appreciate or even accept someone like you."

I wanted to argue with him, but of course it was the truth. "It's hard to accept someone's ability when they use it to destroy half the village." I bit my tongue. Perhaps it wasn't the best idea to say such things when the prince had only just forgiven me for my crimes the day before.

But he only shot me a ghost of a smile. "You're in the right place now—many of the others here were pardoned for crimes they committed inadvertently because of their powers."

I looked up at that.

"Kharankhui has no doubt shown you what she can do, and you've already seen Ivan's power. Grigory and Boris are also gifted with abilities."

I raised my eyebrows at that. That was more people with abilities than I'd ever expected to meet. I remembered Kharan saying something about Boris's strength earlier, and I thought back to the battle with the raiders, but it had all been so chaotic. Grigory could take control of trees—at least, that's how it seemed from my perspective from the sleigh. "Boris's ability is his strength?"

The prince nodded. "He is easily stronger than ten men, and he has a gift for swordplay."

I thought of Boris sitting by the fire, serving his delicious stew. He wasn't an overly large man, and there'd been nothing to indicate he had an ability. I wondered how many others there were out in the world—people I'd met but never knew had a power like mine.

"They all once struggled with control over their power, just as you do now," the prince continued. "They have experience with it, and they can help you—if you'll let them."

I met his dark eyes. "And then will I be forced to join your war?" I asked.

"You will not be forced to do anything—I doubt I could even make you fight if I wanted to," he added with a grin. Almost against my will, my lips pulled back in a return smile. "You have heard, perhaps, that I have been gathering people with abilities like yours." When I nodded, he said, "But even as I have found such people, so, too, have our enemy. They have made many alliances with people with elemental power—earth elementals."

"Earth elementals," I repeated, dumbfounded by all the things I was learning that I'd never even dreamed of in my village.

"Grigory is also an earth elemental, but his power to bend trees to his will is small compared to what the others can do." He narrowed his eyes. "To what they have done already."

As if he sensed we were talking about him, Grigory walked toward us from the other side of the dvor. Kharan, I noticed with a sinking stomach, had disappeared. I hadn't spent much time with her, but she still made me feel like I had an ally. Grigory stood there, staring at me in a cold way for several moments until the prince finally said, "I thought we had concluded our conversation, Grigory."

"Forgive me, Gosudar," Grigory said with a slight bow, "but there is more I must tell you."

"Whatever you have to say can wait," the prince said, and I tried not to take satisfaction from the way he cut off Grigory so completely. "You'd be of greater service to me if you agreed to give Katya a demonstration of your abilities. Go and find Ivan for us, and we will show Katya that her power can be controlled."

The small bit of joy I'd felt at Grigory being put in his place disappeared. The last thing I wanted to do was summon my power here . . . before the prince.

Grigory hesitated for just a moment before he turned on his booted heel and left—presumably in search of Ivan.

"There's been enough talk," the prince said, moving toward the mews with Reys. "It's time we showed you."

The cold spread across my skin as I watched the prince. His face wouldn't look nearly so beautiful when it was splintered into a million pieces by my ice, and I feared that they were all horribly wrong about my being able to control it.

It was decided that the best place for such a demonstration was in the wooded gardens within the palace walls. Ivan must have been close by, for Grigory returned quickly with him. Once we reached the garden, Grigory immediately stood beside the prince, as though in his absence I might have suddenly become a threat.

"Gosudar," Grigory said, "I'm not sure this is the safest place for you to be should things go wrong with the girl."

The look the prince gave him in response was scathing. "It is not for you to decide."

Grigory bowed his acquiescence, but he shot me a look full of such malice that my skin erupted in ice. "What would you have me do?"

"Give Katya a demonstration of your power," the prince said with a nod toward the trees in the garden.

"As you wish."

Grigory walked over to the middle of the garden that was absent of any other plants, the ground covered in snow. Falling to one knee, he placed his palm on the cold ground. He closed his eyes, and there was a great rumbling beneath us. In the next instant, a tree burst free from the earth: small at first, it quickly gained height and foliage until it was a massive oak tree with a wide trunk. Grigory stood back up, and the tree ceased growing. It towered over all the other trees and defied the season with its verdant leaves. The moment Grigory had broken contact with the earth, it seemed that his power ceased to flow. Unlike my own cold fire.

"You make it seem so simple," I said to Grigory, but he only gave me a single nod in answer.

"Katya, can you freeze the tree?" the prince asked, and I looked at the enormous oak dubiously. I'd frozen buckets of water before, yes, and of course my cold fire could freeze anything, but I didn't know how to release the necessary amount of power.

"I'm afraid I would freeze everything else in the garden," I said, "including you."

"If I may, Katya," Ivan said, coming up beside me, his boots crunching in the snow. He held out his hand to me, and slowly, I put my hand in his. He closed his eyes and held my hand. I tried not to pull away. After a moment he said, "You have so much power—it's like an endless, rushing waterfall. To freeze the tree Grigory has created, you'll need a substantial amount of power, yet not as much as you've released in the past."

I nodded. "I'm not sure I've ever released only a moderate amount of power—only a very little, or torrential."

"Then what you must do is think of your power like a horse. So much energy and speed and power are contained within a horse—enough to throw a man, even injure or kill him—and yet a man can control it. Such is the ice within you. If you let it take the reins, it will gladly run freely, trampling all in its path." He looked at me, gaze sharp beneath bushy brows. "But if you use the reins and your body to halt the horse, it will have no choice but to obey. If you imagine your power in the same way, you can learn to control it, just as you would learn to ride."

I decided not to tell them all at that moment that I could barely ride a horse, but I appreciated that Ivan was trying to help me.

"If you lose control again," the prince said, "then Ivan is here to stop you."

I thought of what Ivan had said in the throne room—that he'd barely been able to stop me when I'd released my power on the raiders. "And if he cannot?"

"Then we'll knock you unconscious," Grigory said with a nasty smile, like he hoped it would end up that way.

"You can do this, Katya," Ivan said, patting my hand and stepping back.

Part of me never wanted to access that type of power again, but another part—a darker part—wanted to feel the cold fire rushing from my palms, to feel the delicious warmth chase away the cold. I turned to the oak tree, its leaves fluttering in the wintry wind. My thoughts turned inward, and I could feel that well of power that Ivan had sensed within me, rushing through my veins and coating my skin in frost. If my power was like a horse, then it was a wild one, untamed and unwilling to submit to the bridle. I had one moment when I thought, *I can do this*, and then I released the cold fire, letting it pour from my palms.

Flames of blue licked up the tree trunk, turning it to ice so cold cracks formed. The tree groaned as though it were a person, branches and leaves shaking as the cold fire spread. The temperature dropped still lower, and the cracks in the tree grew larger, until the whole thing splintered. In the next moment, it broke in half, the heavy, frozen boughs crashing toward the ground only to shatter on impact. And still the cold fire raged, flames dancing gleefully toward other trees, toward statues and fountains and benches. I tried to rein it in as Ivan had said, tried to call it back to me, but it continued unheeding.

"Gosudar," Grigory said in a panicked rush behind me, "we must take you away from here. You are in danger."

The cold fire continued to spread, pouring out of me like the waterfall Ivan had first compared it to. I didn't dare turn around and look at the prince or any of the others—doing so would cause the fire to leap toward them hungrily, and not even Ivan would be able to stop it.

"No," the prince said as I fought against the torrential outpouring of cold fire. "I have faith in her."

"Take the reins, Katya," Ivan said.

The cold fire spread to tree after tree, freezing them solid and moving with blue tongues of flame over the already snowy ground to the palace walls, made of stone. I didn't think the cold fire could freeze the stone; the garden, too, was surrounded by a massive stone wall. But it could certainly freeze and destroy everything within the walls. I had to gain control of it and stop the flow of fire—I was feeding it with my own power, and if I could but stop, then the blue flames would lose their momentum. It was what had happened before in my own village.

"She will destroy the palace!" Grigory shouted.

Suddenly, the ground trembled beneath me.

"Stop this, Grigory," the prince commanded, but whatever was happening continued.

Wood burst from the earth all around me, like branches of a great tree that grew underground. They wrapped themselves around me, trapping me even as they froze under the onslaught of my cold fire. They began to tighten until I cried out, and I could hear the prince shouting, but I couldn't make out what he was saying over the groaning of the branches that held me prisoner.

Terrified Grigory would allow the branches to continue to

wrap around me until I suffocated, I thought desperately of what Ivan had said. In my mind, I imagined my power as a great white horse, galloping unchecked across the snowy landscape. I added a bridle and reins and pulled back on them with everything I had within me. The branches groaned as they wrapped still tighter.

"Grigory, so help me God, I will kill you if you do not stop," the prince said, his voice cutting through the wood of the branches.

I pulled back on the reins of the great white horse in my mind, and at last, the cold fire went out. The branches around me, frozen from their proximity to me and to my cold fire, shattered, and I crashed to the ground. Coughing and gasping for breath, I saw three faces: Grigory, brows drawn in determination; Ivan, full of concern; and the prince, whose expression was so murderous I began choking in fear.

It was the prince, though, who helped me to my feet, who demanded that I tell him if I could breathe. If I was all right. I nodded, still unable to speak.

The prince whirled on Grigory. "You could have killed her."

Grigory held up both hands in peace. "She had lost control—she could have killed *you*, Gosudar."

I didn't understand the prince's anger on my behalf, or how he could have possibly come to care for me—not only someone who was a peasant from a tiny village in the middle of nowhere, but also someone he'd just met. But then he made everything clear.

"She is our only chance of defeating our enemy, and you nearly crushed her to death." He looked to me after the words escaped his mouth as though he hadn't meant to say so much.

Foolish girl, I thought viciously. Of course he didn't care about *me*. He cared about what I could *do*. As a weapon.

I was disgusted that I'd been so willing to try to release my power here. That I'd actually believed I could control it. It was clear the prince had only sought me out to test my abilities, to see the power of the weapon he'd acquired.

Grigory was continuing to offer paltry excuses to the prince when I slipped away, back toward the palace and my room . . . and away from the prince.

"Katya," Ivan called after me, but I refused to stop. He caught up to me when I reached the door to the palace. "Are you injured?" he asked. "I can have the healer come to your room."

"I'll be fine," I said, already pushing open the door. "I need to rest."

But I knew what I really needed.

I needed to find a way out of this palace and away from the prince.

Chapter Seven

Alone in my room, I was warm from the inside out, and as I stood before the fire blazing in the wide fireplace, tendrils of steam curled up from my skin. As my body warmed, pain followed: bruising all over my sides from where the branches had wrapped around me, and an aching soreness in my throat where I'd nearly been choked. I wasn't sure if the blazing emotion I felt within me was anger at Grigory for attacking me in such a way or fear that the whole thing had nearly ended in disaster. For once, though, the painful stab of guilt didn't follow. I'd called forth the cold fire, but death hadn't followed.

It would have given me hope had it not been for the prince's reaction. I looked around the room—elegant and richly furnished, just as the tent had been. I was being treated well only to gain my compliance in being used for his war, and I didn't care that he'd said before he wouldn't make me fight. I wasn't so sure that, if I refused when put to the test, the prince would relent.

I wasn't so sure that I would be able to control my power enough to keep from killing them all—friend and foe.

All too soon, the warm feeling inside me faded, chased away by my dark thoughts. Soon I could barely feel the heat from the fire. Exhaustion, too, lowered itself over my shoulders like a yoke. Besides the usual death toll, this was the cost of the cold fire: a terrible fatigue, such that I could barely hold my eyes open. It was because of this that the villagers had so easily caught and subdued me.

I stumbled to the bed on stiff legs as the cold spread throughout my body. As I collapsed and gave in to the exhaustion, I thought of one of the only times I'd been ill that I could remember, and of the smell of herbs and the warm, rough hand of Babushka upon my forehead. As darkness rolled over me like a fog, tears fell from my eyes. I could see her in my mind, as clearly as if she was standing before me.

Sleep, devotchka, she said. *I will watch over you.*

And I did.

I awoke hours later to a knock at my door. Blearily, I opened it to find Ivan waiting for me. He looked apologetic.

"The prince has asked if you will join him for dinner."

Though my stomach once again reminded me it had been

far too long since I'd last eaten, I shook my head. "I would rather rest tonight, Ivan. Could you thank Gosudar for me?"

"You shouldn't go to bed hungry," he said. "It won't be just you and Gosudar. The rest of us will be there—the members of his bogatyr with abilities." *Bogatyr* was an interesting description of them. The prince thought of his guardsmen with abilities as knights? Still, I wasn't yet recovered enough to face them all. I didn't relish an evening full of Grigory's malicious glances and the prince's offhanded remarks on how I might best be used as a weapon.

"Tomorrow, perhaps," I said, and started to turn back to my room.

His stern face looked disappointed. "The dining room is on the first floor if you change your mind."

I nodded and turned back to my room. After I heard his footsteps fade down the hall, I closed my door and leaned against it.

I knew I had done the right thing. Better to be alone, better to not be drawn into more of the prince's manipulations.

Even if the memories of what I'd done began to pull at the edges of my mind again. Even if I missed Babushka and Dedushka so badly it gnawed inside me.

I walked over to the window, which overlooked the river. The water below was frozen still, but soon it would thaw. The air was already losing some of its bite when the sun was high. Spring would follow, chasing away the cold.

But not for me. For me, it was always winter. The cold was trapped inside me like the frozen river. Emotions threatened to crash over me: the aching loneliness, the piercing regret, the bleak sadness. But I let the cold spread to my heart, pushing away those feelings as a stone stands resolute against crashing waves.

For far too long I fought against succumbing to self-pity, but then the growling of my stomach convinced me I had to at least go and seek out food from the kitchens if I wasn't going to attend dinner with the others.

I whirled around and walked to the door, and after a brief hesitation, I pulled it open.

I nearly walked right into the prince.

"Katya," he said, eyebrows raised in surprise.

For a moment, I was struck dumb. "Gosudar," I finally said warily.

His gaze swept over me, brows knitted as though concerned. *He has to be sure his weapon is still functioning properly,* I thought savagely. "Ivan said you would rather rest tonight than come to dinner, but that you hadn't eaten. Did you change your mind?"

"No, I was only going to seek out a bit of bread and cheese from the kitchen."

Once again, his gaze swept over me, lingering where I held my arm protectively over my tender ribs—the area the branches had squeezed the hardest. "You are injured," he said, his eyes turning darker, until the gray looked almost black.

"Just bruised and sore," I admitted so he would stop looking at me in that way. "Enough so that I'd rather just stay in my room tonight, if you don't mind."

"I don't mind," he said, and a little breath of relief escaped me. "What does bother me, though, is your choice of meal. If I had supper brought to your room, would you eat it with me?"

The exhaustion lingered in my bones, my aching ribs begging me to lie down again. "I happen to like bread and cheese," I said, and even I could hear the irritable tone creeping into my voice. Babushka would have given me a hard look, but the prince only grinned.

"I feel badly that you were injured today, Katya," the prince said, and the sincerity in his voice gave me pause. "It wasn't my intention, and I would like to make it up to you."

"You weren't the one who injured me."

His expression darkened. "Grigory has been dealt with."

My skin turned cold. Just how did this prince—one who so many had rumored to be cruel—deal with those who displeased him? Suddenly, the prospect of dinner with the prince didn't seem worth arguing over anymore. "If you insist upon such a meal, then I won't fight you."

"Good. Then I will ask Vera to bring the food up."

I nodded, already turning back to the sanctuary of my room. Once inside with the door safely shut again, I glanced down at my wrinkled rubakha. And when I touched my hair, I knew the pale locks had escaped their braid. Running my fingers through it, I braided it again, and then retrieved a turquoise headscarf from the trunk—perhaps the least ostentatious accessory in there, and even it had golden discs hanging from it that made a pleasant jingling sound as I shook it out—and fashioned a turban that kept my hair wrapped and secure.

It wasn't long before the prince returned, followed by Vera, who bustled in with a tray laden with food and mead. She'd brought a colorful quilt, too, and she laid it out before the fire. "If you bring a few of those cushions from the bed, you'll have somewhere to sit, too," she told me, and wordlessly, I did as she asked. She set the tray on a low table nearby and gestured for us both to sit. "I'll stay to serve you," she said, and I tried not to let my relief show. I wasn't sure I'd be able to keep myself from turning into a frozen statue if I was left alone with the prince.

"Thank you, Vera," the prince said, and she bobbed her head once.

Vera handed us both goblets of mead and bowls of shchi, and although it was essentially the same cabbage soup Babushka always cooked, this one was made with richer ingredients: venison, carrots, onions, basil, and garlic. It was warm and delicious, and I had to keep myself from drinking it down in one gulp. I hadn't realized quite how desperately hungry I was until the soup touched my tongue.

The prince ate slowly, as one who isn't accustomed to ever being hungry does, his manner thoughtfully quiet. He didn't say anything for a very long time, and it allowed me to relax enough to finish my soup. Vera took away our bowls—mine empty and the prince's half-full—and laid out a plate of piroshki. They were baked golden brown, and as I took a bite of the soft crust, it yielded sautéed mushrooms and onions. It, too, was delicious. I took a sip of the sweet mead, to again pace myself from devouring everything like a wolf.

When I'd finished two or three, the prince nodded his head toward the chest. "None of the clothing I sent was to your liking?"

I stiffened, expecting him to be insulted, but instead, a grin played at his lips.

"They were all very elegant and beautiful, but . . ." I trailed off, unsure what to say.

"But . . . ?" he prompted, a single eyebrow arched.

"I wasn't sure any would be appropriate for travel, especially for someone . . . like me."

The amusement continued to tug at his lips, distracting me. "Then they weren't to your liking."

I frowned at the twisting of my words. "That's not what I said."

"Perhaps, but that's what you meant." The grin finally took over, prompting me to smile back in spite of myself.

"I like the red coat very much," I said, glancing at where it draped over a chair near my bed.

He laughed, but it wasn't the rich and full laugh of someone who laughs often. Rather, he almost seemed surprised by the outpouring of mirth himself. "It is a nice coat," he said, the laughter dying back down to burning embers in his eyes. "It suits you."

"Thank you," I said quietly, turning my focus once again to the food and the mead so that I wouldn't have to look at him. I couldn't decide what I thought of him, and that made me nervous.

We ate in silence again for a time, but then I finally asked the question that had been circling in my mind since I arrived. "This war," I said, glancing up from my goblet of mead. "I've known there have been whispers of unrest in the land, and that you had been amassing an army, but I suppose in my ignorance I hadn't thought the threat was so imminent."

He shifted on the quilt with one arm resting on his knee. "That isn't because of your supposed ignorance—I've intentionally hidden how dire the situation is to prevent mass panic. The Drevlians and Novgorodians, once our allies, have now joined forces against us. They make weak attempts at peace, but in the end, we will have no other choice but to fight.

"I told you before that our enemy's element is earth, and they have gathered the most powerful earth wielders the world has ever known. In comparison, I have an army at my command, but it is comprised of humble soldiers incapable of stopping an earth wielder. Kharan is skilled at espionage, Ivan at negating power; Boris has unnatural strength; Grigory has a minimal amount of earth wielder power." He paused and looked at me. "And then there's you."

I shook my head. "Today is the first day my power didn't come with the high cost of killing people indiscriminately. I wouldn't count my ability as an asset."

He looked at me appraisingly. "You were able in the end to stop your power—have you ever done that before?"

It was true that I had eventually gained control over the release of the cold fire, but I wasn't sure if that was due to my own ability or because Grigory's branches had been choking the life from me. "No, but I also don't know if I could do it again."

He nodded confidently. "You could."

Unwilling to argue with him, I changed the subject. "And what of you, Gosudar? Have you no otherworldly ability?"

"I am skilled at swordplay, but no, not anything else that could compare to yours."

"Still, you haven't told me why I must fight this enemy with you—assuming I even had the ability to control my element."

The prince's expression hardened. "So that what has happened to Novgorod and the Drevlians will not happen here."

Confusion knitted my brows together, and I would have blushed at my own ignorance if I was capable of blushing. Instead, frost spread up my neck. "Forgive me, Gosudar, but what happened to them?"

He looked momentarily taken aback, which only made me curse my ignorance all the more. "I have forgotten that you have spent your life in a secluded village. It's no surprise that you wouldn't know. The princes there have taxed their people to death. What they cannot pay in gold, they must forfeit in people—the princes' men sell them and regain their taxes that way. They have designs on Kiev, ones that were set into motion many years ago. Now that the Drevlian prince and the Novgorodian prince have joined forces, I have no choice but to protect my people any way I can. War will be inevitable."

Unease trickled through my mind. In light of such evil, the prince's war sounded almost . . . just.

But as I thought about the realities of battle and of war, my skin turned painfully cold. There would be people trying to kill each other purposefully. And if what the prince said could be believed—that they had gathered those with earth abilities—then they would be slaughtered in the most unimaginable ways.

Worse still was the knowledge that the prince was asking me to do the slaughtering.

"Have all attempts at diplomacy been exhausted? Surely no one wants war."

He laughed darkly. "They do want war. By all accounts, they have taken great pleasure in destroying the soldiers I send to stop them from encroaching farther on our land. Many villages in the north have fallen." He met my gaze. "I need you, Katya."

I tried not to let his words stir me. "You need my power."

"Yes," he said simply.

"I can make no promises," I said, looking at the contents of my goblet like it held the answers to the mysteries of life.

"All I can ask is that you try," he said.

I couldn't deny that I wanted help gaining control over my power. And being here with others like me was more than I could have ever hoped for. All my life, I'd wondered why I had such power. Where I came from. Who I really was. Maybe this was a chance to find out.

Sometimes where we least want to go is where we need to be.

Babushka was wise, but in this case, I wasn't sure I was

interpreting her words correctly. It made me even more desperate to go and see her again.

With my heart beating hard in my throat, I nodded to the prince. But I knew that even if I should gain control of my power, I would never allow it to be used as a weapon.

No matter how I felt about the prince's war.

Chapter Eight

The prince left shortly after, saying I needed to rest, but I thought he'd just gotten what he'd come for: my agreement. I'd gladly given in to the lingering fatigue left behind by the cold fire, sleeping until well past dawn. But it was the banya I sought when I first woke. I needed the cleansing steam and heat—not only for my body, but in the hopes that it would chase away the confusion lingering in my mind. I pulled open the door and went out into the hall, now bright with sunlight and candelabras lit in every darkened corner. Once I made my way down the stairs, I saw Vera bustling by with an arm full of linens.

"Can I help you with something, devotchka?" she asked when she caught sight of me.

"I want to visit the banya," I said. "Would that be all right?"

Her headscarf was a beautiful rich green, and some of her hair had escaped, as though she'd been rushing around this morning. Still, she smiled at me like she had all the time in the world. "Of course. I can go with you if you like. There are fresh eucalyptus branches inside, too—I just put them there myself this morning."

"I don't want to take you away from your chores," I said with a nod toward the linens.

"You won't," she said with a shake of her head. She put the linens down in a pile at the bottom of the stairs. "I don't mind stepping out for some fresh air for a moment."

She led me then to the back of the palace, near the kitchens, and out into the dvor. We continued in the opposite direction from the stables, only a little way from the palace. There stood a little wooden banya, constructed of rounded logs. Smoke puffed heavily from its chimney.

She opened the door for me, and we both stepped into a little room where I could remove my clothing. A rush of warmth enveloped me, and I knew it would be still warmer when I went to the steam room. Vera walked past and checked the next room—the one where the actual bathing occurred. "No one here," she said briskly. "Now, off with your clothes, and I'll bring you something to change into while I wash these for you."

"Are you sure you don't mind?" I said, hesitant both to wear anything else and that she should trouble herself.

She answered with a look that reminded me so much of Babushka I had to swallow hard. She waved her hand at me impatiently.

I did as she asked, handing her my clothing in exchange for a bundle of eucalyptus branches tied together.

"Do you think anyone else will enter while I'm in here?" I asked, glancing at the door behind us. The banya was for everyone in the palace, so it was rather surprising I was able to have it all to myself.

"I very much doubt it," she said, and I felt my shoulders relax. "The women in the palace tend to bathe in the very early morning, and the men like to come here in the evening to relax. The prince, though, he's a little more unpredictable."

"I'll hurry then," I said, more to myself than her.

"Mind the bannik," she said with a little wink as she left.

I smiled to myself at the thought of a visit from a bath spirit; if ever I needed a hint as to what the future would hold for me, it was now.

The door closed firmly behind her, and I brought one of the buckets of cool water with me as I entered the steam room. A large stone fireplace dominated one wall, the fire devouring an enormous pile of wood. Wide bowls filled with water were placed around the room, causing clouds of steam so thick I could barely see. With a sigh of happiness, I ladled the water over myself and rubbed the grime off my skin with the eucalyptus leaves. The sharp, herbal smell perfumed the steamy air, and the extreme heat was enough to penetrate even my icy skin.

My village had a banya, but it was one I couldn't frequent often. Being enclosed in a small space, completely naked, was something I tried to avoid at all costs. I'd learned being vulnerable like that could be humiliating at best and dangerous at worst.

I sat on one of the wooden benches closest to the fireplace and ladled water and used the crushed eucalyptus until every inch of me felt clean. In this thick steam, I wasn't as warm as I'd been directly after releasing the cold fire, but it was close.

I stared at the flames dancing through the steam, using the ladle to dip and pour the water over and over until it was almost hypnotic. Because of this, it was quite some time before I noticed the bannik staring at me from the other bench.

But when I finally saw him, a small man no bigger than a human baby with long white hair and a long white beard, ice raced over my skin so quickly that a blast of steam erupted from me. It hid my nakedness, at least, though I was sure if the spirit lived here he'd seen his fill.

"This is a very nice banya," I said to him, because it was always important to be polite to a bath spirit, lest he use the steam itself to suffocate me. Our village had one, too, but it was much smaller and rarely seen. This one, though wrinkled as an old man, was full and fat.

"*Da*," he said, his voice surprisingly deep and grumbly for such a small creature. "The prince is generous."

I certainly couldn't argue with that, but I was surprised into a watchful silence that he was speaking to me. With one eye on the clouds of steam surrounding the other bench, I wrung out my hair and listened for a moment for Vera's return.

In the thickness of the steam, I hadn't noticed him move closer, but soon, I realized the bannik was on the bench beside me.

"Child of Winter," he said, and I startled. Could he sense the power within me even in this common place? It was a curious name—one I'd never heard before—and there was something about it that brought goose bumps to my arms despite the heat. "Do you wish to know your future?"

This gave me pause. A bannik was typically a good spirit, known to foretell a good or bad future, but he never spoke to do so. It was said that one had only to present one's back to the bannik, and if it was with gentle fingers that he touched one, then the fortune would be positive. If not, then one's back would be rent with claws.

"I haven't had a very fortunate life so far," I said cautiously, "so I fear what the future holds for me."

The bannik released a sound that was like the hissing of steam. "Fear is good . . . until it is not. You may choose not to hear what I have foreseen, but then a decision will be laid before you, and you will make the wrong choice."

A sound came from the other room, and Vera's voice called out, "Katya, I've returned with your clothing. I will lay it out here for you."

"Thank you, Vera," I said, my gaze never leaving the bannik.

I waited until I heard her leave.

"Tell me," I said, my words swallowed by steam.

"The earth will only fall to fire and ice," the bannik said. "Without them, everything you have ever loved will be taken from you."

The ominousness of his final prediction chilled me to the bone. I disliked riddles and wasn't very good at them, but it was easy enough to figure out what he was talking about. Earth most likely meant the earth elementals the prince's enemies had been gathering; ice referred to my power; but fire . . . fire I wasn't sure about. "Who has the power of fire?" I wondered aloud, but the bannik had faded again into the steam, leaving me to think on his words with dread growing in the pit of my stomach.

I left behind the eucalyptus branches I hadn't used as an offering for the bannik, though I wasn't sure I was thankful for what he had told me. I didn't want such responsibility placed on my shoulders. I would have been happier had he urged me to go home to my village, despite the danger that awaited me there.

I found the clothing Vera had left for me in the other room: a plain linen rubakha, and a brocade rubakha in pale blue and gold, trimmed with embroidery and seed pearls. The more ornate tunic was meant to be worn over the other, and as I pulled on the linen one, I found that it reached my ankles. She'd even included soft leather leggings to wear underneath. My boots were waiting for me, which I was grateful for, and I pulled those on beneath the linen rubakha. A matching pale-blue headband, trimmed in seed pearls with beautiful dangling tassels that hung over my ears, helped keep my newly washed hair under control.

As I left the banya, the words of the bannik echoing in my ears, I saw Kharan from across the courtyard. So much had happened since I'd last seen her—most notably the fact that Grigory had nearly constricted me to death with his branches—that a sort of joyful relief bloomed within me at the sight of her.

I made my way across the dvor, and she waved to me when she saw me approach. She was dressed in a long blue-and-black tunic, belted at the waist. Black pants peeked out from the split in the tunic, and she wore a beautiful hat trimmed in silver fox fur. She was leading Daichin, who looked around curiously.

A smile lit her face as she took in my clothing. "I see you finally relented and wore something out of that enormous trunk the prince gave you."

I glanced down at the heavy brocade. "Not by choice. These are the clothes Vera brought for me while I was in the banya. I can only hope she hasn't taken my old clothes away to burn them."

Kharan laughed. "She did the same to me when I refused to take off my deel when I first arrived," Kharan said with a sympathetic look. She nodded toward the stable. "I was just about to go for a ride. Would you like to join me?"

"Yes, a ride would be nice."

She nodded and led me back to the stables, but Ivan caught up to us before we could enter.

"If you and Katya are going riding," Ivan said to Kharan,

"then put her on one of the Vyatka horses, like Dukh."

"Fine, fine," Kharan said, waving him off.

"Is that one of the plow horses?" I asked hopefully as we entered the stables, and Kharan laughed.

"Practically."

Kharan asked one of the grooms to saddle Dukh, which turned out to be a stout dun-colored horse with a black mane and tail and a friendly face. Definitely one of the humbler horses I'd spied in the stables when I'd visited before.

"This will be the perfect horse for me," I said to Kharan, admiring Dukh's stocky physique. He didn't look like he could make it faster than a brisk walk.

She shot me a look. "I thought you were joking before, but I take it you don't have much experience with riding."

I shook my head. "Very little. Our village didn't have many horses."

"Dukh will take care of you, then," she said, giving him a pat. "He'll happily plod along."

At least he wasn't very big. I managed to hoist myself up easily enough. I took up the reins and followed alongside Kharan, and Dukh's pace was slow, as promised.

The palace's paths were winding and full of snow, but I could see areas where, in spring and summer, there would be lovely gardens. Skeletal trees reached toward the sky, surrounded by evergreen bushes peeking out from beneath the snowy ground. As we made our way to the back of the palace, toward the river, there was a small wood-and-glass building—a greenhouse located right off the kitchen. That must have been how fresh herbs were present in last night's soup.

Something else, too: a tunnel carved into the stone that jutted out from the rear of the palace, near the kitchens. I pointed it out to Kharan. "Where does that lead?"

She followed my line of sight. "Ah, that is the escape tunnel for the palace should we ever fall under siege. It leads to the river."

"Has the palace ever been under attack?"

"Not in all the time I've been here at least," she said, but her expression soon turned grave. "Though that may change if the prince's enemies breach the city."

"And you fear that as a possibility?"

"There is no doubt that war is coming; it's just a matter of where and when. I heard enough whispers of it in my travels here."

I glanced at Kharan, who was barely holding the reins, letting her horse have his head and follow the path on his own. "You said before that you and Daichin had come all the way from the steppes. Did you leave willingly?"

"In a way," she hedged. When I stayed silent, inviting her to say more, she continued, "I came because my ability wasn't conducive to nomadic life with my clan, and after my parents"—she paused, her gaze focusing on a spot somewhere over Daichin's ears—"after they died, my grandfather said I should go where my power was useful, so I joined a trade caravan and eventually made my way here."

I could see from the way her face darkened that it still pained her, and that she probably still missed her tribe. "I'm sorry about your parents," I said, knowing the words weren't enough. "I never knew my own, but my dedushka is also no longer of this world."

"We've both known loss," she said, "but we can do our families a far greater service here than we ever could at home. This is what I saw as I journeyed west: the soldiers of our enemy burning villages still loyal to the prince, seizing land, and always searching for people with power."

The picture she painted was a bleak one, and more frightening than I could have imagined. "The prince told me they have earth elementals, but were they able to find others?"

She shook her head. "We are so few and far between. The earth elementals are from a tribe who only intermarry their own. They are said to have come far from here—from the south."

I had to give Dukh a little nudge with my heel to keep him from stopping. "Is Grigory from the same tribe, then?"

"Distantly. His power is diluted compared to theirs."

"Not diluted enough," I said with a dark laugh. "He nearly choked me to death yesterday," I said at her questioning glance. "The prince had made me think I could control my cold fire, and when I ultimately was unable to rein it in, Grigory stepped in to keep me from harming the prince . . . by any means necessary, I suppose."

She made a disgusted sound at the back of her throat. "Were you hurt?"

"Not badly."

"I'm glad. So it was only the shock of what he did to you that allowed you to stop your cold fire?"

I turned her question over in my mind. "I think perhaps it provided motivation, yes, but I did manage to gain control—at least enough to stop it."

She looked at me with eyebrows raised. "That's the first time you were able to exact some control over it, right?"

I nodded. "Thanks to Ivan's suggestion."

"Good old Ivan. I wish I'd had an Ivan growing up," she said with a smile that brought a dimple out in one cheek. "It can be difficult when you don't have anyone else to show you the way. There had been shadow melders in my family, but it was long ago. There was no one living to offer advice. I had to sort of stumble along and try different things on my own. Of course, my power can't hurt others as yours can, so I know it's not quite the same."

"I'm sure it was hard no matter what," I said. "Did you ever think . . ." I trailed off, unsure I should ask, unsure she ever felt that way.

"Just ask. You can't hurt my feelings," she said.

"Did you ever think, 'Why me?'"

She nodded. "Many times." Her gaze flicked to mine. "And you?"

"Every day," I said, my gaze shifting now to the gray winter sky in the distance. "I wondered why I was born with a power that only made me the object of ridicule, or why I was abandoned so soon after birth by my mother, or even who my father could be. But always, I would remind myself that I was not suffering alone in this world. There are many born with a worse fate, and at least I had Babushka and Dedushka, an izba, and food and clothing."

Sympathy lit her eyes, but at least it was not pity. "Your village, though, that was part of the problem for you. At least in my tribe, even though we hadn't had a shadow melder in many generations, they knew of them. You were treated as an outsider by the people you'd been raised with, and perhaps if they'd had ice powers like you, they would have understood."

I stopped urging Dukh on while I contemplated what she'd said, and he came to a slow stop. "There are others, then? Others like me, with the ability to control ice?" I could find them, convince them to help the prince in my place . . . perhaps even learn more about my ability. I would be free to leave, free to return to Babushka . . .

"No." The word cut through my fevered thoughts like a hot sword through snow. Overlooking the frozen river, Kharan pulled Daichin to a stop next to Dukh. "At least, not that I've ever heard tell of in all my days of gathering information."

"I suppose that would explain why the prince is so desperate to place all his hope in someone who has no battle training and who has little if any control over her ability."

Kharan's expression turned even more serious. "All of us are desperate to stop the evil that the Drevlian and Novgorodian princes are committing."

"Forgive me, but how do you know this for sure? Is this just what the prince has told you?"

"I gather information for the prince, slipping through the shadows and picking up things here and there until a great tapestry of their plans is created. There are whispers that the strongest earth elementals can control the very land we walk on—changing its shape, forcing rich minerals from its depths, even felling whole forests. They care nothing for their people—for any people besides the nobles. They would subjugate all the people of Kievan Rus', and beyond, to the steppes—to my own clansmen. They want to amass riches the Byzantine Empire, with its golden palaces, would be envious of."

I thought of the rumors I'd heard of the prince—rumors that had, so far, appeared to have been exaggerated. "You've only heard things, though? Never seen?"

"Yes, I have seen for myself—once, on my journey to Kiev." She seemed to grow pale as the memories overtook her. "I had the misfortune to come upon a Drevlian man with earth elemental powers one night on the shores of the Volga. His ship was filled with people, and by their chains, I could see they were captives. I slipped into the shadows even though I knew there was nothing I could do to help, but I still . . . I still just couldn't ride by like I'd seen nothing."

I could see guilt ripple over her face, and my stomach tightened in sympathy.

"There were others who must have had the same idea—armed men who challenged the captain, who'd come to rescue the captives. The captain met them before they even reached the shores. They'd borne down on him on horseback, swords brandished high, but the captain raised his arms. The ground beneath us trembled violently, and the horses screamed in fear. In the next instant, a great chasm opened, and swallowed the entire battalion of men—horses and all."

A horrified silence descended. "Was that captain you saw . . . was he the only one with such power?"

She shook her head. "No, the clan of earth elementals that the Drevlians have sought out—they have at least fifty who can use such power. Those men and women would be in addition to the combined armies of the Drevlians and Novgorodians."

Understanding was dawning in my mind, and with it, a sinking in my stomach. "To avoid a war, it might have been better to accept their demand for tribute."

Defiance flashed in her eyes. "Never. You think they'd stop at that? The demands would grow larger and larger, until every man, woman, and child was enslaved."

I'd seen how hunger for power and greed could change someone, could make them forget everything that was good and decent in the world. But what Kharan was describing was so much worse. Men who already had all the power, princes instead of small village elders, free to run rampant over the weak.

"Already, the nobility of this land still loyal to the prince have called upon their druzhina, their cavalry and militia, but the numbers are small. And even with their skill, the earth elementals destroy them easily. Much land has already been lost. The prince has the city militia, numbering in the tens of thousands, but we fear even this will not be enough. Endlessly, he has searched for someone with such power, and I have aided him. But my searches produced nothing. Until you."

I watched the frozen river instead of her. "What use can my power be?"

I could feel her staring, and I finally turned to meet her intense gaze.

"Not even earth can stand against ice."

Chapter Nine

After my ride with Kharan, the rest of the day had progressed slowly. With nowhere else to go, I'd returned to my room, only to have my head so crowded with thoughts that I paced like a caged tiger. I thought of the destructive powers of earth Kharan had described; of the ominous things the bannik had said; of the malicious plans of the princes; of the unfounded hope in my own power.

I'd braved dinner with the others in the dining hall but found the prince and Grigory to be missing from the table. While I filled myself with dark bread and smoked fish, hearty borscht with sour cream and fresh herbs from the greenhouse, and honey cakes for dessert, I found myself surprised by how comfortable I was with the others. Especially when Kharan turned to me and said, "We've been told so much about you, but I'm sure you have questions for us. It's only fair that you should know more about our lives, too."

I glanced up to find Ivan and Boris watching me with encouraging smiles. "That's actually . . . very kind of you to offer." I settled for the most innocuous and polite of questions first. "Have you both been at the palace long?"

Ivan was the first to answer in his gruff voice. "I started here as a squire under the prince's grandfather, and was able to become a part of the bogatyri after years of training."

"He's being modest," Boris interjected with a swig of his kvas. "It was only two years, and he was the youngest bogatyr at sixteen."

My eyebrows raised. "That's impressive. Did you meet Vera here at the palace?"

He shook his head, his gaze taking on a faraway look. "No. She is from a little village to the north, and from the moment I met her, I knew I couldn't leave her behind. I was in the area by order of the late prince when I was only twenty—he wanted me to hear the needs of the northern boyars. After I met Vera, I stayed at her village until I convinced her father to agree to let me marry her. And I was just lucky enough that she agreed to come with me here, though I'm sure she regrets it now." He said it in his typical deadpan way, so it was difficult to say if he was being serious or joking.

"Don't say such things," Kharan said. "It isn't true, and you know it."

"Kiev and life in the palace are very different from what

Vera was used to," Ivan explained to me. "She had dreams of a northern farm and many children, but I gave her neither of those things."

"I'm sure she's happy to work here in the palace now," I said, "especially since it's warm all year-round. I know how cold it can get in the small villages, and I didn't even live in one of the northernmost ones."

He smiled and raised his mug of kvas. "You're right about that."

"And what about you, Boris?" I asked. "How long have you been a bogatyr?"

He paused to swallow his bite of bread. "I've been here two years now, but I'm afraid my story is more sad than impressive." He glanced up at me, his warm brown eyes meeting mine. "I was like you once: I'd lost control of my powers and was brought before the prince for my crime. He should have executed me, but instead, he gave me my life back and asked me to join him."

I was so taken aback by this—Boris had always seemed cheerful and friendly and with an easy manner. I couldn't imagine him committing a crime. "You . . . lost control of your powers?"

His face, for once, looked haunted. "I hit a man from my village so hard, it smashed his head like an egg." He looked down at his hand, opening and closing it as though he could still see traces of blood. "It was a small offense—he'd made advances on a girl I was courting—something that certainly wasn't worth the cost of his life.

"I left the village and the girl I loved and I will serve the prince without question for the rest of my life because he had no reason to spare me for what I did. Yet here I am."

I was struck momentarily silent by the similarities in our stories. A moment of anger that turned deadly. The loss of control over our powers that resulted in the loss of someone else's life. And the prince's mercy and pardon. "You didn't mean to kill him."

Boris gave me a sad smile. "I didn't mean to hit him as hard as I did, it's true, but I knew I was strong. I shouldn't have lost my temper. Since I've been here, I've learned to control it, to channel it into my swordplay instead."

"Don't ever shake his hand, though," Ivan said with a straight face that again made it difficult to tell if he was teasing or serious.

Kharan laughed. "Or dance with him. He doesn't know any of the steps, and then he'll crush your foot under his."

"I see you will never let me forget that night," Boris said with an easy grin.

"Never," she said with a flash of teeth.

"That was when things were not so dire as they are now," Ivan said. "When the prince still threw the occasional ball."

"Yes," Kharan said, "though I'm sure it was Grigory who put a stop to them. He loathes dancing." She leaned back in her chair, her hand gripping a mug of kvas. "Where is the prince and that minion anyway?"

"Scouts were sent out after a letter arrived warning that the enemy had defeated the druzhina of the two nobles to the east of Kiev," Ivan said, and Kharan nodded grimly. After everything she'd said on our ride today, even I could recognize the danger. "And then another letter arrived from the Drevlian prince."

"Is that where Gosudar and Grigory are now?" Kharan asked Ivan, and he nodded. "What did the letter demand this time?"

"It began with more of the same—for the prince to hand over his throne to them or else pay crippling tithes."

"And by that you mean people," Kharan said, disgust clear in her tone.

"Eventually, yes," Ivan said. "But this time, they tried a new tack: to ask the prince to join forces with them."

Kharan shook her head, sadness pulling the corners of her mouth down. "As if he could do that after what they did to his parents."

I paused in taking a bite of borscht. "What do you mean?" I asked.

"I suppose the news never traveled to your village," Ivan said. "The Drevlian and Novgorodian princes conspired together to kill the prince's parents."

I sat back in surprise. "I had heard it was the prince himself."

"A particularly cruel rumor," Ivan said with a frown.

"Do you have proof of what happened? Why have they never been apprehended?"

Ivan laughed, but the sound wasn't very cheerful. "They've never been apprehended because they hired a Varangian—a Northman—to do it. But Kharan . . ." He glanced over at her.

"I got close enough to one of the earth elemental's camps—at least before one of their vines found me," she added with a shudder. "They spoke of how two years ago, the Drevlian and Novgorodian princes united to have the prince and princess assassinated because they were hoping it would leave the young prince weak and unable to rule."

"But the prince has never been weak," Ivan added.

"The princess had ties to Constantinople," Kharan continued, "so they didn't want her calling upon her allies to stop them as they slowly took over Kievan Rus'. They even made it seem like the young prince had become impatient for the throne and hired an assassin, allowing it to be traced back that a noble—possibly a royal—from Kievan Rus' had hired him. And with rumors circling like the one you heard, of course Constantinople won't help the prince if they think he killed his mother."

"In answer to your question," Ivan said, "they've never been apprehended for the same reason the prince never has: no one can prove it."

I glanced around at their serious expressions. There was more to this brewing war with the other princes. This was about vengeance as much as it was about defending Kiev.

That night, as I lay in my plush bed of down covered with fur blankets, I felt like I was a fly who'd flown straight into a spider's web.

I didn't see the prince until the next morning. Sleep had been slow to come for me the night before, crowded as my head was with thoughts. The dark rumor that the prince had killed his own parents had been the last thing holding me back, making it difficult to trust that he was as kind as he appeared. And yet . . . I couldn't bring myself to willingly join his army. What did I know of war? Despite what Ivan and Kharan had said of the earth elementals and their princes, it seemed so far away, so removed from my everyday life. The thought of entering a battlefield with the intent to kill as many people as I could terrified me.

Perhaps if I spoke to Kharan about it—if I could get her on my side—then she could help me explain my case to the prince. I'd never had someone I could call my friend before, but I thought Kharan was becoming such a person.

And if she wouldn't agree to help me, then I would have to escape on my own.

I awoke and dressed again in my rubhaka and skirt, which I found to have been cleaned while I slept, thanks to Vera. As lovely as the brocade rubhaka had been, I was grateful to be able to wear my familiar clothing. When I pulled open the door to my room, I prepared myself to ask Ivan where I might find Kharan, but instead, I found an empty hallway. I wasn't sure where to find her, but my stomach made the suggestion that the kitchens might be as good a place as any to start my search, and I agreed.

The enormous oven beckoned me from the hallway, the smell of bread and pies making my stomach growl. Its blazing heat chased away some of the cold from my skin, so for a moment, all I did was bask in the warmth of the hallway.

A servant girl came through the doorway, and when she saw me, bobbed her head in greeting. "Can I get you something to eat?"

"Maybe a bit of bread?"

The girl grinned, showing a dimple on her right cheek. "I can do better than that. Just a moment."

She disappeared back into the kitchen, and when she returned, she had a steaming-hot pie, small enough to fit in my hand, but by the delicious smell wafting from it, filled with meat and vegetables. It was wrapped in linen, and I closed my eyes with a brief jolt of joy when she handed it to me, the heat briefly warming my cold hands.

"This looks delicious—thank you," I said.

"They're the prince's favorite," she said with a wink before going back into the kitchen.

After taking a bite, I could see why. It was a delicious blend of herbs and savory meat and vegetables, warming and filling my stomach simultaneously. With my piroshk leaving a trail of steam, I walked down the hall until I reached the door to the dvor.

A quick scan once outside revealed Kharan to be nowhere in sight, so I made my way toward the stables to see if she might be with Daichin. Before I got there, however, a flash of light—like flames—caught my eye. I turned toward the winter garden, where the prince had me demonstrate my power for him, and again, a flash of flame and smoke danced in the air.

Though the dvor was busy with the comings and goings of servants and guardsmen, no one seemed to notice or concern themselves with the strange fire. I couldn't look away, so I found myself walking toward the garden.

I'd fully been expecting to find servants burning sticks, or leaves, or some other refuse, but I stood stock-still the moment I realized where the flames were coming from.

The prince stood under an old oak tree, its bare branches spread wide above our heads, glittering with ice. His profile was to me, strong and almost harsh were it not for the softness of his lips. His arm was outstretched, and in his hand he held tongues of flames that wavered and danced almost cheerfully.

The earth will only fall to fire and ice, the bannik had said, and I shuddered. Here now was fire.

"You lied to me," I said before I'd even thought to choose my words carefully. The prince whipped his head around to look at me. "You said you didn't have power of your own, but you clearly have the gift of fire."

"Yes, but it isn't strong enough to light anything bigger than a pile of dry wood," he said, and he made a terse, frustrated movement with his hand, extinguishing the fire. "The uselessness of my ability is why I've had to seek out others with power."

"Do any of the others know?" I asked, unable to keep my gaze from his hand. How I wished I could summon a flame to chase away the perpetual cold inside me.

"They do, but we've always known it isn't powerful enough

to be help against the earth elementals." His hand tightened into a fist as he glanced down at it. "But now things are more desperate."

My gaze jumped to his, and I belatedly noticed his jaw was tight, his face shadowed by a light dusting of stubble that seemed to indicate he hadn't slept well. "Because of the nearby attacks?"

"Someone must have filled you in."

I nodded. "Last night. At dinner."

"The boyars had too much faith in their druzhina. They had cavalry and armor and weapons, but it wasn't enough. We didn't get word of the impending attack until it was nearly upon them, and I cannot risk sending the city militia to fight . . . not now. It would leave the city too vulnerable to attack."

He looked so tormented, so distraught, that I unthinkingly said, "I wish I could help you."

"Do you?" he asked with a wry twist to his lips. "Has Kharankhui convinced you so quickly, then?"

I thought again of the bannik's words, and of the nature of fire and ice. "I meant help you with your power. There has never been a fire hot enough to burn me."

His eyebrows rose, as though he was taken aback, but then he grew contemplative.

"Ivan told me that he saw your eagle land upon your arm, with nothing to protect your skin from her talons."

"It's part of my ability. There is ice that coats my skin, hardening it and protecting it against such things."

He looked impressed. "A useful skill."

"I didn't always think so," I said, staring at the blanket of snow coating everything in the garden as the memories of the village children's cruelty flashed through my mind. "But it has been useful with Elation."

"Do you control when the ice spreads?" he asked without a hint of disgust, only curiosity.

"Yes—well, now I can. When I was a child, I had no control over it, but now, I am able to at least dismiss it—much like certain people can train themselves not to react in frightening situations."

"That must have been a difficult thing to bear when you were only a child."

I could feel that pull toward him beginning again, to open up and tell him things and *trust*. But then I remembered that the prince wanted me as a weapon and nothing more. The cold snuck back into my heart.

"It was a long time ago," I said, like the memories didn't still bring me pain as sharp as barbs.

He looked at me like he could see through to how I really felt but decided not to push. "I ask you these things because I'd like to be able to do the same."

He held up his hand, palm toward me, and nodded at my own hand. I raised it, until it was hovering just an inch away from his. My eyes widened. "It's hot. Normally I can't even detect another person's body heat because my own skin is so cold."

"But not hot enough to burn, correct?"

"You can't hurt me with it," I reassured him.

"Will you show me how you coat your skin with ice?" he asked.

I nodded, allowing the cold to spread and spread. He watched almost without blinking, and then a moment later, the heat of his hand increased, until soon there was a flame surrounding it. The flames flickered and glowed, but his skin remained untouched beneath the blaze.

My gaze jumped to his, eyes wide. "Did I teach you that?"

He grinned. "I'm a quick study."

We continued like that, using our powers to coat our hands with flames and ice, until the prince suddenly said, "Attack me."

I glanced around, sure Grigory would somehow sense the prince's intentions and attempt to choke the life out of me again. "I won't use the cold fire."

He shrugged. "Then try to freeze me."

"You're sure?"

"You won't hurt me," he said, one eyebrow arched as he echoed my earlier words.

I could feel the waterfall of power flowing within me, unchecked and wild, eager to be put to use. When I froze buckets of water in the summer, I needed a small fraction of that power. I reasoned this was no different. Still, I hesitated. What if I called forth more than he could handle? What if it was cold fire that leaped from my hands?

"I trust you," he said. "You need to trust yourself."

I searched his face and saw that he meant what he said. Palms toward him, I released a stream of cold air—the same I would have used to freeze water. Instantly, twin flames burned forth from his own hands. For one beautiful moment, the ice and the fire met in the air, a brilliant burst of crimson and azure, until they dissipated in a burst of steam.

With a relieved smile, I looked up at him, and his silvery gaze captured mine. There was a moment where we said nothing, only looked at each other, and the cold tingled over me in answer to the heat rolling off him. And then I remembered he was the prince, and he wanted me to be his weapon—that at this very moment, he was using me—and I took a step back.

"I didn't hurt you, did I?" he asked, concern furrowing his brows.

"No," I said.

"Shall we try again?" he asked.

After a moment, I nodded.

We went back and forth like that many times, the flame and ice meeting to form puffs of steam, but no matter how hard the prince tried, his flames never grew larger. At one point, the cold air I sent his way was too strong and nearly overtook his fire. But he never became frustrated or angry, only resolute.

When sweat dotted his brow, and fatigue threatened to settle in my bones again like it had after the cold fire, the prince raised his hand. "I've tired you. Forgive me."

I shook my head. "I wanted to learn control, and this has helped me."

The prince glanced down at his hands. "I can control my fire, but it never gets any stronger than those small flames. They would only be useful for short-range battles. I was hoping it would respond to your own power, and in a way, it did."

"I'm only sorry it didn't incite yours into a blazing inferno," I said with a smile.

He laughed. "It was enough just to be able to practice with you," he said, his gaze holding mine until my heart beat a little faster. "Will you come with me back to the palace? There is something I want to show you."

Unable to think of an excuse, and admittedly curious, I agreed. He led me back to the palace, past the kitchen and down the main corridor before turning off on a smaller hallway I'd never been down. His stride was purposeful, and I had to hurry to keep up.

Before long, we arrived at a small wooden door. He held it open for me, and I walked through after only a moment's hesitation. Inside, the first thing I saw was an enormous icon corner. There were several icons on display, but the most prominent one was of the Virgin holding the Christ child, her eyes gazing down lovingly at him as his gaze pierced the viewer's.

Prince Alexander crossed himself before the icon, and I did the same, both of us taking a moment to pray, though I was sure we prayed for very different things. I opened my eyes again, and as I did, I caught sight of a beautiful gilded vase. Adorned with red and yellow jewels, it was also intricately enameled; at the center was a firebird of every color of the sunset. The vase was lovely itself, but rising from within it was a feather of such splendid beauty that I couldn't look away. It was gold as no creature on earth is gold, but also the deep crimson of fire, and a bright vermilion. Large as a peacock feather, it shimmered even in the dim light of the candles.

"It was my mother's," he said, when he caught me looking.

"It's beautiful," I said, leaning toward it without even meaning to. "I've never seen a feather like that. This is what you wanted to show me?"

He nodded. "She always told me it was from a firebird."

I thought of what I knew of the firebird legend; that it was a creature who came out only at night; that it was often sought but rarely found; that if a feather was removed, it still glowed like the bird itself. I could see the last was true. I'd thought the feather was illuminated by the nearby candle, but now I saw that the feather itself was emitting a soft glow.

I raised my hand to touch the feather but stopped myself. "Do you think there is truly such a creature?"

"My mother said that they had a different legend in Constantinople, where she was born. She said the firebird was an elemental creature that could summon fire as you do ice."

I gave him a sharp look. "So you believe there's a connection between the firebird and your ability?"

"My mother always said it was our family's legacy, but she wouldn't reveal the truths of it all until I took the throne."

"Did she have power like yours?"

He shook his head. "No, but she said my fire ability came

from her lineage. It didn't manifest until I was fifteen, and as you can see, it's never advanced to more than a very entertaining magic trick."

I thought of how they said Grigory's power was weak compared to the other earth elementals, but that was because he was from a diluted line. Surely the prince's lineage was stronger. "Did your mother say anything about that—about the strength of your power?"

He looked up from studying the glowing feather. "She always said my power was one fit for a grand prince and was tied to the throne, but when I was suddenly forced to take the position, the power didn't grow with it."

I turned his words over slowly in my mind. "Then she probably had plans to tell you how to increase the strength of the power, too, when you took the throne."

That same shadow of grief I'd glimpsed earlier appeared across his face. "I think so, but then, she hadn't known she'd be murdered in her sleep."

My own pain throbbed in response to his. Did the others consider Dedushka to have been murdered? Did Babushka? "And you believe the Drevlians and Novgorodians are responsible?"

"I know they were," he said. "The Varangian assassin was traced back to them. I would have been killed, too, were it not for Grigory."

I started. "What do you mean?"

"He came to me two days before their murders and asked

if I would accompany him to visit one of the nearby boyars. I was eager to go with him because this particular nobleman bred horses." He shook his head in disgust. "I was busy bartering for horseflesh the day my parents were killed."

I started to reach out to him but stopped myself at the last moment. "You couldn't have known. And if you'd been here, you might not have been able to save them."

"I owe my life to Grigory, it's true, but that doesn't mean guilt at being alive doesn't torture me." He looked down at his hands, letting a small flame flicker across them. "And while I mourned, the Drevlian and Novgorodian princes have used these two years since my father's death to slowly take over Kievan Rus'. Any boyar who did not join their side found his land razed and his people taken. They thought I would be too weak to stand against them, and maybe I am"—he looked up at me—"but together . . . together I think we are strong."

This was not my war—had never been my war—but now I was starting to understand the consequences should I do nothing. If the Drevlians and Novgorodians came for us all, enslaved the people of Kievan Rus', and I only stood aside, too afraid to lend my power, how would I feel then? I took a step toward him, until the heat from his body surrounded us both. "I'm still not convinced that I can be of much help, but I will give it to you nonetheless."

He held out his hand to me, and the heat from his body blazed still hotter, until I felt it melt some of the cold inside me. "Katya, you don't know how relieved—"

"Gosudar!" a voice called, and the note of anxiety thrumming through it made us both startle.

Grigory hurried into the room, and for a moment, he only glared at me, as though annoyed to find me there alone with the prince.

"What is it?" Prince Alexander demanded, his body going taut as a bow.

Again, Grigory glanced at me. "I must speak with you privately, Gosudar."

The prince looked like he would refuse, but I didn't want to cause any strife—not when there was clearly something wrong.

"I'll be in my room," I said before the prince could ask me to leave.

To his credit, the prince hesitated before answering me. "I'll come seek you out when I can. I'd like to continue our discussion."

I nodded before giving an awkward little curtsy and leaving. But once outside the room, I wasn't very far down the hall before I overheard Grigory's first words:

"There's been another attack."

Cold pierced my heart. *Where?*

I couldn't bear to stop listening.

"So soon?" the prince asked, a mixture of anxiety and fury in his voice. "The last report was that the armies were still much farther to the north."

"They must have traveled through the night. We didn't expect them to come so close to Kiev yet. But now they draw closer still, which means more villages are exposed to the threat."

"Which villages stand in their way?" the prince asked.

I pressed closer to the wall, my heart beating wildly in my chest.

"All the villages to the northwest of Kiev are at risk."

Northwest. My village was northwest of Kiev. Tears pricked my eyes, and I shook my head. I didn't cry for the villagers—not after what they had done to me—but Babushka . . . I had to see for myself. I should have gone to her—I shouldn't have let the prince and the others make me think my place was here with them. If I had gone back to Babushka and begged her forgiveness for Dedushka, then perhaps I could have done something when they came. Ice rippled over my skin now, and I could feel the great waterfall of power within me crashing down, over and over. Power enough to destroy a village. Power enough to defeat an army.

"Then I will send the militia," the prince said.

"You cannot send them away from the city now; you will need all your resources should they attack Kiev. Your priority must always be the city."

White-hot anger shot through me at Grigory's advice to the prince.

"The villagers are my people, too," the prince said. "I won't abandon them to their fate. You will take a contingent of men to the villages to lend them aid."

"Gosudar, I don't think—" Grigory started.

"That is my command," the prince said, cutting him off.

"It will take me some time to ready the men," he said.

"Do it, then," the prince said. "As fast as you can."

I pushed away from the wall before they could leave the room and find me listening. As I hurried to my room, thoughts crowded my mind. I hadn't been at the palace long, but I knew Grigory: he was loyal to the prince. He wouldn't leave him willingly, and I was sure he'd make every appearance of obeying the prince's command while still taking too long. More time than my village—than Babushka—had.

Grigory and the soldiers might not arrive in the village soon enough to save it, but perhaps I could.

I owed it to Babushka to try, even if all that was left of her was ash. For once my power would be put to the right purpose—saving the one person I loved in this world.

Chapter Ten

I raced up to my room, praying I wouldn't encounter anyone on my way. Every flicker of shadow made me twitch for fear Kharan would appear before me. I wasn't sure that she would try to stop me once she knew the reasons behind my flight from the palace, but neither did I want to put her to the test. My plan was a simple one: after gathering the things I might need, I would seek out the tunnel I'd noticed before on our ride. I only prayed no one would question where I was going.

In my room, I grabbed my coat, and as luck would have it, there was already a table set up with food on a piece of linen—just cheese and a small loaf of bread. Vera must have kindly thought to leave me something to eat in case I hadn't had the sense to seek out something to break my fast earlier. Taking hold of the linen underneath, I fashioned a rough sack that could hold it all. The kvas I quickly drank—I would need my strength—and then added the earthenware mug to my sack. There was a knife for slicing the bread, and I took that, too.

Lastly, I went to the fireplace and took the tinderbox. It would save me much time and energy later when I needed to make a cooking fire.

Back in the hallway again, I hurried as fast as I dared to the stairway that would lead me down to the kitchen. The tunnel I'd seen was at the rear of the palace, facing the frozen river. From my wanderings in the palace, I knew the door must be somewhere near the kitchen.

Heat blasted from the ovens as I passed by, and I thought of the prince. What would he think when he realized I had gone? But I pushed such concerns aside. Worrying would only slow me down.

But no matter where I searched near the kitchen, there wasn't a single door that led to a tunnel. With growing frustration gnawing at my insides, I stalked back and forth from one end of the hallway to the other, willing a door to appear.

On one wall, there was a tapestry with a golden key on a crimson background, simplistic in design, and yet, something about it caught my attention. As I watched, it fluttered, ever so gently, as though moving in a breeze. I glanced around, but there were no open windows.

The tapestry fluttered again as I watched; it hung from nearly the ceiling all the way to the floor. I took a few steps toward

144

the tapestry and pulled it aside. I half-expected there to be just more of the wall, but a wooden door stood behind it. There were cracks in the doorframe where a cold breeze escaped, just enough to move the tapestry.

For a moment, all I could do was stare in disbelief at the door. But then I reached for the iron handle and wrenched it. A cold wind rushed in, billowing out the tapestry and bringing with it the scent of fresh air.

With a cry of relief, I plunged into the passageway, my footsteps echoing as I hurried as fast as I dared over the slick stones. The ceiling was barely higher than my head and dripped cold water onto my neck as I passed, making me shudder. The way was lit by torchlight, which meant someone came down here to light the torches. A flicker of unease raced through me. What would I say if someone challenged me? If they asked why I was here?

It reminded me of being chased before, of knowing I wasn't nearly fast enough, of being struck and bound by chains. My heart raced, and my skin became so hard I no longer felt the cold drips of water.

There were no turns or forks, only a straight tunnel to follow. Before long, the way ahead grew brighter, the light cooler, more natural, and I knew I was nearly there. I slowed my steps, and the way grew so light that I could finally see: a great frozen river lay before me, the sun reflecting off the ice so powerfully it penetrated even the darkness of the hidden passageway.

I made my way out of the tunnel slowly, scanning my

surroundings for the prince's guardsmen. Before me, there was only the vastness of the Dnieper River. I looked up, and far above me loomed the palace, perched on the very top of a hill.

The river was silent as I crept toward the shore. My breath came out in great plumes, and at any moment, I expected someone to shout that I'd been spotted. I wasn't seen, though, and made it to the river's edge safely, only to realize two things. One was that the river only *appeared* frozen. Spring was mere weeks away, and I could see cracks forming on top, and places where the ice was thin, giving way to the rushing water beneath. I'd seen firsthand what could happen if a person ventured out onto a river that wasn't quite frozen.

The other thing I noticed was that there was no other way across.

But as I touched the ice at the edge with my boot, I thought of what Kharan had said, that ice was my element. I gazed out at the wide stretch of river. I'd frozen small buckets of water before, but did I have enough control to freeze the river without resorting to using the cold fire? The ice inside me crept over my skin, until it felt as though I was carved from marble.

I took a step out onto the frozen water, and then another. I thought of holding my hand up to the prince's, of pushing back against his fire with my own cold power. I'd made some progress in my level of control while at the palace, so I tried to push away any remaining doubts. I *had* to make it across this river.

As I made tentative progress away from the shore, I

remembered a time I saw I an elk fall into a frozen river. The ice had cracked and split open so fast the animal had no chance of escape, and I'd stood at the very edge of the shore with my hand clutched to my chest. Its hooves thrashed uselessly at the chunks of ice that had broken off with it. It was torturous that there was nothing I could do. Eventually, Dedushka had shot it with an arrow just to end its suffering.

My ears strained for any ominous cracking, but there was nothing but the wind and my own footsteps. No one, either, to end my suffering should I be swallowed by the ice.

Still, I persisted, pushing past my own fear. I had to make it to my village and defend it from the armies; had to see Babushka again. I thought of Elation, too, of how I could find her again now—anything to stay calm.

A small sound came from beneath my feet, interrupting my thoughts. I froze in place and anxiously scanned the ice. Nothing—no signs of any cracks. Ever so slowly, I took another cautious step and let out a relieved breath. The ice held. It made me want to dash to the other side, but I knew that would be far more dangerous. If the ice was weak at all, my pounding footsteps would ensure its collapse.

I glanced back at the shore I'd come from, and my shoulders dropped. I'd hardly made any progress at all! I wasn't even halfway.

I crawled along at my snail's pace, the pale sun hidden behind the clouds above. I'd only taken a few more steps when another sound broke the silence, this time a definite cracking. I froze again, but when I looked down, I let out a cry of horror. The ice had splintered beneath me. Barely daring to breathe, I turned to look behind me, but there were jagged lines that way too.

The fear was like a wild animal within me, clawing my stomach and snatching away my breaths. Either way I chose to move, the ice could crack, the freezing-cold black water swallowing me without anyone even knowing what had happened to me.

Who would even care? a cruel voice inside me asked. The prince, but only because of the loss of my power.

I thought again of the elk that had fallen in, and I remembered what Dedushka had said. *If only it hadn't run, it might not have fallen through.*

I just had to fight the urge to run and instead take tiny steps. My heart in my throat, I took a step, and then another. The ice splintered, and I bit my lip to keep from crying out.

Help me! I thought to my powers. *Be useful for once!*

But it did nothing except harden my skin. I was too panicked to help myself. I tried to be calm, to think of how I'd managed to control the cold fire at the palace—if only for a moment. And I thought of before, with the prince, only calling enough ice to repel his flames.

In one movement, I bent and touched my palms to the cracking ice beneath me. I reached deep inside me, where it was coldest, and I thought of every moment I'd ever commanded water to turn to ice. The fear and the doubt tried to stop me, but I pushed it aside.

Freeze, I commanded, and icy cold erupted from my palms, shimmering in the sunlight, and so cold it froze not only the river below but also the air itself. Ice crystals rained down as the river solidified.

And then I ran.

Above me, the beating of wings made me risk a glance at the sky. Elation swooped low, a soft cry of greeting. She'd found me!

I wanted to weep with relief. With her by my side, I had a chance. I ran still faster, until my legs and lungs burned, and I welcomed the sensation, because it meant I was free and alive.

I reached the shore and dry land, but I didn't dare let myself stop. Elation continued to soar above me as I ran toward the cover of the woods. Only once I was surrounded by snow-capped spruce and fir trees, towering over me with their branches full of needles, did I allow myself to glance back at the palace.

There was no movement, no sign that anyone had seen me leave. The river, despite the cracks that had appeared, now looked untouched thanks to the cold inside me covering my tracks. No guardsman had noticed, nor the bogatyr, and I wondered if they'd been called to the prince as Grigory prepared the battalion of men to defend the villages.

Elation flew to a low branch, and I held out my arm to her, already hardening with ice before she landed. She looked at me with her golden eyes, and then bowed her head as I bowed mine.

"I've missed you," I said, tears filling my own eyes. "But I don't have time for a reunion. We must go to the village as fast as we can and pray we get there before the enemy destroys it."

She let out a soft cry before taking off again, and I followed at a run.

Hurry, hurry, went every beat of my heart.

We continued through the day and long into the night, until I was stumbling with exhaustion, until I'd made it far past the woods beyond Kiev where I'd first left Elation behind. She flew to a spruce tree thick with needles, and I found a nice pile of branches at the base of the trunk. With the last of my energy, I cleared some of the snow away and fixed the branches so they formed a rough sort of shelter. My ability to withstand extreme cold ensured I wouldn't need to waste time with a fire, and I was too tired to eat. For now, I curled beneath my little hut of branches and fell instantly to sleep, knowing Elation would keep watch.

Tomorrow, though, I would make my way to the village.

And pray I got there in time.

Elation's soft cry awoke me at dawn. The sky was streaked a pale buttery yellow and pink, and my limbs felt heavy, but I knew Elation was right. I had to keep moving.

As I left the cover of the branches, I pulled out the bag of bread and cheese I'd taken from my room. I nibbled just a small hunk of the bread and two or three bites of cheese—it was better to save it in case I had a greater need later on. I was thirsty, too, my mouth dry from the mad dash to the woods, but I was sure I would come across a stream at some point. If not, I could always melt the snow and drink it if I had to.

With the sun behind me, I turned west. I knew my village was roughly northwest from Kiev, and the closer I got to that area, the more I'd recognize the forest and its surroundings. But with Elation with me, I wasn't afraid of losing my way. I had confidence that she knew how to return, and I had the added security of her superior vision. She would see Grigory and the battalion—if he'd even managed to mobilize them so soon—following long before they arrived.

The sense of urgency stayed with me, nipping at my heels though my endurance was low. I walked and trotted as much as I could, but the snow was thick in places and slowed me down, clutching at my legs.

Before I could stop myself, my thoughts turned to the prince. What would he think when he discovered I'd left? For a moment, a little twinge of fear snuck into my stomach. Would he rescind his pardon of my crime? Worse still was the thought of *why* he'd be angry. Would he be upset because I had left despite finally offering my help, or, more likely, would he be upset because he'd lost his weapon?

I hated this line of thinking—hated that it twisted my insides into knots. Just because he'd been kind to me, I expected him to care for me? The thought was laughable.

Just because he was kind and blindingly handsome, I found myself drawn to him? This last thought made me so angry I squished the bread in the sack I was holding, and then I was furious with myself that I'd done so.

Instead, I tried to make myself think of what I'd say to

Babushka if I managed to reach the village. If the villagers didn't chase me away with pitchforks like some monstrous creature—though I could hardly blame them if they did.

That was *if* the enemy soldiers hadn't arrived there first.

I didn't know if Babushka would speak to me at all. I had hope, though, from her words to me before I'd left in the prince's sleigh. Before I was taken not to my execution as my village had thought, but to a palace where I was treated as a guest. Over and over in my head I practiced what I would say to her if I found her alive: I would tell her how terribly sorry I was, that I was only trying to save Dedushka before everything went out of control. That I missed him, too. That I was infinitely sorry for destroying the life we'd had together.

I was full of regret that even though they'd raised me as their own and saved me from dying alone in the woods as a baby, I'd only thanked their generosity with death and destruction.

I walked and ran until I could go no farther, and even then, I pushed on until the sun was setting. It turned the sky a vibrant orange and pink and purple, and all I could do was sit beneath a spruce and stare in a haze of exhaustion at the sunset's beauty. It reminded me of fire, and fire now reminded me of the prince.

Elation had flown off while I was lost in my own thoughts, but when she returned, she had a hare clutched in her talons.

"That's kind of you, but I don't know if I can eat," I said. My belly churned with fear for Babushka. What if I couldn't save her in time?

But Elation only dropped the hare into my lap and stared at me with a glint in her eyes, like she might start ripping into the meat herself and feeding it to me.

"I suppose you mean to say I'll need my strength."

She had a point. The hare would be more filling than just the bread and cheese I'd brought with me.

After gathering the driest wood I could find, I made a neat little triangular pile and used the flint from the tinderbox to light it. While the fire crackled, I skinned the hare with my knife and put it to roast on a spit I made from a stick.

The meat was unseasoned, of course, but still delicious a couple of hours later. After filling my belly, I created another rough shelter with branches to sleep under, leaving the fire to burn cheerfully nearby.

I closed my eyes and tried to sleep, but my mind kept dragging up images of Babushka. Her izba was tucked into the woods beyond the village. Would the enemy soldiers go that far? A twinge of fear snuck up my back to think of facing the soldiers on my own, but I had only to think of protecting Babushka as I'd failed to do for Dedushka, and a surge of strength flowed through my body.

I would do whatever needed to be done.

After a time, I finally fell into an uneasy sleep, but my dreams were full of fire and ash.

The next day began as the one before it: at dawn. I broke my fast on a small bit of bread and cheese as I continued on my way, supplemented by cold, fresh water from a partially thawed stream that crossed my path.

It was toward midday that I saw it: smoke rising above the tree line in the distance. Despair wrapped my heart in chains. It was my village, I knew.

I had no energy left, but still I ran. I ran like a pack of wolves would tear me apart if I stopped. Thick firs and pines reached for me as I raced by, needles brushing my cheek. This was the forest I was familiar with: the same oak tree where mushrooms always grew, the same rotted tree stump that looked like a monster in the wrong light, and the stream, where just beyond lay the elder's house, and the beginning of the village.

Only, as I ran across the stream and out of the woods, there was no elder's house. What remained was a blackened ruin. I was too late. The knowledge stabbed low, cold and hard as a blade of ice.

The stables and the blacksmith were jagged piles of wood and ash. And the other side of the village, the side I'd destroyed with my own power, but where the villagers had tried to rebuild—the frames of the izby still visible—was nothing but skeletal charred wood.

Where were Grigory and his men? How had I arrived here before them?

As I came closer to individual buildings and izby, I saw the dead. They, too, were burned, the elder recognizable only by the tattered remains of his coat, the men who had survived my own attack dead with their paltry weapons nearby, and perhaps the most ghastly, Yana, a girl my own age, whose skin had peeled away from her flesh from the heat of the fire.

The enemy soldiers hadn't even taken prisoners. They'd burned and destroyed wantonly, leaving only death in their wake.

I picked up my pace, running toward Babushka's izba. I could just see it at the far end of the village, almost hidden among the trees, but it, too, was burned and blackened. By some miracle, though, half of it was still standing. Though in this cold wind, the two walls left and no roof were of little use. Elation flew ahead and landed at the top of one of the walls, making a soft little cry.

Anger at those who would do such a thing to an innocent old woman—to an entire village—burned cold and bright within me.

As I got closer, ice coated my skin and I walked along with my heart in my throat. I both did and did not want to see what was in the izba.

"Babushka," I said quietly, and then louder: "Babushka!"

A noise came then, and I couldn't be sure what it was. A breath, a sigh, a rustle. Whatever the sound was, I ran toward it.

Babushka was there, on the floor by the fireplace. She was alive, but even from the threshold I could see that her breathing was labored, her skin burned away by fire, patches of it blackened, other parts as red as blood. Half of her hair had been burned off, and she'd been wearing her red-and-orange kerchief at the time, so part of it had melded to the skin of her face. It was grievous that she was still alive, and I found I couldn't even rejoice in the last chance to speak to her. She had to have been in agony. A pain beyond what little comfort herbs would be.

Too late, whispered through my mind. Too late to help her; too late to comfort her; *too late*.

I knelt beside her. The eye on the side of her face that had not been burned fixed on me, and I choked back a sob. Elation flew to me, pressing her body against the side of my hip.

"I've come to ask your forgiveness, though I do not deserve it," I said. "I've brought nothing but horror down upon this house and village."

"No," she said in a croak. She smacked dried lips and a parched tongue, and I raced outside with my cup to fill it from the well. I ran back to her side and carefully allowed the water to dribble into her mouth. She took precious few sips and then said, "It's not your fault. I knew of your true power, but I never told you—I thought if we never spoke of it, it would never manifest. But I was wrong. And your dedushka died because of it."

Tears welled in my eyes and fell. "He didn't die. I *killed* him."

She took in a gasping breath. "Your true power was too much for this small village. We knew it, and yet we couldn't bear to part with you. There is nothing to forgive. You are our blood." She held my gaze as best she could with the eye that wasn't burned.

I went still. "But you said . . . you found me abandoned as a baby."

"I lied all those years ago. I *am* your babushka."

"Then . . . you know who my mother is? My father?"

"There," she gasped, her gaze shifting to her herbal medicine cabinet. "Bottom of the drawer is false."

Hesitant to leave her, even for the moment it would take to cross the room, I went and pulled open the drawer. Reaching to the very bottom, I found a little notch in the flat wood that I'd never noticed before. I pulled it up, and below it was a small, brown leather book. I took it out.

"That is the truth of how you came to us."

Her voice was fading, and I ran back to her side, grasping her gnarled hand. "The eagle will lead you." I glanced at Elation. Lead me where?

Babushka gave a great shuddering gasp, and I wrenched my attention away from the eagle at my side.

"Babushka, please," I said, tears thick in my throat. "I don't want to lose you."

"I love you," she said. "I love you both."

And then she breathed her last.

Chapter Eleven

I RELEASED A CHOKING TORRENT OF pain. Tears fell unchecked down my cheeks, clinking to the floor as pieces of ice once they came into contact with the chill of my body. I watched Babushka's face for what seemed like hours, as if she might suddenly open her eyes again. Her skin was warm, but she had the stillness that only came with death: no flush of life, no intake of breath, no twitching of her muscles. Finally I bowed my head as her final words echoed in my mind.

I love you both. Who did she mean? Dedushka? I glanced up at Elation. Not her, surely? Although she'd remained by my side as Babushka slipped away.

The little book in my hands seemed to call to me. I'd seen it before—Babushka wrote down all her herbal findings in it. But when I opened it, I found it was so much more than a record of medicinal herbs. It was a journal.

I didn't want to read what was in that book—didn't want to see the moment I'd taken Dedushka's life and Babushka's reaction to it. I flipped to the beginning instead. Just a few terse lines:

She brought us the baby today. Our granddaughter. Our beloved Alexei's only child.

I repeated the name Alexei to myself over and over. My father, it must have been. And with a jolt, I realized my patronymic name, Alexeyevna, finally made sense. Babushka had always said I'd been given that name—the name that should have come from my father—in memory of the son they had lost. But now I saw the truth. Babushka and Dedushka were truly my grandparents—my father's parents. The knowledge of that shook me, until I could barely hold the book in my hands. It didn't give a name for who "she" was. It didn't even say if it was my mother, but somehow, I knew it was.

I flipped through, noting more terse entries.

A beautiful child.

We love her.

We fear for her.

Her powers have not manifested like her mother's, but we fear they will. Still, we cannot part with her.

The eagle watches over her.

I realized that Kharan had been right: I *had* inherited my powers. It felt as though missing pieces from my childhood were falling into place, and yet there was still so much I didn't know. Other than mentioning my father's name, skimming the pages of the book produced no other names, nor any indication of who my mother was. I'd always believed I'd been found, abandoned in the woods, left for dead. But that wasn't the truth. The truth was I'd been given to my own family to raise me.

I just didn't know why.

When Grigory and his men still hadn't shown, I spent the rest of the day gathering what I could find of the dead—in some cases, only blackened remains—and preparing a funeral pyre in the small cemetery behind the elder's izba. The ground was still far too hard to be able to dig enough graves, so I was forced to burn the bodies.

Grimly, I wondered how many other villages had been attacked. Grigory had told the prince that the Drevlian and Novgorodian armies were in this area, and I felt almost betrayed by God that they had preyed on my village—though I didn't wish this on any other. From the northwest, though, we were the closest village to Kiev—perhaps that was why it had been destroyed. I hadn't arrived in time to save them, so I was left to do what I could for the dead. I couldn't give them a funeral, or last rites, and there were no lamenters to wail and gnash their teeth at the fact that they were gone, but at least their bodies weren't lying scattered across the village.

For Babushka, I found a colorful quilt that had somehow survived the attack, and I wrapped her small frame in it carefully.

Despite her age and her small stature, she'd always seemed larger than life to me. She was energetic and driven, and she took up space in a room just from the force of her presence. But now she was little more than bones, most of her body burned away, and light enough for me to half-carry, half-drag to the graveyard.

Even after working to gather the villagers' remains, it wasn't until the quilt wrapped around Babushka's body caught fire that my throat swelled and I blinked back the sting of tears.

There was so much I regretted. The thought of never seeing Dedushka and Babushka again; of not being able to learn from Babushka about healing herbs or Dedushka about hunting and general woodsman skills, or from either of them about the mystery of my power or the truth of my origins. It hurt because these people had raised me, but it was agony to find out after they had died that they were my real grandparents.

While the funeral pyre burned, I swayed on my feet as much from exhaustion as grief, but as I fell to my knees and covered my face with my hands, the grief consumed me like a wild wolf.

But as it so often does, the grief turned to anger, the black emotion churning like the sea. It crashed over me, and I bent at the waist to absorb its blows. I'd been a fool to think this war wouldn't affect me. That I was somehow removed from it—that the village was safe. If only I had been here . . . I could have . . .

Killed them all? The question hovered in my mind. Would I have killed the enemy soldiers to protect Babushka?

An answer bubbled up inside me, carried on the flow of power that cascaded like a waterfall at my center.

Yes.

Yes, I would have killed the enemy soldiers. I would have fought their flames with my own cold fire. What was more— there was a part of me that wanted to hunt down the soldiers responsible for this and destroy them.

But I knew what I must do: return to the prince. Lend him my aid. Strike at not only the small company of soldiers who had leveled my village, but destroy the whole of the enemy's army.

I wanted to leave immediately, but I knew I'd need my strength. It made me wonder: Where were Grigory and his men? Why had they not yet come? I never thought I'd be so eager to see Grigory, but I was desperate for news of the enemy soldiers—where else had they gone? Surely not on to Kiev?

With half the *izba* destroyed, sleeping in a bed wasn't an option, so I curled up on the hearth with my coat as a blanket. I tried not to look at where Babushka had breathed her last, but the spot with ashes and snow kept drawing my gaze.

I love you, Babushka had said, and another sob wrenched its way from my mouth.

Elation landed beside me, a soft cry escaping her as she help- lessly watched me suffer under the burden of my own thoughts.

I didn't know what allowed her to retain her bond with me, her need to stay by my side, but as I succumbed to my exhaus- tion and grief, I was glad she was there.

At least I wasn't entirely alone.

I awoke on the cold hearth of Babushka's izba, my body stiff from the previous day's hardship. But now that I had said my goodbyes and buried the dead, a desperate need to return to Kiev assailed me. I stood in a rush and staggered with light-headedness. When had I last eaten? Part of me didn't care, but another part warned that I would need my strength.

There was a cupboard to the left of the fireplace where Babushka always kept some bread, nuts, dried berries, and buck-wheat for porridge. I opened it to find a good supply of it still there. Eating the nuts and a chunk of bread as I left, I stopped for a moment to stare back at the izba, years of memories press-ing for attention. Before I left, I let my fingers graze along the beautifully carved windowsill that Dedushka had always been proud of, promising myself that one day, I'd return and remove it from the izba to keep it for myself.

Hurry, hurry, a voice in my head kept repeating. What if the same army that had destroyed my village turned its attention to Kiev? What if that was why Grigory and his men had never arrived? Would the others' powers be enough to keep them at bay?

With everything that had happened here, I hadn't let myself think of the prince, but now that I did, it seemed to be what my mind had been waiting for all along. A flood of images and feelings burst free: fear that the prince had been injured juxtaposed with memories of his smile, his silver eyes. Worse, I realized he'd been right about the enemy all along. Kharan, and Ivan, too—everyone had tried to convince me, but I'd been too blinded to listen, too afraid of my own power. I felt the wintery strength within me rise. And I knew: with every drop of power I had, I would help him defeat these monsters who burned the villages of innocent civilians.

I would unleash my cold fire on them, and I wouldn't allow myself to be crippled by guilt.

Headed southeast now, I hurried as fast as I dared. I wished for a horse, or a sleigh, or anything that could make me move faster. Elation flew above me and then ahead to scout for me, before always circling back again.

I made good progress, though the taste of snow and ash lingered on my tongue, slowing my pace every time it triggered the horrible images of Babushka burned and dying. And thinking of Babushka led to questions of who I really was. Questions that swarmed relentlessly in my mind as I kept up my grueling pace.

Night passed, and early the next morning, I was just taking a drink from a stream when Elation plummeted down from the sky.

She physically pushed me back from the direction I was heading and wouldn't let me go any farther.

I understand, I thought to her, *but I have to see what threat I'm up against.*

I crouched down and moved silently forward, until I could just make out movement and voices through the trees and thick snowcapped underbrush. Were they Grigory and the prince's men?

But as I moved to a place where I could see between the leaves, I saw that there were ten men and women, none of whom I recognized. They were dressed very finely, in rich brocade and fur and shiny boots. Their elegant clothing seemed out of place in the wild of the forest. Beyond them, though, was a small company of soldiers dressed in black, the image of a wolf howling on each chest. They were deep in conversation with the finely dressed men and women, and as I crept closer, I could hear their words.

"Prince Stanislav sent us to assist you in defeating the southern boyar," one of the finely dressed women said. "We are to make the very trees turn against them."

The trees, I thought as a cold dread filled me.

These weren't the prince's men at all.

They were his enemies. Earth elementals.

Chapter Twelve

My heart beat so strongly I could hear it echo in my ears. The soldiers were almost certainly the ones who had burned my village, and worse, they had plans to destroy yet another boyar, where no doubt thousands of people would be called to defend their land. Fear warred with a need for vengeance within me, turning my skin hard as ice.

But as I counted the number of soldiers before me, I wondered how they planned to accomplish such a feat. There were perhaps thirty men altogether, and ten elementals—not nearly enough to fight against the druzhina—the men sworn to protect the boyar. Unless the earth elementals were more powerful than even the prince had imagined.

"We must attack before Prince Alexander calls the city

militia to arms," one of the soldiers said, his beard as thick and black as a bear's pelt.

It was a woman in a long coat trimmed in fox fur who answered him. "The princes are not yet ready to take Kiev. Even with our power, we should not try to take the city without the whole army at our backs. Boyar Petrov stands between us and Kiev—we can defeat his druzhina first. Perhaps Prince Alexander will begin to see reason as another of his boyars falls."

Another man—one of the ten dressed as the woman was—spoke at that. "Why must we attempt to take Kiev at all? It seems foolish considering the bulk of the grand prince's army are there."

The woman shot him a frigid glare. "Kiev is the seat of power for Kievan Rus', which you well know. You are merely trying to sow dissent."

"I don't need to sow it—it's already among our people." He stepped closer to her and lowered his voice until I had to strain to hear him. "Why do this, Vanya? It will only mean more deaths. Who knows what allies the grand prince has. Are you so greedy?"

"Yes," she said simply, "I am." When he shook his head in disgust, she continued. "The prince has no allies—the other princes made sure of that. And he's a child. We will overtake him and Kiev easily, and then all Kievan Rus' will be ours. We will help turn it into the mighty empire it always should have been." Her eyes narrowed. "And if you and the two others who agree with you don't fall in line, then, well, we'll just have to grind your bones to dust right along with the prince of Kiev. So tell me, Vasily, are you still with us?"

If there was anyone among those men and women who agreed with him, they did not step forward. After a moment of silence, he nodded.

I was stunned by what I'd heard. Not only did the elementals plan to attack Kiev, but there was clearly some infighting among them about their decision to join forces with the other princes. Even if this one man had been ignored by the men and women here, surely there were others who thought like him.

I realized I was now doing what Kharan was best at: spying. Privy to conversations these men and women would kill to keep from being brought back to Prince Alexander. Unlike Kharan, however, I could not become one with the shadows. They scanned the forest surrounding them warily, and I knew I should hurry back to the prince while I could. He would want to know where they were and what they had said.

Crouched low, I took a few steps back very slowly. Elation walked beside me, and I knew she was smart enough not to take to the sky and draw attention to us. As I continued my backward movement, the sleeve of my coat brushed across the green needles of a fir tree, sending a light dusting of snow down to the ground.

I froze as I watched the snow fall, a chill racing up the back of my neck. It was no louder than the flap of a butterfly's wings, and yet . . .

I could no longer see the man and the woman who had been

talking—the bushes hid me from view—but it was as though I could sense the heat of their gaze.

I took another small step back. A low rumbling came from beneath the ground, causing Elation to flap her wings nervously. I remembered what Kharan had told me, of earth elementals who could split the ground wide open, and I prepared to run.

Suddenly, in an explosion of snow and frozen ground, a thick vine burst from the earth beneath me. Elation screeched a warning, and I bolted.

The vine, as thick around as my leg, shot forward impossibly fast. It wrapped around my ankle and brought me crashing to the ground.

With a scream, I tried to free myself, but the vine grew still tighter until I feared it would snap the bone of my leg. My body went cold and rigid, and I panicked as the vine dragged me back to the circle of people.

In the sky above, Elation screeched again.

No, I thought to her when she flew lower. I was terrified they would catch her, too. *Find Grigory and his men.*

They couldn't be far.

"I thought the trees had whispered that there was a human hiding behind them," the woman said, her dark eyes and darker smile making my blood freeze. "Are you a spy?"

"No," I said, forcing myself to meet her gaze, even as I thought of the devastation that was left of my village. I fought against the vine, but it only squeezed harder.

She tilted her head. "Spy or not, you've heard too much."

The vine slithered up higher on my body like a snake until my arms were restrained along with the rest of me. The woman lifted her hand, and the sharp tip of one thick vine rose above me. My heart beat fast, but I wasn't afraid. My skin had turned to ice, and cold poured off it like mist. I had that defense, at least.

Before I could blink, she brought the vine down toward my exposed throat, but it was repelled by my frozen skin. Again, she tried, only to fail. Meanwhile, the power within me grew. These were the people who had burned my village and killed Babushka. Cold fire was almost too kind a punishment for them.

The dark-haired man stalked forward with sword drawn, and I knew he meant to try his blade against my frozen skin.

He never had the chance.

I released my power in an explosion of wintery fury. The frozen vine shattered into a thousand pieces. The man and woman closest to me froze instantly, and as the cold continued to pour down on them, they, too, shattered. It spread from them to one of the others who was close by: a man in a black fur hat. And the backdraft it created was so powerful, it blew everyone away from me. The wind buffeted my ears, explosively loud as it destroyed everything in a small radius around me.

"Enemy soldiers approaching!" came a shout from one of the men who was far enough away to escape my cold fire.

I looked up to see Elation leading the way above as the prince and an entire contingent of soldiers, including Ivan, Boris, and

Grigory, rode into the clearing. I breathed a sigh of relief—finally they'd arrived. The earth elementals still living and the other soldiers turned to face this new threat. The prince, astride an enormous blood bay charger, met my gaze from across the snowy field. Even from this distance, I could see the recognition followed rapidly by fear contorting his face. As his men immediately dove into the fray, he urged his horse toward me.

Taking advantage of my distraction, a man with a thick, blond beard and black fur hat raised his hand, and a massive tree sprouted from the ground mere feet from me. Thick roots spread in every direction, and as they made contact with my cold fire, they froze and shattered—but more grew in their place. One avoided the cold fire and grasped hold of me just as the vine had. I screamed and fought as it lifted me into the air.

"Katya!" the prince shouted.

But before he could reach me, the tree's trunk split down the middle, opening wide like a cave, and the massive root that kept me imprisoned threw me inside. With a groan, the gaping hole in the tree closed around me, and I was trapped.

I was encased in darkness, my rapid heartbeat and heavy breathing the only sounds I could hear. Fear threatened to suffocate me, but the burn of anger within my chest kept me from giving in to terror. I loosed my cold fire again, and the tree was not impervious to it. The cold spread, blue flames dancing powerfully, and a terrible cracking and splitting sound echoed around me. The tree was thick, but it would not be able to withstand the cold fire for long.

I kicked at the trunk in front of me until cracks appeared, letting in slivers of light. Again and again I hit with the ball of my foot, until finally the tree was frozen enough to shatter. I burst through the hole I'd made, only to find that the battle had gotten worse for our men.

The earth elementals and enemy soldiers had moved to intercept the prince. Boris, Ivan, and Grigory fought around him—but it took all of them just to keep the earth elementals at bay. Enemy soldiers joined the fight, but Boris wielded his sword in a powerful arc, and two or three men fell at once.

Meanwhile, the earth elemental who had encased me in the tree came toward me again, and before he could summon another tree to delay me, I sent the flames of my cold fire racing across the snowy ground, where they greedily spread over his body. He fell frozen to the ground.

I took a step toward the prince and the others, but I couldn't let the cold fire rage out of control; I was afraid if I moved closer to the battle, I would burn ally and foe alike. I thought of what Ivan had told me, of imagining my power like a horse that needed to be guided. But trying to wrest control of my power was siphoning even more of my strength.

The prince fought powerfully with his sword, easily striking down the enemy soldiers. But then he was targeted by one of the earth elementals, a woman with fiery red hair. She lifted her arms to the sky, and the ground beneath us trembled. In the next instant, an enormous oak tree uprooted itself and was lifted into the sky as easily as a child plucks a dandelion. She held the tree—the trunk of which was as wide as two men standing with arms outstretched—aloft and it was clear that she meant to launch it at the prince.

Fear clutched at me with razor-sharp talons, and I realized with a start I didn't want him to be killed—couldn't bear for yet another person I cared about to die—so I ran. My cold fire leaped ahead of me, burning across the snow, and I knew if I could only reach the elemental before she released that tree, then I would rein in my power. I would do it. I *had* to.

I ran faster than I'd ever run, fleet of foot from years of hiking through snow and forest underbrush, but still, I was not fast enough. The distance was too great, and the elemental was too far away.

She launched the tree at the prince.

In the next instant, though, just as the massive tree began to fall toward the prince, Boris appeared in front of him. With a shout loud enough to be heard clear across the field, he held out his hands. There was a powerful wave of energy from him, and then the tree flew back at the elemental.

I stopped halfway across the field as the tree sailed over our heads. It crashed on top of the elemental with a horrendous *boom*. She was crushed beneath it.

But just as she was defeated, another took her place. This time, enormous vines exploded all around the prince, too numerous for even Boris to defeat with his superior strength.

Vines didn't stand a chance under my cold fire, I knew, so I sprinted even faster toward the prince.

The vines towered above him, twisted and green, barbed and terrible, and swayed like snakes before a strike.

Ivan and Grigory shouted and moved to stand in front of the prince, swords upraised. With his other hand, Grigory brought forth twisted branches of his own, and they attempted to hold the vines down, but still more and more vines burst forth from the ground. The prince and his men cut many of them down, but more sprang up in their place.

Before I could reach them, another elemental called forth hands of stone that burst from the ground and held fast to my ankles. With a cry, I sent flames of my cold fire down toward the stone, but they could not make the rock cold enough to shatter. I would have to kill the elemental. I sent flames racing over the ground toward him, but then the prince was knocked down, his sword flung aside.

I cried out in horror as pain rippled through me, thinking of Ivan, who had been the first to show me kindness and mercy after all I'd been through at the village, who gave me a crimson coat and insisted I wear it, and Boris—Boris, with his friendly manner and his dark past, who loved cooking and grew herbs and had been unfailingly loyal to the prince. The prince's face was a mask of fury as his flames grew exponentially hotter. He was like a blazing inferno, like being cast in the depths of hell, and his sword was a blur as he matched Stanislav blow for blow.

By the time I reached the elemental, my cold fire burned and leaped across any who were still alive, reaching the enemy soldiers who hadn't fallen and any of the prince's soldiers who were still close enough.

Grigory and Ivan and Boris pulled the prince to safety,

calling frantically for the soldiers to escape before my cold fire consumed them all. The horses screamed and plunged along with the men, but all I could think about was vengeance. For my babushka and for the prince. The fire raged uncontrollably, but then I saw Boris lay the prince gently on the ground, blood spilling out around him, staining the snow red.

The wild horse of power that galloped inside me stumbled at the sight, and I took control. I bridled it; pulling it to a halt so fast that the weakness nearly made me fall. I ran to the prince's side, barely noticing that everything around me was frozen: the ground, the trees and bushes, but most of all, men and women—both enemy and ally. They'd shattered when they froze, and their broken bodies lay scattered about in bloodless piles. I closed my eyes to the sight of it. I couldn't think of it now.

Grigory tried to keep me away, but I ignored him and knelt at the prince's side. Fear clawed at my insides: Had the vine punctured something vital? As I examined him, I saw that it had pierced his chest just below his right shoulder. I nearly cried with relief. Too high to hit the lungs and the wrong side for the heart. Still, the pain had to be unbearable. He was conscious, though, his silver eyes meeting mine.

"Are you hurt?" he asked me, and I snorted a laugh.

"How could you ask me that?" I said, my voice, to my embarrassment, wavering like I might shed tears. Inwardly, I thought of how Babushka would react in this situation. Her calm, pragmatic attitude that would immediately force everyone around her to obey her without question. As far as I knew, there was no one else here who could treat the prince for this injury, else he would have stepped forward. There was only me.

I turned to Ivan, who hovered nearby. "Did the vine pierce through his back?" Everything I ever learned from Babushka crowded in my mind. If there was no exit wound, punctures were prone to infection.

"No," Ivan said with a worried grunt. "Do you have knowledge of the healing arts?"

I nodded tersely. "My babushka was a master healer." I pointed to the prince's beautiful black fur coat. "We need to remove this so I can see how extensive the wound is." I turned toward Boris. "I will need you to tear off a good portion of the linen from your tunic."

He nodded and immediately started stripping his clothing off, while Ivan and Grigory assisted the prince with removing his coat. Sweat beaded the prince's brow, and his teeth were tightly clenched, but he never cried out.

Finally, the coat was off, and after asking Boris to use his strength to tear the prince's beautifully embroidered kaftan, too, I was able to see the wound.

It was terrible. Deep and at least the width of two of my fingers, blood poured from it. I'd seen injuries like this one before in my village, but never on someone like the prince. Someone I cared about. And as ice bit into my stomach at the thought of him dying, I knew I couldn't let it happen. I couldn't let him die. I held my hand out for Boris's linen tunic, and he gave it over to me quickly. "Ivan, keep constant pressure on the wound to staunch the bleeding." I turned to Boris again. "Is there any water? I need to clean the wound."

He nodded and raced back to where the other soldiers on horseback kept their distance from me.

"We need to get the prince back to the palace," Grigory said, his tone dripping with more venom than usual, "where a *real* healer can care for him."

I turned to him, ice in my voice and in my gaze. "If we don't get the bleeding under control now, he won't make it to the palace."

"All because of you," Grigory snarled back. "Because you left, and the prince followed."

"Don't blame Katya," the prince said weakly, and I shushed him immediately.

"I left to try to save my village—something *you* should have been doing," I said to Grigory. "But you never arrived."

His eyes narrowed. "Your village was never a priority. The boyars were."

I knew I shouldn't let his comment hurt me, but it still pierced my heart to think that saving Babushka and any of the other villagers wasn't a priority. What hurt more than that, though, was the little question that suddenly rang in my mind: Had the prince been the one to make that decision?

Boris returned with a waterskin before I could demand further explanation, and I was forced to focus on the task at hand. I instructed Boris to support the prince so he was tilted slightly on his injured side. The prince winced and grew even paler. I tried to work as quickly as I could. "Ivan, you can stop applying pressure now," I said, and we all watched nervously as he pulled the linen away. The blood continued to flow, but it was a trickle compared to the gush of before. I poured the water over the wound, until only watered-down blood gushed forth, praying I'd done enough to stave off infection. There was no telling what the vines had brought into his body. They could have even been poisoned.

"I'll need more cloth," I said to Boris, "something I can pad the wound with, and also strips." He immediately ripped more from his tunic. With the last bit of water, I wet the linen and pressed it into the wound, wishing I had access to Babushka's herbs, before covering it with another dry piece of linen. I used the strips to secure it to his body, tying them under his arm and over his shoulder blade. He was more muscular than I'd anticipated, and the cloth strips only just fit.

"We must get Gosudar to the palace," Grigory said.

I glanced up at him. "How far is the journey?"

"A day's ride," Ivan said, his concern pulling his mouth down into his beard. "We didn't bring a sleigh."

"I can ride," the prince said, wincing as he sat up. "Bring me my horse."

Ivan and Boris looked at me, while Grigory hurried to do as the prince asked. "Will it be too much for his injury?" Ivan asked.

"How else will I get back to the palace?" the prince

demanded as he came unsteadily to his feet, waving Boris's attempt to help him away.

He had a point, though I watched him closely for fear he'd be too weak from loss of blood. The snow was saturated where he'd lain, and it was amazing that he could stand much less ride.

The beautiful bay horse was brought to the prince, and Boris helped him mount. The prince gathered the reins in one hand; the other he kept crossed over his heart, and I knew it was because it pained him to let his arm hang down.

"Are you sure you're all right to ride?" I asked, shielding my eyes as I looked up at him against the winter sun.

"Thanks to you."

Ivan came with a horse for me, and I recognized Dukh, the one I'd ridden only a few days ago with Kharan.

It felt like a lifetime.

The others mounted their horses, and then we started back for Kiev. Though we had won the battle, the men were silent, everyone's gaze frequently landing on the prince before darting away again. He stayed mounted, though the farther we got, the more tired he appeared, his tall stature drooping and his head lolling.

I'd done all I could on the battlefield, but the real danger was infection.

I wouldn't let death have him. Not after losing Babushka.

Chapter Thirteen

WE RODE THROUGH THE NIGHT, PUSHING the horses and refusing to stop so we could get the prince back to the palace as soon as possible. Despite reining in my power, I was still fatigued to the point that I fell asleep riding. At one point, I would have slipped off my horse's back had it not been for a well-timed cry of warning from Elation. She had flown with us, taking turns soaring above us and riding on my arm. I wouldn't leave her behind this time, especially after the prince said she wouldn't have to stay in the mews. By the time the moon had risen high above us, we'd returned.

When we rode into the dvor, Elation flew to the very highest tower and surveyed the city as though she were its new master. It brought a small smile to my face, but as the prince rode past and I could see how pale he was, the smile quickly faded. He hadn't complained once about his shoulder on the way back, but the long ride had taken its toll.

Vera, who had come to meet us on the steps of the palace like she had the day I arrived, gasped when she caught sight of him. "Merciful heavens! I *knew* this was a terrible idea. How badly is he injured?"

She bustled over to him as Ivan and Boris helped him off his horse. I dismounted, too, already thinking of the herbs I'd need now that we'd arrived at the palace. Babushka's journal might have more insight, and I patted my coat pocket to be sure it was still there.

The prince was barely able to hold himself up. "I made it here, didn't I?" he said with a grim smile.

But in the next instant, he collapsed to the ground, blood weeping again from his wound. I let out a cry of surprise, my throat tight as I momentarily panicked that he would die here on the cold ground. I waited for anyone else to take control of the situation, to tell the others what must be done to help him, but then I realized they were waiting for me.

"Boris, carry him to his room," I said urgently. "Vera, if I give you a list of herbs I need, can you find them for me?"

She nodded. "Yes, they should be in the greenhouse."

"Then I will need comfrey, yarrow, and white willow."

"I'm familiar with yarrow and white willow, and I can ask the gardener about comfrey."

"I'll need clean linen and water, too," I said, and she put her hand comfortingly on my shoulder.

"I'll get everything you need."

Grigory blocked her path. "Now that we're back at the palace, it's the healer we should call to tend to the prince, not this girl." He dismissed me with a wave of his hand.

"I've been trained by the best healer in the country," I said, "and I know exactly what needs to be done to treat his wound."

"She kept her head on the battlefield," Ivan said, coming to my defense.

"And it'll be a sight better than bloodletting and leeches," Vera added.

"I agree," Ivan said. "Go get the things Katya requested, Vera. He turned to Boris. "Could you carry Gosudar to his room?"

Dismissed and overruled, Grigory watched Boris walk past him with the prince, a frown twisting his face.

Boris made his way up the stairs as quickly as he could, which turned out to be faster than even I could go, and I wasn't burdened with an unconscious prince. He turned right at the top of the stairs, the opposite direction from my own room, and I trailed behind. Soon, the rugs became so thick my boots sank into them, and all the windows were made of stained glass. It was a bit overwhelming when combined with the painted ceiling, the fabric upon the walls, and the numerous torches that had now been joined by candelabras.

Just ahead was a set of double doors, each made of a wood so dark it was nearly black, carved with crowned eagles. I ran ahead to open the door for Boris so he could easily carry the prince in.

Boris strode over a red-and-gold rug and laid the prince

gently atop his enormous bed, drawing back the heavy brocade curtains so we'd have clear view. He didn't stir.

Before I could go to the prince's side, Boris said, "I'll remove his clothing so he's more comfortable."

He began removing his boots first, but I caught myself staring and inwardly shook myself. "I'll wait outside."

I turned back to the doorway, passing a roaring fire in a fireplace big enough for three men to enter side by side. Back in the hallway, I nearly ran into Kharan, who was rushing toward the prince's room.

"Katya," she said, surprise widening her eyes. There was a moment when I was almost afraid she'd be angry that I'd left without saying goodbye, but then she threw her arms around me. "I didn't know you'd returned! I'm so glad to see you," she said breathlessly. She pulled away and took a step back. "What happened to the prince? Ivan said he was wounded?"

I nodded, glancing back at the doors of his room. "We encountered earth elementals and soldiers—the same who destroyed my village and killed—" I choked on the last word, tears pooling in my eyes. I'd been so focused on the prince's wound that I hadn't let myself think of Babushka dying.

Kharan touched my arm. "Was it your babushka?"

I nodded again, tears now running like rivers down my cheeks. I brushed them away impatiently.

"I'm so sorry, Katya. I knew that's where you must have gone when they found you missing. Of course you'd try to defend your village—I only wish you'd waited for the prince's men to help you."

"It would have been too late," I said tightly, remembering Babushka's badly burned face. "I barely had the chance to say goodbye."

She shook her head sadly. "And the soldiers who destroyed your village . . . ?"

Ice crept over me, freezing my tears. "Dead."

"Good," she said with feeling. "Especially if they managed to injure the prince first." She glanced back at his room. "Is it serious?"

"A vine punctured his chest just below his right shoulder. I worry that the vine was tainted."

She sucked in her breath. "Will he live?"

I chewed the inside of my lip while my insides churned. I didn't know the answer to that—was too afraid to imagine the possibility that he wouldn't.

Boris appeared again in the doorway. "Katya? You can see him now."

Kharan followed me into the prince's room. Inside, it was far too warm. The fire in the massive fireplace was gobbling up an enormous pile of wood, but even the smell of burning was not enough to hide the coppery scent of blood that hung thick in the air. On top of it was something else—something I'd smelled before when I helped Babushka with her herbalism and healing. It was the slightly sweet, rotting stench of infection.

I hurried to the prince's side.

His pale form was swallowed by the linens and furs of his bed. I watched his chest for a moment, but his breathing was so shallow the blankets barely moved. I could hear Babushka's voice in my head, *Remove those furs from the bed! Bring cool water.*

The smell of infection was strong. The wound from the vine had festered—despite my efforts to clean it—and I saw that I was correct: the vine had been tainted. Like a poison, it had caused a terrible reaction within the prince's body. He shook violently beneath his pile of blankets, though I knew without even touching him that his skin would burn to the touch. I wrenched all but the thinnest blanket off him. He tried to open his eyes, but they rolled back in his head.

Even where I stood beside him, heat poured off his body—like when he'd summoned the flames.

"He's burning up," Kharan said, her face awash with concern.

I thought of the prince's smile and kind words, and my heart constricted. I knew what came next: convulsions, followed inevitably by death. He had almost reached the point where he was beyond the help of herbal remedies.

Comfrey, yarrow, and white willow, Babushka's voice demanded in my head. They were the only things that could save him now.

I turned to Kharan. "Will you find Vera? Beg her to come with the herbs as fast she can."

Kharan raced away, and I turned back to the prince. I placed my hand on his forehead, and instantly, steam began to rise from my hand.

The prince didn't have time for me to apply herbs—he was minutes away from convulsing. I had to bring the fever down just enough to let herbs take over. There was something else that might help, if I dared. My power was cold enough to shatter people like glass, but if I only touched him for a second, it might cool his body and break the fever.

Or it might shock his system and kill him.

With a trembling hand, I touched his forehead again. It was so hot, especially compared to my frigid skin, that it was like touching a flame. Still, I kept the tips of my fingers there and took a breath. His shaking grew more violent, and I gritted my teeth, willing the convulsions not to start. I thought of all the times I'd touched water and turned it instantly to ice, but I had to temper such power, so I thought of the brisk cold of a river in spring.

Tendrils of steam continued to rise from where my skin touched his, and then it faded away.

The shaking stopped abruptly, and then the prince became so still that I jerked my hand away. *Please let me not have killed him.* I was so close to his face as I searched for any sign of improvement that I could see each individual black eyelash.

His breathing changed from shallow and pained to deep and relaxed, and I let out my own breath in relief. And then his piercing gray eyes met mine.

"Katya," he murmured, "please don't leave again." And before I could even respond, his eyelids fell closed.

I searched his face, tension rippling over me. He was safe from immediate danger, but his wound had still not been treated properly. Without the herbs to treat him, the fever would return as surely as the sun rises.

❖❖❖

At long last, Kharan and Vera had returned with what I needed. We were lucky the herbs we needed grew in the palace greenhouse. While they'd been gone, I'd consulted Babushka's journal, but I found that my instincts for what herbs he'd need were correct. This gave me the confidence to continue to treat him. Perhaps I had learned more than I'd thought in all those years at her side.

Vera had turned as white as bone when she saw how ill the prince was. Kharan had been called away almost immediately by Ivan, who needed to discuss with her what they'd found during the battle, and how narrowly the prince had avoided yet another attack on a boyar.

But now, as I soaked a cloth in yarrow and white willow for his fever, I was at war with myself. I didn't regret leaving the palace and going to Babushka, but Grigory's insidious words were worming their way into my mind. Should I have told the prince I intended to go to my village? If I had, there was no guarantee he would have let me. I tried not to feel responsible for what had happened to him, but it gnawed at me and wouldn't relent. I looked at him lying so still and almost lifeless on the bed, searched his face for any signs of waking, but there was nothing. He'd said my name before and asked me not to leave, but it was hard to say whether he truly recognized me, or would even remember seeing me in his delirium.

"You seem to know your craft far better than the healer the prince employs," Vera said by my side, drawing me out of my thoughts. She carefully draped the herb-soaked cloth across the prince's forehead. "I've told Gosudar many times that the healer does nothing but apply leeches. He'd have been better off sending for an herbalist in the village."

"I don't know nearly as much as my babushka," I said, my breath hitching on her name. The pain pierced my chest, making it difficult to breathe. "I tried to absorb as much as I could when I helped her."

"Well, you know enough to save Gosudar from a terrible fever. I knew he should have remained behind in the palace when they left to intercept the enemy," she said, her expression turning dark with regret. "He grew tired of waiting for Grigory to ready the men. It was only when the prince threatened to go himself that Grigory finally finished his preparations."

I glanced up at that. "Grigory told me that my village wasn't a priority, that he meant to give aid to the boyars only."

Vera smiled. "That might have been *his* plan, but it wasn't the prince's. As soon as he discovered that you'd left the palace— which, admittedly, took far too long—he wanted to go after you."

"He wasn't going after me to bring me back?"

She tilted her head, considering. "He wanted to be there to help you save your village, and he hoped to convince you to come back, but his primary goal was to protect his people . . . and you."

I watched her for a moment to see if she was telling the truth before glancing back down at the prince. "Are you sure he wasn't just afraid his favorite weapon would be killed?"

She looked at me sharply. "Devotchka, I have known the prince since he was just a baby. I think you have misread his intentions toward you."

"Perhaps so." I pulled back the blankets on his bed to expose the puncture wound just below his shoulder. "And do not praise me for saving him just yet," I said with a grim nod toward the wound, which was bright red with infection. "If I can't heal this wound, then the fever will return even worse than before."

"I have faith in you," Vera said with a definitive nod of her head.

I tried not to let her words affect me, but they warmed me much more than they should have. I didn't think anyone had ever trusted me, much less said they had faith in my abilities. But even as I thought that, I remembered one person who had: the prince.

I focused on crushing the herbs for the poultice, wrinkling my nose at the scent of comfrey—it was nearly as bad as the smell of an active infection. The yarrow, with its spicy scent, at least masked some of the odor. But there was nothing that healed as quickly as comfrey. I crushed the leaves of both until the comfrey turned the mixture brown. It would stain everything it came in contact with—including the luxurious linens on the prince's bed—but I was sure he wouldn't mind if it saved him in the meantime.

"That smells like death," Vera said, wrinkling her nose at the crushed herbs.

"Yes, but the wound should look noticeably better in the morning," I said. He should be feeling better, too, hopefully enough that he wouldn't have to remain bedridden.

"Will he need more of these poultices?" she asked, watching me as I worked.

I nodded. "He'll need a fresh poultice of these herbs every day, maybe even twice a day if it isn't so painful for him. Crushed garlic and honey will help his body fight off the infection, too."

"I can get those from the kitchen for you. And the herb that smells so terrible—that one is called . . . ?"

"Comfrey," I supplied. "And this one is yarrow."

I slathered the pungent mixture of herbs onto clean linen and then brought it to the prince's bedside. I gently pressed the herbs into his wound with the linen. "Could you bring me another strip of linen, please?"

Vera came with the linen, watching everything I did carefully.

After threading it underneath his arm—with Vera helping me lift him up just slightly—I tied a knot with the other piece of linen to secure the poultice.

"White willow bark will help with the pain, too, when he wakes," I said. "It can be steeped to make a tea."

"Should I go prepare that now? In case he awakes?"

"Yes," I said, suddenly feeling exhausted now that the danger had passed.

"You should take yourself to the banya, and then rest, devotchka," she said, her kind eyes softening as she reached out and touched my shoulder. "I will leave supper for you in your room."

"Thank you, Vera," I said with a relieved smile.

As soon as she left, I placed my hand on the prince's forehead again. He was still very warm to the touch, but no longer burning, even to my cold skin. I looked down at him, and for a moment, I couldn't move. Now that he wasn't in danger of dying, all I could think of was how his face seemed sculptured from marble. His chest and arms, too, were more muscular than I'd thought. He looked strong and capable now that he wasn't shaking and delirious from fever.

"I'm glad you didn't die," I whispered, and was surprised at how powerfully I meant it.

Chapter Fourteen

After a quick visit to the banya—I would have stayed longer just to luxuriate in the hot steam, but I was too wary of encountering the bannik again—I retreated to my room, so tired I could barely lift one foot in front of the other.

So when a vine wrapped around my foot and dragged me into a darkened room, I could do no more than scream until I was silenced by leaves.

Grigory stood before me, his face contorted with rage.

The leaves still kept me from crying out, from demanding to know what I was doing here.

"When you left, I thought the Holy Saints had finally taken pity on me and brought my prayers before God. But then the prince said he couldn't let you face the Drevlians and Novgorodians alone; I begged him not to go, and I prayed that they would kill you." My eyes widened, and I struggled even harder against the vines, letting my skin grow colder and colder. I knew I'd be able to free myself, but I didn't want to destroy the whole palace with my cold fire.

"Because of *you*," Grigory said, his voice more like a growl, "the prince believes he has a chance against the earth elementals. I had advised him to surrender before all of Kiev is taken by force, and he was nearly convinced . . . until we heard tell of *you*." This last word was spat in my face, and suddenly, Grigory's animosity toward me from the very beginning made sense. He wanted the prince to surrender, but I had given the prince— given all the others—hope.

But it was *why* he'd want the prince to surrender that made the cold burn even brighter across my skin. "Why would you expect the prince to do such a thing? To give up his throne?"

"I believed the prince was powerful once—a force that could unite all of Kievan Rus'—but I now know I am mistaken. I kept him safe when they came for his parents, gambling on the fact that one day, his elemental fire ability would strengthen, but it never did. He isn't strong enough to hold out against the Drevlian and Novgorodian princes and the earth elementals. The weak have no hope of ruling."

"You're on their side," I said with a dawning horror.

He leaned closer to me. "I will always choose the winning side." He took a step closer to me. "Prince Alexander wrongly believes you to be his savior, but even if you are powerful enough to defeat the earth elementals, the prince will never be able to rule this country. If I kill you, though," he said, a mad glitter in his eyes, "then the prince will have no choice but to surrender."

The vines began tightening around me, but I'd had enough. The cold inside built in power, until I could no longer hold back. It blasted free from my palms, icy cold air that streamed around him like a snake made from snow crystals. It was beautiful, pure white and shimmery, but deadly as fire. The force of its power blew him back, and he crashed to the floor.

This power wasn't on the same level as the cold fire, though, and it took only a moment to realize why: I was exhausted. Panting with exertion from the battle, from the long journey home, from healing the prince. Still, I couldn't let this pathetic creature attempt to intimidate me anymore.

The cold settled over me like a snowy mantle, and I stalked toward him where he lay stunned on the floor.

I grabbed a knife from his belt.

I held it to his throat. "Did you really think you could kill me?"

He held up both his hands in surrender, but I shook my head.

"You are a traitor to the prince, and once he knows of it, it is *you* who will surely be killed." I didn't know this for sure, could hardly think straight with my mind fuzzy from exhaustion, but still, the threat was taken seriously, for his eyes grew as wide as the moon. "Here is what you must do: leave. Leave this palace and the city, and only then can you be sure you will not be tried as the traitor you are."

I pressed the tip of the blade against his throat to make sure he understood and tried to hide the fact that I was nearly swaying on my feet.

And then, from out in the hallway, Ivan called my name. I could have cried with relief. "In here," I called back.

To his credit, and to Grigory's detriment, when Ivan came in and took in the scene, he did not immediately pin me as the aggressor. "What has happened?" he asked instead, warily.

"Grigory wanted to kill me in the hopes that he could finally convince the prince to surrender to his enemies."

Ivan's gaze narrowed. "I thought you had given up that faulty line of thinking, Grigory."

"I told him he could leave the palace and never return, and then perhaps he wouldn't be tried and executed for treason."

Ivan was silent for a moment. "The better course of action is to restrain him in the dungeon until the prince can be made aware of what has transpired." His eyes narrowed. "Especially of his attack on you."

"Then"—and finally I did sway on my feet—"then perhaps you could make sure he is taken to the dungeon?"

Ivan nodded once. "Yes, of course."

He yanked Grigory to his feet.

I watched for a moment as he dragged him away, and I nearly collapsed with relief. Ivan would easily be able to restrain Grigory, for he could always negate his power should Grigory try to use it on him.

I didn't even remember making my way to my room

afterward, but I must have, for soon enough I was there. Too tired to eat the food that had been put out by Vera on a tray, I fell onto my bed, unable to even cover myself with the furs.

But as I succumbed to sleep, thoughts of what Grigory had said plagued me.

He had more than implied that he'd known there was going to be an attempt on the former prince's and princess's lives, but had chosen to save Prince Alexander. He'd only supported the prince because he believed him to be more powerful, and now I couldn't help but wonder how deep his treachery went. How long had Grigory been allied with the enemy?

And worse still: Had he been the one to arrange the assassination of the prince's parents?

The next day, I slept far later than I ever had, until it was well into the afternoon. I awoke slowly, the sleep not letting me go easily. A woman stood beside my bed, wearing a red-and-orange headscarf, and for a moment, I thought it was Babushka. But then I remembered.

"I'm sorry to wake you, Katya," Vera said, "but the prince is asking for you."

I sat up in a rush. "When did he wake?"

"Not long before you. Ivan has already been in to tell him of what happened last night. But he wishes to hear it from you, too."

The memories of what had happened with Grigory slowly trickled into my mind. I could only hope he was locked away in the dungeon, unable to do any more damage to the prince.

I hurried out of bed, dressing in my own clothing, which was once again perfectly clean. "Thank you for cleaning this for me, Vera," I said, and she smiled. "I should have been awake hours ago. The prince's bandages will need to be changed."

Vera put one hand on her hip. "What both of you needed was to sleep. There is no greater way to heal."

I did feel stronger now that I'd had rest, but still, I could hear Babushka's scolding in my mind: *You overslept and neglected your patient.*

"By all the saints!" Vera exclaimed, her gaze on the uneaten tray on the other side of my bed. "Have you not eaten?"

I shook my head. "I was more tired than hungry last night."

"Eat now, then," she said, handing me a hunk of bread with a determined look on her face. "The prince can wait another moment or two."

I didn't want to—I was too anxious to check on the prince's wound—but then my stomach took control of my hand and made me reach for the bread before I could protest. Vera watched me until I ate every bite, and then she pushed a cup of water in my hand, too. When she was satisfied I'd at least broken my fast, she led me to the prince's room.

I walked through, my heart in my throat. I'd been in his room before, of course, but it was different knowing he was awake and fully able to communicate. I tried to think of Babushka and how she would handle the situation; how she would bustle in and be completely focused on the prince's healing.

But then, Babushka wouldn't be in any way attracted to the prince.

The room smelled of the herbal poultice when I walked through the doorway, and I was both surprised and pleased to see the prince had recovered enough to be sitting in a high-backed wooden chair, the carved arms so smooth from age the wood shone in the light of the fire.

"Katya," he said, coming to his feet when he saw me enter, and I hurried to his side.

"Don't make any sudden movements or you could reinjure yourself," I chastised. "I shouldn't have left your bandages unchanged for this long. Forgive me, Gosudar."

"There's nothing to forgive." He took a step closer to me, his gaze holding mine. "And please, do not call me by such formalities. Call me Sasha—the nickname my mother gave me," he said when I looked at him questioningly. He gestured to another chair before the fireplace. "Sit, please."

When I had done so, he continued. "Katya, you must know I'm completely in your debt. Not only for saving my life from this injury, but after one of my own men tried to kill you." His expression darkened, his jaw tightening. "Ivan told me he came upon Grigory after he had attacked you here in the palace, and that you had accused him of treason."

I nodded once. "He was angry that I gave you hope in defeating your enemies. He wants you to surrender to the Drevlians and Novgorodians."

The prince—*Sasha,* I corrected myself—nodded grimly. "Grigory has counseled surrender many times of late—I just hadn't realized how far he would go to have that scenario come about." A muscle in his jaw flexed. "I take the threat to your life very seriously, and he's lucky no harm came to you. I have ordered him kept in the dungeon Ivan secured him in until he can be questioned and dealt with."

I gazed into the fire, remembering my last thought before I'd fallen asleep. "Do you think it's possible he had anything to do with the death of your parents?"

The prince looked taken aback. "You suspect his treachery runs that deep?"

"I don't know. I only know he implied that he had known the assassination would occur, and that he'd only protected you because he thought you would be able to fully harness your elemental fire."

"And now he imagines me to be weak," the prince said pensively. "You've given me much to think about. My parents were killed in their beds at night, and we've always thought whoever hired the assassin would be one who was familiar with the palace's layout. The other princes—they have been to this palace many times, have stayed here, feasted here, even been baptized here. It wouldn't have been a stretch to think either of them could have provided the right information to the assassin."

A little sliver of cold anger stabbed inside me to think that either way, the deaths of the former grand prince and princess had been orchestrated by someone who had known them well. "Did you ever suspect anyone else?"

"I'd like to think we had," he said with a shake of his head, "but I don't think that's true. I fear the truth is worse than I'd imagined—that perhaps Grigory had been conspiring with the enemy."

"I'm sorry, Gosud—Sasha," I corrected myself when he gave me a look. "It seems the Drevlians and Novogordians are a greater threat, too, than I'd been willing to admit."

"We didn't expect the earth elementals to be so close to Kiev. I suspect if you hadn't been there, we might not have all escaped with our lives."

His mention of the earth elementals made me realize I'd never told him what I'd overheard. With his injury consuming my thoughts instead, I'd completely forgotten.

"You have reminded me that I overheard them talking—the earth elementals," I added when he gave me a questioning look. "They spoke of their plan to attack Kiev, but they wanted to wait until they had more forces. In the meantime, they wanted to intimidate you by continuing to terrorize your boyars and their druzhinas."

The muscle of his jaw tightened. "I don't take the deaths of my people lightly."

I thought of my own village, laid to waste. "I know you do not. Though from what I heard, not all the earth elementals are in agreement with the plan to overthrow you and kill so many innocents."

"What do you mean?"

"There was one man who stepped forward and argued against attacking Kiev—argued against the entire plan to overthrow you, actually. He wondered what the gain would be for the earth elementals and why they should align themselves with princes who have killed so many. But a woman who seemed like she was their leader threatened him—and anyone else who agreed—into silence."

Sasha was quiet for a moment. "This is an interesting thing you overheard. I had wondered if all the earth elementals were blindly following the princes. It seems they, too, are hesitant for war."

"Maybe so," I said, "but the leader also made it seem like there were few who would agree with the man's dissent."

Sasha nodded slowly in understanding. "And those who do agree with him will be threatened or killed."

"Yes," I said, thinking of the woman's words and the man's cowed reaction to them.

"Thank you for telling me," he said, and his gaze held mine. "Though it pains me that you were so brutally attacked after overhearing."

I gave him a small smile. "An attack I not only survived, but returned tenfold."

He laughed lightly. "This is true. Ice like fire," he said, his gaze drawing me in more.

"I'm sorry you were injured though. Your wound," I said, standing, "may I take a look at it?"

He nodded. "It hasn't been as painful since you applied the poultice."

When he began to shed his clothing, I bit my lip and studied the flames of the fire. Still, I could see him from the corner of my eye. He undid his belt and let it drop to the floor before carefully removing the tunic with a wince. This, too, fell to the floor. When his chest was bare but for the bandage, he sat down. He glanced up at me. "Or should I lie down on the bed?"

"No," I said a little forcefully. "No, the chair is fine."

Despite his having slept through the night, the linen still looked clean but for a circle of blood from the wound. Just thinking of the warning signs I needed to look for when I examined him helped to bring a sense of calm over me. This was familiar ground to me, and therefore, stable.

"It may hurt a bit when I pull this away," I said, pointing to the linen covering his wound, "but I need to be sure there are no longer any signs of infection."

"I'll try to be the model patient," he said with a smile that was more of a grimace.

As gently as I could, I peeled back the linen from his wound, but parts of it had adhered a bit to his skin where his body had started to heal. He sucked in his breath with a hiss, and I glanced at him. "I'm sorry to cause you pain."

When I saw the wound beneath the skin, I was relieved to see no red streaking, pus, or any other signs of infection. The area was still red and raw, but certainly healing. "You'll need to continue eating garlic to stave off infection, but it's much better." I looked over at the small table where I'd first prepared his poultice and was pleased to find it still had the necessary herbs.

"I'll prepare another poultice," I said, moving toward the table of herbs and water.

"It's healing quickly, thanks to you," he said. "Perhaps you will consider staying on as my healer."

It surprised me how much such a thing appealed to me. To be a healer like Babushka had been in the village, to do something everyone would recognize as a valuable role. Being a healer for the prince was infinitely better than being a weapon. Still, I would keep my true thoughts to myself. I turned and smiled at him. "Perhaps."

"Why did you leave, Katya? I would have let you go to your village if you'd asked," the prince said, watching me. "Have I made it seem like I would forbid you anything? Because I assure you, that's not the case."

"So I would have needed your permission?" I asked, quietly but firmly.

He let out a frustrated breath. "No, but when I first discovered you had gone . . . and Grigory had not yet roused the militia . . . I will admit that I was afraid for you."

"Because you didn't want to lose the chance to use my power against your enemy?" I hadn't intended to say it; I immediately regretted it, for his expression could only be described as thunderstruck.

He didn't answer at first, only reached out and touched my arm, so that the warmth from his body mingled with the cold from mine. "I was afraid because I care about you. Despite everything you've been through, you've never been anything but courageous and resilient. But even knowing that, I wasn't sure why you'd leave. Especially after your village treated you the way they did."

"I overheard you and Grigory talking about the threat to nearby villages. It wasn't the other villagers I wanted to save—it was my babushka. I couldn't bear to be here, safe, while she was in danger." I could feel his intense gaze on me, and I ground the herbs still harder in the pestle.

"I am sorry, Katya. I'm sorry for your loss and the destruction of your village."

"My babushka was still alive when I made it there—barely. Long enough for me to make amends," I said quietly. Long enough to discover some of the truths of my origins.

The sound of the pestle grinding was the only sound in the room for a moment.

I brought the poultice and the fresh linens to his side, and he looked up at me. "Amends for what?"

Carefully, I spread the aromatic poultice into his wound. "Because I betrayed her kindness with death."

When I placed the clean linen over his chest and bound it, he touched my hand with his. "It wasn't your fault."

I shook my head sadly. "It was my fault. Just because it wasn't my intention doesn't leave me blameless in their deaths. In *his* death."

"Will you tell me what happened?"

I made a noise that was like a creature in pain and took a step back. "You already know."

"I know what your village elder told me."

"I'm sure he told you the truth," I said, already turning away.

"Please," he said, stopping me. "I would hear it from you."

I didn't want to relive that terrible night, but it was his calm silence that encouraged me to speak. It wasn't until I was in the midst of telling him that I realized how much I needed this, how much it had been eating me from within like a poison. The prince listened quietly, even as my voice faltered, even as I told him I'd killed Dedushka.

"I'm sorry for what happened to your dedushka," he said as I swallowed tears. "I'm sorry you were pushed to that point."

"But you see, it was my fault. And now I have lost them both."

For a moment, there was only the soft crackling of the fire before us. I thought he would finally see what a monster I was, how the villagers were right all along, but then he said, "I think you were trying to protect someone you loved, but you didn't know how. I know what it feels like to lose the people who raised you—it's a pain I wouldn't wish on anyone, especially you."

I met his gaze, somehow only just realizing how much we had experienced similar things . . . despite my being common born and he the grand prince of Kievan Rus'.

"There is something I would ask you," he said, holding out his hand for me to sit in the chair across from his again. "A request."

I nodded as I took my seat.

"Given what you overheard just before the battle, that they will soon have enough forces to march on Kiev, I have no choice but to seek out alliances from Constantinople—the city my mother was princess of before she married my father. It's time I set things straight with my mother's family—that they know the people of Kievan Rus' are not to blame for my parents' deaths. That *I* am not to blame. If I had their army—even a small part of their army—I could easily defend Kiev and go on the offensive on behalf of the nearby boyars, too." He leaned toward me. "But I must do this quickly. I plan to journey south in only a few days. Will you accompany me?"

My gaze jumped to his. "Travel . . . all the way to the Byzantine Empire?"

He nodded. "Kharan will come along, too, as well as Ivan and Boris and other members of my bogatyri. And you will have your tent."

The last made me smile in spite of my fear of leaving my homeland for the biggest city in the world. "Forgive me, but what good would it be for me to come along?"

"Because I think you can help me—there's so much more I think my mother never told me about the fire ability I have, and I think Constantinople holds the answers. There is also someone we will meet on this journey who can give you greater advice on how to control your power—how to bend it to *your* will." His gaze caught and held mine as he turned toward me. "But the selfish truth is, I just want you to come with me."

This silenced me like nothing else could. Part of me was

afraid of his words, afraid he didn't mean them, and even more afraid he did. I hadn't dared hope that I could form a friendship with the prince, but now . . . now I didn't know what to think. And the journey itself—so far from Kievan Rus'—that was farther than I'd ever traveled in my life. But I thought of my village and Babushka. Of the powerful earth elementals, and I knew:

I would no longer sit back and do nothing.

"I will go with you," I said. "Someone needs to look after your wound."

He laughed. "Whatever you must tell yourself, so long as you come. Now, I've kept you from supper, I'm sure."

I checked his bandage one more time. "Be sure to eat and rest, especially if we are to go on this long journey so soon."

"I don't know about resting, but I can certainly eat," he said. "Be sure to seek out Vera and do the same."

I dipped my head. "Good night."

"Katya," he said, and I stopped, "I'm glad you're coming with me."

"Thank you, Sasha," I said, willing my skin not to ice over with embarrassment. "I think I'm glad I'm coming with you, too."

I felt his gaze on me as I left, and a little tendril of warmth stirred inside me, chasing away the cold.

CHAPTER FIFTEEN

IT DIDN'T SEEM TO TAKE SASHA long to recover fully. Only a few days later, as the morning dawned overcast and winter gray, we received word that everything was ready for our journey, as the prince's men had used the time he spent recuperating to prepare. There were two sleighs carrying supplies—food, weapons, trunks of clothing, and the tents. One sleigh remained empty, and I wondered if it would be for Sasha while the rest of us rode horses.

The horses called to one another in the dvor and stamped their feet, ready to be off, as I slowly made my way toward the chaos in my newly cleaned rubhaka and red skirt. I'd found a coat as white as snow to wear on top, made of wool and silver fox fur. Vera had helped me pack a trunk, and in it she'd piled the beautiful clothing the prince had given me; I didn't dare argue with her, for she seemed determined.

On my arm was Elation, who'd spent the past two days sleeping in my room at night and hunting in the nearby woods by day. I wasn't sure she'd travel all the way to Constantinople with us, but I didn't want to leave her behind, especially now that she was the only connection I had left to my past.

"Katya," a voice called, and I turned to find Kharan moving toward me. She was leading Daichin, and he looked more alert than I'd seen him before, with head held high and ears pricked forward.

I hadn't seen her since she returned from her latest mission— to find just how close the Drevlians and Novgorodians were to marching on Kiev. Not close enough that the journey had to be aborted, but still, there was an anxiety in the air. The city militia, too, had been called to arms, and there were soldiers everywhere. They were heavily concentrated around the palace; I was sure we would find them at every gate. Even in the distance, I could see archers patrolling the wall.

"I was relieved you agreed to come with us," she said, taking hold of my arms and touching both of my cheeks with hers in greeting. "The prince had mentioned that he would ask you, and I was afraid you'd say no and leave me alone with these bearish oafs."

I smiled, and she smiled back, and for a moment, we were just two friends about to embark on an adventure . . . until I remembered all that it entailed. "I'm sure I'll be glad I've agreed to come, too—I know we will see things I've never even dreamed of before, but I'm also intimidated by traveling so far."

She gazed out into the distance, as though she could already see the marble city. "It will all be worth it once we reach Constantinople."

I thought of traveling far beyond the boundaries of Kievan Rus', of entering an empire I couldn't even imagine. "This journey will test us all, I think."

All around us, men started to go to their horses to prepare to leave. I looked for the prince and for Ivan and Boris, but I didn't see them yet. I stepped closer to Kharan and lowered my voice. "The Byzantines, they are kin to the prince?" She nodded. "Then why did they not believe the prince when he said his parents were assassinated?"

"They believe they were assassinated; they just don't know who is to blame. The Drevlian prince and the Novgorodian prince were once part of Kiev. It is only in the past two years that they have established their princedoms—with the help of the Varangians—the Northmen," she added when I looked confused. "The Byzantines blame all of Kievan Rus' because they don't know who was responsible, and even the prince is under suspicion for the death of his mother, the Byzantine princess."

"How could they think that? It's horrible."

"They were killed in their beds," Kharan said, her voice a mere whisper now. "With the palace well guarded, it had to have been someone close to them."

Ivan and Boris entered the dvor then, followed by the prince, and Kharan said no more about it. I watched Sasha talking to his bogatyri, a smile on his young face, surveying with approval all that had been prepared. Now that I knew him better, it was hard to believe I had ever thought him capable of all the terrible things I'd been told. But as fierce as his reputation was, I could also understand how such rumors would influence the Byzantines.

"Katya," Sasha called, interrupting my thoughts. "Come. This is for you."

I walked over to where he stood by the sleigh, his hand on the reins of a beautiful white horse. He gestured toward the sleigh beside him, and suddenly I realized he meant for me to ride in it—while everyone else rode horses. "Oh no, I couldn't. This is a sleigh for the prince, not the likes of me."

He laughed. "Well, this prince refuses to ride in a sleigh, so it's for you."

I shook my head again. I wouldn't do that—like some highborn lady. "Forgive me, Gosudar," I said, unwilling yet to call him by his nickname in public, "but I won't sit in a sleigh while everyone else rides."

Ivan leaned against the sled near me. "Have you ever ridden long distance on a horse? You'll be so sore you won't be able to walk."

I shook my head obstinately. "I would still rather ride."

"Very well, you win," the prince said, his tone wry. "Get her a horse," he said to the nearest man. "One of the desert-bred mares."

"Yes, Gosudar," the man said, hurrying off toward the stables.

The prince returned his attention to me. "But don't complain to me if you're as sore as Ivan promises you will be."

"I won't complain," I said, thankful just to be riding like everyone else.

Everyone else mounted their horses while I waited for the servant to return, the prince's mount standing out among the rest as elegant and beautiful, with a long flowing mane and tail. When the servant finally returned, it was with a mare of pure white, nearly as regal as the stallion the prince rode. As I looked closer, I realized it was the same horse I'd admired in the stables all those days ago.

"That is Zonsara," the prince said. "She is from the deserts of Arabia, and she is the dam to the horse I ride now."

I reached up to pet her silken neck. "She's beautiful," I said, and a quiet laugh escaped me when she turned and snuffled my hair.

"They are bred for endurance, so they will take us far."

He nodded toward the servant then, who offered me a leg up. Elation took to the sky, and I mounted the well-behaved mare. I had some difficulty arranging my rubhaka and skirt until it was comfortable, so I was glad I wore soft deerskin leggings beneath.

"Onward," the prince called, and his horse let out a squealed neigh as he wheeled it around.

I could feel my own horse eager to be off, her muscles taut with anticipation, but she waited for my command. I squeezed my legs lightly as Kharan had taught me, and my horse followed the others at a trot.

The empty sleigh came last. I turned to look at it, remembering when I'd arrived as a captive. Now I was willingly accompanying the prince to a foreign land.

But as we trotted through the palace gates and beyond, I thought of what Kharan had said: that the Byzantines couldn't trust the prince.

If they no longer allied themselves with him, then what would happen when we entered their city?

It seemed the entire city of Kiev had come to see us off. Everyone from waifs on the street to merchants dressed in fine furs to nobles riding on horseback. They waved and cheered as though we were on a great crusade. Perhaps we were. It felt so different from when I'd first arrived in Kiev that the juxtaposition was as surreal as a dream.

Before long, we passed through the gates, the horses sludging heavily through the snow. Kharan and I rode side by side, her smaller horse keeping pace with my long-legged mare.

The prince had brought two of his falcons; they rode silently with their blindfolds on, tied securely in the sleigh carrying supplies. It made me sad to see them bound and flightless, as beautiful as they were.

Elation flew in slow, lazy circles to keep pace with the horses. I watched her for so long that my neck became stiff, until I was satisfied that she was staying with us.

When I returned my attention to where we were going, I

realized it was through the thick forest that bordered Kiev to the south. Enormous pine trees towered over us, their branches blocking out much of the sun. It was much colder in the shade, the snow thicker and more difficult to plod through.

Kharan's pony had fallen behind, but now she urged it on until he was level again with Zonsara. "You would've fit in well with my clan," she said, her eyes on Elation. "We hunted with eagles."

I turned to her in surprise. "You hunted with eagles? How did you train them?"

"I never had one of my own, but my cousin let me fly his. They trained them the same way you would any other animal—with food."

"I can't even imagine falconry with an eagle," I said, thinking of how enormous Elation was. The hares she so often brought me were small prey; eagles could easily hunt and kill a deer. "You must miss your clan."

Her smile turned nostalgic. "Sometimes. But then I only have to remember why I left. I have no talent with any of the things that makes my clan who they are: I can't hunt. I was terrible with the reindeer. I can't sew or cook or tan hides. And normally, a member like that would have been given *something* to do, but I did have one talent—one that no one else had. I could shadow meld, and as soon as my grandfather discovered that, he urged me to follow my fate and not to waste such an ability in the wild steppes where it was next to useless."

"I can't imagine such an ability being seen as useless—by anyone."

She laughed. "It's useless to anyone who has no need for spying and subterfuge. What good is it to reindeer herders?"

"That's true enough," I said with a smile. As the sound of the horses' hooves on snow lulled me, I thought of my own uselessness at the village. I'd been able to help Babushka with herbalism and healing, but she was far more talented than I. I'd gathered herbs for her, but Dedushka was better at finding them when he went hunting. All I'd managed to do was bring death and destruction to a peaceful village.

I glanced at Kharan, her face partially in shadow from the trees. "Do you regret leaving your clan?"

"Never," she said. "Do you?"

My answer leaped to the tip of my tongue, and I was surprised by what it was.

"Not yet," I said.

Maybe not ever.

We rode and rode until my legs shook as violently as leaves in a summer storm. When the prince finally called for us to stop, I feared I wouldn't be able to dismount on my own. I watched as the others practically leaped off their horses and fell upon the tents, pitching them at an alarming rate.

The prince himself helped, but when he saw me still mounted, he came to my side. "We rode hard today," he said, squinting up at me past the dying sun. "Did Zonsara carry you well?"

I forgot my shaking limbs for a moment and leaned forward to pet her silky neck. "Yes, very well. She was as smooth a ride as I could hope for."

He smiled and moved closer to me, so close his coat brushed against my leg. "And yet, you are stuck up there on her back." Embarrassment stole over me, but before I could say anything, he held up his hand. "Come, let me help you. Ivan needn't know he was right."

Relieved, I started to let myself tumble down, but then I stopped myself. "You're sure it won't hurt your shoulder?"

He answered by pulling me down off the horse. I bumped into his chest as my knees threatened to buckle, but his arms kept me from falling.

"I'm sorry," I said. "I didn't think my legs would fail me quite so spectacularly."

He shook his head. "Riding has a way of doing that to a person, especially if you aren't used to traveling far."

Hesitantly, I touched his arm as I straightened to meet his gaze. I'd looked into his eyes many times before, but there was something about *this* moment that made my heart beat a little faster. There was something there, something I hadn't noticed before, and it made everything around us disappear. Perhaps it was because we were embarking on this epic journey together, or maybe it was because whenever I was with him, I felt warm. Even through his wool coat I could feel heat, as though I stood close to an open flame rather than a man.

He seemed on the verge of speaking, of either breaking

the spell or drawing me further into it, and I couldn't bear it either way.

"Are you sure you don't have a fever again?" I said. "You feel so hot."

"I think that's just because you feel so cold. Why don't you come sit by the fire to warm up? The journey has been long and tiring."

I allowed him to lead me to the fire, where someone had helpfully rolled some fallen logs so that we might have a place to sit. I sat down, and as I did, I saw our men start to pitch the blue-and-gold celestial tent that had been mine when I first traveled to Kiev.

I nodded in the tent's direction. "Shouldn't that one be yours? It's a tent fit for a prince."

He smiled as he poked the flames with a stick. "It is indeed a beautiful tent. How kind of you to offer it to me, too." He turned to look at the progress being made on raising it. "I wonder, though, where you would sleep? I'm sure I could make room for you if that's what you're offering."

I straightened my spine. "Of course not."

He laughed, and the sound made my skin harden into ice.

"Forgive me, Katya, I was only teasing you. I know you are not a maiden such as that, but I must admit," he said as he leaned closer, "if you really had offered such a thing, I wouldn't have said no."

As I was unused to apologies, it took a moment for his words to register. "You're right," I said slowly, "I am not a maiden who would do something like that."

That was what I said, but how I actually felt was something else entirely. It was Kharan who saved me from any further discussion on the subject when she sat down heavily on the log next to me.

"I never thought I'd see the day when you were tired," the prince said to Kharan, and she snorted.

"Yes, well, I wouldn't be if you hadn't given Katya the long-legged mare to ride. Daichin insisted on keeping up with her, and I spent most of my time fighting him to stay at a reasonable pace. It didn't work, and now we're both exhausted." She gave the pony in question the evil eye, which he seemed to ignore.

"Katya may let you stay with her in the celestial tent should you wish for furnishings that are a little less . . . rustic . . . than the ones you usually enjoy," he said with a pointed look at her leather tent, still rolled neatly in a pile at her feet.

"My *furnishings* are perfectly comfortable, thank you," she said. "And in any case, Katya never agreed on such an arrangement."

"Oh, I wouldn't mind," I said, but the prince interrupted.

"She offered up her tent to me just moments ago," he said, and I sucked in a breath, "but was horrified when I nearly accepted, so I thought she'd prefer your company instead."

Kharan looked between the two of us for a moment before letting out a laugh. "You don't think it's foolish to tease someone with such volatile power, Gosudar?"

"I can't help it when she makes it so easy to do," he said.

"Well, thank you, *Katya*," Kharan said pointedly, "but I doubt you want to sleep in the same tent with a horse, so I'll just stay in my own."

"It makes little difference to me, honestly," I said, glancing at Elation, who was even now landing in a nearby tree, "since I will be sharing mine with an eagle."

"Horse manure or eagle *govno*," she said, "I'm not sure which is worse."

The prince laughed as I shook my head. "Actually, I've never seen Elation do such a thing—at least not in front of me."

Kharan snorted. "Then your eagle must not be an animal after all. Perhaps it is a spirit guide instead, because Daichin has absolutely no qualms about that." She glanced over to where the pony was eating his weight in grain. "Still, there is no better way to stay warm."

"If you don't mind the smell," the prince added, and Kharan grinned.

"Gosudar," Ivan interrupted, and we all turned. He stood not far from the fire, his black coat dusted with snow. "We have pitched your tent."

"Very good, Ivan. Thank you."

The prince stood, and I followed his line of sight to a tent that must have been five times as large as the celestial one. It was so black it blended in with the night sky, but the edges were visible due to elaborate silver scrollwork that stood out like the stars. Cheery warmth was coming from within, as though a fire and many candles had already been lit for him.

"Do you want to see it?" the prince asked when he noticed me staring at the tent in awe.

I glanced at Kharan, suddenly unsure. I'd been to the prince's room many times in the palace, but for some reason, a tent beneath the stars seemed even more intimate. She only shot me a look of amusement and lifted her eyebrows.

Ordinarily, I would say no to any situation remotely this intimidating, but tonight, with his easy smile and the moon so bright above us, I couldn't refuse.

He offered me his arm, and I took it, like I was some high-born boyar lady. Up close, the tent was even more beautiful. Amid the black, tiny silver threads were sewn throughout, and the effect mimicked the night sky.

He held aside the flap, and I entered before him. Inside, it was lavishly furnished. A large bed had been constructed with a feather mattress and furs, and nearby was a wide table and chairs with a leather map spread on top, no doubt showing the path to Constantinople. A fire pit in the center provided warmth and light, but I was surprised that the most illumination was coming from another icon corner set up perpendicular to the prince's bed. There, the firebird's feather glowed brightly.

"You brought the feather with you?" I asked, unable, as before, to take my eyes off the shimmering gold of it.

"I thought I should, considering that we will be traveling to my mother's city. Perhaps it will attract the creature that dropped it, and then I can ask it as one fire creature to another."

I tilted my head as I studied it, remembering what he'd told me about it. That the Byzantines had their own legends about the firebird. "Perhaps you're not waiting on a *that* at all. Maybe you're waiting on a *who*."

His expression turned pensive. "I'd be a fool to discount the possibility of that. Especially when I have surrounded myself with people with otherworldly abilities." He crossed over to the feather and held it between his thumb and forefinger, twisting it around and around. It threw the colors of fire around the room, so that it seemed like he held rubies and topaz instead of a feather. "Though in all my encounters with those with power, I've never seen anyone transform into anything else, much less a bird of legend."

Well, that was true. I'd only seen Kharan transform into shadow, and I wasn't sure that was the same thing. "Perhaps we can find out more in Constantinople."

He grinned. "You just said 'we.' Does that mean you intend to help me?"

"I will endeavor to be useful while we're there, but I doubt I'd be better at gathering information than Kharan."

He snorted. "No one is better at that particular skill. That's not to say you don't have your own means of getting people to tell you things. There's something about you that makes me feel like I can tell you anything."

I surprised us both by laughing. "That's a pretty thing to say, but I don't believe you. No one tells me anything, least of all anything of importance. If you'd like an example, I just learned a few days ago that my babushka is truly my babushka though she'd always told me otherwise, and that I have both a mother and a father, though I'd always thought I'd been left abandoned in the woods to die."

He looked stunned for a moment but recovered quickly. "That must have been shocking to learn, but I can only see this as good news. Did she tell you their names? I wish you had told me before—I would have sent Kharan to see what she could find."

"I only know my father's name. She didn't have much time to tell me anything before she . . ." It was as if my tongue refused to work in my mouth. Refused to pronounce Babushka's death. But the prince understood—the concern in his gaze made his eyes look as dark as the night sky. "She gave me a journal, but I have read it cover to cover and have found nothing useful. She never calls my mother by name."

He nodded thoughtfully. "Still, it is enough that we have your father's name. When we return to Kiev, we will see what we can find of him."

"That is very kind of you," I said, relief that I would have his assistance taking away some of the bite of the worry that had plagued me.

"I'm glad I can do something kind for you. I know there are some . . . intimidating rumors about me. Hopefully I've shown you they aren't true."

"I have to admit I was afraid at first," I said with a little glance his way. "But I quickly realized they were wrong. How did such terrible rumors start?"

"They were spread by my enemies," he said with a frown. "And it's been particularly harmful to my alliance with the Byzantines." He glanced over at me. "I'm sorry if the rumors caused you distress. I'm far from perfect, and I do have a terrible temper, but I don't think I'll cut you into tiny pieces and drink your blood. You needn't fear that at least."

But as I looked into his eyes, and he mine, I wondered if there were worse things than physical pain. Things like falling in love with a prince—someone I could never be the social equal of.

Chapter Sixteen

WE CARRIED ON MUCH THE SAME the next day and the day after that, until we were so far south that spring was winning the battle over winter. All around, the trees were budding, birds sang merrily, and wildflowers forced themselves through the melting snow. On the third day after leaving, we stopped to change over the supplies from the sleighs to wagons, for the snow had melted enough that wheels would be more efficient. The men did this as easily as they took apart and rebuilt the tents and camp each night and morning.

Despite my saddle sores, Zonsara was a joy to ride. Though she appeared as a hot-blooded horse—her tail lifted and streaming behind her, her nostrils flared—she carried me as though I was a baby she'd been entrusted with. Even when we strayed from the path one day, accidentally flushing a mother nightingale from her nest directly at us, Zonsara did not shy away. Each night at camp, she waited quietly and patiently as I slithered off her back, my legs no more trustworthy than a newborn fawn's. And yet, I didn't want to rely again on Sasha to help me off my horse.

Ever since the first night, I'd also avoided being alone with the prince again—a fairly easy feat when he was spending more time with his bogatyri the closer we came to Constantinople. Nothing had happened that night—not really—but the heat of his gaze and my answering interest frightened me almost as much as losing control of my power. I was afraid to care for him. Afraid to be hurt when I knew he was the grand prince and I was an abandoned girl with no family and no village. And though I had agreed to help him, I was afraid that he still valued my abilities above all else. More than that, I knew the cold, cruel twists of this world. The more I cared about someone, the more likely I seemed to be to lose them.

Sometimes because of my own hand.

Even befriending Kharan made me nervous, though she had proven to be impervious to any of my moods. If I was quiet and tense, she spoke of things she had seen or heard on her travels (like the people she'd encountered who rode elephants like horses just as Dedushka had always told me) so that I couldn't resist engaging in conversation. If I became so lost in my own thoughts that I could barely pay attention to my surroundings, she turned our steady march south into a riding lesson. The last I greatly appreciated because I knew next to nothing about riding—only enough not to fall off my horse on our long journey.

And Kharan was a superior horsewoman; Daichin did anything she asked of him. She frequently dropped her reins to reach across and forcibly push my heels down or adjust my grip on my own reins, and Daichin didn't even blink. Once she even kneeled upon his back, her spine perfectly straight while Daichin trotted then cantered then galloped, to demonstrate the importance of balance.

After two full days under her tutelage I had no hope of kneeling on Zonsara's back, but at least I could make her walk and trot and stop when I wanted her to.

"You're doing well," Kharan said, as I trotted to catch up to her and Daichin and slowed Zonsara to a walk again.

"You're a good teacher," I said, giving Zonsara a pat on the neck. "Only I wish I could go off trail a bit to practice leading her. I think Zonsara is mostly following the others, especially Daichin."

Daichin snorted when he heard his name, and Kharan smiled. "We're about to make camp, and there's a stream just there," she said, indicating the silvery water burbling happily to our left. "You could follow it for a while when we stop, and then you'll know if you can guide Zonsara on your own or not."

I glanced ahead, to where the prince led with Ivan close behind. "Do you think I should tell the others?"

"I'll vouch for your character and swear you didn't intend to escape," Kharan said, light teasing in her tone.

If I had any intention of escaping, I wouldn't get far. I couldn't ride well, certainly not at a gallop, and I had no supplies—everything was in the wagons.

I didn't have long to wait before we stopped. Over the next hill and through the trees, there was a little clearing, large enough for us to make camp. The horses all nickered happily; they knew they'd soon get bags full of grain and some well-deserved rest.

I felt a little twinge of guilt at denying that to Zonsara, if only temporarily, but at least I had a small bit of sugar to reward her for the delay.

"I won't be gone long," I said to Kharan and turned Zonsara's nose off the trail and toward the stream. She flicked her ears back and forth for a moment, as though unsure she should be leaving the safety of the herd, but a little flicker of happiness went through me when she decided to listen to me.

Behind me, I could hear one of the men question where I was going, but Kharan answered, "Where she's supposed to." The man said nothing else, but I think that was only because most people were a little intimidated by Kharan. She could, after all, learn your deepest secrets without you even knowing.

But soon, all thoughts of everything else drifted away as I followed the silver stream. It burbled cheerfully over rocks as Zonsara lent the soothing sound of soft hoofbeats to the water's melody. When we went around the next bend, the trees thick on both sides of the stream, I sat back on my hipbones like Kharan had taught me.

Zonsara immediately responded by halting, both ears flicked

back to listen to my next request. I preferred to think of it that way—as asking rather than commanding. Whether animal or human, we all responded better to being asked instead of told.

I gave her a little pat, and then squeezed lightly with my calves. She walked on again, her head bobbing in time to her smooth gait.

We continued for a few more minutes, until I started to feel a little bubble of worry that I'd strayed too far. I had an hour yet before the sun went down, but I didn't want to be caught alone in the woods after dark. Not only because it would be more difficult to find my way back, but also because there were countless stories of the creatures that inhabited the forests at night—not beasts, but ancient creatures that had their own legends. Some were kind and beautiful, like the firebird. Others . . .

I just didn't want to run into the others.

But just as I thought I'd better turn Zonsara around, I saw the stream emptying into a pond up ahead, the water reflecting the blue of the sky and the green of the trees. But most important, it was unfrozen.

It had been so long since I'd seen any body of water without at least blocks of ice floating on it that I couldn't resist going to the water's edge. I dismounted Zonsara and gave her the sugar cube I'd kept from the tea Kharan had brewed that morning. She was so well-trained, I didn't think I'd have to tie her up, and she was already eyeing the tender grass and plants that grew near the pond.

The water looked so inviting that I bent down to touch

the surface of it and found it to be warmer than my skin—not entirely surprising since my skin always felt like ice, but pleasant all the same.

A soft rustle of wings sounded from above, and Elation came to land on one of the trees nearby. She looked down at me, quietly surveying the pond.

Zonsara snorted, nose-deep in greenery. A glance at the sun told me I still had a little time—it hadn't quite dipped below the tree line. I pulled off my boots and sat down by the edge, putting my feet in the water. The stream fed into the pond with the most soothing sound, and for a while, all I could do was watch the hypnotic ripples across the surface, my mind quiet for the first time in a long time.

The longer I watched, though, the stranger the ripples looked—swirling round and round in the center of the pond, bubbles forming beneath. Something was rising from the depths, and I tilted my head to try to figure out what I was looking at. Green, with shimmering scales like a fish. But when the water calmed, I saw that it was a girl, only a little smaller than I was.

Above, Elation screeched a warning.

The girl grinned at me, her mouth full of teeth as sharp as knives. Her hair was so long it touched her knees, and it shimmered in the dying sun. I knew what she was, just as every peasant in Kievan Rus' knew of her kind: a rusalka—a water spirit. This wasn't like the familiar bannik. A rusalka was a malevolent spirit.

Behind me, Zonsara whinnied nervously. My legs twitched—I wanted to run, but I knew the rusalka would catch me before I could even get to my horse. And anyway, I didn't want to leave my boots behind.

It was early for this spirit to be out—summer was usually the time when everyone knew not to swim alone in lakes and ponds. But maybe the fact that we were already farther south than I'd ever been explained why a rusalka would be in a pond in the first days of spring.

She tilted her head at me, and even this small movement made my heart pound and my skin turn to ice. The rusalki were spirits of women who had drowned, and in their misery, wanted to drown others just as they were. At least, that's how the stories had always gone. I'd always suspected there was more to it than that.

Despite my fear, I forced myself to say something. "I didn't mean to disturb you. I'll just put on my boots and be on my way."

"You haven't disturbed me," she said, her voice like water over rock. "Were you seeking a warm pond to bathe? You look like you have journeyed far."

There was kindness in her tone and in her expression, but I knew it had to be a trick. Everyone knew the rusalki liked nothing more than to drown any person who entered their water. "It's not warm enough for me to bathe in, but I was just so happy to find water that wasn't frozen that I couldn't resist at least putting my feet in."

She smiled. "It's much warmer in the middle here. It is I who warms the pond, and I haven't quite reached the edges yet. Come," she beckoned, her hair moving with her arm, "you will see."

"That's a kind offer, but I should get back to my camp," I said, noticing with a little shiver of unease that the sun had dipped far too low.

I stood, but before I could step out of the water, she called out again. "Please don't go. I never have any visitors, and I'm terribly lonely. Won't you at least stay for a moment and talk?"

Her eyes were dark as night, but round with sincerity. Still, I didn't want Kharan to be reprimanded because I'd stayed away too long. "Perhaps I can come again on our return journey, but I must go now."

I took one foot out of the water, and that's when I was hit with a massive wave, as though I was swimming in the Black Sea instead of a small pond. It sucked me back toward the center of the pond, wave after wave crashing over my head, pushing me under the water. I didn't have time to take a breath before my mouth filled with water again.

Panic fluttered inside me like a bird caught in a net. I barely knew how to swim, and my clothes were heavy and sodden. I fought toward the surface only to be thrown back again. My lungs burned, and desperation tore at me.

Water was part of my element, I thought in my panic; I couldn't let it defeat me.

I focused on the cold covering my skin, on it radiating from the core of me. I thought of the release of explosive power I'd unleashed on the raiders and my village, on the elementals in the forest. I wouldn't need such power here. I only had to freeze the pond—just as I had the river when I escaped. Beyond the water, I thought I heard hoofbeats, and a flicker of worry entered my mind. Had Zonsara fled?

When next the wave pushed me beneath the surface, I stopped trying to fight it physically. Instead, I let the cold spread until it was emanating from me. Colder and colder, and as the wave rose up, it froze beneath me, shoving me to the surface. I gasped for breath.

It sounded like someone shouted my name, but the ice grew, drawing my attention to the center of the pond.

Like cold fingers, my power reached for the rusalka. Her eyes were huge with fear and her grin was long gone.

I let the ice grow until it gripped the rusalka; she screamed as the bottom half of her body became encased in ice. "You tricked me! You pretended to be a mere mortal, but I see that you aren't. You're a daughter of Winter."

She emphasized winter as though it was a person rather than a season, and it so surprised me that I stopped my ice from spreading further. The bannik, I remembered, had called me something similar. "You know who my father is?"

Her eyes were on the icy water so close to the middle of the pond, but she glanced up at me. "Not father—mother."

I thought of Babushka's journal. Of how she never mentioned my mother by name. Could this be true, or was the rusalka merely trying to trick me?

"I find that hard to believe."

"Anyone with eyes for the creatures of the Old World can tell that you are no ordinary mortal."

Despite my wariness, I found myself desperate to know. "Who is she?"

The rusalka shook her head. "I will not invoke her name here, not when spring has already come. Go to the old witch in the woods—Baba Yaga. She will help you."

We'd all heard the stories of Baba Yaga, a witch who lived in the woods, wiser than any other, but with a taste for human flesh. "I'd rather not become a meal for a witch."

"It's no trick," the rusalka said. "She won't harm you for the same reason I won't, and she may tell you more besides. It's your choice."

Was my mother so powerful then? That this spirit and Baba Yaga would fear her wrath? It seemed unlikely, after all that I'd experienced in my village.

"And how would I find this witch?"

"You must travel east to the deepest part of these woods, until the sun and moon have switched places."

I didn't know why creatures such as the bannik and rusalka chose to only speak in riddles, but at least she had given me a direction—if I dared to believe her.

I kept my eyes on the rusalka as I backed toward the shore, walking carefully on the ice I'd created. Just as I reached solid ground, I turned to the sound of hoofbeats and found Sasha riding his own horse while he led Zonsara. "Katya, thank God, I was so worried when I found Zonsara galloping into camp without her rider." He fell silent when he saw how wet I was and then looked to the middle of the pond where the rusalka was held prisoner. "What happened?"

"I invited her to stay and talk with me," the rusalka said before I could answer, "but she deceived me into thinking she was an ordinary mortal—not Winter's daughter." Her eyes had that strange light of hunger in them as she looked at Sasha, but he wasn't foolish enough to approach the water.

"You are fortunate she's unharmed, demon," Sasha said. To me, he said, "Come, we should get you dry."

Heedless of how dripping wet I was, Sasha helped me remove my sodden coat only to replace it with his fine fur one.

"Wait," the rusalka said as I walked toward Zonsara. When I turned back to her, she pointed to the ice. "My pond."

"Leave it," Sasha said. "Perhaps it will save someone else's life by preventing this demon from drowning them."

I hesitated. "I gave her my word."

I walked to the edge again, the rusalka watching me from the water, and Elation watching from above. In all likelihood, the spirit could free herself after I left, but I was sure it would take some time. I'd thawed my ice only one other time before: when I'd accidentally frozen water in a horse trough. But that was a much smaller amount of water. Trepidation twisted my stomach at the thought of trying to thaw the pond, but I wouldn't let myself back away now.

When I touched the ice, I thought of how I'd called the ice to me, how it traveled over my skin. Only this time, I recalled it.

With a hiss, I winced as the cold seeped into me. The ice receded, the water melting again as the cold spread over my skin instead.

I stepped back, and the prince strode over to me. Clouds of cold billowed from my mouth with every breath. "Are you all right?" he said in a low voice.

I nodded. "Yes," I answered, but my teeth chattered viciously.

"Can you ride?"

"I won't do that to Zonsara—I'm soaking wet," I managed to say.

He gave me an exasperated look. "Then I suppose we'll walk."

After gathering up the horses, he stayed close by my side, but I wouldn't take his proffered arm. If I was to master myself and my power, I couldn't let something like that disable me.

I glanced back at the pond, but the rusalka was gone.

Daughter of Winter.

But who was Winter?

Camp wasn't far, only a ten-minute walk away. The prince was thankfully quiet the whole way, though I could tell he wanted to say something. He was waiting, it turned out, for me to change into dry clothes.

Barely the moment after I had donned my rubhaka and skirt. Thankfully, Vera had included one set of plainer clothes for me, suitable for travel—the prince called out to me from the other side of the tent flap.

"You may enter," I said after a glance at Elation, who watched the tent entrance just as I did.

The prince ducked as he came through the flap, a steaming earthenware cup in one hand. "For you."

"Thank you," I said, and took a sip of the warm kvas.

"You shouldn't have left on your own," he said, his voice quiet, but his eyes gazed back intensely. "You could have died. Again."

"It wasn't my intention to endanger myself," I said, trying very hard not to feel chagrined. "I only wanted to test out my riding ability when I was on my own."

His body tensed. "You didn't tell me you were leaving, and no one could say for sure where you'd gone."

"But Kharan—"

"She should have told me right away," he said, his words cutting into mine. "What if that creature had managed to overcome you?"

"Forgive me, Sasha," I said, surprised at just how upset he seemed to be. "Obviously I didn't know there would be such danger, but in any case, I was able to protect myself."

"You're right—you were able to defend yourself in the end. It was only when I came upon you, drowning in the pond like that . . ." His jaw flexed as he trailed off, looking pained. "But it may be partially my fault for not conveying to you how dangerous are the woods we travel through. They are not as wild,

I suppose, as the woods in the north, where every moment you may chance upon a creature of legend. Still, there are enough here—enough to do you harm or even kill you. We are safer in numbers." His tone had grown increasingly passionate the more he spoke, and now his whole body was tense.

"I'm sorry, truly," I said. "I hadn't realized the danger, but I can't say I entirely regret the encounter . . . not after what I learned from the rusalka. She said I was the daughter of Winter, and that Baba Yaga could tell me more."

His eyes narrowed. "You can't mean to take that demon's advice—Baba Yaga won't answer your questions. Surely you've at least heard of her in your village? She'll trick you and torture you, and you'll be glad when you finally die."

Though his words made me quake, I didn't flinch away from his gaze. "That name, though—daughter of Winter. The bannik in your banya said something similar."

This gave him pause. "You spoke to the bannik?"

"I did. He called me child of Winter, and he told me that earth would only fall to fire and ice. I can't help but think he meant us."

The prince was quiet, my words clearly turning over in his mind. "I've never known the bannik to speak to anyone in all my years spent at the palace, much less give a prophecy." He looked at me closely. "And your babushka never spoke of Winter as a person?"

I shook my head. "No. I never knew I had a mother and father until recently. Babushka might have known the truth, but she never conveyed it to me. All my life, I've wondered who my real parents were, who had been cruel enough to leave a defenseless baby alone in the woods. If there's a chance I may learn the truth, then I must take it. Wouldn't you?"

He looked away for a moment, his jaw tightening, and I held my breath. "My first instinct is to refuse. It's too dangerous, and we don't have much time to spare." I opened my mouth to argue, but he continued, "However, I offered before to help you find your father, and this could lead you to the truth about both your parents. Not only that, you have willingly joined me in my own quest to find out more about my power. It's only fair that I should aid you in yours."

I let out my breath in relief. "Thank you, Gosudar."

"Sasha," he corrected with a smile. "But we will have to leave tonight—after dinner." Again he glanced away, this time to the tent entrance. "And we will have to do so without Ivan noticing. You may ask Kharan to accompany us if you wish— she can be discreet and even disappear if needed—but I cannot risk anyone else. I doubt Baba Yaga would allow an entire army to march into her domain anyway."

"I understand, and I am loath to risk anyone else, too. I appreciate your help more than you know."

"I'm glad to give it," he said.

I nodded toward the tent entrance. "Shall I help Kharan prepare dinner now?"

"If you'd like. Perhaps she will know more about Winter and even Baba Yaga. She has traveled farther, heard more stories, and seen more than I ever have."

He held open the tent flap graciously for me, and I stepped through. "Thank you," I murmured, and he caught hold of my wrist.

"You can always change your mind. I'd rather not put you at risk like this."

My heart beat a little faster as I felt the heat of his hand on the sensitive skin of my wrist. I tried to tell myself that he only didn't want to risk losing my power, but the excuse fell a little flat even in my own head. "I know, but I feel I must."

He nodded and released my wrist. "I'll see you at dinner, then."

I hurried off to find Kharan and help her prepare the food.

Perhaps she would know more about what to expect from Baba Yaga.

Chapter Seventeen

I found Kharan carefully transferring round river stones the size of her fist from an open fire to an iron pot. Nearby was an enormous earthenware platter filled with chunks of meat and vegetables. She looked up when I approached.

"I thought you could use some help," I said. "I hope the prince didn't force you into cooking for all of us."

She grinned. "No, but I wouldn't mind having you here to help. I haven't had the chance to make one of my clan's recipes in far too long. Not that I'm especially good at cooking."

"It looks delicious already, though—what's it called?"

"Horhog," she said. "The meat used is typically sheep, but I had to make do with the deer the men killed earlier." She pointed to the hot stones. "We use these to roast the meat like in an oven. It's the easiest, best meal when you're camping."

"That's ingenious. So how can I help?"

"The meat needs seasoning."

I nodded and found the requisite salt and pepper, liberally seasoning everything like she asked. When I was finished, she dumped the whole thing into the pot with the hot rocks and closed the lid.

"There is something I discovered today, when I went out on my own on Zonsara."

She raised her eyebrows. "Do you mean the rusalka?"

I smiled. "Is there nothing you don't know about? How have you heard about the rusalka already?"

She sat down on the ground near the fire and invited me to sit next to her. "I assure you, it took no interrogation skills. The prince was incensed when you both returned—he was ranting about the rusalka and the pond the entire time you were drying off and changing."

So Sasha *had* been holding in his anger with me. I glanced around us to be sure no one was close enough to overhear. "The rusalka said something to me, and I'm hoping it's something you'll know about."

She must have recognized my serious tone, for she leaned closer, her brows drawn. "I will help you if I can. What did she say?"

"She said I was the daughter of Winter and that Baba Yaga could explain more about where I came from. She spoke like Winter was a person—my mother. And this isn't the first time

I've heard someone use Winter in connection to me." I told her all about the bannik and how he'd called me child of Winter. And I told her of Babushka's journal, how frustrating it was that it lacked a name for my mother.

Kharan was quiet for a moment as though deep in thought. "There are legends in the north of a queen with complete control over ice, but I never learned more than that."

That was more than I had known, at least. "And what of Baba Yaga? The prince has agreed to come with me to find her, and I would like your help, too, if you are willing. Do you know anything about her?"

Kharan grinned. "It's amusing to me that you Rus' believe Baba Yaga to be a single person."

I shook my head. "I don't understand. So, Winter is a person, and Baba Yaga isn't one but many?"

"Baba Yaga is the name for a bone witch, and there are many, but they are always very powerful." I didn't think I wanted to know why they were called bone witches, but then Kharan told me anyway. "My grandfather always said they used bones to divine, and whether they were animal or human was hard to say."

I shuddered. "The prince wanted me to ask you to come, but I can't do that. It's too dangerous."

She gave me a look. "I'm coming. What kind of friend would I be if I didn't try to help you find out more about your own mother?" Though I was happy she thought enough of me to call herself my friend, I still was reluctant for her to endanger herself. "You won't be able to stop me," she added with a little nudge of her shoulder to mine.

Beaten, I let out a breath. "That's true, and I can't say I'd mind the company. But when we reach the bone witch's hut, it would be best for you to stay hidden."

"I can agree to that. Though her eyes may be able to detect even my shadows."

Cold fingers touched my spine, and I hoped seeking out such a creature would be worth it. More than finally discovering the truth about my parentage and even my abandonment, I wanted to find out more about my power. I wanted—no, *needed*—to be able to control it. And the possibility that I might finally be able to assert my will over my ability was enough incentive to seek out a witch.

Even a bone witch.

Though the horhog had been delicious, I hadn't been able to stomach more than a few bites. My mind had been racing too far ahead, picturing the way we would have to travel to reach Baba Yaga. How far would we have to go? And even if we made it there, would the bone witch be forthcoming about my mother?

Now, as I stood in my tent after having changed into my old rubhaka, skirt, and boots, I waited for the sound of voices to fade, to signal that everyone had finally gone to bed. I glanced back longingly at my own plush bed; so many days on the road had brought a weariness to my body that made me glad for a bed at the end of every day. Of course, it was this same weariness that would cause the others to seek out their own tents, too.

It was quiet and still while I waited for Kharan and the prince.

And it was the smallest of noises from outside that alerted me to a presence. I pulled back the flap of my tent.

"Are you ready?" a voice whispered behind me, and I froze nearly solid.

"Kharan," I whispered back, and she materialized in the light of the candles.

"You'd be terrible at espionage," she said. "I thought for sure you'd expect me once you opened your tent."

"I'm afraid I'm not omniscient."

She let out a soft laugh. "Well, you have to be if you want to play this sort of game."

"Then what will happen next?"

She tilted her head as though considering for a moment. "We'll retrieve our horses, and the prince will meet us on the path."

I grinned. "I'm not sure whether that's omniscience, or that you and the prince formed a plan in advance."

"Don't question my powers of foretelling," she said. "Let's go."

She led the way, and the only sounds in the quiet camp were the winds through the trees and the soft stamping of horse hooves. It was still and silent as we reached the dozing horses, but as soon as we got closer, many pricked their ears forward, hoping for more treats. Daichin let out a soft whicker when he saw Kharan, and Zonsara bobbed her head as though hoping I'd come just to scratch her forehead.

"They won't be so happy to see us once they realize we want them to go out again into the cold night," I said, obliging Zonsara with a forehead scratch.

"Probably not," Kharan said, and then untied the rope that kept Daichin secured next to the other horses. "But we can give them plenty of treats when we return."

As silently as a shadow, she pulled herself astride, and it was then that I realized we had no saddles. No bridles, even, other than makeshift ones from the halters and ropes.

Kharan watched me as I stood by Zonsara's side, desperately trying to decide how I'd pull myself up.

"Tonight will be a more advanced riding lesson," Kharan said.

I smiled grimly as I grasped hold of Zonsara's withers. If I couldn't even mount my horse, what good was I against a bone witch?

With an awkward little jump, I managed to flop my belly onto her back. The mare snorted her displeasure at me and swished her tail, but she held still, even as I swung my leg over her heavily.

Kharan was already riding away by the time I got my legs untangled from my skirt, and I squeezed my legs around Zonsara a little too firmly. She shot forward, nearly unseating me in the process.

Kharan glanced back at me, and I smiled sheepishly.

The beating of wings alerted me to the return of Elation, who followed us by making lazy circles in the sky. Her presence comforted me, made me feel stronger. Like maybe I'd be able to face Baba Yaga and live to tell about it.

We stayed silent as we rode along, the horses not making much noise on the freshly thawed earth. I'd almost forgotten what Kharan had said about the prince until a horse neighed behind us, nearly unseating me again.

"Hello, Gosudar," Kharan said. "I take it you made it past your own guards?"

He grinned. "As you see." He turned his gaze on me. "You can still change your mind, Katya."

"No, it must be now."

"I had to try one last time," he said with a nod. "Then we will accompany you and help you in any way we can."

"Thank you," I said.

"Do not thank me," he said with a shake of his head. "To let you face this level of danger alone would be the worst sort of idiocy."

He gave his horse the signal to move forward, and we fell into a staggered line, with Kharan in the lead, Zonsara and I following, and the prince bringing up the rear.

"Baba Yaga isn't always evil in the stories," I said hopefully. "Sometimes she offers wisdom."

The prince made a scoffing sound. "Yes, but you won't know which story this is until you're in the midst of it."

The truth of that made me fall silent, and again I prayed I

wasn't leading everyone into unnecessary danger.

Soon I would know the truth.

Or be dead—depending on Baba Yaga's mood.

Despite the moon lighting our way, it took us most of the night to reach the center of the woods. The trees grew thicker and thicker, until their branches and needles all but blotted out what little light came from the night sky. We had passed the rusalka's pond long ago, weaving deeper into the forest. Many times we had hesitated on which path to take, but it was Elation who seemed to lead us where we wanted to go. Her circular flight patterns would indicate the way—east or west—and eventually we came to a place where the trees were so thick the horses could barely move.

And then just as I feared we wouldn't be able to continue, we spotted flickering lights. I tried to dismount, but the prince stopped me. "Let Kharankhui go and see."

When I turned to look at Kharan, she had already melded into the shadows, leaving Daichin nearby. It seemed to take far too long before she'd returned again, and by then, my skin was radiating cold.

"The hut is unoccupied," she said quietly, appearing beside Daichin but somehow not spooking him. "The lights we saw are flames flickering within lanterns."

"If there are lanterns, then surely someone will return soon," I said. I didn't want to have traveled so far only to not find Baba Yaga at all.

"I think it's safe to approach," Kharan said, and Sasha nodded.

I gave Zonsara a little squeeze with my calves, but Sasha came up beside me on his own horse and reached for my arm. "Let me go first. Please," he added when I thought about refusing.

When he'd passed through the thick trees, I followed and brought Zonsara up short. Before us was a little clearing, in the center of which was a hut constructed with what I thought at first was wood. As I moved closer, I realized it wasn't wood at all, but petrified bone. I turned to look at Sasha, and he was grimly inspecting one of the lanterns whose flames had drawn our attention. They, too, were made of bone. Skulls—though these were still white. The flames danced within, completely independent of any wax or oil to burn.

"Interesting design," Kharan said, as though this wasn't the most terrifying structure we'd ever seen.

"She makes light of things when she's afraid," Sasha said to me, and Kharan glared.

"With good reason," I murmured, placing my hand on Zonsara's neck. The horses were shifting restlessly, and I thought it was only their good training that kept them from bolting.

Just then, a piercing neigh broke the silence, and all three of our horses froze, their ears pricked and tails lifted at the sound. A rider entered the clearing on a blood-red charger, and the moment the horse's hooves touched the outer ring of the grass that surrounded the hut, the sun rose behind it. Beyond, the trees were still veiled in darkness. The night sky remained unchanged in that part of the forest, and it was as if the clearing we found ourselves in was something apart from the main world. I looked at the transformation in awe: this is what the rusalka had meant by the sun and moon changing places in the sky.

The charger and its rider came closer, and as they did, our horses backed away. The rider wasn't a man at all—at least, he had the form of a man, but he was made of fire. His whole body crackled, and his eyes were dark as the night sky just beyond.

He raised a sword—also made of fire—and his charger lowered its head.

There was a moment where I thought, *He means to attack us, and I will fall from this horse.*

His horse leaped forward, and at the same time, Sasha grabbed me and pulled me off Zonsara. My lovely mare turned and bolted, but with me pressed close to Sasha's chest, he managed to keep his own horse under control. Sasha's mount pivoted out of the way just before the man of fire could run us through with his sword.

"He is made of fire," Sasha said into my ear, and now both he and Kharan were desperately trying to evade the blood-red charger and his rider.

"Fire," I repeated dumbly, my body a pillar of ice.

"You can do this," Sasha said, and he maneuvered his horse around again, staying just out of reach of the flaming sword.

My heart was in my throat. "I could kill us all."

"You won't." His voice was pure confidence.

The charger swung around again, and above us, Elation cried out a warning. There was no time. If I didn't stop him, Sasha and Kharan would be killed.

I reached deep within myself, like sinking into an icy cold pond, and grasped the frozen power. I forced all doubts aside. With the picture of the flaming rider in my mind, I unleashed the ice.

A torrent of icy air so cold it froze the ground it passed over rushed toward the rider. It blasted him off his horse, freezing him instantly. The horse reared, letting out a piercing scream. Where the ice had touched its side, there was a terrible streak of frozen hair and flesh.

The rider himself was trapped in ice, though he hadn't become so frozen as others I'd done this to. He hadn't burst into millions of ice crystals, perhaps because his own body was made of fire. Still the cold continued to pour from me, and if it hadn't been for Sasha's warmth radiating so powerfully from him, I feared it would freeze him, too.

"Enough of this, Daughter of Winter," a voice boomed across the clearing. Instantly, the flow of my ice dissipated, as though an unseen power had reached out and stopped it.

A woman stood in the doorway of the hut, seemingly shriveled and bent and old—even ancient—but then she strode over to the frozen rider like a soldier of twenty. She touched him with a hand as gnarled as a twisted tree root, and the ice melted away. His flames returned, and she touched his charger's side. It healed instantly, and the horse calmed.

Then she turned to us. Her small gray eyes were so deep in the folds of her face it was hard to see them, but I could still feel the intensity of her gaze. It seemed to paralyze me as easily as my ice had frozen the rider. She'd prevented the flow of my cold fire and melted my ice so easily! It was obvious her powers were far greater than mine.

"You nearly destroyed my servant," she said.

"My apologies," I said, as contritely as I could manage without betraying my fear of her, "but he would have killed us."

"And so he would have done to any trespasser."

"We've come because the rusalka said you might have answers—"

"I know why you're here," she said, interrupting me with a shake of her head. She walked back toward her house, and when none of us made to follow, she beckoned. "Come. I will tell you what it is you want to know."

Sasha's arm tightened around me when I tried to dismount, and Kharan gave a single shake of her head. "How do we know you won't kill us the moment we walk through the door?" he demanded.

"You already passed the test by defeating my servant." She grinned, her mouth full of missing teeth. "Besides, I could kill you out here just as easily."

The beating of wings, and then Elation flew just above our heads, coming to land on the gate made of bone.

Baba Yaga glanced at her before turning and walking into her house.

"I think it's safe," I said to Sasha, taking in Elation's relaxed position.

His arm finally loosened its iron grip on my middle. "Very well."

He dismounted first to give me room to swing my leg, and I slid to the ground next to him. After securing the horses to the fence—also made of bone—Sasha, Kharan, and I followed Baba Yaga into her hut. Elation remained outside, but close by.

Despite the forbidding exterior, the inside was warm—almost welcoming. It was small, with a blazing-hot oven on one side and a small cot on the other. Two spindly chairs and a roughly carved table sat near the oven, but Baba Yaga was already stretched out in a wooden rocking chair—the only comfortable-looking piece of furniture in the house.

"Come and sit beside the fire," she said, gesturing toward the small chairs.

Sasha pulled out both from under the table and gave them to Kharan and me, and then he stood behind us, arms folded over his chest.

"Now you may ask your question," Baba Yaga said, her eyes falling closed.

"Who am I?" I asked. Before I could even really think about what I was asking.

One eye opened. "Such a question. To answer that properly, I must tell you a story. It isn't a happy one."

"I'd still like to hear it," I said, my heart beating rapidly in my chest.

She sighed, came again to her feet, and shuffled toward the fire. "Gaze into the flames," she said.

I glanced back at Sasha, and he nodded. Kharan, too, seemed to think it wouldn't put us in any greater danger than we were already. As soon as the three of us were watching the fire dance and beckon, Baba Yaga threw a handful of powder into the flames.

We shielded our eyes as the powder caused the fire to billow out with smoke, but I soon found I could breathe just as easily as I had before. The smoke was white, but as I continued to watch, colors emerged, swirling and beckoning until I couldn't look away.

"Long ago, in the coldest part of the world, a woman emerged with complete control over water and air," Baba Yaga said, and as she spoke, her voice brought forth images in the smoke. A woman with hair so pale it was almost the color of snow, eyes like blue crystal, robed in a cloak of white and silver. Her every step brought forth snow, and her breath filled the air with snowflakes. She was beautiful, but her face could have been carved from marble.

"She built herself a palace of ice," Baba Yaga continued, and the icy castle appeared before us, impossible in its crystal-clear construction, "but no one would venture so far north, nor survive the brutal cold of her home. She was queen of all she surveyed, though no living subjects populated her kingdom.

"For a time, this pleased her. She sought out animals who could survive the cold: foxes and wolves, bears and lynxes, rabbits and birds. She befriended them, and they worshipped her as their queen."

The smoke shifted again, showing the queen surrounded by creatures of all kinds. A wolf slept at her feet at the bottom of her icy throne; a bear with fur as white as the queen's robe allowed her to pet its cub as though they were both domesticated dogs; foxes bounded in the snow before her as she walked in a forest crowned in white.

"After a time, though, the queen grew lonely. She left her great ice palace in the north and traveled south, but as she did, she found that she brought winter with her. Anything she touched turned to snow and ice, and it wasn't long before anyone she met begged her to leave again."

The smoke showed us this: the path the Ice Queen made, turning everything along it white. Anyone she met recoiled from her, frightened by the cold emanating from her. It pierced my heart; I knew how she felt, this woman who might have been my mother.

"She retreated to her palace, and as she did, Spring overtook the land. Winter envied Spring with her cheerful flowers and busy animals, who everyone was so overjoyed to see. No one was happy for Winter to arrive, and this wounded her heart."

The smoke showed us Spring, who was a girl with skin like a chestnut tree, with hair as rich as freshly tilled earth, with eyes greener than newly budding leaves. She wore a gown that trailed flowers in her wake, the color of the morning sky. In contrast, Winter looked pale and frighteningly beautiful—austere as a statue.

"Winter stayed in the North, where her ice and snow would not be greeted with disgust, and for far too long, Spring reigned. From the ice itself, Winter created a globe that would reveal to her the rest of the world, and she sat for I know not how long on her throne, watching Spring's influence over the land."

The globe was the most colorful thing in Winter's ice palace, and the sun rose and fell in rapid succession over and over without her ever moving. She ignored even the animals who came and went. I didn't know this snow-white queen, but it was still heartbreaking to see such sadness.

"She would have sat there until the end of the world, but it was her animal friends who had had enough. The strongest among them—the wolves and bears and lynxes—joined together, and with two restraining the queen, the other destroyed the orb. Winter, in her madness, fought against the wolf and lynx who held her back, and she froze both into statues beside her throne of ice."

We watched as Winter fell to her knees, sobbing beside the two frozen animals that had only been trying to help her, and I felt an answering lump rise in my throat. I knew what it felt like to hurt someone I loved.

"Free from the influence of the orb, she once again left her great ice palace in the North and traveled across the white world, turning the land to snow and ice as she went. But in the South, she came at last to a lake that had refused to freeze over.

Hope bloomed within her at the sight of it—perhaps there was something that could stand against her power. She stood beside it and reached down to touch the water, curious what liquid water would feel like against her hand, but it froze the moment her fingertip hovered above it. She cried then, and her tears were like diamonds."

I thought of all the times I'd felt alone in my village, and I knew a little of the loneliness she must have felt, though I'd at least had Dedushka and Babushka on my side.

"A simple hunter watched from the woods, carrying his brace of rabbits over his shoulder. When he saw the beautiful lady crying beside the now-frozen lake, he was moved to pity."

The hunter was dressed warmly, in a thick wool kaftan and pants, tall leather boots that appeared hand-made like my own. He wore a fur hat, but his hair was still visible around the edges, golden-brown—a few shades darker than my own—as his neatly trimmed beard.

"He comforted her and spoke to her as a man would speak to any beautiful woman, but not as a mortal would speak to as powerful a creature as she."

The smoke showed the hunter touching her on the shoulder in comfort, but as Winter looked up to meet his gaze, the hunter's warm brown eyes widened as though ensnared by her beauty.

"She stayed with him in a cabin by the woods, and she kept her powers frozen within her, so that she would not kill him with her touch, although this took its toll on her, in spite of her depth of abilities. Slowly, they fell in love, and when the moment came for them to act on that love, the second it was over, Winter lost control over her power and the hunter was frozen as quickly as the lake had been."

Tears fell from my own eyes as Winter fell sobbing over the now-still body of the hunter she'd loved. I tried desperately not to look at Sasha, as the terrifying realization crashed over me: if I grew too close to him, could I lose control over myself and kill him?

"Horrified by what she'd done, Winter sought help from the only one she knew who had the power to thaw her ice: Spring. Spring agreed to help, but never again could the hunter be restored to his human form. He became a shadow of what he once was. The loss of the hunter and what Winter had done to him froze her heart, and when the baby was born, the product of that love, she could no sooner care for it than a stone could care for a sparrow."

A baby, small and innocent and swaddled in white fur, hair golden-brown as the hunter's, eyes crystal-blue as the queen's, lay in a basket. Animals of all kinds kept watch over her, but Winter herself looked as unmoved as stone. Watching the baby in the smoke—the one that could be me—ripped me apart.

Sasha leaned forward and touched my shoulder, his hand blazing hot against my own cold. His sympathy undid me, and I was helpless to prevent myself from crying.

Baba Yaga continued, "So she sent it away to be taken in by mortals, for the child was half-mortal herself, and she gave it all the gifts she herself possessed, but with her mortal father's ability to temper them."

A younger Dedushka and Babushka were shown finding the baby in the woods, and then there could be no doubt as to the baby's identity. Sasha squeezed my shoulder gently as I took in a great shuddering breath.

Just beyond the trees, snowy white animals could be seen, though my grandparents had never noticed. Winter had given me away, but it comforted me to see that the animals were clearly charged with my protection until I was found by my family.

The smoke dissipated, and Baba Yaga came again to her feet. "You are the daughter of Winter, with all the powers of snow and ice at your command, but the mortal side of you will always fight to temper the power within." Her sunken gaze turned to Sasha. "You've chosen well, prince. Along with the firebird, she is the most powerful elemental in all the world."

CHAPTER EIGHTEEN

I COULD FEEL BOTH Sasha AND Kharan looking at me. Their intent gazes only made Baba Yaga's pronouncement more daunting.

"I'm only glad you were able to help Katya discover the truth," Sasha said, reaching out and touching my arm. He turned back to Baba Yaga. "You mentioned the firebird, though. What do you know of it?"

Baba Yaga walked to her door. "I only agreed to answer one question. You are no longer welcome here."

Disappointment flashed in Sasha's eyes, but he gave her a slight bow. "We thank you for the information you gave us."

"Be gone with you," she said, her gaze returning to me.

Kharan and Sasha walked through the door, but before I

could reach it, the bone witch made a gesture with her hand, and the door slammed closed.

I turned to her, my pulse leaping in my throat. "Will you not let me leave, too?"

"Katya!" Sasha's voice sounded through the door, followed by Kharan's. They beat on the door, but to no avail.

The bone witch grinned. "You heard what I said. You are the most powerful elemental in the land. Why would I give you up?"

Ice coated my skin. "Because I am not yours to keep."

"I have a servant of flames, but not a servant of ice," she said, stepping just a little closer. "You would make an excellent addition."

I floundered for anything that might save me from my situation. "You said I passed your test."

"And so you did. But that only entitled you to the answer to a question. I said nothing about you leaving."

Panic began to well up inside me, causing the air around me to grow colder and colder.

"None of that," Baba Yaga said, and as she gestured again, bones from the wall stretched out and gripped me with skeletal hands.

Sasha called for me again, his voice taking on a more desperate edge.

"Please," I said, "I cannot stay here."

"You'd rather be servant to that boy-prince?"

My eyes narrowed. "I'm not his servant."

"You are his weapon," she said, head tilted. "Perhaps worse

than a servant." The cold around me grew until my breath was coming out in plumes of white smoke. She watched me for a moment with her hooded eyes. "If you can free yourself, then I will let you go."

My gaze jumped to hers. "Do I have your word?"

"Yes. Break the bones that hold you prisoner, and I will set you free."

I didn't fully believe she'd keep her word, but I had to try. I thought of how easily I had fought back against the rider of flames, how quickly I'd accessed the power within me. But that was in defense of others. My power was slow to come when it was only for me.

I closed my eyes, let myself follow the cold emanating from my skin right to its source, deep inside. But before I could grasp hold, it danced away, just out of reach. I strained against the bones holding me captive, willing the cold to spread. Nothing happened. My power ignored me, just as it always did when I had need of it.

When I opened my eyes again, I found Baba Yaga watching me closely.

"Katya!" Sasha called again, only this time it was followed by a great *boom* as the door rattled on its hinges.

Baba Yaga's gaze slid to the door. "I think it's time I removed your friends from my yard before they destroy my door." She glanced back at me. "You have until I summon my servant to free yourself. If not, your friends will surely be killed."

With that, she threw open her door and raised one gnarled hand. Instantly, a screamed neigh rang out again across the clearing. My blood turned to ice in my veins.

"*No*, please," I shouted at the witch, but she kept her back to me.

The thunder of hooves rattled the hut, and I could practically see Sasha and Kharan turn to face the new threat.

I fought against the skeletal hands digging into my upper arms. The hoofbeats grew louder and louder. I thought of how easily Sasha and Kharan would be cut through by that flaming sword. And suddenly, my power was there, rushing to the surface of my mind like a geyser.

I grabbed it and launched it outward in an explosive rush. At that moment, I didn't care if I destroyed the bones restraining me and the entire hut besides.

A burst of icy cold wind, and then everything exploded around me. The wind I produced was so cold that the bones holding me splintered and broke into dust around me. The cold bloomed still outward, until the very bones holding up the hut began to freeze.

I let it spread, let the cold continue to emanate from me until it was as though I was a mountain watching impassively as a blizzard unleashed its destruction upon the land.

The bone witch seized a staff, somehow not frozen, and with great effort, drove it down onto the floor of her hut. A counter-wave of power knocked me back. It broke my hold on my own icy abilities, cutting off the flow of the blizzard that was decimating her hut.

I found myself on my back, looking up at the sky where the

ceiling and roof should have been.

Baba Yaga came and stood over me. "You are fortunate that my hut's bones will grow back."

"Sasha," I said weakly. "Kharan."

"They survived," she said. "Thanks to you."

I pushed myself up to a standing position, willing the hut around me to stop spinning. I'd bashed my head upon the floor when her power first hit me. "Then am I free to go?"

"Go, but remember this: you are at your most powerful in defense of another."

I didn't waste any time; I walked straight out of the hut before she could stop me again. Kharan and Sasha were waiting with the horses. Elation cried out at the sight of me, still perched on the gate of bones.

Baba Yaga's words only confirmed what I'd already suspected. I thought of all the instances my power had rushed easily to my fingertips: in defense of Dedushka, against the raiders when I thought they'd kill Ivan, and just now, to keep the rider of flame from killing Sasha and Kharan.

Before I could mount Zonsara, Sasha strode over to me and touched my chin. "Are you hurt?"

His kindness nearly undid me. I hadn't realized how terrified I'd been, how emotionally drained I felt, until this moment. I shifted my gaze to Kharan to keep from crying. She looked a little shaken—her face paler than normal. "Yes, but we should go before the bone witch changes her mind about letting us leave."

In answer, he brought Zonsara forward and helped me onto her back. I settled in, thankful my horse hadn't been injured or lost when the rider attacked us before. We walked the horses out of the clearing, and there was a terrible moment when I was afraid we wouldn't be able to escape. The sun was high on our side of the forest, but beyond, it was dark still. We crossed through easily enough, and I breathed a sigh of relief.

In the darkness and quiet of our trip back, everything I'd learned from Baba Yaga replayed through my mind. Without the experience of the smoke showing me everything that had happened to the Ice Queen, it was almost hard to believe it had happened at all. It seemed a fairy tale, dark and strange.

"Kharan," I said, riding closer to her and Daichin, "what the bone witch said—was it the same tale you'd heard? Of a queen in the North who lives in an ice palace?"

Kharan glanced at me, and I was glad to see the color in her face was back. "Yes, but our stories are different."

She had even Sasha's attention now, who had slowed his horse to stay close enough to listen.

"How so?" I asked.

"We know her for what she is: one of the original elementals."

I glanced at Sasha, confused. "Original elementals?"

"They are the ancient beings who first had an affinity for each element, who we are all supposedly descended from. Only . . ." She trailed off with a glance at Sasha.

"Only what?" I asked, my stomach once again in knots. In

the short time I'd known Kharan, I hadn't seen her look unsure, but she did now.

"It's very rare to find a direct descendent," Sasha said, his expression contemplative. "I've spent two years searching for elemental users, and I've never heard even a whisper of a direct descendent. I didn't know they existed anymore."

"Most of us have diluted abilities," Kharan added, and now even she was staring at me.

The way they watched me, like they'd suddenly discovered I had two heads instead of one, made my skin erupt in cold. "But surely there must have been others with an affinity for ice?"

Sasha shook his head. "I've never heard of someone who could do such a thing besides Winter herself. I never truly believed the rumors from your village until I heard from Kharan and the others what you did to the raiders. I thought I was just saving you from the cruelty of people who would chain you and trade you to a prince many of them thought would only kill you."

To hear that I wasn't so similar to the others with abilities as I'd always thought, that in fact my power was unusual and frightening, after I'd already learned so much about myself that my mind could hardly absorb it all, was like the final snowflake that brought on the avalanche. I sat back on my hip bones hard, and Zonsara obediently came to a halt.

"Are you all right, Katya?" Kharan asked, bringing Daichin to a stop next to me.

"You are more powerful than I'd ever guessed," Sasha said, his tone taking on that of the prince instead of the Sasha I knew as my friend, "and we cannot risk you falling into the wrong hands."

Anger, bright and cold and terrible, crashed over me. Zonsara threw her head in the air, her nostrils flaring.

"For the last time, *Sasha*," I said with no little amount of contempt, "I am not a weapon for you to control."

Sasha looked at me sharply. "I don't understand your anger, and I certainly don't think of you as a weapon. That's the whole point—*I* don't, but the Drevlian and Novgorodian princes would." His whole body tensed, and his horse tossed its head. "If they should learn that you have such abilities, they will stop at nothing to capture you. And they would force you to use your power through torture."

I flinched at the bluntness of his words, but I saw Kharan nod once, grimly.

"It wasn't a lie when I told you that I care about you. I might have thought of your ability as a weapon before I knew you, but it wasn't long until I saw that you are so much more. Someone who deserves to make her own choices. I offer you my sincerest apologies for thinking of you so wrongly, but I assure you, I don't think of you that way still." He bowed low from atop his horse. "Forgive me."

I could feel my heart want to harden against him. I was afraid to trust; afraid to allow myself to believe him. But then I looked at him—at a prince's low bow to a peasant girl—and I knew he hadn't meant to offend me. Was it the hunter's merciful side of me that thawed the ice of my heart? Whatever it was, my anger evaporated, leaving me exhausted beyond measure. "I forgive you," I said, and his shoulders dropped as if he'd been afraid I'd say otherwise.

"Then let us find the way out of these accursed woods and seek out our tents," Kharan said, pointing Daichin back the way we'd come.

Sasha urged his horse on, and then we wearily followed Kharan.

"It will be dawn soon," I said, glancing toward the sky already lightening in the east. "We will have little time for sleep."

"Have no worries about that," Sasha said. "We've made good time so far, so I don't think even Ivan will protest if I demand an extra day of rest."

I glanced back at him with a smile playing at my lips. How good a bed would feel after all we'd endured this day.

"*Now* I forgive you," I said, and the three of us laughed the laugh of those who have had too little sleep and far too much emotion.

But even as the laughter faded, unease still gripped me.

For this newfound power was a treacherous thing. Only time would tell how much it would cost me, but I knew it had already cost my freedom.

Chapter Nineteen

Sasha was true to his word and gave us a full day and another night to rest before we left again in the morning for Constantinople. Everyone must have needed the time to recuperate, because once we were back on the road, even the horses had far greater energy. Our pace was better than it had been in the beginning. Refreshed as I was, my mind was racing along, for I'd had far too much time to think.

All my life I'd thought that my mother—perhaps even my parents—had abandoned me to die. That they'd touched their infant baby and felt my ice-cold skin, hardening before them like marble, and recoiled in horror. I'd imagined they took me out to the woods because they could not bear to do the deed themselves. I'd always believed it was by the grace of God that

Babushka had found me. But now I saw that it was more than that. Winter had wanted me to be discovered, though this only led to more questions. How had she known my grandparents would find me? Had she sent word to them? And where was my father when Winter brought me to my grandparents' village?

Elation swooped lower from the sky, one golden eye on me. She was part of this, too, but I wasn't sure how. Was she the animal familiar Winter had chosen to keep watch over me? Golden eagles nested far to the north, so it wasn't outside the realm of possibility. She was intelligent enough to understand me, I was sure, but I wished she could communicate back.

The thoughts circled round and round in my head, distracting me completely. So it wasn't until long after we'd stopped in the middle of the day for a brief meal that I realized the landscape had changed. Everything around us was green and in bloom. Not only that, but it was warm—warm enough that even I could feel the difference in temperature. We approached a settlement in the distance, but it wasn't large enough to be Constantinople.

It was the tang of the salt in the air and the calls of birds I was unfamiliar with that hinted as to where we were before we ever crested the hills.

The sea.

And as the horses and wagons finally made it to the top of the highest hill, I saw the sea spread out before us. Endless water, waves crashing on the shore, a bright blue sky stretching above the midnight blue.

And ships. Everywhere, ships. There were several different types, but the most prevalent among them had square sails and hung low in the water.

Sasha rode his horse over to mine, a relaxed smile on his face.

"Where are we?" I asked, taking in the ships with wide eyes. I remembered a story Dedushka had told me about the first grand prince of Kievan Rus'—a Varangian, one of the men others called Northmen. They were strong fighters and expert tradesmen, and Dedushka had said they traveled as far as their ships could carry them.

Amusement danced in his silver eyes as he looked at me. "You didn't think we'd ride all the way to Constantinople, did you?"

I had, actually. I'd never learned the geography of the land beyond the woods of our village, so to me, the location of Constantinople might as well have been across a desert instead of a sea.

"We will sail across the Black Sea," he said.

A ripple of cold unease spread over my skin at the thought of sailing across such a vast body of water.

Elation flew past us, aiming for the sea as though wanting to look for herself at the water we would soon sail across. Seabirds fled the moment they saw her, screeching terribly in their fear.

"I have never been on a ship," I said, my hands tight on the reins.

"You will be safe, Katya," he said. "I have arranged for the greatest Varangian navigator to give us safe passage. I think you will find his wife and you have much in common."

My brows drew together at this pronouncement as I couldn't imagine what I would have in common with a Varangian sailor's wife, but I kept silent. I would soon see for myself, I was sure.

Sasha urged his horse on, and we followed. We wound slowly down the hills to the port town, and the closer we got to the ships, the more details I noticed. Carved runes, colorful shields over the sides, and dragon-headed prows. The most distinctive ship among all the others was one with a red skeletal dragon on its sail. It was the type of sailing vessel that instantly filled people with trepidation just laying eyes on it. This was the ship that Sasha led us to.

Sasha, flanked by Ivan and Boris, rode to where the ship was docked, just beyond the wooden pier. Waiting there was a tall, broad-chested man, his hair long and golden. He wore a black-and-silver tunic, but his arms were bare. His pants and boots seemed to be of the highest quality, and the claymore he wore by his side had a beautifully ornate hilt. It was clear he was no ordinary Varangian sailor.

As Sasha dismounted and clasped hands with the Varangian man, a woman came forth from the ship, dark in every way the Varangian was golden. Her hair was as black as night, and even from the little distance I was away, I could see that her eyes were dark as crow's feathers. She, too, was dressed in finery that suggested she was also not a simple sailor. She wore a dark-blue gown, heavily embroidered with silver threads, but it was unusually fashioned. There were no sleeves, and it was cut open at the skirt to reveal leather leggings and tall black boots. She also carried a sword, the hilt and pommel as black as her hair.

She clasped hands with Sasha, her gaze traveling to Elation flying overhead. She said something to Sasha then, and he gestured for me to join them.

I dismounted hesitantly, uncomfortable under the scrutiny of the two strangers.

"Katya," Sasha said when I approached, "this is Ciara, queen of Mide and Dubhlinn, and Leif Olafsson, king consort of Mide and Dubhlinn, and jarl of Bymbil and Skien."

A king and queen. If I could blush, I knew my face would be bright red. My body turned cold instead. I curtsied as best I could.

"Did I say all your titles correctly?" Sasha asked.

King Leif grinned. "You left out a few of our accomplishments—destroyer of giants, savior of worlds—but I suppose it's enough for now."

Queen Ciara glanced at her husband with what looked like exasperated amusement before turning those dark eyes back to me. "I asked about your eagle," she said, and I noticed that though she spoke the same language as I did, it was accented differently than the king's.

"Her name is Elation," I said, unsure again.

"And she is yours?"

My gaze slid to Sasha for just a moment. "She has accompanied me since I was a child."

"At least it's not a crow," King Leif said, and a smile played at Queen Ciara's lips. I could see it was a joke of some kind between the two of them, but it meant nothing to me.

"I know something of animal familiars," she said to me. "There is just something in her . . . eyes that caught my attention. She is highly intelligent, yes?"

For a moment, I considered lying, but I felt Sasha watching me too, so I dared not. "She is."

"Very interesting," Queen Ciara said, almost to herself. To me, she added, "She is beautiful and will be welcome aboard our ships should she need a place to rest."

"Thank you, highness," I said, relieved that Elation would be allowed on the ship with us—something I hadn't even considered when we first embarked on the journey.

"Your horses and supplies will go on the knarr," King Leif said, pointing at a ship with a much wider and deeper hull than the one with the skeletal dragon sail. "Everyone else will ride on my own ship."

"How long will it take us to arrive in Constantinople?" Sasha asked.

"A full day and night and the morning besides," King Leif said. "If the winds are favorable."

"It won't be a comfortable trip," Queen Ciara said, "but it will at least be quick."

King Leif shook his head. "After all I do to make sure you're comfortable, my queen, this is what you tell our passengers?" To Sasha and me, he added, "She has never liked to sail, so her opinion cannot be trusted."

"A Varangian who doesn't like to sail?" I asked, and then was horrified when I realized I'd spoken out loud.

King Leif laughed heartily, the sound ringing out across the shore. "Ciara, my love, what would you have done five years ago if someone had accused you of being a Northman?"

Queen Ciara only smiled and turned to me. "That is because I am not a Northman—a Varangian as you call them—at all. I am a Celt."

"The only beautiful Celt in all the world," King Leif added, and her eyes narrowed at him.

"My sisters are beautiful," she said.

The king made a noise of exasperation. "Yes, fine, your sisters are beautiful as well."

A Celt and a Varangian—I found myself fascinated because I had always heard they were bitter enemies. But as I watched them together, I wondered if the rumors had only been exaggerated, much as they were with the prince.

Lost in my own thoughts, I didn't hear the remainder of the king and queen's conversation with Sasha, but soon they finished and turned back to their ship. The breeze blew warm, salty air as Sasha came to my side.

"I chose them because no one will be able to guard us better," he said, his eyes narrowed against the glare of the sun. "And now that I know the truth of your abilities, I'm glad I chose two of the most powerful warriors the world has ever known."

I considered his words for a moment and thought about the thrum of power I felt in the air just being near the king and queen. "What elements do they control?"

"They don't, as far as I know. But the king is undefeated in battle, and the queen has the ability to overtake a man's mind and control him."

I felt my face pale. "What a terrible power."

"She has other abilities, they say, but some are more secretive than others. Perhaps Kharan has heard more. I had hoped that you might find comfort in knowing someone like her— someone with abilities considered frightening."

His comment was casual, but as I turned to look at him, *really* look at him, I could see that he wanted to help me. I couldn't remember a time someone had considered my feelings in any way, so this moved me.

"Thank you, Sasha," I said, and I meant it.

All this time we'd been together, and I still didn't know what to think of him. Prince and ruler? Friend and protector? And there was something else, something when he smiled at me or when our skin touched that seemed to thaw some of the ice inside.

It frightened me more than a queen who could control minds.

The ship was uncomfortable as promised, but I loved it all the same. There wasn't much room for us all, but the lilt of the ship and the spray from the sea, the wind in my hair, was all so new and exciting that for the first hour I did nothing but hang my head over the side to stare at the water below. I was on my own in a small space at the bow of the ship, or as alone as I could be in a ship full of people. King Leif had a full set of thirty men to row, and even this number seemed to be half of the ship's capacity. Sasha and the king and queen had all gone to the stern of the ship and seemed to be deep in conference. Kharan had found a seat near the bow of the ship, too, but she seemed to be as enamored with the water and waves as I was. Nearly all the prince's other men were on board the knarr, save Ivan and Boris, who stood near Sasha.

Elation flew above us, keeping pace with the ship, her wide wingspan casting a shadow across the middle of the ship.

I lost myself to the wind and the waves, images of my mother's story replaying in my mind, weaving themselves into the unbelievable fairy tale that was my birth story.

I didn't hear Sasha approach until his hand touched my shoulder. "Are you ill?" he asked, his voice gentle.

I glanced up at him with a smile as I realized he thought I was seasick. "No, I just wanted to feel the spray on my face."

He smiled back. "I'm glad to hear it because it would be miserable to spend the journey with a churning stomach." He gestured to the small bit of room beside me. "May I sit with you?"

"Of course," I said, and then almost immediately regretted it when the whole side of him was pressed up against me, blazing hot against my own cold skin. We had shed our heavy coats and were dressed in our lightest-weight tunics, so I could easily feel the hard muscles of his arm.

"I spoke to the queen about you," he said after a moment. "She is the one I told you of before—the one who may be able to help you with reaching the full potential of your powers."

My whole body tensed. This was what it always came back to with the prince: using my powers. "How kind of you," I said, and I couldn't keep the frost from my tone.

He looked surprised and then wounded, but I refused to thaw. "I wasn't thinking of what your powers could do for me. I was thinking of how you were almost unable to save yourself from Baba Yaga."

"It's hard for me to believe that, especially when you know now what I can do."

He reached for my hand, his warm and strong against my icy one. "I care for you, Katya. Not because of what you can do, but because of who you are. I can't even explain to you how I felt the moment that door to the bone witch's hut closed with you still inside." For a moment, he looked haunted. "I was ter-rified I'd never see you again. *You*. Not your power."

I glanced down at his hand gripping mine, a lump form-ing in my throat even as a strange warmth filled my chest. I thought of the fear that had held me in a vise when I'd believed the flaming rider would kill Sasha and Kharan. "I was afraid, too—afraid I wouldn't be able to stop the rider in time." Some of the ice coating my skin receded. "If the queen has advice for me, then I will gladly accept it."

"I'm sure she can help you," Sasha said, finally releasing my hand, albeit reluctantly.

"Your shoulder is better now?" I asked, my voice tight. It had been many days since I'd had to treat the wound; it was healing beautifully.

"Yes, thanks to you," he said. "Though I have to admit, I miss the excuse of having you come to my tent."

I glanced at him, and his gaze ensnared me, causing my breaths to come faster.

"Katya," an unfamiliar voice interrupted, and I looked up to find the queen watching us. Embarrassed, I tried to put some distance between the prince and me, but only ended up nearly falling off the bench for my efforts. If she noticed my awkward display, she thankfully didn't react to it. "Would you speak with me? I have heard there is much we have in common."

"Yes, Your Majesty," I said, and hastened to my feet.

She walked to the stern of the ship, where there were far fewer people and we could have relative privacy. "You have unique powers," she said, and it was a statement and a question both.

I flinched. "Unique is . . . a kind word for what they are, I think."

She looked at me knowingly. "You're afraid of them?"

I started to say that I was afraid of what they could *do*, but then I realized she was right. I was afraid of having any powers at all. "Yes."

"And have you struggled, then, with controlling them?"

I thought of all the many times I'd lost control over my powers once I'd fully unleashed them, but I also remembered my recent successes: against earth elementals and even Baba Yaga herself. "Yes, I have failed on many occasions, though I've managed to assert my will upon them lately, at least to some degree. What plagues me the most is how much it drains me."

"I was once like you," she said, her dark eyes taking on a far-away look. "Afraid of my powers, unable to understand them, which on one occasion, nearly cost me my life. Worse"—and now her gaze shifted to the king at the prow of the ship—"it nearly cost the life of the one I love."

She had my full attention now, as it was clear to anyone with eyes that the queen was someone who was formidable. "What did you do?"

"You must stop being afraid of your power," she said, turning back to me. "You are not a monster, Katya. I have known you for only a very short time, and even I can see that. But you think you are, and because of that, you hold yourself back."

To my horror, tears pricked my eyes. "You don't know what I've done," I whispered.

"It wouldn't change my opinion if I did. But know this: not having an understanding of your power will only cause you to continue to hurt people."

As if sensing my distress, Elation landed on the edge of the ship, mere feet from us. Her golden eyes bore into the queen's. I walked over to her and touched the soft feathers of her head. *Be still*, I thought, *I am only upset because I know she is right*.

"My power doesn't always listen to me," I said, surprised by how true that was. I thought of the times I'd tried to recall my power, only for it to ignore my attempts.

She watched me for a moment. "It was on this very ship that I learned to control my own power. Where someone much wiser than I said I had been using it all wrong. I had to completely relearn how to access it."

"How did you do that?"

She smiled, but the expression seemed to be toward a memory replaying in her mind rather than to me. "A woman who agreed to mentor me in it properly motivated me. You must do the same. In many ways, your power is like another being living inside you. And just like a person, you must find what motivates it. Only then will you learn to access its full potential."

"Did you ever stop being afraid of your own power?"

A knowing smile played across her lips. "Much more than that. I revel in it."

I thought of the terrible destruction I'd brought upon my village, of all the people I'd killed, and worse still, of the moment I'd been glad to bring justice upon those who had treated me so badly. Even now, the memory of that warm feeling sank teeth of guilt within me.

"If you'll let me," the queen said, "I'd like to help you learn more about your power. It's a part of you. It shouldn't be something you're afraid of."

I dipped my head in thanks. "I'd appreciate any help you can offer."

She gave me a small smile before walking away to join her husband at the bow of the ship.

Despite what the queen had said, I didn't think my power

would ever be something to delight in.

But I was more afraid of the day it would.

The queen left me alone with Elation and rejoined her golden husband at the prow of the ship. He wrapped his arm around her and drew her close, and despite her cool demeanor, she leaned into his touch. It was clear they didn't care who saw. I looked away though, feeling as though I'd witnessed something intimate.

The sun glinting off her blue-black hair, Kharan joined me at the stern of the ship. "It took everything in me not to shadow meld while she was talking to you," she said, her eyes on the dark queen. "I dared not because I was sure she'd be able to detect me."

My eyebrows arched at that. "You think she could see through even your shadow form?"

"I have no doubt," she said with no little awe. "They say the queen once commanded an army of undead soldiers—they had died, but she raised them with dark power and used them to conquer most of her land and the Varangian land besides."

A little shiver chased over my skin. It was difficult to believe, and yet I did believe it. Power rolled off both the king and queen in waves. "She would make a terrifying enemy."

Kharan nodded before leaning closer. "What did she say to you?"

"She gave me advice on how to better understand my power," I said hesitantly. "She said I'd have to overcome my fear and find what bests motivates me to use my abilities."

Kharan fell silent in thought for a moment. "That's true. Even with my shadow power, I had to learn not to be afraid of disappearing forever." She grinned. "But I got over that fear very quickly as a child."

I could imagine disappearing into the shadows might be frightening for a child at first. "How did you learn not to be afraid?"

"I discovered how fun it was to spy on people," she said, amusement dancing in her eyes. "Even in a small tribe, there are intrigues and conflicts—though perhaps minor compared to the ones in the palace."

"I envy you your power sometimes. I think it would have been useful to be able to disappear in my village."

Her mouth turned downward momentarily in sympathy. "Your village was truly awful. I've been wondering about that ever since we learned the truth of your parentage. Why that village? Why so far south? The Ice Queen must have had her reasons."

"She did have her reasons—the village was that of my father's parents. That was something I learned when Babushka left me her journal, but what I haven't been able to figure out is what happened to my father. Baba Yaga never said for sure that he was dead."

She turned her attention to Elation, who'd seemed to be tracking our conversation with her intelligent eyes. "If only Elation could tell you."

Elation flapped her wings mightily for a few moments before

taking off into the bright blue sky high above us.

"One other thing I've heard whispered of about the queen," Kharan said, "her mother is like yours—one of the Old Ones of her land. She is half-immortal, too."

"Half-immortal," I repeated. I looked again at the queen, wearing her power as easily as one wore a cloak. It was hard to believe I had anything in common with her. Yet she had taught her power to serve her, had both conquered and brought about peace.

What could I do with my own?

CHAPTER TWENTY

THE SKY WAS AWASH WITH A deep black when I awoke, the stars glittering above and below, diamonds reflected onto the dark blue of the sea. The sea was so calm, and the water so dark, that it looked like I could simply lean over the side and pluck a star right from the surface. It stole my breath; I didn't think I'd ever gazed on anything so beautiful. I wasn't sure what had woken me, but I couldn't be upset when it enabled me to appreciate such views.

I sat up slowly, noting the deep, slow breaths of Kharan beside me. King Leif had provided us with leather bags to sleep in, lined with soft fur. The king, I saw, was still awake, sitting close to the mast and gazing at the stars. Navigating, perhaps?

But as I continued to survey the ship, I noticed Sasha sitting nearby. The light of the moon and stars illuminated his face, and I could see he was deep in thought. As though I were the tide and he the moon, I found myself drawn to him. My heart beating unsteadily, I slithered out of my soft leather bag and stepped carefully over other sleeping forms to his side.

The starlight glinted off his light gray eyes, his hair dark as midnight, so that for a moment, he appeared as though he was wrought from the night sky itself.

He turned when he heard me approach, and the light in his eyes turned from cold starfire to warmth. "You couldn't sleep?"

The heat of his gaze seemed to transfer to my body until I nearly felt warm. "I could at first, but now I'm glad I did wake." My face tipped back toward the sky. "I don't think I've ever seen something so beautiful."

"I have," Sasha said, his eyes drawing me toward him again.

The quiet of our voices and the relative privacy we had with nearly everyone else asleep combined to make our conversation seem far too intimate. I was too afraid to ask what he meant. Too afraid I already knew. "You seemed lost in thought."

He mercifully didn't try to fight my change in subject. "I was thinking of how I haven't been to Constantinople since I was a child, of how I stayed in the imperial palace and was treated like the son of a princess of the Byzantine Empire." His face darkened. "But now I'm hardly welcome in the city, much less the palace."

I remembered what I'd heard about the Byzantines with-drawing their alliance with Kievan Rus', and my heart ached for the prince. Still, I wanted to hear the story from Sasha himself. I knew how badly rumors could be twisted. "Why have they barred you from the palace?"

A muscle flexed in his jaw, and his whole body tensed. "My blood kin believe I was capable of murdering my own parents, never mind that I was little more than a child at the time. They were both killed in their beds—stabbed—so it had to have been someone who knew the layout of the palace helping the assassin. The Byzantines believe that someone was me."

Kharan had told me as much before we left, but it meant a lot to hear it from Sasha—that he trusted me. The pain radiated off him, and I couldn't help but reach out and touch him if only for a moment. "How terrible to be accused of something you didn't do, and to your parents no less."

He glanced down at where I was touching his arm before looking back up with a ghost of a smile. "I'm surprised you believe me. Wasn't it you who feared I was the monster rumored about from village to village?"

"Yes, but that was before . . ." I trailed off, unsure what exactly I meant. Before I got to know him? Before I realized he was nothing like the beastly prince the rumors said he was?

"It's nice to be believed, though I know I little deserve it." He shook his head. "For all my sins, I would never do something so evil."

Kharan had once said that the assassin who'd killed his parents was a hired Varangian, but as I looked at the Varangian king, his form regal and strong in the moonlight, I knew he would never be hired as an assassin. He was too conspicuous and memorable. "Have you known the king and queen long?"

"No. I haven't known them at all, but only communicated through letters before this day. I knew we needed to sail to Constantinople, and the Varangians have an active trade route there through the Black Sea. I asked them when they next planned to sail into the city, and then I paid them a hefty sum for our passage."

I watched the wind rustle the skeletal dragon sail. "I hope it will be worth the price."

He smiled grimly. "They are the only reason we will be admitted into the imperial palace, but I plan to take full advantage of it."

I knew what it felt like to be exiled from a place where I should have been welcomed, and it twisted my heart to discover just how much the prince and I had in common. "I'm sorry you won't be admitted as the prince you are, Sasha," I said.

"If I can prevent the other princes from destroying Kievan Rus', then it'll be well worth the pain of being barred from my mother's city."

"What is the palace like?"

His expression softened in memory. "More beautiful than I can describe. So large it's like a city by itself, and more gold and marble than you've ever seen. I just remember being a child and thinking everything seemed impossibly enormous. My neck ached by the end of our visit there because I'd kept my face tilted upward the whole time. Then it was ruled by my grandfather, but now, two sisters are co-rulers."

"Two sisters ruling together?" I said in surprise. "I didn't know such a thing was possible. The palace sounds like it's just as astounding. I've never been anywhere at all, so I'm sure I'd be amazed even if it was little more than a hut."

He grinned. "It's as beautiful as the bone witch's hut was terrible."

"I'm glad you can joke about it," I said with a shudder. "I think I will have nightmares for years to come."

This time it was he who reached for my hand. "I only joke because it helps distract me from what nearly happened to you. I'll have nightmares of *that* for years to come."

His gaze turned warmer and warmer, until an answering warmth grew within me. He bent his head, and before I knew what he was doing, he pressed a kiss to the back of my hand. It was like being branded with fire, the way it thawed the ice that had risen to my skin at the thought of his lips touching me. It terrified me, but at the same time, my mind raced ahead. What would it feel like to have his lips on mine?

But something held me back. I thought of what I'd seen in the fire at the bone witch's hut. Winter, if she was indeed my mother, had ended up killing the man she loved by losing control over her power. What if I was destined to do the same?

Before, we'd been interrupted by the queen, but there was no one who would stop us this time.

"I should go back to sleep," I said, gently pulling my hand from his.

He looked down for a moment before nodding. "Of course."

"*Spokoynoy nochi*," I said, before turning back to the sleeping forms in the middle of the longship.

I risked one more glance at him before I lay back down, his strong form silhouetted against the starlit sky. He reminded me again of a wolf, though this time, it was of one that was very much alone.

At long last, we arrived in the port of Constantinople. The water was crowded with ships, and beyond that rose the great white city. I recognized the Varangian longships with their dragon-headed prows; the now-familiar knarr ships were there in abundance, too. There were other ships, ones I wasn't as familiar with, with three sets of rowers. They were even larger than the longships. Beyond the port itself, the most striking thing about the city was that it was entirely enclosed in white walls of marble. The walls were formidable, and it became readily apparent why the city had been, so far, impregnable.

Seabirds called to one another overhead, but Elation kept silent, staying perched near my side. The birds drew my gaze upward, and beyond the harbor, rising up from the first hill of the seven hills of the city, was an enormous structure surrounded by four towers and topped with a golden dome that glinted in the sun.

A warm breeze stirred my hair from where it lay heavy on my neck. We had all brought clothes appropriate for standing before the empress in the imperial palace. I wore a rubhaka of soft blue-and-gold silk, studded with pearls. It hung heavily on my body and was belted at my waist with a golden braid.

Peacock feathers were embroidered all over the fabric, and the neckline was fit for a princess, with pearls and blue sapphires. Yet underneath it all I still wore my deerskin boots.

Kharan, too, had donned her most elegant outfit, with what looked like a robe in the most gorgeous gold-and-black brocade. As she moved closer, the golden threads caught the light, shimmering like molten flame. It was covered with flowers, but there was something else among the blooms—an animal of some sort. A wolf?

"That's beautiful, Kharan," I said with a nod toward her elegant clothing.

"Thank you," she said with a relaxed smile.

"Another deel?"

She smiled. "You remembered. And yes, this one has the pattern of my tribe."

Sasha walked over to me, close enough that my breaths came a little quicker.

I tried not to think of the way he had kissed my hand, nor the way his gaze had captured mine. "Is that the palace?" I asked.

"No," he said, his voice rumbling in my ear, "that is the basilica of Hagia Sophia."

"A church! It's enormous."

He laughed. "The palace is much larger."

His laughter and the spectacular scenery seemed to loosen something within me, and I took a step toward the side of the ship and just breathed it all in. It wasn't long before King Leif's longship docked, and the two other ships that had accompanied his—the knarrs—did, too. Sasha helped me from the ship and onto a wooden pier, his hand lingering on mine so long I wondered if he would continue to hold it. Ivan soon joined us, though, and then he did release his hold, and the chill that returned to my hand felt like a cold gust of air after being seated in front of a warm fire.

The king and queen disembarked, and then they ordered their horses and ours as well brought forward from the knarr.

"Tell the others," Sasha said to Ivan while we waited on our horses, "only the five of us will accompany the king and queen. Everyone else must stay with the ships."

"Yes, Gosudar," Ivan said, striding off immediately toward the knarr.

A clatter of hooves announced the horses, and two let out piercing whinnies as though relieved to finally be on land again. Ivan brought Zonsara over to me, and as I stroked her soft neck, I watched the Varangians bring forth the king's and queen's mounts. They were both war chargers, at least two hands taller than my own mare and much wider. The queen mounted a horse as dark as night, and the king rode beside her on a stormy gray stallion. But even with such an impressive display, it was Sasha who held my attention on his blood bay mount. The prince's eyes surveyed the city possessively, his bearing tall and strong in the saddle, and it was as if a Byzantine prince was coming home. True enough, whether the Byzantines would accept that or not.

In the chaos of disembarking, I'd forgotten about Elation, but she let out a soft cry as she flew above me. Without thinking, I held out my arm, and she landed, gently.

"I don't want to leave her behind," I said to Sasha.

"Bring the eagle," he said. "She is tame enough with you that she will pose no problem, and I'm sure there have been stranger sights in this golden city than a girl and an eagle."

"Thank you, Gosudar," I said, slipping back into formal address now that there would be eyes upon us and ears to listen. But I touched my forehead to Elation's soft feathers before smiling at the prince, and his answering smile was warm. I knew he understood how much it meant to me.

With Kharan mounted on Daichin, and Ivan and Boris on their two horses, we followed the king and queen off the pier and toward the massive wall. The king and queen had come to discuss trade with the Byzantine Empire, and so they would accompany us to the imperial palace.

Though we were still outside the city proper, the sights and sounds of the sea were alive around us: fishermen shouting instructions to one another as they brought in great nets full of fish, ox-drawn wagons rattling along as they hauled their catches in a long line toward the city, and over everything, the smell of the sea, salty and distinctive.

We headed south along the wall a little way, until there before us stood a gate, one that was everything I would expect from this extravagant city.

"The Golden Gate," Sasha said beside me as I brought

Zonsara to a halt just to stare at it for a moment.

It towered above us, so high it would take Elation quite a few breaths to fly to the top. Zonsara barely reached the third marble block, and there must have been thousands. There were three archways, but we were headed for the one in the middle—the largest. It was flanked by columns so tall I could hardly make out the details on them, though I could see they were ornate. My gaze was continually drawn upward, until there at the very top, I saw six statues: four golden elephants trumpeting in the middle and two winged female figures on either side.

"What are those statues there?" I asked Sasha, pointing to the winged figures in particular.

"Winged Victories," he said. "They represent the fortune and triumph of the city."

It was becoming obvious why Sasha wanted to renew his alliance with the Byzantines. Their wealth and power was clear. We passed through the gate, and then it all lay before us: a city of marble and gold.

Inside were a great number of people, and though many were dressed the same in modest linen garments that were straight and undefined, the array of colors was beautiful. Reds, oranges, yellows, blues, greens—all in intricate patterns. There were others like us, though, who were clearly from other parts of the world, indicated by the different ways we dressed. It made me feel a little less distinctive in the extravagant rubhaka I'd chosen to wear.

We rode on and on, the narrow streets and the number of

people forcing us to ride single file. All around us were marble and columns and architecture I had no name for, but all were ornate and beautiful. There was a particular design that was repeated often: a peacock feather in the marble. It reminded me of something, and it took numerous sightings of it before I finally realized what it was: the firebird feather the prince kept with him.

But before I could think on that further, we arrived at the palace.

It would have been more accurate to say we arrived at a small city within Constantinople, for that is what it seemed like. There were buildings upon buildings encased within more marble walls with a gate guarded by men in armor with spears. Beyond the walls was the sea, shimmering with sun-kissed blue water.

The king and queen stopped to speak to the guards, and once we were all admitted, I saw that Sasha was quiet, that telltale muscle in his jaw flexing. I wanted to reach out to him, to tell him it would be all right, but of course I knew no such thing. Ivan and Boris rode past me, and soon Daichin walked beside Zonsara.

"We will have to watch the prince closely once inside the palace," Kharan said, her voice quiet. "There is nothing that makes him angrier than the accusation that he killed his parents, and I wouldn't put it past the empresses to do just that."

I thought of the tension coiled in his muscles already and tightened my hold on the reins. We had just passed through many examples of this city's power and strength. I wouldn't want to put it to the test. "Perhaps I can freeze him if he cannot restrain himself," I said, and Kharan snorted a laugh.

I was only half-joking.

We rode by yet another colossal structure, this one like two elongated horseshoes joined together. I looked at it in wonder, sure I'd never seen anything like it.

"That's the Hippodrome," Kharan said when she caught me staring. "The Byzantines hold races there. They actually let everyone come to watch. Like the Roman Colosseum of old."

All was quiet now as we passed, but I could imagine what such an enormous structure sounded like when it was full of screaming people.

On and on we rode, winding past countless buildings of marble. At long last, we came to a building at the rear of the complex, with a dome for a roof and so many windows they sparkled like diamonds within the marble blocks. More guards waited, and when they caught sight of the king and queen, they marched down to greet them.

"We have come at the invitation of the Empress Zoe and the Empress Theodora," Queen Ciara said, and the guards bowed their heads in acknowledgment.

Grooms appeared as though magically summoned, and they held the king's and queen's horses while they dismounted.

"Please allow us to bring your horses to the imperial stables," the lead groom said, and soon there was a servant for every one of our mounts.

A boy a year or so younger than I came to take Zonsara. He eyed Elation warily. "The imperial palace has a mews," he said uncertainly, but I shook my head.

"Thank you, but the eagle stays with me."

A guard came forward, then, with more insignia upon his tunic than all the rest had. "We cannot allow you to bring such a dangerous creature into the palace. It could be a threat to the empresses."

I could understand his reasoning, but still, I couldn't bear to send her to an unknown mews, blinded and tied to a post. "Then I will wait outside with her."

Sasha appeared by my side. "Of course you will not wait outside. You wanted to see the palace."

"Weapons are permitted as long as they are kept sheathed," the guard said, "but we cannot allow a potential weapon with wings into the throne room."

"It'll be fine," I said to Sasha, while trying not to look longingly at the palace.

The sound of boots on marble announced Queen Ciara's presence as she walked up to the guard. He looked at her, his gaze ensnared. "I can vouch for this girl that her bird will pose no danger to the empresses."

Very slowly, the guard nodded his head.

Queen Ciara smiled. "Thank you. Now, will you show us the way to the throne room?"

She took a step back, and the guard stood blinking for a moment, his face pale. "Yes, this way," he said, and he sounded like a man just awakening from a dream.

There was a part of me that wondered if she'd used her power just now, but I didn't stop to analyze it. In truth, I didn't want to know.

When the horses were taken away, we followed the guards up the steps and into the palace. If the city itself had been ornate, then the palace was extravagant. Mosaics were embedded in the walls, with images of not only the saints and Christ, but also unusual depictions. One was of two hounds catching a frightened hare, and as I had once been hunted like a rabbit myself, it made me shudder. Even the furniture was impressive: overly large and carved beautifully, containing vases studded with gemstones, sculptures wrought from precious metals, even figures carved from ivory and onyx.

As we continued to walk down the polished marble hall, we passed a forest of columns, the same peacock feather design found within. But just before we reached the throne room, another mosaic stopped me. It was of the firebird; this time I was sure of it. Its wings were outstretched, and fire surrounded it. The mosaic was done in reds, oranges, and yellows, and surrounding the whole piece was gold that gleamed in the light of all the lamps.

A warm hand touched my arm, and I turned to find Sasha waiting for me.

"I may be imagining this, but it seems like this whole city has an interest in the firebird," I said.

He gazed at the mosaic, sorrow pulling at the edges of his

mouth. "This was commissioned by my mother before she left for Kiev. It was she who had an interest in it." He walked away as though looking at the mosaic pained him, and I followed after one last glance.

Before us, the king and queen were being admitted into a room beyond a wide archway. The moment I followed them through the door, my breath caught in my throat. Soaring above me was the same dome I'd seen from outside, but now it was a ceiling of golden mosaics depicting a holy scene of Christ and the angels. From afar, the colors used were incredibly lifelike, such that it seemed like God himself was gazing down on us.

Guards and servants lined the walls, each standing in front of a marble column of the circular room. At the far end were two ivory thrones, upon which sat two empresses. One was fair and beautiful, even in her old age, and the other was younger and plain, but with kind eyes. It was hard, though, to note the features of either's face as they were both covered head to toe in gold and precious gems. Both wore ornate golden crowns, heavily filigreed and studded with rubies, emeralds, and sapphires. Their kaftans and tunics were gold and vibrant purple, with emeralds and pearls sewn directly into the silk brocade. Both of their kaftans were beautifully embroidered: the younger empress's kaftan had a depiction of the Blessed Mother with the Christ Child, and the older empress's kaftan had a floral scene of red roses with sharp green thorns.

Aside from their beautiful clothing, they wore matching

looks of lofty indifference, as though they were carved statues themselves.

The guards first announced that we were in the presence of the Empresses Zoe and Theodora, two sisters who reigned together on the throne—I couldn't help but admire the obvious power of these two women. We bowed or curtsied before them—some of us lower than others, according to rank. The two empresses regally nodded their heads at the king and queen, but when the guard announced Sasha's name, a crack of emotion ran through the perfect facade of their still expressions.

"King Leif Olafsson and Queen Ciara of Mide, you are most welcome here," the older Empress said, the one named Zoe. "We have waited for the chance to open trade with two people known the world over for their trade prowess."

"The pleasure is ours," Queen Ciara said with a dip of her head.

"We very much look forward to speaking to you about how we can both benefit from such an alliance; however"—her eyes narrowed at Sasha—"I don't remember extending an invitation to the prince of Kievan Rus'."

King Leif glanced back at Sasha. "Surely he isn't unwelcome here. Are you not kin?"

The empress lifted her head even higher in the air. "Distantly. His grandfather was emperor once, but he is no longer living. My sister and I are from a different bloodline, and the prince is very much one of a kind." She glanced at him pointedly. "Now."

The implication was clear: he was alone now because his parents were dead. I thought of what Kharan had said about the prince's temper when it came to his parents' deaths and slid my gaze to him cautiously.

"Even the other princes—the Drevlian and Novgorodian—have cut ties with him," the empress continued.

"Well, he is here now," Queen Ciara said, and all eyes fell upon her. She had a way of commanding a room. "And so he will remain until we set sail again in two days. The faster you hear what he has to say, the faster he will leave."

Empress Zoe's face suddenly looked pinched. It was Empress Theodora, though, who next spoke. "What is it you seek, Prince Alexander?"

"I have come because this empire was once an ally of Kievan Rus'. We are in the midst of a war—the boyars are being over-whelmed, their land seized, their people taken and sold by the very men who should be protecting them—and our enemies move ever closer to Kiev. Soon, we will be overtaken."

Empress Zoe lifted her eyebrows as if to say, *And so?* "For-give me, Prince Alexander, but I fail to see why I should lend you aid and risk my own people. As you said, my empire was *once* allied with yours. But then a Byzantine princess—your mother—was assassinated. Her line has been severed. The party responsible should bear the burden."

My gaze flicked to Sasha's, my heart constricting at the empress's harsh words.

"As the son of a Byzantine princess, I am requesting your

help," the prince said, and I could see by the set of his shoulders that it was a blow to his pride to have to continue to ask for help, but he did it for his people.

"Even if I recognized you as such and we could determine that you are entirely innocent, what would my empire have to gain through alliance with yours? By your own account, it seems you have nearly been overtaken."

"Because my enemies aren't the only ones who have people with power fighting for them," he said, tension evident in the stiffness of his shoulders. "We would fight on behalf of the Byzantine Empire should we be called to arms."

I glanced at Kharan to see if she was surprised by Sasha's words, but she only continued to look at the empress. Was Kharan willing to fight for the Byzantines?

Empress Zoe smiled, but it was a cold, mean gesture. "I have heard whispers that you were amassing your own army, but I doubt very much you have found people with the same scope of power as the Drevlian and Novgorodians have, nor so many."

I stared at the prince, unable to help myself. Ice burned across my body, freezing my skin. Would he mention me and tell her of my cold fire? What would she say then?

"Then you refuse to uphold the alliance forged when my mother married my father?" he said, and the ice receded—marginally.

"Our alliance died with them."

The prince's hands curled into fists beside me, and very slowly, I reached out to touch his arm. *Peace*, I thought. Heat radiated off him, and my body answered with a biting cold that poured from my skin.

His voice sounded restrained as he answered. "Then I have one last request." He waited for a moment until she nodded once before continuing. "I would like to speak to anyone who knew my mother, and especially those considered to know her best."

She tilted her head at him from the throne. "Hm. Are you planning a coup?"

"I have my reasons for wanting to seek them out," he said, his voice barely more civil than a growl, "but you have my word I mean no harm to anyone in this city."

"How reassuring it is to have your word on that," Empress Zoe said, "because prince or no prince, you'd be arrested and tried for murder just like anyone else."

Peace, I thought again as his arm twitched beneath my hand.

"I understand," he said with what sounded like great effort to be civil.

On her throne, Empress Theodora stirred. "There is someone in the palace who knew your mother well. Aemilia, a servant who was once handmaiden to the princess."

She nodded toward a nearby hovering servant, who hurried to her side. She whispered something to him, and he strode away purposefully.

Empress Zoe shot her sister a glare.

"Thank you, Empress," Sasha said, and this time he sounded sincere.

The empress's gaze fell upon me, rooting me in place. "You there, girl. You are very brazen to bring a bird of prey such as that into our throne room. Though it seems tame enough."

Elation watched the empress without blinking, but stayed motionless.

"She will pose no harm, Empress," I said, pulling the arm that Elation was currently perched on closer to my chest.

"That is a relief that my sister and I will not be attacked in our own palace." She turned to the nearest guard. "I'm surprised one of the guards didn't stop you bringing such a weapon here." Her voice rang out across the throne room, filled with disparagement.

The guards said nothing, but I saw a few shift uncomfortably. It reminded me of the lead guard we'd encountered before we entered the palace, and it confirmed that Queen Ciara had influenced the guard's decision about Elation.

"Now then," Empress Zoe said, turning back to the king and queen and very clearly dismissing Sasha, "tell us what you've brought."

While the king and queen regaled the empresses with all the goods they'd brought for trade on the other heavily laden knarr, the rest of us followed Sasha to an alcove to wait for the handmaiden.

"You did well bearing the empress's provocation," Kharan said to Sasha, her arms crossed over her chest.

Sasha glanced at me. "Katya had a hand in keeping me calm. I felt the anger rise in me like smoke from a fire, but then it was like it was doused by cold water."

I was taken aback. Had I truly been able to influence him as I'd imagined? Though it must have been the same as when I was able to lower his fever.

"Say the word, Gosudar, and I will gladly show these empresses just how powerful the prince of Kievan Rus' is," Boris said, with a mad grin.

"You're a fool," Ivan said in a growl. "Be silent. That's how you'll help us best."

Boris let out a petulant grunt but said no more.

Before long, the servant returned with the handmaiden. She was young, though still older than I, with dark hair and eyes and dressed in a beautifully embroidered linen tunic in the Roman style with a gold pin to hold it in place. When I looked closer, I realized the pin was of a firebird with wings outstretched.

As soon as she laid eyes on the prince, her eyes began to shine as though she was holding back tears. "Your Highness," she said, bowing her head. "I am Aemilia, your mother's hand-maiden. I'm sure you don't remember me, but I remember you. When you last visited this city, you were only a child. How you look like your mother now! It both pains me and brings me such joy to look upon her beloved face again."

Sasha reached out and touched Aemilia's slim shoulder. "I do remember you—you made sure I had a steady supply of sweets. For that, I am eternally grateful."

She laughed. "It was the least I could do."

"Will you help me again?" he asked, his gaze turning serious.

"Of course."

He glanced around, and I followed his line of sight to the nearest guard, who was out of the range of hearing—but only just. Sasha leaned closer and lowered his voice. "I've come seeking information on the firebird."

I thought of the feather illuminating the prince's trunk on board the ship, and the flames that he could summon from his palms. In spite of myself, curiosity gripped me.

Aemilia closed her eyes for a moment, as if saddened, before nodding. "I will help you, but we will have to leave the palace complex. The information you seek is in the heart of the city, guarded by a sorcerer of considerable strength."

Cold spread over my skin. First the bone witch and now a sorcerer?

"He'll be no match for us," Boris said.

"Be silent, fool," Ivan growled.

Aemilia shook her head. "You misunderstand me. He has been waiting for you, guarding your mother's secrets."

"Lead on, and we will follow," Sasha said.

Aemilia bowed once and strode away purposefully. The others and I followed. As we walked, I thought of what the empresses had said, how any hope that the Byzantines would help us had been dashed. Now the only hope left was that Sasha would learn about his power.

Earth will only fall to fire and ice.

I had to pray it was true.

Chapter Twenty-One

Aemilia led us through the labyrinth of narrow streets in the heart of the city. We wove past both grand buildings like we'd seen before and smaller buildings that were becoming increasingly run-down. Eventually, we were surrounded by nothing but ramshackle homes, some without doors. Ragged cloth served as a sort of curtain that hung in the doorway to give a modicum of privacy. Here there were no columns, no ornate carved marble statues, nor shiny gold. This part of the city looked like it was in a different world from the one we'd just seen.

We'd left behind the king and queen with the empresses, and now it was only the five of us: Sasha, Kharan, Ivan, Boris, and me. I stayed next to Kharan, just behind Aemilia, while

Ivan and Boris flanked Sasha.

At long last, Aemilia stopped before a house that was perhaps slightly less ramshackle than the rest. It had a true door, one of wood, and above the doorframe were symbols painted in gold: a feather, the moon, a sword, and an eye.

Aemilia glanced around her before taking a step forward and knocking once on the door. A man, one I couldn't see with any clarity for it was dark and gloomy within the house, answered. Aemilia spoke to him for a moment in their language, and then she turned to Sasha.

"This is the home of Septimus, the sorcerer I spoke of. There isn't much room within, so perhaps it would be better to leave one or two people outside if you don't mind."

"Ivan, Boris," Sasha said, "please keep watch out here."

Sasha stayed by my side as we followed Aemilia into the house. Kharan came last, closing the door behind her.

The inside of the house was cramped, and even without Ivan and Boris, we took up nearly the entire space. It was lit only by a few candles, so it was difficult to see anything clearly. There was only a narrow cot, a single chair, and a table, but the rest of the house was filled with a variety of containers: copper urns and clay bowls and ceramic pots. Many were beautifully embossed with intricate designs or with painted scenes of flora and fauna.

"Prince Alexander," Septimus said, his voice tired and gravelly, "you are welcome here."

He stepped more into the light, and I could finally see his

face—old and lined, but with a strong bone structure that suggested he had once been very handsome. His hair was gray and cut short, his clothing simple but clean.

Sasha bowed his head. "I'm relieved to hear you speak our language; my Latin and Greek are barely passable."

"I have made a study of languages to better be able to speak to any who come to my house, just as I learned yours to be able to speak with you."

Sasha leaned toward the old man. "You knew I would seek you out?"

"Not in the way I'm sure you're imagining. I don't have the Sight, but your mother wrote to me and said one day you would come looking for answers, and I was to provide you with the means of attaining them."

I glanced at Kharan to see if she was making sense of this—of why his mother would go to such lengths rather than tell the prince herself. I could see Sasha wondering the same, and Kharan's dark eyebrows were drawn together as though she was as confused as I was.

"We knew you weren't to blame for what happened to your parents," Aemilia said softly, "for your mother had suspected their lives were in danger, and it certainly wasn't from their only son."

"What she couldn't foresee, however, was when the terrible event would occur," Septimus added, "and for a while, she hoped she was wrong. She told us that she was merely acting on suspicions that couldn't be proven, but she wanted to plan for the worst just in case."

"And I failed you," Aemilia said, tears falling freely down her cheeks now. "I failed to come and take you away like the princess asked of me. She knew how it would be for you if they were killed; she knew you'd stand accused. But word didn't reach the palace until weeks after it had happened, and the empress forbade anyone from going to Kiev. All trade from the port was blocked."

"By then I was old enough that people could suspect me of being guilty—sixteen is old enough to kill one's parents," Sasha said bitterly. "You shouldn't blame yourself, though, Aemilia," he added. "I couldn't have abandoned Kiev and my people even if you'd offered to take me away."

"And now forces gather to challenge your rule," Septimus said.

"Yes, which is why I seek information on the firebird. With its strength, I might have the chance to defend Kiev the way I should."

Septimus nodded thoughtfully. "What do you know of the firebird?"

"Very little. I know it's likely not a bird at all," he said with a glance at me, "but instead someone with a powerful fire elemental ability. I have fire elemental ability, but it's nothing compared to what the firebird can do. My mother made it seem as though my power could grow, but not until I took the throne. I thought if I could find the firebird, then maybe I could learn to unlock my own power, but though I've tried to uncover the secrets of my mother's family and even of the feather passed down to her by her own mother, I've never been able to." And then he reached inside his tunic and retrieved the gleaming feather, which lit up the small hut like the sun.

"The firebird feather," Aemilia said breathlessly. "I haven't seen it since the princess was a child."

"It's not, actually," Septimus said, and all of us turned to him with matching expressions of confusion.

"It's not . . . what?" Sasha asked.

"That's a peacock feather and not a firebird feather at all."

Sasha's expression turned confused and then angry in rapid succession. "How could it be a peacock feather? No peacock I've ever seen has glowed like this."

"I think a demonstration would help to illuminate the situation." Septimus turned away toward a cabinet and opened its doors. From within, he retrieved a gold box.

When he opened the box, a single flame was inside, floating slightly above the bottom of the box, and burning as though lit by some phantom source. It flickered softly, but its light was as bright as the feather Sasha held.

"May I?" Septimus asked, holding out his hand for the feather. Reluctantly, Sasha handed it to him, watching him closely all the while.

Holding the feather by the quill, and the box in the other hand, he dipped the feather into the flame. Sasha hissed in his breath, and Aemilia cried out, but all of us fell silent when we saw that the feather didn't burn.

"Explain," Sasha said, the flame reflecting in his eyes, turning them golden instead of silver.

"This is a peacock feather infused with the flame of a firebird," Septimus said, twisting the feather this way and that. It was none the worse for wear despite having been dipped in fire. "You were right when you said before that the firebird wasn't a creature at all, but a person. But a true fire elemental is so rare that the legends have gotten the story slightly wrong, as legends do. A fire elemental has such complete control over fire that he or she can command it not to burn. Thus, an everlasting flame can be created from almost anything."

I glanced down at Elation, thinking of the bird who had given that feather. "Even an animal?"

Septimus considered for a moment. "I would venture to say yes. That is likely how the story of the firebird being an actual bird began."

Sasha stared at the feather like his entire world had suddenly shifted. "Do you know how my mother came to have this, then?"

"It was passed down in her family, from the one who carried the blood of a fire elemental."

"What are you saying?" Sasha asked, and when he glanced at me, I knew he was thinking of the small flames that he could summon—the ones he could never command to grow larger. "That I'm kin to a fire elemental?"

"I'm saying you're the descendent of one," he said. "Your mother knew it ran in her bloodline, for her father, the emperor, had that power. It tends to skip a generation, which meant that the chances of you having it were extremely likely."

Sasha looked stunned. "Why wouldn't she have told me? All this time . . ."

"There is only one way to determine if you are a fire elemental or not." Septimus held the golden box aloft. "You must walk through fire. I doubt your mother wanted to entrust such a secret with you before you were ready, when you might have tried to do that very thing. And what if your father's blood was enough to dilute your mother's? What if you walked through the flames and burned to death? She wouldn't have risked such a thing."

"And then she was killed," Sasha said, his voice pained.

"She knew she might not be able to convey these family secrets to you herself, so she put things into motion that would allow you to discover the truth about yourself when it was time." He held the box toward Sasha so that it illuminated him, the flame dancing off the strong bones of his face. "Do you wish to see if you have this power within you?"

"Yes," he said without hesitation.

I glanced at Kharan, who by her expression, seemed to be feeling the same amount of dismay. "Gosudar," she said, "might it not be better to be cautious?"

He didn't answer her, but instead turned to Septimus. "What happens if I do not have the power of a fire elemental?"

"You will burn."

This did not seem to alter his decision in the slightest, for he only nodded.

"Why does the prince have to enter fire to access his power?"

I asked Septimus, thinking of my own. I'd been born with my power.

"Do you remember tales that a firebird must rise from the ashes of its predecessor? For it, the fire does not destroy, but rather gives it life. It's the same for a fire elemental. The fire is purifying, life-giving. It will bring the power that lies dormant in the prince's blood to the surface."

"*If* he has enough of that blood," Kharan said with a heavy dose of skepticism. "Otherwise, it'll just burn him alive."

Sasha sent her a silencing look. "I can summon a small flame and it's never burned me. I must do this. It's worth the risk if it means I might be granted the power to defeat our enemies."

Septimus bowed his head once. "Then come, we must go deep within the earth, to a place outside the city, where we will be safe from the flames and from prying eyes."

"That sounds like a tomb," Kharan said.

Both Septimus and Sasha ignored her, but I had to hope that wasn't some sort of premonition. If Aemilia was unsure about the test the prince must complete, she didn't show it. No one in this city seemed to be on our side, so I had trouble believing they were just because they said so.

"Wait," I said as Septimus turned toward the door. "Forgive me, but is there some way you can prove that you're acting on the princess's wishes? You have that flame, I know, but how are we to know how you obtained it?"

I expected a reprimand from Sasha as Septimus turned to me with gray eyebrows raised, but he only waited for Septimus to respond.

"You didn't look at the inscription on the box," he said, handing it back to the prince.

Sasha took it and carefully turned it over. "*Pro filio meo Sasha: de cinere surgebis*," he read aloud slowly. "For my son Sasha: from the ashes you will rise."

He met my gaze, and his eyes were full of wonder, as though his mother had resurrected before us and spoken the words herself.

"She believed in you," Septimus said quietly, "and I do, too."

"Does this convince you, Katya?" Sasha asked, and by his sincere tone I could see he truly wanted me to answer.

I thought of what the bannik had said about fire and ice. I thought of the flames around Sasha's palms that had never burned him. But most of all, I thought about how he had helped me when I wanted to discover who my mother was. Who I really was. "Yes," I said.

Sasha nodded once. "Then let us go."

The others went out the door, but before I could follow, again Sasha took my arm in his. The heat of him was enough to be felt through my clothing.

I watched him for a moment. "Did you suspect the truth—that you were the firebird?"

"No, but I thought my mother knew of its location. That was before I realized it wasn't a creature at all—thanks to you."

I nodded thoughtfully. "And do you think you're going to burn to death?" I hoped I was only saying this in jest.

He grinned. "I hope not, but if I do catch on fire, perhaps

you can douse the flames with your ice?"

"I suppose I can lend you my aid," I said with an answering grim smile, "but let's hope it doesn't come to that."

We followed Aemilia and Septimus as they led the way through the city to the marble quarry, where we would see if Sasha would rise from the ashes—or be burned to death in front of our eyes.

As the sun began to dip toward the horizon, we reached the very outskirts of the city, high atop the hills, where the marble quarry was located. The entrance to the quarry was made up of enormous marble blocks that stood far above our heads, roughly cut into rectangles instead of the polished designs found in the city. The workers had already left for the day, but Septimus lit the torches at the entrance. In front of us was a doorway of darkness, so deep the torches did nothing to illuminate what was within.

"Once inside," Septimus said, "we will be surrounded by marble so thick, the flames won't be able to escape."

"Then what will you use to make a fire?" Kharan asked.

"You will see," Septimus said, already moving toward the dark doorway. "Prince Alexander, if you will open the golden box and hold it aloft, we'll be able to find our way even in this darkness."

Sasha did as he was asked, and the flame was so bright, we could suddenly see all the way to the back of the entrance, where a ladder leading down waited. We kept close to the prince and the light as we made the long descent.

When at last we reached the bottom of a great marble cavern, every movement echoed loudly, and the darkness would have swallowed us were it not for the single flame in the golden box. The prince held it aloft, and when he came across torches, he bent to light them, but Septimus's loud voice stopped him.

"Do not use that flame!" Instead, Septimus brought forth a tinderbox and lit them with that. "That flame you're holding would burn through the torch and possibly eat through the marble itself."

A trickle of fear ran down my spine at the prospect of such power. It was like my own, wild and untamed.

"Then how am I to walk through it if you cannot light anything with it?" Sasha asked, his tone sharp.

"I will show you," Septimus said.

He stepped forward to the center of the cavernous space, far from all of us, who were pressed against the wall of marble. Kharan was beside me, while Ivan and Boris flanked Sasha, both radiating their displeasure at this turn of events. Neither wanted their prince to take such a risk, but he had been deaf to their concerns. Aemilia stood apart from us, watching closely.

Septimus raised his hands and spoke two words in Latin: *"Rete luminus."*

A net of light appeared before us, woven into the air itself, glowing a soft blue that reflected dully off the marble like a bruise. I glanced at Kharan, and I was sure my expression matched her look of awe.

Septimus gestured for Sasha to bring the flame to the net. "Now you may light it."

Sasha held the golden box with the flame close to the net of light, and instantly, it caught on fire, blazing like an inferno. The heat was terrible, enough that even I could feel it penetrate the frost that covered my skin.

I felt the cold rise in me in answer, coating my body in ice to combat the heat. I took a step toward Sasha, concerned that his clothes would catch on fire as close as he was.

As though he'd heard my thoughts, Septimus said, "You will have to disrobe, Prince Alexander. The flames will destroy your clothing."

"I must walk through the flames naked?" he asked, a nervous grin playing at the edges of his lips.

"Yes," Septimus said.

The prince took off his clothes without hesitation, beginning with his beautifully embroidered tunic. It fell to the cavern floor, and the reflection of flames danced over his skin. I turned my gaze away, only to find Kharan watching dispassionately, as though this was something she saw every day. Ivan and Boris wore similar expressions, though perhaps Ivan watched the net of flames with a touch of nervousness. Aemilia was the only one who had her eyes averted. I dared to look again, and now Sasha was completely naked, his back to the rest of us, facing the fire before him.

The muscles in his back flexed, and I tried not to let my gaze stray lower.

It seemed we all held our breaths. The quarry was heavy with tension.

The prince glanced back at me over his shoulder, just once, and as our gazes caught and held, I was glad I hadn't averted my eyes. He gave me a confident flash of teeth, and then he strode through the flames.

A cry escaped my lips despite myself, for the fire blazed so powerfully we all had to shield our eyes. When I could look again, I saw nothing but the flames, and my breath hitched in my throat.

Had it burned him to ash?

That last smile he'd given me kept replaying in my mind over and over until tears welled in my eyes and then froze against my ice-cold skin.

Suddenly a figure stepped toward us from the other side of the net, orange and red and gold flames creating the image of a man, one made entirely of fire. None of us said anything, none of us breathed. It was as if I'd frozen us all.

Only Septimus was capable of movement, and with the golden box outstretched, he walked toward the fiery figure of Sasha. "You must touch the fire again."

A finger made of flame reached for the box. The moment he made contact with the fire inside, the flames receded from his body with a powerful *whoosh*, as though a tempest had manifested in the quarry.

Sasha was left completely untouched by the fire that had raged over his body—his hair and skin without ash or singe.

But naked. Very, very naked.

Ivan was the first to recover, to bring the prince his clothing, but still Sasha remained unembarrassed. "I didn't burn," he said with wonder. "Katya, did you see?"

"Yes, Gosudar," I said, keeping my eyes on the floor. He seemed in no hurry to put his clothes back on.

"Gosudar, there are ladies present," Ivan reminded him gently when Sasha merely stood and stared at the net of flames.

"Oh yes," Sasha said distractedly, finally consenting to being clothed again.

Septimus raised his hands over the net of light and dispelled it with a few muttered words. He turned toward the prince. "The fire recognized the power in your blood. It will obey you now."

Sasha glanced down at his own hands like he'd never seen them before. He held them, palms up, and suddenly, twin flames as bright as the peacock feather sprang to life above his hands.

He met my gaze, a slow smile overtaking his face as the light of his flames turned his silver eyes golden.

There was no mistaking it now:

The prince was the firebird.

Chapter Twenty-Two

Septimus led us back out of the quarry, and we emerged to find that the world had darkened around us. Elation flew over as soon as she caught sight of me, having waited at the entrance for us. The moon rose like a beacon in the night sky, but even its luminance was challenged by the lights of the city, which spread before us, twinkling like the stars as lamps and torches burned.

I couldn't stop imagining the prince as a man on fire, consumed by flames and yet still alive.

"I cannot thank you enough for your help, Septimus," Sasha said, and the sorcerer bowed his head.

"It was my pleasure to help you unlock your family's legacy. I hope it will serve you well in protecting your land and its people."

"We may not be welcome at the imperial palace," Sasha said, "but there must be somewhere we can find a good meal."

"The finest food in the Mediterranean can be found here," Septimus said. "I know of an inn that has the best fish and wine."

"Will you join us? And you, Aemilia?" Sasha asked. "I would like to thank you both properly."

"It would be my pleasure," Septimus said.

"Of course," Aemilia said with a bow.

We were silent as we followed Septimus back through the city, all still in shock, it seemed, from what we'd witnessed. Ivan kept sneaking Sasha looks like he was afraid he'd suddenly combust.

"This could make all the difference," Kharan said to me, her expression calculating. "Fire is strong against earth."

I thought of Sasha walking through flames hot enough to burn through marble, and hope blossomed within me. The Byzantines had refused to aid us, but perhaps his newfound power would be more than enough.

The city was still alive, even at this time of night. We passed many people traveling through the streets, some returning home after a long day's work, some visiting shops that were still open, and others seemed to be exploring the city as we were. Only this time, we didn't have far to go. Septimus led us to an inn on top of one of the seven hills of the city, where he spoke a few words to the innkeeper, and we were immediately ushered to the roof.

It was readily apparent why such a location was chosen for anyone who came to the inn to dine, for the whole city stretched before our eyes. In the distance, I could make out the domed roof of Hagia Sophia and the tall columns of the imperial palace.

Sasha ordered a feast of seafood, fresh greens, herbs, bread, and olive oil to be brought to the rooftop. He even remembered Elation and gave her a leg of goat to eat, which she graciously accepted.

It was the freshest-tasting fish I'd ever eaten, delicately cooked in butter and wine and herbs. The bread was light instead of dark, and the olive oil was liberally poured over everything.

"This is delicious," Boris shouted after almost every bite, all trace of his seasickness gone, and his appetite returned in full force. "Is it not?" he asked, and we all nodded, mouths full.

"It may even be more delicious than anything you've made," Kharan said, a teasing smile pulling at the corner of her lip.

Boris dropped his knife, a line of worry creased between his brows. "Are you serious?"

"No, of course not," she soothed as she poured herself another glass of wine.

Satisfied that his own cooking skills were not inferior, he turned his attention to the innkeeper and spent nearly half an hour asking every detail of the preparation of the meal. The innkeeper was patient, though, and answered his every question. When he was finally able to extricate himself from the conversation, he walked over to Sasha and bowed.

"If His Highness would permit, there are musicians staying here who would like to play for you." It was clear that Septimus had told the innkeeper that Sasha was a prince, and we were being treated well accordingly.

"Yes, send them up," Sasha said.

The innkeeper bowed again, left, and returned a few minutes later with a trio of musicians: two men and one woman. All three wore elaborately brocaded tunics with colorful geometric patterns; they were similarly styled, except the woman's tunic had very full sleeves. She was veiled, but her dark hair peeked out at the top of her forehead, and her eyes were shining with anticipation. She carried no instrument at all, and I wondered if she would be singing. One of the men, his beard neatly trimmed, carried a lyra, a stringed instrument that had the most hauntingly beautiful sound—I'd heard it before in my own village. The other man carried a slim reed instrument that I'd never seen before.

They tuned their instruments for a moment in the corner of the roof, and then they began, their song slow and lilting. It was like the night sky, dark and intense. But then the woman opened her mouth and sang, the words unknown to me, and the tempo increased until it was like a tempest swirling in the darkness. The music moved through me, making my heart beat until it followed the same fast-paced rhythm.

My gaze was drawn to the prince, and as I glanced his way,

he stood and came over to me. His expression determined, he held out his hand. "Will you dance with me?"

I nodded and took his hand, the music filling me with an abundance of energy. He pulled me close, and the heat of him enveloped me, chasing away my own aura of cold. The music led us, and we danced at a wild pace. This was no courtly dance, not one of civility and restraint. It was wild and free and breathless as a storm.

I couldn't tear my gaze away from him, and when the music slowed again, only then did I feel like I could take a proper breath.

Even with one song ending and another beginning, the prince didn't let me go. He held me close, and said in my ear, "Now I may finally be worthy of you."

I laughed. "Is a prince not worthy of a peasant?"

"I thought you'd understood after hearing Baba Yaga's tale of Winter. You are the Ice Queen's daughter, which makes you a . . ." He lifted his eyebrows in question.

"A princess," I said, realization dawning.

He grinned and spun me around. "And even if you were not, you'd still be the most powerful elemental, far greater than a mere prince."

"That's debatable, but I'm having far too much fun dancing to argue."

The music sped up again, the lyra and the woman's voice beautifully matched.

The prince pulled me even closer to him, his strong arms wrapped around me as we followed the music's frantic tempo.

We danced until a sheen of sweat covered the prince, and even I felt warm. While we'd been enjoying the music, the others had been enjoying the wine. We returned to find Kharan entertaining the others with tales of reindeer and hunting with wolves, her eyes bright from drink.

The prince held out a chair for me, and I collapsed into it with a smile. He sat in the chair next to mine after pouring us each another goblet of wine. One of the candles had gone out on the table, and the prince lit it with a flick of his fingers. I envied his control.

"I suppose with this newfound power you won't have need for mine," I said as casually as I could while the prince took a sip of wine. I wasn't sure what I wanted his answer to be.

He set his goblet back on the table. "How can you say that? Don't you remember what the bannik said? Fire and ice are unstoppable against earth." His gaze met mine. "That is, if you'd be willing to stay with me when we return."

I met his eyes. "I want justice for Babushka and all others like her. I want revenge on the earth elementals and the soldiers alike. But I fear that my power is still not under control. At the battle after I discovered my village destroyed, I killed some of your soldiers along with the enemy. And then there's Dedushka and what happened in my village. I'm terrified I'll do it again. Worse, when I release the cold fire—truly release it, not just freeze water of a pond or river—it drains my energy."

The prince was deep in thought for a moment. "Perhaps if you had somewhere for that energy to go—something that could contain it for you, for a time. Then it wouldn't continuously pull power from you. Much like the flame in this box vanquished my own flames."

"In the quarry—how did you do that so easily?"

"Because I can feel it inside me, part of my blood, waiting for my command."

Perhaps that was the piece I was missing: the prince was used to giving commands. He had grown up giving orders for others to follow, whereas I'd been raised to do as I was told. And to not ask questions. Especially about my power.

It made me think of what Queen Ciara had said to me before: that I was afraid. All my life, I'd tried to avoid using my power since all it brought me was censure and ridicule. And then when I did, it brought death and destruction. Seeing the prince use his so naturally and easily made me feel both ashamed and determined.

It was time I accepted the truth: my power could make all the difference in this war, and I would gladly make myself into a weapon if it meant saving the people of Kievan Rus'.

Much later, after the musicians had left, and the wine had been drunk, we made our way back to the ships. The innkeeper offered us lodging, but the prince was anxious to leave for Kiev as soon as possible, and he hoped to meet with the king and queen tonight after they had dined at the imperial palace.

Boris had been sent to deliver the message asking to speak

with the king and queen, and to retrieve our horses. Septimus and Aemilia had returned to their homes, so it was only the four of us and Elation as we entered the shipyard. Elation perched comfortably on my arm, no doubt full and happy after her own feast on the inn's roof.

"The food and drink was too delicious," Kharan said, dragging her feet. "I wish we could sleep for days."

She threw her arm around Ivan companionably, and he shook his head. "And you have had too much of it."

"Why must you be so serious, Ivan?" Kharan said with an exaggerated eye roll.

He answered her with a grunt, and as she laughed, a commotion rang out over the shipyard, drawing our attention. Shouts, wails, and the rattle of chains came from just beyond where the two knarrs were moored. It was coming from a ship.

Kharan stopped laughing immediately, her eyes clearing of mirth.

The prince glanced her way. "Kharan" was all he said, and she melded into the shadows.

We waited for what felt like an eternity for Kharan to return, all of us tense—even Elation, who trained her eyes in the direction of the sounds. She could understand me, but I wished to understand her, for I was sure she could see far more than we could from where we stood.

"Are the king and queen's ships in danger?" I asked Sasha. "Are pirates attacking?"

He didn't take his eyes off the direction Kharan had

disappeared. "No, I suspect those sounds are from something far worse than pirates."

Elation turned her head toward a spot just beside the prince, and suddenly, Kharan appeared. "It's a Drevlian ship," she said.

"And its cargo?" the prince asked with a grim expression.

"Captives. I could hear their cries for mercy; they are Rus'." Anger flashed in her eyes. "Others, too, from the steppes."

"What will they do to them?" I asked, but there was a sick feeling inside of me that made me think I already knew.

"Sell them," Sasha said. "This is why the empresses denied my request for aid. If the Drevlians are here, we can be sure that the empresses have sanctioned—and possibly even encouraged—their trade."

Disgust and a cold fear for them gripped me. I knew what it felt like to be bound, to be handed off to someone who could do any number of horrible things to you. But I'd been held prisoner by a prince who'd given me a tent, a room in a palace, and soon, my freedom. These captives wouldn't have the same fate.

"We have to save them," I said, my hands curled into fists at my side.

Ivan narrowed his eyes before turning to Kharan. "How many soldiers did you see?"

"At least twenty," she said.

Ivan leaned toward the prince. "Gosudar, this seems to be too dangerous a situation. We'll be far outnumbered, and we won't have the support from the empresses. If anything, they may be complicit in the Drevlians' trade."

The prince straightened his spine and met Ivan's gaze without blinking. "They are my people. I won't abandon them to their fate."

Ivan sighed and bowed his head. "Yes, Gosudar. I await your command," he added formally.

"You and I will engage the men," Sasha said to Ivan. "Kharankhui, Katya, you will lead the captives off the ship and to safety while we engage the Drevlians."

"I can kill them all myself from the shadows, Gosudar," Kharan said, and the prince considered for a moment.

"We don't know whether an elemental will be on board," he said. "If so, you won't be able to do it alone, and we can't risk them moving the captives before we can rescue them. No, it has to be all of us working together." Suddenly his silver eyes were on mine. "Though if you wish to stay behind, Katya, I will understand."

Anger over the captives' plight and a desperate determination solidified within me, hardening to ice. "I couldn't live with myself if I didn't help."

The prince smiled at me approvingly. "I just wanted to give you the choice." He looked toward the knarr. "But first, we will need weapons."

After we'd returned briefly to our own ships and retrieved weapons—a broadsword for the prince, a dagger for Kharan and one for me that I had no hope of wielding properly, a sword and bow for Ivan and a longsword for Boris—we made our way to a hill just above the port, where we had the perfect vantage of the Drevlian ship. It had a single mast with a billowing white sail, and many men on board. As we got close enough to see with clarity, the captives were located toward the stern of the ship, chained to the mast. There were people of all types: men, women, even children. At the sight, rage boiled up inside me, tightening my grasp on my dagger.

"Fire arrows until we draw them away from the ship," the prince told Ivan, and he nodded. The prince turned his attention to Kharan and me. "When you see that the majority have left the ship, you and Katya work on freeing the captives."

"Yes, Gosudar," Kharan said.

Ivan got into position, plucking an arrow from his quiver and drawing his bow back. He sighted carefully for a moment, let out his breath, and let the arrow fly. It flew straight and true, slamming into the chest of one of the Drevlian men. He fell as all the others on board froze. Ivan nocked another arrow and let it fly again, this time hitting a man near the mast. When he, too, fell, the Drevlians finally realized where the arrows were coming from. While some fired back with arrows of their own, others began to pour off the ship like ants from a mound.

Ivan continued to fire upon them until they were too close for arrows to be effective, and then the three men met them head-on with their swords. The prince was a blur of movement, cutting down the Drevlians easily, and Boris took out many with broad strokes of his sword. There were more men than we'd thought, as more appeared from within the ship's hull.

Elation lent her help without being asked, flying at the enemy with talons outstretched. My heart caught in my throat as I saw them try to fend her off, but she was too fast for any of their swords to connect.

Kharan and I tried to make our way to the Drevlian ship, but there were so many men now that the way was blocked. "Go," I told her. "You can at least begin to help the captives. I will follow when I can."

"Be careful," she said before becoming a shadow that melded into the darkness, invisible.

I'd have to help them here—now—or they'd be overwhelmed.

Some of the Drevlian men saw me standing to the side, like a foolish doe caught in a hunter's sights, and rushed toward me. Immediately, my skin turned to ice. *Do something else*, I thought to myself savagely, my hand still curved around the dagger.

"Katya!" the prince yelled, fighting to get to me. Suddenly, his sword ignited with fire. He swung the flaming sword toward the men, and screams of agony and the smell of burning flesh filled the air.

I glanced down at my dagger. The cold power seemed to hover inside me, waiting. I thought of how naturally the prince had taken to his own power, and determination filled me. I grabbed hold of my power and pulled it toward my weapon, imparting my icy energy to the dagger. Three men were mere inches away now, and I swung at them. A blast of ice shot forth from the weapon, hitting them in the face. It froze them instantly, and they fell, dead before they even hit the ground.

Above me, Elation screeched a distinctive cry, calling my attention to her. She was circling a trio of horses and riders, with more horses being led behind. In the lead were the king and queen.

Elation drew them to our battle, and I watched for a moment as the king and queen changed direction from the ships to the hill we fought on.

The thunder of hooves announced their arrival, and both the king and queen had swords drawn. They joined the fray without hesitation, their swords flashing in tandem.

"Who are we fighting?" King Leif asked as he viciously cut down one of the Drevlians. "Wasn't I just saying it had been too long since we'd battled, my love?"

"The gods must have heard your pleas," Queen Ciara said with a grin.

Sasha kicked an attacker away and swung his sword. "They are my enemies, and they have taken my people captive."

I watched in a sort of horrified awe as one of the Drevlians suddenly turned on his fellow men, cutting down as many as he could, while the rest gave him a wide berth, their faces twisted with fear. For a moment, that same fear gripped me—it was like he was suddenly possessed. But then I remembered Queen Ciara's power.

I'd seen a glimpse of it before with the palace guard, but witnessing it during a battle was truly frightening.

"Where are the captives?" Queen Ciara asked as she cut down another attacker.

I thought of her mind control over the Drevlian man, and suddenly, I knew how we could easily free them from their bonds. "Will you come with me?" I shouted to her over the chaos. "Bring him," I said with a nod toward the bloodied man she had possession of.

I sprinted down the hill, and she followed on horseback before leaping off when we reached the Drevlian ship.

"The people are bound by chains," I said.

The queen was silent for a moment, as though deep in thought. "He knows where the keys are kept—in the captain's quarters." Her head shot up. "But the captain is—"

She was cut off by the ground beneath our feet ripping open. The man the queen controlled plummeted into the gash in the earth, and the queen and I fell to either side, scrambling to avoid falling. In the next instant, the hole closed, swallowing the man like a colossal mouth of earth.

A man with green eyes as bright as spring grass stood over us, smiling a malevolent grin. He was richly dressed, in a brocade tunic, finely woven pants, and polished leather boots. "Is it the two of you who've caused so much trouble for my men? Let me guess, I've captured one of your loves, and now you've embarked on a daring quest to save him."

The queen looked at him like he was less than the dirt beneath her boots.

"We don't know the captives you have on your ship

personally," I said, my voice as icy as my skin, "but neither do we need to."

"Then you'll die for nothing," he said, and before we could even react, the ground tremored beneath our feet again.

The queen shoved me aside, so hard that when I landed I could hardly draw breath. A yawning chasm opened in the earth again, prepared to swallow us whole.

"You could take control of his mind," I said breathlessly.

"I could," she agreed, "but I'd rather see what you can do."

The ground trembled again, and we rolled out of the way. I stood and pulled free my dagger. Reaching for that icy-cold power, I seized it, coating my dagger in its energy. The chasm closed again, and I slashed the dagger toward the Drevlian captain. Ice shot toward him in a blast of cold air, but he raised his hand, and a tower of earth rose from the ground and blocked the ice.

In the next instant, he sent the earth flying toward me. I lifted my arms to shield my face, and it was deflected harmlessly off my icy skin.

Elation's screech echoed in the harbor as she dove toward the captain, talons outstretched. He dodged her at the last moment, narrowly avoiding his eyes being torn out of his face.

"Does the eagle obey you?" the queen asked. "Can you communicate with it?"

"I can put thoughts into her mind," I said, "and even though I can't hear a response, she has always seemed to understand."

"I have a plan for her, so I will see what I can convey," the queen said, and her face immediately took on a look of intense concentration.

Elation seemed to pause in midair, as though listening.

Meanwhile the captain had been raising towers of earth again, and he aimed them for Elation. Fear for my eagle gripping me, I took advantage of the captain's distraction and imbued my dagger again with ice. Another blast of freezing winter air shot toward him as Elation banked and changed direction.

With two of us to contend with, the captain was unable to defend himself. He prevented my ice from cutting him, but Elation attacked him from behind, tearing into the side of his neck with her talons. With a scream, the captain enclosed himself in a wall of earth.

The earth wall that had hidden the captain exploded in a shower of rocks and sand. He emerged, striding toward us with murder in those green eyes, his neck fully healed.

This time he lifted huge rocks from the ground high above our heads, and it was clear that he would rain them down upon us. I thought of how cold I could make things, cold enough to freeze and shatter. He let the rocks fly toward us, and at the last second, I raised my hands and thought of ice.

Cold shot from my palms, coating the rocks above us in a layer of ice so frigid the rocks exploded into tiny, shimmering pieces.

I glanced back at the queen, who was watching with her arms crossed, as though she was overseeing a training session instead of a real-life battle.

"Your defenses are good, but you lack imagination for how to kill people," she said. Her gaze shifted to the sea mere feet away. "Perhaps something like this."

It felt like a hand of iron gripping either side of my head, but before I could make a sound, images filled my mind: me reaching toward the sea, one hand outstretched, calling the water to me. The image changed to the water being imbued with my wintry power, freezing solid, and flying toward the Drevlian captain like swords of ice.

The pressure on my head disappeared, and when I became aware of my surroundings again, the queen watched me with her dark eyes. "Sorry about the headache—I thought it would be easier to show you what I meant."

And as soon as she mentioned a headache, a splitting pain pierced my skull. I held my head with one hand, narrowing my eyes at the queen.

While I'd been in the grip of the queen's mind control, the captain had opened multiple chasms in the ground beneath our feet. Somehow, the queen and I had managed to avoid them, but we wouldn't be able to avoid them for forever.

The captain lifted the earth from the chasms, hovering the dirt and stone high above our heads. He meant to crush us beneath it. I looked toward the water, and my mind filled with doubt—I'd never summoned water to me like that. With a shake of my head, I pushed it aside. I let my mind fill instead with the image the queen had planted there: of me summoning the water and transforming it to ice.

I lifted my arm, willing the water and air to obey my command. With a powerful burst, a cascade of seawater came flying from the harbor. A thrill ran through me that it had actually worked. I thought of the way the black water could look: like swords of ice. And the next instant, they were soaring toward the Drevlian captain.

He managed to stop two or three with spiraling towers of earth, but he could not stop them all. They pierced him cleanly through the chest, and as he fell, a terrible triumph rushed through me.

Before he'd even hit the ground, the queen moved toward him and pulled a set of keys from beneath this tunic. "The other tried to hide the location of the keys from me in his mind, but of course, there's no hiding anything from me."

She strode toward the Drevlian ship, and I followed. Above us, Elation flew with one eye trained on me.

Beyond us were the captives. Kharan knelt down before them, talking to them in soothing tones.

The queen tossed me the keys. "You can be the hero today."

As soon as I climbed aboard, all the captives' eyes were on me. Some were huddled and weak, others crying; still others had faraway looks like they'd given up all hope. A little girl, perhaps only five or six years old, cried for her mother. The sound tore at my heart. The men who would take a child captive—those were the real monsters.

As they registered the keys I held in my hand, they seemed to come alive again.

I found the main padlock where all the chains ran to the mast, stuck the key in, and turned it. It sprang free with a satisfying click. I passed the keys to Kharan, and she went to each individual lock where the captives were chained together. At last, they were all free. The ones who knew each other—or had at least come to know the other after being chained on a ship for days—wept and held one another. A woman from another part of the ship ran to the little girl who had been crying and scooped her into her arms. I felt sickened that the cruelty of the captain was so extreme that he would separate a mother and child.

They turned to me, then, and began a chorus of thanks in various languages, some even accompanied by bows, and I could only smile at them and nod with tears in my eyes. I was so relieved that we had saved them.

From behind us, there was the sound of boots ringing out on the gangplank, and then the prince, King Leif, Ivan, and Boris appeared. The prince had streaks of ash across his cheeks and forehead, the king was covered in splashes of blood and grinning, and Boris was the cleanest one of all. The moment the former captives recognized the prince, they swarmed toward him, bowing and thanking him for his help in saving them.

The prince took my hand and pulled me to his side. "You have Katya to thank for that, not me. She is the one who defeated the captain of this ship."

"I didn't do it alone," I said as they resumed their profuse thanks.

The woman who held the now-quiet child came and touched my arm. "Thank you for saving my daughter. I will have nightmares for many years to come of what might have happened, but I can at least comfort myself with the knowledge that none of it came to pass."

I gave her a little bow, too overcome to respond with words.

"We will grant you safe passage home," the prince said, "if you can stomach being on a ship for two more days."

"We would ride in rowboats tied behind your ship if it meant we could see our homes again," said a man with a still-healing black eye and a swollen face.

"No need for that," King Leif said. "There is room on one of the knarrs now that we emptied it of its cargo." He turned and gestured to one of his men who waited on shore. By his drawn sword, I assumed he'd aided in the fight against the Drevlians. "Erik will escort you," he told the former captives.

As the people followed Erik, the prince turned to me. "I know I have no reason to fear for you, but I cannot help myself. You aren't hurt, are you?" His gaze swept over me.

"No," I said, and he looked relieved. "Were you injured?

"No. My newfound power ensured a decisive victory."

I smiled. Stated like a true prince.

I watched the people shuffle by, in various forms of weakness and injury. "If ever I needed a reason to solidify my desire for vengeance and join your battle against these enemies, it would be what I've seen here today. I want to fight beside you to end it." I shook my head. "Little though I know of actual battle."

"Just as the bannik said to you," he said, his expression serious. "Fire and ice."

I nodded. "Together we have a chance to stop them."

He took a step toward me, and before I could take another breath, he pulled me into his arms. Shocked by the sudden contact, my skin turned as cold as marble. As the extreme heat of his body melded with the extreme cold of mine, tendrils of steam wrapped themselves around us. He pulled away just far enough to look at me, and the moment our gazes met, I could see the warmth of desire reflected in his silver eyes. His hand touched my cheek, the heat searing through the cold. My heart hammered away in my chest as his head bent toward me, my eyes fluttering closed just before his mouth descended upon mine. Hot and cold—for a moment, I was afraid the ice inside me would hurt him, but it didn't; his own heat seemed to cancel it out. He deepened the kiss, and I pulled him closer, pushing away any thoughts that he was a *prince* and *what was I doing*?

All too soon, he pulled away.

"I—" I began, but then he kissed me again.

"I've wanted to do that for a long time," he said finally, a grin pulling at the corners of his mouth.

A blush, leftover from the warmth he'd shared with me, crawled up my neck. "I'm thankful I didn't freeze you to death," I said.

"I don't think you can." He took my hand and leaned closer. "Our powers seem to complement each other."

It did seem that way, but of course, I hadn't been unleashing

340

the cold fire. It made me wonder, with ice prickling all over me, if his own fire would be powerful enough to withstand it.

Despite what Ciara had shown me, of the well of power deep within myself and how to access it, fear still kept me in its iron grip that I would fail.

But then I thought of the captives we'd rescued, and I knew: I'd do anything to keep that from happening again.

Chapter Twenty-Three

We sailed for home that same night. King Leif was used to navigating by the stars—and possibly even leaving under cover of darkness—and both he and the prince thought it was best to leave immediately. They didn't know if the Drevlians were here by the empresses' invitation, but it was a good guess that they were. We had to leave before the city retaliated or more Drevlian allies arrived. The king and queen sent word to the empresses that because of a nearby battle so close to their ships, they would be setting sail early. They of course omitted any mention of their own (or even the prince's) involvement.

Under a sky brilliant with stars, the ships cut through the black water. Everything was quiet as we were all recovering from the battle, and I should have been sleeping, too. But my mind was restless with everything I'd witnessed today: the prince's newfound powers, the battle, the defeat of the captain. Most of all, though, my mind kept replaying my dance with the prince on the rooftop . . . and the kiss just before we set sail. This pull toward Sasha was seductive but frightening at the same time. We had a common goal now, but what would happen when the battle was over? Would I still be expected to live in the palace? Would I even want to?

I rolled to my other side, and found that Kharan, whose leather sleeping bag was beside mine, was still awake, too. Her expression seemed to be pained.

"Are you all right?"

"I'm fine. There's a scratch on my side that's bothering me, but it's shallow."

I sat up. "Should I put a poultice on it? Are you sure it's not deep?"

She pushed me down. "I'm fine. We're both tired. I already wrapped it before I lay down to sleep."

I reluctantly relented, and we fell silent for a moment. There was shifting beside me, and then Kharan was watching me again.

"So," she said, eyebrows raised, "I can't help but noticed that *moment* between you and Gosudar."

I shifted a bit before shooting her a side glance. "How long have you been waiting to ask me that?"

"Since the moment it happened," she said, giving me a little poke in my side. "And so? How was it?"

I covered my face and flipped onto my back. "I can't stop thinking about it," I mumbled into my hands.

"Did he burn your lips?"

I let out a strangled laugh. "No."

"Do you want him to do it again?"

"Yes."

She smiled at me, her teeth white in the light of the moon. "That's good, because I think he very much wants to kiss you again."

This had my full attention. "Why do you think that?"

"Because I know things."

I gave her shoulder a little nudge. "Yes, but *what* things?"

She sighed as though she was exasperated, but I knew she was loving every second of this. "I overheard him talking to Ivan when you first came to the palace. He said he didn't expect you to be so beautiful, and he wanted to know what you'd been like when Ivan had gone to retrieve you from your village. Ivan told him that you'd been fiercely brave, and the prince said that from the moment he first saw you, he could tell there was a pillar of fire trapped within all your ice."

Beautiful. Fierce. A pillar of fire. Did I really deserve such praise? "I cannot believe he has such feelings for me."

"Any fool can see he loves you."

Surprise shot through me. "Love? No one said anything about love."

"You didn't see how he reacted when he discovered you'd left for your village."

344

I thought of the intensity on his face when he'd found me, but still, I couldn't imagine . . . "Even if he was upset—"

"He was *terrified*. And it quickly turned to rage when he realized Grigory hadn't left yet."

I tried not to let her words affect me—tried not to let that hope bloom. I wasn't sure how I felt about the prince, and love. . . . I didn't have much experience with love. "Still. Even if he reacted that way, I'm sure he'd behave the same no matter who it'd been."

She propped her head with her hand, under her chin. "You think so, do you? Well, I can see it's no use talking sense into you tonight, and I'm tired. But I think what you need to ask yourself is: Why *shouldn't* he love me? Why are you so afraid to let yourself be loved?"

Silence descended over us as we both gave in to our need for sleep, and as I finally drifted off, I thought of Winter's tale, and how she'd eventually killed the hunter she loved—my father—despite being able to control her power far better than I. Sasha was a powerful elemental instead of a mere mortal like my father, but still, fear coiled itself around my heart. If even my powerful mother had lost control, then how much worse would my own fate be?

The morning dawned warm and bright, and I awoke to find Elation watching me. Her eyes seemed to be trying to say something to me. Not for the first time, I wished I could understand. I stood and went to the stern of the ship where the queen was alone, gazing out at the water.

She turned when she saw me. "You did well against the captain once you overcame your fear and hesitation."

"Thank you, but I think most of it was luck."

"No, but I did have a thought. You wrought the most damage with your power when it was beyond your control, yes?"

I hadn't thought of it that way, but I supposed it was true. Both with the villagers and with the raiders, I'd only thought of stopping them—in any way possible. "Yes, but then I can't rein it in."

"I understand that, but I did you a disservice by treating your power like mine: it isn't like that. I was trained as a warrior for one thing, so I have always been able to use my abilities like an extension of my fighting ability. But you don't have such training."

"So what should I do?"

"You may not have training, but that doesn't mean your power doesn't know exactly what to do. Yours is raw, elemental power. Like a winter storm. It doesn't need your help causing destruction. But it *does* need your help in reining it in. A storm in winter will blow until its energy is spent, right?" When I nodded, she continued. "But that's what your power has been doing to you. It uses you until you deplete all your energy and lose consciousness. It's this aspect of it that you must gain control of."

I shook my head with a little self-deprecating laugh. "Yes, well, then I may as well not use it at all, for I have no idea how to stop once it once it's set free."

"You must think of what would keep a raging winter storm at bay," she said. "I may not be able to see the future, Katya, but I can see that you are determined. Never underestimate your strength of will."

"You've given me much to think about," I said. "I cannot thank you enough for all of your help."

"I'm glad to give it."

We fell silent again for a moment, gazing out over the dark water. But then I remembered. "I never had a chance to ask you more about Elation—my eagle," I clarified when she turned and looked at me. "You could read her mind, right? I know she understands me, but I've always wished I could understand her, too."

"You were right," the queen said to me. "The eagle can understand everything perfectly. Only"—she paused with a glance at Elation who was perched nearby—"*she* is actually a *he*."

I stared at the queen for a moment, slow to understand. "That can't be true. Look how large her wingspan is! The females are always bigger than the males."

"I heard his voice," the queen said firmly. "It's true, he's much larger than any eagle I've ever seen, but then, coupled with his superior intelligence, it's clear he's no ordinary bird."

Elation watched us with an intent look in her—his?—eyes, as though following the conversation. "When you . . . entered his mind," I chose the words questioningly, unsure if that was the right way to describe it, but she nodded. "When you did that, he spoke to you?"

"Yes," she said, glancing toward Elation, "which is why I think he is more than he seems. I can enter an animal's mind to an extent, but it's not like a human's. They don't form thoughts with words, for one thing, but instead, with images and sounds and smells. The eagle, though, told me about himself with clearly spoken words."

I held my breath. "What did he say?"

"He said he has lost much of his past before he was entrusted with your care, so you are 'the sky, the sun, the trees' to him. He sees himself as your guard, but he cannot remember who first commanded him to protect you."

I watched Elation silently for a moment, absorbing what the queen had said. If Elation had been with me from the beginning, then it was reasonable to assume Winter had been the one to command him to watch over me.

"I think I know who it was," I said. "He truly can't remember?"

She shook her head. "He loses more pieces of his memory every year."

There was obviously more to the story—like how an eagle came to have such unusual intelligence—and I felt like the answer was hovering just out of reach.

"I'm glad to know even this much about him—thank you," I said.

"There's much to be said for an animal you can connect

with," she said with a melancholy look in her eyes, "especially if they're willing to go to battle with you."

"He certainly is willing to fight," I said, thinking of the way he used his talons.

She smiled. "I had a horse like that once. He was just as much a warrior as I was."

"I'm sorry he's no longer with you."

"I am, too," she said with a sad little laugh. "There has been no replacing him. Ah, but let's talk of other things." She seemed to forcibly push the sadness away, her whole body straightening until she appeared as once again an invincible queen.

The queen tilted her head for a moment, watching Elation. "There may be something I can do for you and for your eagle. Would you allow me to touch your mind again? My powers have grown of late, and I may be able to form a connection."

"I'm willing to try anything at this point," I said, the curiosity burning in my mind.

I felt the queen's powerful mind reach out and snatch mine, dizzying and headache-inducing, but just as I thought I couldn't stand the sensation anymore, a sound drew my attention.

The scratching of talons on the wooden floor, and then Elation moved closer. I turned to look at him, and as I did, he bowed his head toward mine. Unsure what he meant, I mimicked the gesture. Feathers brushed my forehead, and then as suddenly as a bolt of lightning, images burst into my mind.

I saw the hunter, young and hale as he gazed into the crystalline eyes of Winter, the eyes that were the same as mine.

The images skipped ahead, dancing over scenes of their love: passionate kisses and long looks, laughter and shared food, talking long into the night.

Until the moment he turned to ice. In my mind, as though it was my own memory, I saw Winter's eyes go from hooded and relaxed to wide with unspeakable horror as she realized the hunter was dead. Only he wasn't. Not entirely.

Spring was able to heal him, but she didn't have the power to reanimate him in his human form. And this time, the image showed him transforming, light warm and golden as the sun's rays pouring over him until he was no longer a man. Feathers erupted over his body as his face shrank and transformed into the sharp beak of an eagle, though the color of his golden eyes remained. His legs and feet became the slender ones of an eagle, ending in wicked talons.

He screamed, but it was the battle cry of a raptor.

Winter didn't flinch, or cry, or show any emotion at all. She could have been carved from stone. She held out her arm to him, and he flew awkwardly to it, wrapping razor-sharp talons around her flesh.

The images skipped again, to the hunter watching as Winter's belly grew and grew, and I could feel his anguish from our connection. Every day he lost pieces of who he was as a human. He could understand Winter but not respond, and he was forced to watch her heart slowly turn to ice.

As the memories progressed, they grew hazier, as though the hunter was losing his grasp on them. Desperation rose in me, and I reached for the smoky tendrils of images as they flitted past me.

Finally, the baby—*me,* I realized—was born, and as Winter held me in her arms, tears fell like diamonds from her eyes.

I cannot risk hurting her as I did you, my love, she said to the hunter, and he let out a piercing cry, but could no sooner speak to her than a real eagle could. But as he was currently doing with me, he flew to her shoulder, bowed his head, and as soon as he touched his forehead to hers, they could communicate.

He tried to convince her to keep me, that she wouldn't harm me because I shared her blood. Already, he could feel the cold radiating off my infant body. But she refused—she wouldn't risk it. Eventually, the hunter relented. The only humans he trusted to care for me were his own parents, and I would at least be raised in an ordinary village.

The images danced ahead again, to Babushka and Dedushka meeting the hunter in his eagle form, and Winter with all her snowy white animals surrounding her, in the forest. Winter held me while the hunter flew close to Babushka and Dedushka on a nearby branch. Both Babushka and Dedushka stared at this bizarre menagerie with shocked looks on their faces—shock inching toward fear. Winter encouraged them to move toward the eagle, and Dedushka finally took a step forward. The hunter bowed his head, as he'd done with me, and just as I had, Dedushka mimicked the gesture.

Expressions flitted across his face—surprise, horror, wonder, and a dawning understanding. At last, he turned to Babushka, who had been waiting none too patiently, her arms crossed defensively over her chest.

"This is our son," Dedushka said, nodding toward the eagle before turning his attention to the baby in Winter's arms, "and that is our granddaughter."

Babushka paled, but she was a resilient woman, not prone to emotional outbursts, nor did she ever doubt her husband. She simply nodded, as though knowing she could get more detail about the strange interaction later, but for now, all she asked was, "What do they want us to do?"

"Raise her as your own, but never tell her of her true parentage," Winter said, and though her face still held that cold stone exterior, her voice wavered. "I cannot risk her seeking me out, not before she is strong enough. Only then may she be able to resist my power." She glanced at the eagle. "Only then may she be safe."

"The eagle—our *son*," Dedushka corrected himself, "is to stay with us. He wishes to watch over the babe."

Babushka was quiet for so long, Dedushka took a step closer to her, as though afraid she'd become overwhelmed. But then she moved toward Winter, arms outstretched.

Winter handed the baby over with only a shimmer of hesitation, but still her expression revealed nothing. But Elation felt pain enough for both of them, grief for what Winter was giving up, grief that he could never be the father he wanted to be.

And then the images of everything else in his mind faded like smoke on the horizon. There was only one thing he could remember now with any clarity: me.

But as he looked down upon the baby—upon me—he swore: he would always be there to look over me.

I pulled away from Elation with a gasping breath.

Elation was the hunter.

Elation had once been my father.

The prince came to my side while I was gazing out at the water, deep in thought. I felt him before I heard him, the heat rolling off his skin.

"What has you so lost in your own thoughts?" he asked.

"So many things," I said with a glance up at him. "Some of them more unbelievable than others." I didn't have to look over my shoulder to know that Elation was there. Watching over me as he always had.

"Try me," Sasha said with a small smile.

"The queen helped me discover the truth about Elation—why he's so intelligent."

"He?" Sasha asked, confusion touching his brows.

"He's as large as a female eagle and extremely intelligent because he was once human."

I watched him for a moment, and he turned to look at Elation. "Once human," he repeated.

"Yes, he was the hunter who fell in love with Winter. My father."

And now the prince did look taken aback, but as usual, he recovered quickly. "Then that explains why he has looked over you all this time and can understand you."

I nodded.

Sasha looked at me again. "But it's a cruel fate to never be able to talk to you. Or hold you. Especially after what you endured in your village."

I gave him a sad smile. "Or to never be able to truly speak to his daughter."

And then he pulled me into his arms, surprising me enough that my skin went cold, but eventually, I relaxed into his chest. I could feel his breath stir the hair at the top of my head, and for once, I felt safe.

We stayed like that for a long time, while dark clouds passed overhead and the ship raced over the water, sending a light spray over us. I thought of what the queen had said about my power. She was right in saying it was like a winter storm. When I pictured the well inside me again, I could see in my mind's eye how it had overflowed and unleashed itself upon my enemies. The problem, though, was that I had no idea how to rein in the power of a winter storm.

I remembered a blizzard that had borne down upon our village like a demon one cold night in winter. The wind had howled like wolves, the snow so thick we feared we'd be buried alive in our houses.

But then I thought of the one thing everyone in all of Kievan Rus' turned to when the wild winds of Winter beat at their doors:

Fire.

I glanced up at the prince. "The queen said something about my power that I'd never thought about before."

His voice rumbled behind my chest. "Was she able to help as I'd hoped?"

I nodded. "I think all this time I've been slowly gaining more control over the smaller aspects of my power—like turning water to ice—but it's the cold fire that has always been the problem. The queen likened it to a storm, and I think she's right. It's like a storm raging out of control with me as its energy source; it takes and takes, and I still don't know how to stop it once it's unleashed."

The prince looked pensive, gazing out over the water as he considered. "Did the queen have any insight?"

"She said I should consider what can stop a winter storm, but . . ." I trailed off, thinking of my earlier realization about fire. I didn't want him to risk himself.

"Ivan was able to stop you before." He searched my face, and it was as if he could see my concern written plainly upon it. "Do you think my flames may be strong enough to stop the cold fire's advance?"

I shook my head. "It's far too risky—for everyone involved. What if your power failed and the cold fire burned you and everyone else? I couldn't live with that."

"These aren't innocent civilians who will be fighting with us. These are soldiers who know not everyone will survive, but they do it for the good of Kievan Rus'. And there's something else I should tell you about the Drevlian and Novgorodian princes. Something Kharankhui discovered."

A chill chased over my skin.

"They are earth elementals themselves," he said, "though many years ago when they attempted to take over Kiev, they were weak, barely able to produce vines like the ones we saw in my throne room. They have the same mother, and it was she who had such a power in her bloodline, though she herself had been frail and didn't live long past her younger son's birth."

"But you think they are stronger now?"

"I know they are," he said, grim-faced. "Kharankhui has heard that they have done nothing but train these past few years. There is no earth elemental stronger. It will be no small thing I ask of you, Katya, and now that I've fallen in love with you, I don't know if I can ask it."

My breath caught in my throat as he gazed down at me. He loved me. I didn't know what to say, or how to express the depth of feeling I had for him—*I love you, too* seemed like far too simplistic a response.

"So tell me once more," the prince said. "Tell me that you wish to fight. Because if you do not, then I will do everything in my power to keep you safe."

I turned so I could see him properly. "I not only wish to fight . . . I *will* fight. I have been given this power for a reason, and I will use it for good."

He nodded once, his strong arms wrapping around me again. "Together then."

The earth will only fall to fire and ice.

❖❖❖

We made landfall late the next day. Sasha wanted to immediately start the long journey back to the palace, and despite my
initial trepidations at using my power, I could no longer let fear
hinder me. Not after seeing the captives firsthand. The people
who would suffer if we failed to stop the princes.

I glanced back at the prince, at the sun glinting off his dark
hair, and a flash of his kiss went through my mind. I remembered the feel of his heat on my lips, on the way he'd melted
some of my ice. But horribly, it only made me fear for him . . .
for what would come. I feared I would lose him just as I'd lost
everyone else—if not by my own cold fire, then in battle.

I pushed those thoughts away and instead focused on the
task ahead. The plan was to ride back to Kiev and assemble the
militia, call to arms all the druzhina who still lived, and march
upon the princes in first Iskorosten, which was the Drevlian
capital and the closest to Kiev. From there, we would ride on
to Novgorod.

While the prince spoke with the former captives and
Kharan waited to give aid to the ones taken from the steppes,
Ivan and Boris retrieved the horses from the knarr. I stood
apart, watching as the people we'd rescued fell to their knees
onshore, some even kissing the land they'd probably thought
they'd never see again. It only reaffirmed my desire to help
protect them from the other princes. If we didn't stop them,
those same people could easily become captives again. The
thought both filled me with a cold dread and strengthened my

resolve; there was much at stake should we fail.

I glanced up at the prince, and he seemed to be having similar thoughts, his jaw tight as he watched the former captives.

A horse's neigh and the sound of hoofbeats drew our attention from the people. The prince tensed as he turned toward the sound.

A small group of men rode toward the prince, and I thought I recognized one or two from the palace. The prince strode toward them, and I followed, the hair on the back of my neck standing on end at the expressions on the men's faces. They looked as though they carried the weight of a thousand rocks upon their shoulders. Whatever they would say would not be good news.

"Gosudar, we are glad to see you back in Kievan Rus'."

"Thank you," the prince said with a terse nod. "What news?"

The soldier looked like he'd be sick, and an answering stab of fear shot through me. "The Drevlians and Novgorodians have launched an attack on Kiev and its surrounding areas. Many villages have been burned to the ground, and the palace itself is under siege."

Before the prince could respond, the king and queen appeared beside him. "What has happened?" King Leif asked.

The prince remained calm, though the color drained from his face. "My city is under siege. The surrounding villages too."

The king and queen shared a look. "We listened to your plea for help before the Byzantine empresses," King Leif said, "and though they did not honor your alliance, we would like to offer you ours."

The prince closed his eyes for a moment as though praising God. "Thank you. You cannot know how much this means to me . . . to all of us."

The queen smiled. "It is no hardship. The king always relishes the chance for battle. In fact, I think he was disappointed you hadn't asked him for it on the ship."

King Leif laughed, but the prince looked chagrined. "My apologies to you both. I had only thought of how much you have already aided us. I was loath to ask for more."

"We have only a small contingent of men—fifty in total," the queen said, "but it is yours."

"And you will have the queen," the king said with a grin. "She is worth fifty more."

The prince asked questions: When had the enemy arrived? Who was protecting the palace? Had any of the civilians been evacuated?

Precious little was known, and too much time had been lost waiting for us to arrive. They had no idea what we would be walking into when we made it back to Kiev.

Kharan and Ivan soon joined us, and each was apprised of the situation. When Ivan learned that the city had fallen under siege, his face grew pale under his bushy beard, and I knew he feared for Vera. We all did. Before long, the ships were emptied of men that could be spared—some would have to remain to guard the king and queen's ships—and our horses. The wagons of supplies, though, would slow us down.

Once we were mounted, the prince came and addressed us all.

"We must ride ahead of the wagons," Sasha said. "It's our only chance of reaching Kiev in time. If all is not already lost," he added, jaw clenched tight. "Our horses were bred for endurance, and we must push them to the limit." He glanced over at the king and queen's war chargers. "If you do not wish to push yours as hard, we will understand."

"They will keep the pace," the king said confidently.

Sasha nodded. "Then onward."

The pace was set to grueling, but it wasn't nearly fast enough. With every beat of my heart, and every stride of powerful hoof-beats, I prayed that we wouldn't be too late.

CHAPTER TWENTY-FOUR

WE DIDN'T SLEEP. WE BARELY ATE. We only kept on a mad pace toward the city. The horses were tiring, but we kept pushing them. If Kiev fell now, then all was lost. The Drevlian and Novgorodian princes, along with their earth elemental allies, were poised to take over all of Kievan Rus'.

But on the second day, Kharan fell from Daichin, crashing to the forest floor in a heap. Her little pony let out a frightened neigh, not daring to leave her side.

I threw myself from Zonsara's back and ran to Kharan, while the others halted and circled around. Sasha dismounted, too.

"Kharan," I said, falling to her side. "What happened? What's wrong?"

Her eyes fluttered open. "I should have told you."

I searched her face. "Told me what?"

"One of the Drevlians . . . his sword," she managed, her face terribly pale. She touched her side. And suddenly, I remembered her look of pain on the ship, her brushing off my concern.

"Does anyone have a knife?" I demanded, and Sasha immediately handed one to me.

Feeling sick, I cut through Kharan's beautiful deel to reveal her ribs. There, beneath bandages, was a wound raging with infection.

"Oh, Kharan," I said, my heart pounding in my ears. I could feel under my hands that her body was blazing with a fever. "You didn't tell me how badly you were hurt."

"What can we do?" Sasha asked, his face awash with concern.

I'd brought herbs and supplies with me, but they were in the wagons . . . at least a day behind us. "I must ride back to the wagons to retrieve my supplies," I said. "I have precious little with me now. She may not survive without them."

The prince looked stricken for a moment before nodding. "Boris," the prince said, and Boris rode over closer, "you will stay here with Kharan and Katya. The rest of us will go on ahead."

I recognized the wisdom in this, but still, I was terrified for the prince to face the enemy without me.

"I'm sorry," Kharan said, and tears spilled from her eyes.

"No," I said, my stomach churning, "this is my fault. I should have asked to see your wound the next morning."

"I should have told you the truth," Kharan said.

"I will forgive you if you do not die," the prince said, and she managed a choked laugh. He turned to me. "I cannot say I'm devastated that you will not be riding immediately into danger like the rest of us," he said, reaching out to touch my face.

I leaned into his hand. "And I cannot say I'm thrilled to see you ride into danger without me."

And then he was pulling me into him and wrapping his arms around me, kissing me as tears froze upon my cold cheeks before melting again as they came near the heat of his body. I pressed myself into him, molding my body to his. His kiss was a burning heat, a painful goodbye, a promise. His hands plunged into my hair as he deepened the kiss, and I could feel his desperation.

He pulled away all too soon, huge palms on either side of my face.

He pressed one more kiss to my lips, gentle this time. "Heal her, as you did me," Sasha said, touching my face one last time. "And then return to me."

"Don't get yourself killed," I said, tears stinging my eyes.

He smiled and mounted his horse again, but he made no promise to me that he would stay alive. And as I looked back at my friend laid out on the ground, stricken with infection and fever, I was terrified I would lose everything I loved.

Again.

Once I treated Kharan with the herbal poultice I had remaining from the prince's shoulder wound, I left her in Boris's care while I rode as fast as I could back to the wagon for more. White willow, in particular, was missing, and I needed it to bring down her fever.

Kharan had repeatedly told me how sorry she was before succumbing to the pain and the fever and falling unconscious. The wound was shallow, and it hadn't been infected when she'd first told me of it on the ship, so she didn't think it necessary to ask for an herbal remedy. I told her not to be ridiculous. She'd braved much for us. And of course I knew it was my fault: I should have asked to see it, should have insisted on applying a poultice. The only consolation was that the fever hadn't progressed as far as Sasha's had, and I hadn't needed to use my power to bring her temperature down.

Zonsara sensed my anxiety, her tail twitching in irritation, but though she'd barely had a rest, she responded instantly, cantering as fast as I dared to spur her on through the thick trees.

It took us half a day to reach the wagon, and by then, I was so pale from fear over Kharan and Sasha that the soldiers guarding the wagon took one look at me and immediately fell to their knees, fearing Sasha had been killed.

"He was alive when last I saw him—he had to ride on ahead," I assured them. "I've come only to retrieve my supplies."

But when I turned to ride back, Zonsara was standing splay-legged, blowing hard from her nostrils, and I knew I couldn't push her again that day. The anxiety ate at me even as I fed her kasha and water, rubbed her down and allowed her to graze.

It wasn't until hours later, when she appeared rested enough to keep a pace faster than a walk, and my fear had broken through my skin and was now gnawing on bone, that I was able to return to Kharan.

Boris had kept her warm and sheltered, but she was still feverish—shaking and pale. I made a tea from the white willow and changed her poultice out for fresh herbs. Before long, she was resting easily. I watched over her, even as my mind raced ahead to Kiev. I feared for Sasha until it felt as though I'd split apart. Not being with him to join in the battle was torture, but I also wouldn't have wanted anyone else here with Kharan. It tore me in two, and I paced throughout the night, alternating between checking Kharan's temperature—which was falling—and imagining what might be happening with Sasha.

Sometime before dawn, I'd finally given in to sleep, after Boris had made us all some hearty stew. I woke up some hours later and was surprised to find Kharan up and feeding Daichin her leftover kasha.

"You look much improved," I said, coming to her side.

"Thanks to you," she said. "I'm sorry I cost us so much time. You must be half mad with worry."

I shook my head. "Stop apologizing when you know I'm the one who should have asked to see the wound the next morning."

She smiled wanly. "I doubt I even would have let you."

I sighed. "I'm only glad to see you better so soon."

"There's something to that, I think," she said. "How quickly people respond to your treatment."

I looked at her questioningly. "I only use the herbs as Babushka did."

"Yes, but I was terribly ill, possibly dying. And now, today, I can ride." She watched me for a moment. "And wasn't it the same for the prince?"

I thought back to when the prince had recovered from the festering of his wound. He, too, had been out of bed the next day.

"Yes, I think you're right."

"A useful skill since we're about to join the war," she said with a grin.

"And you're sure you're well enough to ride?" I asked, reaching out to touch her forehead. It was cool to the touch, and her color had completely improved.

"Yes." She turned toward Boris as he approached. "It might have been Boris's stew, actually—perhaps I'm giving credit to the wrong person."

He laughed. "You are better. That is all that matters."

She touched my arm. "Are you ready? If we push ourselves today, we may not lose as much time."

I nodded. "Let us pray God gives our horses wings."

Let us pray we are not too late.

Hurry, hurry. That was the thought that drove us on. That pushed our horses.

Zonsara picked up on my anxiety, as I'd learned horses do, but still I held her in check. Many times she broke from her smooth canter to a gallop before I had to pull her back, my heart hammering wildly in my chest. I'd learned much about riding in the time since I'd first left Kiev with the prince, but still I feared being thrown—not because it would possibly injure me, but because it might delay me from reaching the battle.

Zonsara fought me still, snorting and tossing her head when I slowed her pace once again. A sweat was breaking out on her neck and shoulders. Finally, I realized I was making her waste more energy by holding her back than by letting her run.

I loosened my death grip on the reins, and she hesitated for a brief moment, as though she didn't really believe I was letting her have her head. But then her stride lengthened as she stretched out into a full gallop.

I leaned low over Zonsara's neck as she raced along, a mixture of slush and leaves kicking up in her wake. Elation flew ahead, casting his long shadow. The horses raced to keep pace. My heart beat furiously as cold dread gripped me. I was afraid I'd be too late. After all I'd learned, after all I'd lost, I couldn't bear to lose anyone else.

I couldn't bear to lose *him*.

Our horses' endurance was once again put to the test, as we kept them at a pace just shy of absolute exhaustion. We stopped twice: once for water, and once to rest for precious little time.

Only a few hours later we awoke, and then we were racing toward the rising sun again. With each beat of Zonsara's hooves, I felt the power within me grow like a thunderhead on the horizon. Cold leaked from my palms, until a stream of snow began to fall behind us. It built and built in power, until the very air around us began to change temperature. Zonsara snorted, and her breaths came out in great plumes of white. In the sky above, dark gray clouds formed. More power spilled out of me, and I did nothing to stop it.

Please, I thought, as Zonsara brought us closer to Kiev, and the storm I brought with me strengthened, *please let them be unharmed. Let Sasha be unharmed.*

My mind tortured me with images of the people I'd come to care for: Vera lying unmoving on the ground, Ivan with a sword through his chest, and Sasha . . . Sasha impaled again by vines, this time through his heart.

The dark-gray clouds pressed lower, and it was as if the clouds were feeding off the energy pouring out of me. *Hurry, hurry,* the voice whispered, and the storm above grew stronger.

The snowfall increased, the flakes larger, and a wind picked up until it was howling along to the beat of my heart.

At long last, we burst from the cover of the trees. The branches reached toward us like they wanted to pull us back, and the storm ripped needles and twigs free, swirling them around in the snow until there was a whirlwind behind us.

We crested a hill, and then Kiev spread before us, and I pulled Zonsara to a halt with a strangled cry. Boris raced on ahead, desperate to give aid to Ivan and the others, while Kharan dismounted and immediately melded into the shadows. The city had been overtaken by thorny brambles and vines so thick, only the tops of the palace towers could be seen. But worse was the battle taking place in the flatland before the gates of the city.

It was a chaotic, writhing mass of people and weapons. The cacophony so terrible it rippled across the land and vibrated in my teeth: the clang of swords, the shouts of men, the screams of horses. There were so many: the prince's city militia battled enemy soldiers, and the king and queen's Varangian men fought among them. But of course, this was no ordinary battle. A group of elementals, scattered around the edges of the field, hurled enormous boulders that crashed down upon the mass of people, crushing bodies and breaking bones as they landed. There were chasms in the ground, much like I'd encountered with the ship captain, yawning open, ready to swallow anyone who took a wrong step.

And towering above it all were creatures I'd never seen before. Craggy and roughly formed, they were like giant men made of earth. I could only deduce they'd been created by an earth elemental. The prince's men fired upon them with arrows, swung shining blades of swords at them, but they only continued their heavy march, crushing anyone in their enormous hands who came close enough.

Shining like a beacon of hope through all the chaos was the prince, who burned brightly, lit with his elemental fire. Relief hit me so powerfully I let out an explosive breath. He was alive. The sword he carried was also burning, and it cut through soldiers easily. Any vines that reached for him, tearing through the earth like the fingers of giants, were cut down by the prince's sword. Yet even with such powerful flames, he still had to dodge the flying boulders and the towering earth men.

The fire wasn't enough. The storm within and above me strengthened, blowing snow in a whirlwind. It danced around me, as though waiting for my command.

I scanned the battle for the others: for Ivan and the king and queen. I found Ivan, fighting perilously close to elementals, and when he got near enough to one who was hurling boulders, he touched him, sucking away his power in a rush. The boulder the man controlled fell on his fellow soldiers instead, and though I couldn't see his face with clarity from this distance, I could tell from the way he held his body that he was horrified. But in the next instant, he was cut down by Ivan's sword.

The king fought powerfully with his sword, his men staying close to him as they cut through enemy soldier after soldier.

And just when I was scanning the battle again for the queen, she galloped toward me on her all-black charger, spooking Zonsara, who let out a snort of disapproval.

"The princes are inside the city," she said, "and none of us can make it past the brambles. Not even the prince's fire can burn it; it's too green. You can see if your power is effective against the brambles. If you can get inside, Leif and I will take care of the soldiers outside. Get to the palace, defeat your enemy princes, and the war will be won."

A rumbling like thunder drew my attention away from the queen before I could respond, and Zonsara pranced in place.

One of the enormous earth-men was lumbering toward me, his face as craggy and featureless as a mountain.

"A golem," the queen said grimly. "Two of the earth elementals summoned them early on. My ability is no good against them—they have no mind to control. You'll have to try ice." And then she was gone, racing back toward the battle and the king.

The golem picked up speed.

My mind raced, trying to decide what to do. I scanned the field. No one was close enough to be in the path of the cold fire should I release it, but still, I was hesitant. I thought of the battle with the Drevlian captain, and I tried to think of how best to attack this golem. But then I remembered what Queen Ciara had said: that it was better *not* to think when using my power. With my heart hammering painfully in my chest, I forced my eyes closed.

Icy fingers of wind caressed my cheek, waiting to be unleashed. I could feel the power in the air, a storm ready to destroy all in its path. It asked, and I loosened my hold. Like a geyser, the power poured out of me.

The cold wind was the first to be set free. It churned and strengthened in magnitude until Zonsara's mane blew back in my face as she hunched against its power. It pushed ahead of me until even the golem's progress was slowed.

Many of the men engaged in battle stopped to gaze around themselves as the wind knocked their blows off course and rendered even the giant boulders useless. Everything was swept away by the gusts, taking them far out to the forest beyond.

The winter storm within me asked for more, and I gave it. The temperature dropped violently, cold enough for even me to feel it. I sent it toward the golem, and it hit the creature with a blast of icy air and snow and ice. It took another step forward, but then it froze before my eyes. It crashed to the ground and shattered into pieces of frozen earth and rocks.

As though I'd shouted my arrival to everyone on the field, it drew their attention.

The winter storm continued to churn.

Over the heads of those locked in battle, I could see the prince's blazing fire. He was racing toward me, and with a shot of horror, I realized he meant to do as we'd discussed before: to use his power to stop my own.

The earth elementals on the outskirts of the battlefield refocused their attention on me, sending everything in their power toward me. Boulders were picked up again and hurled in my direction, but the cold fire reduced them easily to rubble. Golems were sent lumbering toward me, only to be frozen and smashed to pieces.

The storm became like cold fire, blue flames spreading across the earth. It burned a path before me, freezing the ground and boulders and golems and anyone else in its path. A flash of the aftermath of the destruction of my village went through my mind, and I clenched my teeth.

The prince was shouting something as he ran, and his men came to attention, turning their heads toward him before finally running to the other side of the field—out of the path of my power.

Still, some of them weren't fast enough. The cold fire passed over them, freezing them so powerfully they shattered. I whimpered.

And then the prince made it to the middle of the field, his flames burning powerfully, spreading outward in an arc all around him. They continued to grow, until he looked like an avenging angel with fiery wings outstretched. His men were behind the wall of fire, and I finally understood what he meant to do: he was shielding them from my wintery power with his flames.

The swirling blizzard finally reached him, and my heart was in my throat as I watched it crash against the fire. Thick steam rose in the air, the hiss so loud I could hear it from my vantage high on the hill.

I urged Zonsara on, and she shot forward, racing down the hill. We stopped just at the edge of battle, where the ground was littered with the broken, frozen bodies of the enemies. The steam dissipated just enough for me to see the prince. He was uninjured, the fire around him still blazing brightly.

I flung myself from Zonsara—I didn't want to ride her over the carnage of the fallen enemies—and ran toward the prince.

He met me in the middle, dousing his fire like snuffing a lamp. And when I was close enough, he pulled me to him, pressing me against the heat of his body. His hands plunged into my hair—hot as brands, but they felt so good against the permanent frost of my own body—and he kissed me like we'd been parted for years instead of days.

"I cannot tell you how happy I am to see you—even in the midst of a battle," he said with a shuddery sort of relief. He glanced up at the snowstorm churning above us. "And you brought winter with you."

"I thought I'd try my hand at being a warrior," I tried to say flippantly, but ended up choking on the last word. "I killed some of your men—I couldn't stop the cold fire, and you saved the rest, but—"

The prince looked confused at first, and I was horrified to think maybe he didn't know, maybe he hadn't seen what I'd done, but then as his gaze scanned the battlefield, he returned his attention to me. "Katya, you didn't kill any of my men. You saved them."

"But, I thought . . ." I trailed off as I looked around me. How could I have even known which men were on whose side? And then I realized it hadn't really been the prince's men I'd seen at all, but instead, the men and women from my own village. It was like reliving a memory, only this time, I got to wake up and find out it was only a nightmare. Relief hit me so powerfully, I closed my eyes—despite the sounds of battle around us.

"They're all alive—the ones who hadn't already fallen," he added with a heavy weight of regret clear in his tone. "But where is Kharan? Were you able to heal her?"

"Alive and well," I said with relief. "She shadow melded shortly after we arrived."

He nodded approvingly. "I never doubted you'd be able to help her."

I returned my attention to the battle. We might have defeated the enemies here, outside the city, but the most powerful ones were inside. Behind brambles as thick as trees. I turned to look at them now, and they were more wicked up close than they'd been at a distance, the thorns as long as swords, with terribly pointed ends, and the vine itself as thick around as an oak.

"The queen said you need my help with the brambles. The princes are inside?"

He turned his attention to the brambles. "Perhaps ice will be more effective. Even the power of my flames did nothing but produce a terrible black smoke without hurting the plant."

I thought of the way my wintery power could eat through half a village and shatter entire izby. "I can get you into the city."

"Good. And then I want you to stay here."

I recoiled. "Stay here? While the others risk themselves? While *you* risk yourself?"

He looked as unperturbed as usual, except he was saying something drastically different. "I don't want to risk the life of the woman I love—even for the sake of my city."

He was trying to distract me with declarations of love, and even though my heart pounded to hear such a thing, I couldn't let it affect me—not yet. But I also knew the prince well enough to know I shouldn't bother arguing.

I should just go ahead and do what I wanted to do—how could he even stop me?

"I'll take care of the brambles," I said, and I raced away before he could say anything else.

He called my name, but I tapped into the winter power within me again, fueling the storm until the wind howled around us, snatching away every word.

Chapter Twenty-Five

The brambles rose above me, sharp and malevolent looking. They were like what man's idea of nature should be: wicked and cruel as an evil heart. They had grown so thick and intertwined with each other that the gates of the city were no longer visible. The city looked like it had been made from brambles instead of stone.

I thought of the princes inside, both of whom were powerful elementals themselves, and a desperation for this to finally be over caught me by the throat.

I closed my eyes and felt for that welling of power again. The wind turned so cold it left a layer of frost over my skin, and I urged it to go colder still.

Burn, I thought.

Cold poured from the palms of my hands, a wind visible to the naked eye, blue tinged and silvery white. It bit into the brambles in front of me, turning them to ice. But as the first layer of thorns froze, the ones behind them grew thicker.

Suddenly, the unfrozen brambles lashed out, snatching at me like the vines had done to Sasha when we'd first battled the elementals in the woods. The wickedly sharp thorns would have pierced me through if it wasn't for the ice of my skin, but still I screamed in surprise.

Suddenly, I was certain I would fail. I thought of all the times in my village when I had been seen as next to useless, where the cold coating my skin was a source of amusement. Was this another instance of my ineptitude? The others were counting on me to break through these brambles and free the city, but all I'd succeeded in doing was getting myself caught.

Elation cried out above me, helpless to lend his aid.

Despite the fear of being crushed, I closed my eyes and tapped into that seemingly endless well of power within me.

And then the prince was there in a blaze of fire and light. He swung his sword at the brambles that held me prisoner, and they shattered where they'd come into contact with the cold fire still pouring from my palms. I crashed to the ground, and he pulled me to my feet.

My very first thought was not relief or even gratitude, but that I could have saved myself. I *needed* to save myself.

"Are you hurt?" he demanded.

"No."

"Then let's work together to break through these."

I nodded.

The cold fire poured from my palms as the prince shattered the brambles with his fiery sword until we finally made it to the gate. The winter storm still churned above me, and I found that if I channeled some of my power into the storm instead of the cold fire, I could at least stop freezing everything around me. But I knew that eventually I would have to find a way to cut the flow of power.

I'd worry about that later. After the princes were defeated.

I stood aside while the prince's men—Ivan, Boris, and others I recognized but didn't have the names for—came to open the gate. It wasn't meant to be opened from this side, though, so I wondered if they would break through somehow. But then Boris raised his hands, and with a push from his powerful arms, the heavy door came crashing down.

The prince's men entered first, but we were fast on their heels. Elation flew above us, and I wished for his gift of sight.

When we saw what waited for us inside the city, though, we came to a halt. There was no one around. No voices, no movement, no animals. No sign of life. And then we saw why: around each house, the door had been barred shut with the same brambles that had a death grip on the outer walls of the city. These were smaller, to be sure, but still formidable enough that the people were effectively trapped inside their homes.

The prince's fire blazed brighter, and through the flickering flames, I could just make out the tension in his jaw.

"We will save them, Gosudar," Ivan said, his own expression carved from stone, "but not yet. The princes have to be our priority. Defeat them, and we will win."

It was sage advice, but for a moment, it seemed the prince might let his fire consume him. It blazed higher, spread wider, until his men were forced to step back. Finally, the prince nodded. "We'll find them at the palace."

We raced on ahead, through the eerily silent city, and as I took stock of the men following the prince, I realized Kharan was still missing. She must have remained shadow melded and was even now making her way to the palace. There was a desperation in the air, a need for Sasha to confront the princes and retake the city.

Before we could cross the river, a contingent of enemy soldiers came pouring over the bridge, but when Sasha moved to intercept them, Ivan held him back. "We can't afford any more delays," Ivan said. "Let the militia fight them."

Reluctantly, Sasha nodded as a wave of men behind us came to meet the new threat.

We went forward with only his bogatyri. We crossed the river—over the bridge this time as it was no longer frozen—and then the palace loomed ahead. It was strangely devoid of the brambles that plagued the city, as if the princes wanted us to come face them unimpeded. It made my blood run cold, for I knew it was a sign that what they had in store for us was worse than thorns.

Once we reached the courtyard of the palace, the prince came to a stop, and Elation flew to the highest turret, watching from his lofty perch. At the top of the steps waited two men, dressed in beautiful winter coats: one golden and trimmed in fox fur, the other black and trimmed in what looked like bear fur. They resembled the animals whose fur they wore, one with tawny hair and sharp, clever features, the other with dark hair, wide features, and a hulking figure made worse by the bulky coat. Other men accompanied them, guardsmen it seemed, with swords in their hands as they watched us warily. And another familiar man who made my heart sink when I saw him.

Grigory.

"Hello, Prince Alexander," said the prince with hair like a lion's mane. "We wondered if you'd make it this far."

I wanted to reach out to Sasha, to at least see how he was responding to coming face-to-face with not only his enemies but Grigory's treachery, too, but the fire around him was like a shield. It obscured his face in flames.

The other prince stood with arms crossed over his chest, dark and shadowy as the other one was fair and golden. Warily I looked around for the elemental who could have created the brambles, but all I saw were ordinarily dressed guardsmen. The elementals we'd defeated on the battlefield all wore coats with green-and-gold embroidery that had seemed to designate their status as earth wielders.

"Mikhail, Stanislav," Sasha said with a tone of derision, "I've come to retake my city."

"You're welcome to try," said the fair one, the one Sasha had called Mikhail, "but we'll kill you as easily as we killed your parents, even with that weak little campfire you surrounded yourself with."

Sasha's flames burned brighter, and I tensed, expecting sudden violence. Instead, a dark laugh escaped him. "I doubt it. Unlike them, I am not asleep."

Mikhail's expression seemed to lose some of its arrogance, but he shrugged. "Then we will kill you fully awake."

Mikhail made a signal to his bogatyri, and as they rushed toward us—including Grigory—vines erupted from beneath our feet in every direction. They weren't as thick or impossibly dense as the brambles on the outside had been, but they were growing larger as we watched. Before any of us could respond, Sasha's flames burgeoned in a blinding flash of light. They spread from vine to vine, rendering them to black ash instantly. Many of the guardsmen wore expressions of dawning fear, like they hadn't truly realized what the fire surrounding the prince could do until they saw it turn the vines to dust.

Still, they'd been commanded to attack, so they bravely continued, and I forced myself to watch as they, too, were decimated by Sasha's fire as easily as the vines had been. I watched because I knew the princes were far more powerful than the guardsmen, and that they sacrificed them like mindless pawns. I let this knowledge fuel the power growing within me, and snow began to fall as the wind picked up. The princes on the steps looked unintimidated—Mikhail perhaps slightly more irritated—but Stanislav hadn't moved or said a word.

"Impressive," Mikhail said in a condescending tone, "but now it's our turn."

I tried to brace myself, but how could I? I had no idea what they could do.

Mikhail leaped from the top of the steps. He landed with a *boom* that echoed through the courtyard, so hard that it left a circular indentation in the hard ground. Sasha ran toward him, fire blazing, but it wasn't fast enough. Mikhail jumped back, and with hand raised, he summoned the circle of earth to lift. It was a wheel as wide as three men. He sent it flying in a blur toward Sasha, who tried to slow its impact with a burst of flames but ended up having to dodge. The wheel of hard-packed earth and rock crashed into many of his men, killing them instantly.

By the time we had registered what happened to the men, Mikhail was already moving again. From a different part of the ground, he summoned another wheel of earth and sent it flying toward Sasha.

I pushed away all thoughts of doubt and offensive or defensive tactics and just *responded*. The power within me lashed out with a sudden burst of cold wind that both blew the massive wheel off course and froze it, so when it finally landed, it shattered harmlessly.

I felt a gaze on me, heavy and malevolent, and I looked up to find Stanislav had moved while our focus had been on Mikhail. Now he watched me appraisingly. He brought his hands together in front of his chest, and as he did, the earth shook beneath us.

Elation, I thought desperately, sending an image of what I needed from him: to fly toward the people and knock them away from the cracks developing on the ground.

With a cry, he came, his wings tucked close to his sides as he dove in a dizzying fall. He pulled up at the last second and flew like an arrow through the midst of men, forcing them to jump aside just before the ground split open.

It was a yawning chasm, worse even then the one the Drevlian captain had created. Deep and dark and endless. It separated us—Sasha and Ivan and Grigory on one side; the guardsmen, Boris, and me on the other side.

Mikhail continued his barrage of earth and rocks, while Boris did his best to keep them from slamming into any of us.

And then Sasha faced off with Mikhail, struggling to get close enough to destroy him with fire. Every time the flames blazed, hot enough for me to feel them across the chasm, Mikhail was still able to summon a wall of stone and earth strong enough to deflect the powerful fire.

I thought of the brambles and the way Sasha and I had worked together to break through them. I could do the same with the walls of earthen stone. Sasha moved and attacked again, but Mikhail raised his hand, and another wall appeared out of the earth. I felt for the power burning within me, focusing on freezing the wall.

I'd forgotten about Stanislav.

The ground rumbled threateningly beneath me, and I turned and ran. Splintery cracks appeared beneath my feet. It was like being on the ice again, only this time, if I fell, I had no hope of pulling myself out.

A pillar of earth appeared in front of me, cutting off my

escape. Just as I was about to change direction, the ground beneath me gave way. A horrible plummeting feeling, like my stomach had suddenly fallen out through my feet, and then talons dug into my shoulder. With a piercing cry, Elation lifted me free of the chasm, depositing me on the other side, near Sasha.

Sasha turned to me, and I could see the panic for me reflected in his eyes, but I shook my head. "There's no time for that. We must work together like we did with the brambles."

He nodded once, and then the fire around him spread until it crackled and blazed. He ran toward Mikhail with sword held high, and predictably, Mikhail produced another wall of earth with a taunting laugh.

I stared at the blockade he'd created, pictured it freezing in my mind, and then I channeled all the power of winter in a blast of cold air. It hit the wall, and only a moment after, Sasha shattered it with his sword.

Mikhail was too shocked to stop the next attack. Sasha ran him through with a sword of blazing fire, and his body burned away to ash before our eyes.

Breathing hard, Sasha turned to Stanislav. "Mikhail is dead. Surrender now, and perhaps I will be merciful."

Stanislav smiled, the gesture more frightening than friendly. "Mikhail talked too much anyway."

He lifted his arms, and the ground rumbled again, even louder than before.

"Be prepared to run," Sasha shouted, and we all kept our eyes on the ground, expecting the telltale cracks to appear.

But Stanislav only laughed, the sound like rocks grating

against each other, as he bizarrely stripped out of his coat and tunic. And then pieces of the ground ripped away and began flying toward him: clods of earth, rocks, and even pebbles. They coated him like a suit of armor, until he was no longer recognizable.

He loomed over us, taller and wider than even the golems in the field had been. He looked invincible.

"Stay back until we need you," Sasha told me, and I nodded reluctantly. I'd never wished for skill in battle, but I did now.

Swords bounced off Stanislav's body with earsplitting *twangs*; the earthen rock he'd covered himself with was harder than steel. Even Boris's superior strength was no match.

"My turn," Stanislav said, and it was like a mountain speaking—deep and rumbly and loud.

He swept his arm out, simultaneously stomping hard with his left foot, and knocked the heads of six men. The force crushed their skulls, but before the rest of us could react, the ground shuddered so violently, we lost our footing. Sasha recovered first and blazed brightly as he ran at Stanislav. He was aided by Boris and Ivan, who fought with swords as both their abilities seemed useless against Stanislav.

More of Sasha's men recovered and joined the fight—another six bogatyri—and swords rang out as they tried in vain to weaken Stanislav's armor.

Sasha's fire burned so hot that the other men had to step back, and we watched hopefully as the earthen stone armor seemed to melt, but then it hardened again, seemingly more impenetrable than before. I would have to try—I couldn't stand by and obey orders while everyone risked their lives.

I reached for that power, like dipping a bucket into an overflowing well, and thought of nothing but freezing Stanislav—of stopping him, any way I could. The cold fire shot toward him, silvery and blue, coated him in a layer of frost, and nothing more.

He laughed again, the sound reverberating through me, and then he attacked the men in a flurry of powerful blows of his fists. He killed the bogatyri easily. Sasha tried to shield Ivan and Boris, but Stanislav was impossibly fast despite his size. He dodged Sasha and struck them down with blows that left them cracked open, red and bleeding on the snow-kissed ground.

I cried out in horror as pain rippled through me, thinking of Ivan, thinking of *Vera*, as Sasha's flames grew exponentially hotter. He was like a blazing inferno, like the depths of hell, and his sword was a blur as he matched Stanislav blow for blow.

Sasha might fall. The insidious thought passed through my mind, ripping out my heart. I had once thought him a cruel monster, but here was the *real* monster right before my eyes. And he stood the best chance of winning.

I couldn't let that happen.

I'd let too much of my power flow to the storm above us, and though it howled and gusted with snow and pieces of ice, it was nothing to a man coated in earth and stone. I thought of Winter, who could create an entire palace from ice. Whose briefest touch could freeze an entire lake.

Doubt tried to whisper in my mind, but I shoved it away. I'd already failed Ivan and Boris and all the other men; I wouldn't fail Sasha. The queen had said my power was like a storm, but the truth was the storm was me and I was the storm. I could command it.

Return to me, I thought to the power churning in the storm above me.

I spoke to it as I spoke to Elation, and I could feel a response, like hearing a distant voice in the wind. A whirlwind swirled around me then, faster and faster, until I was caught up in a storm of snow and ice. I couldn't breathe, couldn't even blink. I opened my mouth to scream, and suddenly, all that power flowed back into me, burning my lungs with ice.

My heart beat stronger, and I breathed out the power of a winter storm.

Sasha dodged Stanislav, but the edge of Stanislav's fist hit Sasha's shoulder, and the force was enough to knock Sasha to the ground.

I took a step toward them, and the earth below me froze solid. And then another step, until I was racing along the ice I'd created, faster than I'd ever run before. Just as Stanislav bent to deliver the final blow to Sasha, I got there first, shielding Sasha with my arms spread wide.

"Katya, no!" Sasha shouted as Stanislav delivered his blow.

At the same time, I released my power.

It exploded out toward Stanislav, freezing his body in the air as it blew him back against the steps of the palace. The earth and stone that had coated him burned in the cold fire, shattering like glass as he made contact with the unforgiving palace. Stripped of his armor, Stanislav was just a man again, but he tried to push himself up.

The cold fire I'd unleashed continued to siphon my energy, creating another winter storm that whirled around me, gaining power as it froze the ground, the very *air*.

I had to finish this.

But just as I took another step, someone stepped out of the shadows of the palace. Kharan, her dark hair whipping around her face in the terrible wind I'd created, grabbed hold of Stanislav and slit his throat in one fast motion. He fell, blood spilling upon the steps, finally dead.

It was over, but even as relief filled me, fear held me in its talons. The battle was over, the war won, but I couldn't stop my power.

The storm grew, snatching even the breath from my lungs, my vision darkening until I couldn't see. Still, it pulled from me more of the energy that kept my heart beating.

And then through the blinding wind and snow and ice, I saw red-and-gold flames.

"Take my hand," the prince shouted at me over the storm's roaring winds. He was lit up like the sun, the heat from his blaze penetrating even the winter storm that surrounded me.

"I don't want to hurt you," I shouted back. Whose power was stronger? What if mine consumed him, too?

His silver eyes looked golden in the flames. "You won't." He stepped closer, and the wind from the storm that held me at its heart raged against his flames. Fire and ice met, repelling each other like two opposing powers.

I could feel the wintery power inside draining away the mortal part of me, and the edges of my vision darkened as my heart slowed. It would consume me, at least the part of me that had come from the hunter, and I didn't know what would be left. Ice? I swayed on my feet, swept along by the force of the wind and snow and ice. Still, I wouldn't reach for him.

The prince pushed forward, step after step, until finally he grasped my arm. The cold inside me fought like a wild animal against the blaze of his heat, and for a moment, I thought it would destroy us both. But then, as surely as a fire can chase away the cold teeth of winter's night, the prince's fire made gains on the storm within me. His fire melted the snow and ice, the heat warming my body until slowly, there was no more ice that threatened to consume me.

The wind died down at last, and my legs crumpled beneath me. Sasha caught me before I could fall to the ground, gathering me close to his chest.

"It's over," Sasha said, and I wasn't sure if he meant the storm he'd tamed within me, or the battle with Stanislav, or even the entire war. All were true.

I met his gaze, the heat of him enveloping me, and my heart quickened. This time, I didn't wait for him to kiss me. I wrapped my arms around his neck and pulled his head down until his lips met mine. The kiss was desperate, burning heat.

It warmed my blood, even as cold tears of relief slipped down my cheeks.

He brushed away my tears. "I thought I'd lost you to yourself."

I thought of the way my heart had slowed while the storm I'd created pulled away my energy. I shuddered. "You pulled me back from the brink."

"It would seem our powers were made for each other."

Chapter Twenty-Six

We were relieved to find that many of Sasha's guardsmen had survived the battle against the Drevlians and Novgorodians, though the loss was still far too high. But against all odds, Ivan had not been killed . . . yet. I bent over him, examining his gaping wound, and called for the herbal poultice to pack it and keep his insides from spilling out.

He was unconscious but still breathing shallowly, and I worked quickly, thinking of Vera should I fail. Beside him was Boris, who was beyond help, and Grigory, who had been killed by them before he could kill the prince with his treachery.

As I heard Babushka's voice in my head, telling me what I must do to save Ivan, I also thought of what Kharan had said: that I had healed her. More memories poured through me then—of times when Babushka had saved men who seemed past saving. When even ordinary herbs were enough to bring them back from the brink of death. I thought of how badly she'd been burned herself, yet she had survived long enough to speak to me, long enough to tell me where the journal was. And then I realized: she had the power to heal.

And she was my grandmother by blood.

I finished treating Ivan's wound, and he was carried off to bed to be tended by Vera, but I knew that he would live. He might be scarred, but it would not cost him his life.

Others, though, were not so fortunate.

Sasha had lost more than half of his militia, and there were even losses of the king and queen's men, though both the king and queen had survived with only scratches.

Blood stained the snow surrounding the palace, and the brambles took many days to clear. The smoke from the fires after cutting them down and burning them stung our eyes for a week.

I was given far too much attention for my so-called heroism, so I always deferred to Kharan, who'd delivered the final blow and ended the war.

"I kept to the shadows," she had said when I asked her how she'd come to be there at the perfect moment, "and I'd meant to get there far sooner than I did." Her expression looked pained, and I knew she was thinking of Boris.

"You cannot blame yourself for that," I had said, and I tried to tell myself the same.

"I was needed in the city—I helped many guardsmen stay alive, at least, and finally, I made it to the palace."

"I couldn't have defeated him without you," I had said, and meant it. My power had already begun to rage out of control by the time she'd appeared.

I knew what I'd have to do, but I was delaying.

Finally, after the city had been cleared of brambles, we were able to give Boris and the others royal funerals. Villagers came from the farthest reaches of the land to lament their deaths, and to thank them for their sacrifice. Sasha buried them all in the graveyard reserved for nobility.

I'd relented and dressed in one of the gowns Sasha had gifted me with long ago, ice-blue and silver, studded with pearls all the way to the throat. It had a matching kokoshnik—a head-dress heavy with pearls. And still with all this finery, I felt a cold wind blow from the north, calling me.

When the funeral was over, Sasha linked his arm through mine. The tears were still caught in my throat. I had saved the prince and even Ivan but failed Boris.

"He would be happy that you saved Kievan Rus'," Sasha said, because he could read my moods easily now.

I nodded because I didn't trust my voice.

He stopped and turned me toward him. "Stanislav killed him, not you. Do you understand?"

"I do," I said, because I did, but it didn't mean I would stop blaming myself. Not yet.

We walked toward the palace, and before we reached the

steps, I halted. "Sasha, I think it's finally time to talk about it. Now that the city is safe . . ."

He cut me off with a kiss. "You want to leave? Where will you go?"

North, I thought, but didn't say.

"I will marry you," he said. "I *want* to marry you."

I smiled. "I cannot. Not yet."

"I love you more than I've loved anything in my life," he said. "I think I've loved you since the moment you stood before me in the throne room." He took my hand. "After all we've been through, you're such a part of my life—a part of *me*—that I don't think I can ever be without you."

"I love you, too," I said, though it still felt like my heart was breaking.

He stilled. "But it's not enough?"

"You're the prince," I said, expecting it to be explanation enough. I couldn't ask him to come with me. I couldn't ask him to leave his newly won throne.

But then he pulled me into him and kissed me until I couldn't breathe or think straight, and the icy cold of my skin melded with the heat of him, wrapping us in steam.

"Where you go," he said, "I will go."

And I thought of Winter and the hunter, and I knew I wouldn't let that be our fate.

EPILOGUE

THE SUN HAD BARELY RISEN WHEN I rode Zonsara out of the royal palace and through the quiet city. I checked to be sure I had everything: bare essentials I'd need for travel. Since it was summer, I hadn't had to pack heavily. Zonsara could easily subsist on the rich grasses, and I could forage in addition to the meals Elation would help me catch.

The field where we'd defeated the earth elementals was finally clear of the fallen trees—which had been chopped up and distributed to the villages who'd lost everything in the hope that they could rebuild. But there were still horrible scars in the earth, scars to match the ones most of the princedom were recovering from.

Though as the first buds of spring could follow even the worst winter, Kievan Rus' would recover from the evil machinations of the former Drevlian and Novgorodian princes. New princes had been chosen, and they were eager to work with Sasha to repair the land. Already those who had been enslaved by the Drevlian and Novgorodians had been freed, and Sasha had commanded that all of his people be tracked down and liberated.

I could no longer put off the journey I'd thought about since the moment Baba Yaga had shown me Winter's ice palace.

I headed north, in search of my mother.

Just as I urged Zonsara into a brisk trot, I heard hoofbeats sound out behind me. I steeled myself, expecting to have to argue with Sasha again, and I was surprised to see not just Sasha, but Kharan as well. Both dressed for travel.

"You didn't think we'd let you go alone, did you?" Sasha asked, a gleam in his eyes.

"But you're the prince," I said, glancing back at the city. "How can I take you from your palace?"

"The land is at peace, and now I am free to help the woman I love."

My heart beat faster, a great weight lifting from my shoulders, and I realized I desperately wanted them to come with me.

"We were there when you first learned of Winter's story," Kharan said. "Don't we deserve to find out how it ends?"

I thought of that moment in Baba Yaga's hut, both terrible and beautiful all at once. "Yes, of course you do."

Sasha had moved his horse closer to mine. "To the ends of the earth, remember?"

I smiled as the sun broke free of the clouds and warmed our faces. He leaned closer, and I was drawn to him like a moth to a flame. "I remember."

He kissed me, and in that kiss was the seal of a promise: I would never have to be alone again.

Author's Note

When I was a little girl, I loved the Soviet-era cartoons that featured characters from Russian folklore: magic horses, the firebird, Peter and the Wolf. They were my first introduction to Slavic fairy tales, and I was transported by the characters, costumes, and beauty. I grew up reading about the dark stories of Baba Yaga and Vasilisa the Beautiful, Tsarevich Ivan, the Firebird, and the Gray Wolf. I loved how they were both frightening and beautiful, with characters both wise and foolish. As I delved into research of Slavic countries and Russia in particular, I wanted to find a time period that would lend itself to a fantasy world where Baba Yaga could exist alongside a girl with the power to harness winter itself.

Through the White Wood is set during a little-known time in

Russian history, in the eleventh century, when the country was young and ruled by a grand prince instead of a tsar. At the time, it was known as Kievan Rus' and was made up of Slavic tribes from eastern Europe, first banded together by a Varangian—another name for a Viking—prince. I partially chose the time period for its proximity to the setting of *Beyond a Darkened Shore*, but also because the young Russian country was rife with conflict. This makes for a more interesting story.

This is a work of fantasy, so I did take liberties with the historical elements, but culturally, I tried to stay true to what life was like at that time. While I'm by no means an expert, I was aided by the excellent *Kievan Russia* by George Vernadsky, which is seen to be the definitive work on the time period.

There were a few times I tweaked history to suit the story. For example, the Drevlians did revolt against the grand prince of Kiev when they grew tired of paying tribute, but this occurred two centuries earlier than the time of *Through the White Wood*, and the revolt was quickly crushed. Novgorod was originally the capital of Kievan Rus', but later became its own republic, and were never enemies of Kiev. However, there was a period when three princes sat on the thrones of the Drevlian territory, Novgorodian territory, and Kiev itself. These three princes went to war with each other when the Drevlian Prince, Yaropolk, had his brother Oleg, who was prince of Kiev, killed. The Novgorodian Prince Alexander was forced to flee until he later returned with a Viking army and defeated Yaropolk. This was the inspiration for the political conflict Prince Alexander must deal with in *Through the White Wood*.

Empress Zoe and Empress Theodora really did jointly rule the Byzantine throne, but only for a short time in 1042. Still, I couldn't resist the fantastic imagery of two female empresses—sisters—ruling together, and so I tweaked history a bit to have them in my story. Kievan Rus' did have a trade route to Constantinople, thanks to the Varangians (Vikings), and the Byzantines did intermarry with the Rus', but I fabricated the political intrigue and support of the Drevlians and Novgorodians to work with the plot of *Through the White Wood*.

Though the people of Kievan Rus' converted to Christianity under Grand Prince Alexander in 988, Slavic pagan beliefs still lived on through folktales and a lingering respect for and personification of the seasons. The people of Kievan Rus' very much saw the seasons as an eternal struggle between the sun and cold, and I tried to bring some of this to life with the personification of Winter. I only mention a few of the supernatural creatures and spirits of Slavic folklore, such as Baba Yaga, the rusalka, and the bannik, but there are so many more. As with the historical aspects of the book, I took some creative liberties, and I hope my readers—particularly those who specialize in Russian history and lore—will indulge me.

Glossary

Baba Yaga: A well-known figure in Russian fairy tales. She is a wise old witch who is sometimes portrayed as helpful, but usually malevolent, and is characterized as riding around in a mortar and pestle while her hut spins about on chicken legs.

babushka: Russian for *grandmother*.

bannik: A bathhouse spirit in Slavic lore. People used to leave offerings of soap, water, or fir branches to the bannik to keep him appeased. He was said to be able to tell the future by gently running his fingers down one's back if one's fortune was good, and raking one's back with his claws if one's fortune was bad.

bogatyr (plural: bogatyri): A trained warrior much like the knights of western Europe.

boyar: The noblemen of Kievan Rus'; these were feudal lords who were ranked just below the grand prince. They provided military support and tribute for the prince.

dedushka: Russian for *grandfather*.

deel: Traditional clothing worn by the Mongol tribes and Turkic people; could be made from wool, silk, or brocade. It can be worn by both men and women, and it looks like a belted robe or overcoat. It can be plain or extravagantly embroidered.

derevnya: A Russian village too small to have its own church.

devotchka: Russian diminutive for *girl*.

dvor: Russian for *courtyard*.

Drevlians: A warlike tribe of people who paid tribute to Kievan Rus'.

druzhina: The military company of men who served under the prince and the boyars in Kievan Rus'.

dobroye utro: Russian for *good morning*.

Gosudar: A title of respect for the prince, similar to "Highness" in English.

govno: Russian for *shit*.

grand prince: The highest-ranking member of the aristocracy in medieval Kievan Rus'. The first grand prince was actually a Varangian (Viking).

horhog: A traditional Mongolian meat dish, made from heating stones in an open fire and using them to slowly cook the meat and vegetables.

izba (plural: izby): A Russian house made of wood, similar to a log cabin.

kasha: Russian porridge made from any number of grains, but especially buckwheat.

Kievan Rus': A powerful East Slavic state ruled by the Grand Prince of Kiev. It was also the birthplace of three modern-day nations: Belarus, Ukraine, and Russia.

knarr: A merchant ship used by the Vikings to transport livestock and other goods.

kokoshnik: Traditional Russian headdress.

kvas: Traditional Slavic drink made from fermented rye bread.

Novgorodians: People of the city-state of Novgorod in modern-day Russia.

piroshok: A hand-held bun that can be baked or fried and filled with a number of different things, such as meat or vegetables (especially cabbage).

pryaniki: A Russian spice cookie traditionally made at Christmastime; also known as honey bread.

rubakha: A Russian tunic, usually made of linen, and often embroidered.

rusalka: A water nymph of Slavic mythology. Originally the rusalki were seen as life-giving: they came out of the lakes and rivers in the spring and gave water to the crops. But later on in history, they were seen as more malevolent spirits, who could drag unsuspecting victims under the water and drown them.

shchi: A Russian cabbage soup; a staple food of Russia along with kvas.

shuba: A long fur coat.

spokoynoy nochi: Russian for *good night*.

upyr: In Slavic lore, this is a creature who feeds off the life energy (usually blood) of another person; similar to a vampire.

Varangians: The name given to Vikings while they occupied and ruled the medieval state of Kievan Rus'. They traded and pirated all down the vast river systems of medieval Russia, all the way to the Black Sea and Constantinople.

Vyatka horse: A breed of Russian draft horse from the former Vyatka region, now endangered.

Acknowledgments

Deo gratias.

This book was born from my love of fairy tales, particularly Russian ones, but also from my deep and abiding love of Strong Female Characters Who Can Do Really Cool Things. I am so thankful to be sharing this story with you, and it's with the help of so many talented and supportive people that it could be brought to life.

Thank you to my husband for being supportive since day one, when I said, "I think I want to write a book." I love you forever and always.

For my mom and dad, who always believed in me no matter what and have always been endlessly supportive in every way.

For my in-laws, Mike and Carol, who have always been so proud and supportive—and they were always happy to take the kids any time I needed time to write!

For my editor, Alice Jerman, for falling in love with not just one but *two* of my books and working tirelessly again to make sure it was the absolute best version it could be. It's been such an absolute pleasure to work with you! I love our chicken chats best of all.

For my agent, Brianne Johnson, because she has made all my writerly dreams come true. You are the absolute *best*. She even doesn't mind when I have to whisper to her on the phone from my pantry so the kids don't hear me, or put her on my car's Bluetooth with all the kids in the back . . . actually, she may not have known about that last one.

For everyone at HarperTeen, for all their hard work on this book—most especially for the gorgeous cover that was everything I could have hoped for and more.

I have an enormous family, and every single one of them is supportive and encouraging to an incredible degree. Thank you to all of you—all my aunts and uncles (including my favorite aunt and uncle); all the family I gained when I married my best friend; all my cousins, most especially my cousin Kelsey Cox, who has always been my partner in this writing journey through her inspiring and insightful critiques. Let's have another publishing NYC trip extravaganza sometime soon! Love you, cousin.

I have an amazing group of friends, so thank you for all the playdates, book club meetings, and hundreds of text messages, all of which helped me keep my sanity as I navigated being mom to four extremely small (but so, so adorable) children and writing/editing a book.

Thank you to the Electric Eighteens, who got me through